Reviewers acclaim T. Davis Bunn's first novel, *The Presence*

"Davis is a masterful storyteller. His first book promises to be an international bestseller.... It will leave you deeply and spiritually moved and challenged."

KEN CORLEY
Full Gospel Business Mens Fellowship International Naples Chapter

"Bunn uses a fresh approach for fiction and turns readers toward the presence of God. Compelling writing blends humor with a stirring plot to make this book a good choice."
Moody Monthly

"I admire its vivid characterization and conversational language, the sincerity of its message. Truly a parable."

ANTHONY NYE, S.J.
Head of the Jesuit Diocese London

"*The Presence* is a great novel portraying the power of the Lord in the life of a public official. It leaves me more determined than ever to seek His presence continually."

LAURENCE DAVIS
Chairman North Carolina Democratic Party

"... interesting, entertaining, inspiring and instructive. I highly recommend it."

CAROLYN R. ALBERT
Lutheran Libraries

"It's a great book."

JACK BUNDY
Naples Daily News

"A well-written, gripping exploration of relationships, this story is one you will want to read and reread. I could hardly put it down.

CLYDIA D. DeFRESSE
Church & Synagogue Library Association

"His premises are fascinating ... a major talent with great potential in our market."

BOB HUDSON
*Co-Editor
A Christian Writer's Manual of Style*

"*The Presence* is powerful, refreshing.... We can look forward to more writing from Bunn.... There is great value in well-crafted fiction that embraces a Christian world view."

LIS TROUTEN
Twin Cities Christian

Books by T. Davis Bunn

The Maestro
The Presence
Promises to Keep
Florian's Gate

T. DAVIS BUNN

A NOVEL

Florian's Gate

BETHANY HOUSE PUBLISHERS
MINNEAPOLIS, MINNESOTA 55438

Published by Bethany House Publishers
A Ministry of Bethany Fellowship, Inc.
6820 Auto Club Road, Minneapolis, Minnesota 55438

Printed in the United States of America

Library of Congress Cataloging-in-Publication Data

Bunn, T. Davis, 1952–
   Florian's Gate / T. Davis Bunn.
      p.   cm.

  I. Title.
PS3552.U4718F57   1992
813'.54–dc20   92–7191
ISBN 1–55661–244–3   CIP

THIS BOOK IS DEDICATED
TO MY WIFE'S FAMILY
AND TO THEIR POLISH HERITAGE.

Tę książkę pragnę dedykować Rodzinie mojej żony.

*Tylko dzięki Wam mogłem napisać tę opowieść,
tylko dzięki temu co Wy przedstawiacie—tylko
dzięki Waszej niekończącej się gościnności,
Waszym doświadczeniom, którymi dzieliliście się
ze mną, Waszej mądrości życiowej i Waszej miłosci
dla mojej Iziuni.*

*Otworzyliście przede mną swoje domy i swoje serca
i pokazaliście mi ten inny świat, który dane mi
było poznać tylko przez Was. Tylko dzięki Wam
pokochałem Wasz jakże piękny i jakże tragiczny
Kraj. Dzięki Wam Polska będzie zawsze częścią
mnie samego.*

T. DAVIS BUNN, an American with many years of experience as a businessman in Europe, now lives near Oxford, England, with his wife, Isabella, and devotes full time to writing. The research for this powerful story has ranged from the elegant antique showrooms of contemporary London to the dreadful chambers of Auschwitz prison camp of fifty years ago.

"And I said to the man who stood at the gate of the year: 'Give me a light that I may tread safely into the unknown.' And he replied: 'Go out into the darkness and put your hand into the hand of God. That shall be to you better than light, and safer than a known way.' "

MINNIE LOUISE HASKINS

Quoted by King George VI in his annual Christmas address to the British nation in 1939, on the eve of World War II.

AUTHOR'S NOTE

All antiques mentioned in this book do indeed exist. Prices quoted here are either the result of recent sales or current market estimates.

CHAPTER
1

Jeffrey Sinclair swung around the corner to Mount Street in London's Mayfair district and greeted the wizened flower seller with, "It looks like another rainy day, Mister Harold."

The old man remained bent over his rickety table. "Too right, Yank. Mid-June and we ain't had a dry day since Easter. Don't do my rheumatics no good, s'truth."

"How much for the white things up there on the shelf?"

"What're you on about now?" The man straightened as far up as he was able, shook his head, said, "Chrysanthemums, Yank. Chrysanthemums. Didn't they teach you anything?" "I can't say that before coffee. How much for a bunch?"

"A what?" The man squinted at Jeffrey's double armful. It was an Edwardian silver punch bowl, chased in gold and sporting a pair of intricately engraved stags locked in mortal combat. It was filled with disposable diapers. "Got old Ling in there?"

"Yes."

The old man snorted. "Better bed'n I've ever seen. How much that thing worth?"

"It's priced to sell fast at seven thousand pounds." About twelve thousand dollars. "Maybe your wife would like it for her birthday."

That brought a laugh. "The old dear'll be gettin' the same as last year, a pint at the pub. You're a right one, walkin' 'round these streets with a silver jug for a birdbath."

"It's not a jug." He spotted Katya walking toward them and felt his heart rate surge by several notches. She was sheltered within a vast gentleman's anorak, which she wore to hide the fancy clothes required for working in his shop. The hood framed a pixie face.

She greeted him with a smile that did not reach her eyes, said "Good morning, Mr. Harold."

"Hello, lass." Wizened features twisted into a delighted smile. "Been keepin' you waitin' again, has he?"

She shook her head, said to Jeffrey, "I'm doing research at the library this morning, and I need a book I left at the shop." She peered into the vessel, asked, "How is Ling?"

" 'Ere, let's have a look." The old man's blackened fingers peeled back the upper layer, exposing a baby bird about three weeks outside the egg. "Blimey, he's a runt. What you figure him for?"

Jeffrey knew at a glance that he would have to reply. Katya had a way about her on days like this. She moved within an air of silent sorrow, a shadow drawn across unseen depths. Jeffrey could do little more than watch and yearn to delve beneath the surface and know the secrets behind those beautiful eyes. "Katya thinks it's a robin, but we're not sure."

The bird was sleeping, its gray-feathered body breathing with the minutest of gasps. Its wings were nothing more than tiny stubs covered with the finest of down. It looked far too fragile to live.

"What's he eat?"

"The vet said we ought to buy this special formula, but we couldn't find it anywhere. So Katya's mixed up baby food with birdseed and some mineral drink. Ling eats enough of it, that's for sure.

"The girl's right, Yank. Never did trust them doctors." He reached out one finger and nudged the little body. Immediately the bird leapt upright, its tiny beak opened just as wide as it could, its scrawny neck thrust out to a ridiculous length.

"Look what you did now." Jeffrey's exasperation was only half-faked. "He'll drive me crazy until I can get the shop opened and his formula heated."

The old man remained bent over the tiny form, a smile creasing his unshaven features. "Reminds me of how my littlest one, Bert, used to go on. Lad could eat a horse. Mind you, he made a lot more noise than this runt, Bert did."

"I've got to go now, Mister Harold." Jeffrey said, and started down Mount Street. "Bring a bunch of those white ones by the shop, okay?"

"I would, Yank, if I could figure out what in blazes you're goin' on about," the old man replied, turning back to his table. "Around these parts we sell flowers by the dozen."

The bird kept up a continual high-pitched tweet the entire way down the block. Jeffrey handed the bowl to Katya, fished in his pocket, drew out and inserted the round ten-inch strong-box key in the special slot. He turned it once, punched the four numbers in the alarm box set in the red brick wall, turned it a second time, and sighed with relief when the locks unsheathed with a loud click. A year on the job, and he still got the jitters every time he had to open early.

Nine months previously he had forgotten the numbers, and while he was fishing around in his wallet and trying to remember what different sequence he had written down— subtract one, add two, do the first last, whatever—the sky had split open and the gods of war had been set loose. Alarm bells shattered the quiet of the six o'clock street, lights flashed, and a loud wailing began to slide up and down the scale. The racket caused him to drop his wallet into the slush of yet another half snow, half rain that had turned his first winter in London into a seemingly endless grayish hue. Heads popped out of louvered windows to scream abuse. The police raced up with yet more flashing lights and wailing sirens, and it was only after another half hour of browbeating from all sides that Jeffrey managed to break away, slip inside, and begin another day at the office.

That morning all went as it should, except for Ling's endless cry and Katya's silent distance. Ling had been named by Katya, who had said The Ugly Duckling was too long for something that tiny. Katya was his sort-of girlfriend. The sort-of was from her side, not his. As far as he was concerned, today would have been a fine time to set up house. This morning, in fact. Right now, not to make too big a point of it. But he couldn't—make a point of it, that is—since Katya made it perfectly clear that she wasn't interested.

Hers was not a lighthearted attraction, but rather one which remained surrounded by walls and hidden depths even after seven months of their being together. Her hair was very dark, almost blue-black in color, and cut very short in what used to be called a page-boy style and what now was referred to as functional. It was very fine hair, and it framed her face with a silky aura that shimmered in the light and shivered in the softest breeze. Her eyes were wide and grayish violet and very expressive, her mouth somehow small and full at the same time. Hers was a small, perky face set upon a small, energetic body. He loved her face, loved the quiet fluidity of her movements, loved the way she smiled with her entire being—when she smiled, which was very seldom. Katya was one of the most serious people he had ever met.

Only once had he seen the seriousness slip away entirely, when they had gone to Hastings for the day and spent an unseasonably hot early May afternoon on the beach. After a laughter-filled swim in absolutely frigid water, she had toweled her hair and left it salt-scattered, happy enough to be warm and wet and in the sun for a while. From behind blank sunglasses Jeffrey had examined this strange woman in her brief moment of true happiness, and wondered at all that he did not know of her. Her mysterious distance was a crystal globe set around the most fragile of flowers, protecting a heart from he knew not what. And as he looked, he yearned to come inside the globe, to know this heart, to taste the nectar of this flower.

That time on the beach remained one of the few moments of true intimacy they had ever shared. And even then Jeffrey had almost managed to mess it up—without intending to, without understanding what it was he had said, without knowing how to make things better.

They were lying on a shared beach towel after their swim, enjoying the rare day of summer-like heat that warmed away the water's chill. Katya sat supported by her arms, with her head thrown back, her uplifted face and closed eyes holding an expression of earthly rapture. Jeffrey lay beside her, turned so that he could watch her without her seeing him, knowing that he should understand her better to feel as he did.

She opened her eyes, squinted at the sky, then pointed upward and said brightly, "Look, that's where God lives."

"What?"

"Over there. See the light coming through the clouds like

that? When I was a little girl I decided that it happened when God came down and sat on the clouds. That's why they lit up with all those beautiful colors. And that big stream of light falling to earth was where God was looking down at people to see if they were behaving."

"Do you believe in God?"

She turned and looked at him with clear gray-violet eyes that gave nothing away. "Don't you?"

"I used to. I used to feel as if God was around me all the time."

"He is."

"Maybe so, but I couldn't ever seem to find Him when I needed Him." Jeffrey settled his hands behind his head. "I guess I stayed really religious for about three years. Then when I was seventeen I started going through some bad times. I ended up deciding that if God wasn't going to help me more than He was, then I needed to stop relying on Him and learn to help myself. So I did. I didn't mean to let religion slide, but I guess it has. No, I know it has. It just never seemed to matter very much to me after that."

She looked down at him for a very long moment. "That is the most you have ever told me about yourself."

You're not the most open person either, he thought. "I guess I've never had anybody seem all that interested before."

She kept her solemn eyes on him, and for a moment Jeffrey thought she was going to bend over and kiss him. Instead she turned her face back to the sky, said, "I ran away from home three times when I was six. That's what my parents called it, anyway. What really happened was I went running over to where God was looking down. I wanted to ask Him to make the bad things go away. But I never could get there in time. Sooner or later the light would go out and I knew God had gone to watch other people somewhere else."

He lay and looked at the still face, with its delicate upturned nose and upper lip that seemed to follow the same line of curve. Her chin, too, rose just a little bit, as if carefully planed by a gentle artist. "Did you have a lot of bad times as a kid?"

She lay down beside him, her breath causing her breasts to rise and press against the suit's flimsy fabric. Jeffrey decided he had never seen a more beautiful woman in all his life. "I didn't have anyone to compare with," she replied. "It seemed pretty bad to me."

"Do you want to tell me about it?"

She met him once more with that same level gaze, as though searching inside him for something she couldn't find. "I don't think so," she said. "Can I ask you a question?"

"Sure."

"Have you ever thought about giving God another chance in your life?"

"No," he replied honestly.

"Why not?"

"What for?" He turned his face to the sky. "Why should anything be different this time?"

"Did you ever think that maybe you'd understand why you had to go through what you did, if you'd give Him a chance to explain?"

"Why didn't He explain it then?"

"I don't know, Jeffrey," she said, her voice as calm as her gaze. "Maybe you weren't listening. Or maybe you were listening for something that He didn't want to tell you."

For some reason that struck a little close to home. He countered with, "What about you? Did you find all the answers you were looking for when you were little and hurting and went looking for God?"

"No," she replied. "But I kept looking, and now I do."

"You mean you found an excuse." Her certainty irritated him. He sat up, said, "You went looking for a reason to believe in a God who let you be hurt when you were a little defenseless kid. So you found one. If I wanted to, I could come up with a thousand perfectly good reasons. But it doesn't mean God exists."

She raised up to sit beside him. "You don't understand."

"You're right."

"I found understanding because I let God heal the pain. That's when it started to make sense, Jeffrey. So long as I was still hurting, I couldn't see beyond my pain. But when the wounds healed and the pain left, I was able to see the real reason. The only reason. You can too."

"You really do believe, don't you?"

"With all my heart," she replied simply.

He shook his head, turned to face the sea. "Crazy. I thought I'd left all that stuff back home."

She rose to her feet in one fluid motion. "I think I'm ready to go now."

"Why?" He looked up at her. "There's another two or three hours of sun left."

"I'm going home, Jeffrey." She began slipping back into her jeans. "Would you please take me?"

Jeffrey entered the shop and watched Katya walk to the back, retrieve her book, and leave with the fewest of words. He stood for a moment in the center of the shop and felt the vacuum caused by her silent passing. He sighed, shook his head, and carried Ling's bowl back to the cramped office space behind the stairwell. He set the bowl carefully on a Queen Anne rosewood table and turned on the hotplate. While he prepared the formula and washed the eyedropper, he occupied himself with a rundown of the week's activities.

It was going to be busy, with a major buyer over from America, one of his paintings up for sale at Christie's, the Grosvenor House Antique Fair getting under way, and his boss coming in that Wednesday from goodness-knows-where. A buying trip, that much he knew. Probably from somewhere on the Continent, but he wasn't sure. Where Alexander Kantor bought his antiques was the best-kept secret of the international antiques market. Not to mention the basis for endless speculation and envy.

The most likely rumor Jeffrey had heard was that over the years Alexander had maintained relations with the Communist leaders of Eastern Europe. Now that they were out of business, he was making the rounds as a staunch supporter of the new democracies. Yet not the minutest bit of proof had ever been unearthed. The only thing known was that Alexander Kantor, the sole and rightful owner of the Priceless, Ltd antique shop of Mount Street, had more formerly unknown treasures to his credit than any other dealer in the world.

Jeffrey Allen Sinclair, former consultant with the McKinsey Group's Atlanta operations and currently Alexander Kantor's number two, filled the eyedropper and began feeding the mixture into the pitiful little mouth. Ling took it in with great swallows that wrenched his entire tiny frame.

After five mouthfuls, he slowed down, pausing and weaving his little skull back and forth, then coming up for one last gulp before collapsing.

Jeffrey slid his hand under the fuzzy little body and was rewarded with a rapturous snuggle. Ling loved to be held almost as much as he loved to be fed. Jeffrey smiled at the trembling little form cradled in his fingers, extremely glad that nobody back home could see him right then.

He had taken in the bird the night they found it, since Katya had class the next day and didn't want to leave it alone in her own flat that long. He had kept it because it brought Katya over to the shop every afternoon. No question about it, the bird was a much bigger draw than he was. For the moment, anyway. Jeffrey had big hopes for the future.

By the end of that week Jeffrey was hooked on the bird and wouldn't have given Ling up for love or money. If Katya wanted the bird, she'd have to move in—or at least that was what he was planning to insist on if she ever asked, which she didn't. Katya had an uncanny sixth sense that steered her clear of all such uncharted waters.

When baby was fed and burped and packed between pristine sheets, Jeffrey set up the coffee brewer, then started opening for the day. He flipped the switch to draw up the mesh shutters over the main window, turned on the shop's recessed lighting, and began opening the mail.

Just as the coffee finished perking, the front doorbell sounded. Jeffrey walked forward with a smile of genuine pleasure and released the lock. "And a very good morning to you, madame."

A visiting American dealer named Betty greeted him with, "Does it always rain here?"

"I seem to remember hearing somewhere that Boston's weather wasn't always that nice."

"Maybe not, but we get breaks from it. The sun comes out to remind us what's up there."

He led her toward the back of the shop, asked, "Did you sleep well?"

"I never sleep well in London. My body is not accustomed to being under water. I need to breathe air that doesn't smell like the inside of an aquarium. I'm growing webs between my toes. Next comes oily feathers so the water will roll off."

He helped her off with her coat. "Some coffee?" he offered.

"Thank you. I'm beginning to understand why you make it stronger than my nail-polish remover. It's intended to warm your bones on days like this." She handed him a heavy plastic bag. "A little offering toward your continuing education."

She always brought a stack of recent U.S. magazines; he always played at surprise, but his gratitude was genuine. They were those she worked through on the transatlantic flight, and passing them on to Jeffrey was as good a way as any of tossing them out. But he had been in the business long enough to know that having a buyer perform anything that even resembled a courtesy was rarer than genuine Elizabethan silver.

He leafed through them in anticipation of a slow afternoon's pleasure. There was the *Architectural Digest,* at five bucks a pop; *Unique Homes,* filled with full-color full-page ads for the basic sixteen bedroom home and rarely showing anything valued at less than a million dollars; *HG,* the restyled *House and Garden,* struggling desperately to attract the yuppie reader; *Elle Decor,* basically concentrating on the modern, but just snooty enough to give him the occasional sales idea for a piece that wasn't moving; and a variety of upscale magazines to teach him what there was to know about the slippery notions of American taste—*House Digest, Southern Accents, Colonial Homes, Connoisseur Magazine.*

"These are great, Betty. Thanks a million."

Betty shook a few drops of water from her short-cropped gray hair. "I've been here eight days now. No, nine. This miserable misting rain hasn't stopped once. Or correct me if I'm wrong. Perhaps I blinked in the wrong place and missed the glorious English summer."

"It has been pretty awful. But we had a few days of beautiful weather back in May. Hot, sunny, crystal blue skies. I even went down for a day at the beach."

"Impossible. I refuse to believe that London could have had sunshine. It would have made the front pages of every paper around the world."

He smiled. "Come on downstairs, there's something I'd like to show you."

He led Betty down the narrow metal staircase to the basement. It was a simple concrete-lined chamber, void of the upper room's stylish setting. The floor was laid with beige indoor-outdoor carpeting and the low ceiling set with swivel lamps on long plastic strips.

"I've been saving this for you," he said, reaching up to turn a lamp toward the space beneath the staircase.

The light shone on a gateleg table, one so narrow that with both leaves down it was less than eight inches across. It was simple oak, burnished for over three centuries by caring hands until the original finish glowed with fiery pride.

Betty ran a practiced hand over its surface, bent and inspected the straight-carved legs, pronounced, "Definitely Charles the Second. Late Jacobean."

"I thought it might be."

"No question about it." She raised up, her eyes lit with undisguised excitement. "I know just where this is going."

"You're not supposed to let it show, Betty."

"You don't have any idea just how special you are, do you? I've never seen so many twisted definitions for honesty as I find in this trade." She walked back over, patted his cheek. "Did you know you're already gaining a reputation?"

"Who says?"

"One the other traders would kill for, I might add. Of course, they treat the concept of honesty as something they can buy." She chuckled, shook her head, turned back to the table. "What a true work of art. It deserves to go to a home where it will be appreciated, don't you think?"

"I wish I could afford to keep it," he confessed.

"Don't worry. That too will come."

"How can you be so sure?"

She did not look up. "Less than a year in this game, and already the word's getting out about you. Just be patient and don't give in to greed when the opportunity arises. How much for the table?"

"Five thousand. Pounds."

She gave a single nod. "High, but fair. Set to allow me an honest profit, no need to argue or bicker or stomp around in pretended rage. And you don't carry another Jacobean piece in the entire shop, do you? No, of course not. You really were holding it for me, weren't you?"

"The minute I saw it, I knew you'd flip."

"I'm too old and set in my ways for any of that, I'm afraid. But I do love it and you are a perfect sweetheart to think of me." She gave him a from-the-heart smile, another rare gem in this trade. "Now how about some of that coffee of yours? Still making it too strong?"

"I'm trying to get it to where it'll take the tarnish off my spoons," he replied, leading her back upstairs. "I'm not quite there yet. The last batch melted the silver."

"It's difficult for me talk about antiques without talking about my love of antiques," she said, once they were back upstairs.

"You always say that when we start talking."

"Well, it's true." She accepted her cup, took a sip, made a face. "Good grief, Jeffrey. You're going to melt my inlays."

"Too strong?" he asked politely.

"Pour some of this out and fill it halfway with milk. Maybe I'll keep my stomach lining."

She watched him doctor her cup, took another sip, gave him a nod. "I do believe I'm going to be able to drink this batch without gagging."

"Coming from you that's real praise."

Betty settled back and began what for them was the favorite part of their time together. As she sat and sipped her coffee, he sat and drank her words.

"When you think of antiques in the United States, you have to ask yourself how the pieces got here. Some of the early items were brought over by wealthy families. We tend to see all of our ancestors as having arrived in rags, packed into the holds of sailing ships like cattle. For many, many people this just was not true."

She stopped to taste her coffee. The cup was one of a set of Rosenthal, so delicate the shadow of her lips could be seen through the porcelain. On the outside was painted a pastoral scene in the tradition of the early Romanticists; with either excellent vision or a magnifying glass one could make out genteel ladies under frilly parasols watching gentlemen in spats lay out picnics while being watched by smiling cows and prancing horses. In the background was a mansion in the best Greco-Italian-fairytale style.

"In most instances, the wealthier families traveled over with their own craftsmen. They intended to build their homes, you see, and skilled workers were as hard to find then as now. Once the main house was completed, these craftsmen would begin to make furniture."

They were seated in the little office alcove behind the

stairwell. Between the banister and his desk Jeffrey had set a nineteenth-century screen, whose three panels were inlaid with ebony and mother-of-pearl in a European parody of a Japanese garden scene. His desk was a real find, an eighteenth-century product that appeared to have been carved from one massive piece of fruitwood. Its front was curved to match the wood's natural grain, with the two drawers made from the panels that had been cut from those very places. The legs were slender and delicately scrolled, matched by four short banisters that rose from each corner of the desk top. They in turn supported thin panels no more than two inches high, carved to depict a series of writing implements—quill pens, inkstands, knives for sharpening, miniature blotters, tiny books.

"You have to think of American antiques in terms of where people settled, moving from the East to the West, and adapting as they went along," Betty continued. "The same is true between the different settlements in the North and South. In the North you had Chippendale, you had Sheraton, you had craft shops where you found so-called manufactured pieces. These were mostly copies of styles originating in Europe, usually from either France or England, but lacking many of the really intricate details. American craft shops tended to go for higher quantities, you see. And there were fewer people with the really refined tastes who would be willing to pay the outrageous sums required for delicate inlay work."

At the front of the shop, beige lace curtains formed a backdrop that allowed in light, but also restricted the view of passers-by to the lone semi-circular sideboard standing in solitary splendor on the window's raised dais. The remainder of the shop was designed to create an air of genteel splendor. Pieces were placed with ample room to breathe, as Alexander Kantor had described it to Jeffrey upon his arrival. Recessed ceiling lights were arranged to cast the sort of steady glow that was normally reserved for art galleries, with their hue and brilliance individually set so as to best bring out the wood's luster. The whole shop smelled vaguely of beeswax polish and wealth.

"The big southern plantations occasionally had craftsmen so talented that pieces could be identified by their quality," Betty went on. "If you hear of such articles going on the market today, they are usually sold as collectors' items or works of art. The prices would place them in your range, which for American antiques is very rare."

The two back walls of his office space were decorated with original steel engravings, the prints so detailed as to almost look photographed. Beside his desk stood a set of antique mahogany filing drawers, probably used in the director's office of an old shipping company, as each drawer was embossed with a brass anchor and the sides had carvings of a compass face. In the ceiling corner above the filing cabinet swiveled a miniature video, which piped its continual picture to a security company located down the street. An enclosing barrier had been erected to the side of Jeffrey's writing desk in the form of mahogany bookshelves. They stood a full nine feet high, and were fronted by a series of miniature double doors, each the height of two shelves and containing hand-blown diamond-shaped glass set in brass frames. The shelves contained Jeffrey's growing collection of books on antiques.

"Most of the affordable fine pieces came from the northern craft shops, since many were manufactured in lots and not as single pieces. This meant that as the professional class developed, their front hallways and living areas had tables and cabinets and sideboards imported from somewhere up north."

Set in the ceiling corner across from his office alcove was a round convex mirror, through which Jeffrey could watch the entire shop while seated at his desk. Keeping half an eye always on the store was by now old habit, although the front door—the shop's only entrance—was always double locked. Entry during office hours was possible only once he pressed the release button by the banister, then walked forward to personally throw the latch and open the door. Even with all the smaller items safely locked in the pair of Edwardian glass-fronted jeweler's cabinets, unless it was with a very trusted client like Betty, Jeffrey never sat down with a customer in the store. Never.

"When I was a little child my mother used to take me on what she called her buying trips. I was the only girl, and I had four older brothers. When we went off together like that it was the only time in those early years when I felt as if I could just enjoy being a girl."

Betty talked with a soft southern accent which had been

gradually whittled away by years of trading all over the East Coast. Her shop had been located on Boston's Beacon Hill for more than three decades, but her work took her from Texas to Canada and back several times a month. Her shop was the source of only a fraction of her income. Auction houses called on Betty to identify unknown pieces. Interior decorators in ten states had her on retainer to seek out antiques that would fit into the residences and executive offices and fine hotel lobbies they were hired to adorn. Wealthy households would ask her to keep a look out for something to fill an empty space. Something elegant, they would often say, not knowing themselves what they wanted besides the status of owning an almost-priceless one-of-a-kind. Something expensive. Betty had a way of listening that bestowed respect upon such a customer, and that was what many wanted most of all. Respect.

"I was raised in Virginia—I believe I told you that before. My parents were what you would call middle class, and there were not a lot of antiques that had been handed down. When my mother and I went off to buy, we were looking for pieces that would go into our own home. Those were some of the happiest days I have ever known, getting up early and traveling off to some country antique store or a market somewhere, just me and my mother, eating in nice restaurants and talking girl-talk. Very precious memories. My love of antiques started right then and there."

Betty was a smallish woman who carried herself so erect that she appeared much taller than she was. She dressed with an artist's eye, conservative in color and extravagant with materials. Today she wore a midnight-blue crepe-de-chine silk dress with a matching cashmere jacket, and for a necklace had a small antique pocket watch hung from a gold rope chain.

"My mother did not have a lot of money. Most of what she spent on antiques she saved from her weekly shopping, putting it in a little pewter sugar bowl until it was full, and then off she'd go. Back then there were not many antique shops. This was back in the mid-thirties, just as the Depression was lifting. Times were very hard, even for a relatively well-off family like mine, and this was really her only diversion.

"A lot of black people in the rural areas had been given

furniture and cut-glass bowls and even some crystal from the homes where they had worked. Back in the twenties, as people became wealthier, they wanted to discard these old things and buy something new and store-bought. That was what it was called in the South, although most of the rural families purchased from catalogs—store bought goods.

"My mother was a very sweet person, and during the very hard times had organized a church group to help the poorest of these families with food and children's clothes and medicine. People remembered her kindnesses, and now that she had some money and wanted to buy these old things, they would try to help her. So she would drive down these country roads, often nothing more than dirt tracks, and someone would come out on the front porch and say that so-and-so had a pretty piece of pressed glass or a chiffarobe or flow-blue, which was a special kind of pottery china with a pretty blue design on it, and they needed money and wanted to sell it.

"I bought my very first antique in that way. It was a little blue chicken of hand-blown glass that you could open up and keep candy in. A woman let us go up into her attic and go through a trunk filled with old glass wrapped in old newspapers, and she let me buy that chicken for twenty-five cents. It had probably taken me six months to save up that many pennies—money was still very hard to come by, especially for a child. I still have that piece. It sits on its own special little shelf in my kitchen."

The phone gave its querulous demand for attention. "Excuse me." Jeffrey picked up the receiver, was greeted with distant hissings and pops. "Priceless Limited." There were a couple of crackling connections. "Hello?"

"To whom am I speaking, please?" The voice was cheerful and heavily accented, the words fairly shouted.

Jeffrey raised his voice in reply. "This is the Priceless antique shop. Can I help you?"

"Jeffrey?" The gentleman's unspoken laughter called above the line's crackling. "Do I have the pleasure of speaking to Jeffrey Allen Sinclair?"

"Yes." Jeffrey tried to place the voice, came up blank. "Who is this?"

"Ah, an excellent question. Who is this indeed?" The laughter broke through, a most appealing sound. "I fear you will have to ask that of our friend Alexander. How are you, my dear boy?"

"I'm all right," he said, giving Betty an eloquent shrug.

"Splendid. That is absolutely splendid. Alexander has spoken so much about you I feel we are already the best of friends."

"He has?"

"Indeed, yes. Has Alexander arrived?"

"Not yet." Jeffrey was almost shouting the words. "He's supposed to be here the day after tomorrow."

"No matter. Please, Jeffrey, do me the kindness of passing on a message to Alexander. Would you do that?"

"Of course."

"Splendid. Splendid. Tell him the shipment is ready. Do you have that?"

"Got it."

"Excellent. And now, my dear boy, I bid you farewell. I do so hope that we shall have an opportunity to meet very soon. Until then, may the grace of the Lord Jesus Christ, and the love of God, and the fellowship of the Holy Spirit be with you always."

Betty watched him hang up the phone, said, "That sounded curious."

Jeffrey scribbled busily, replied, "I get all kinds of weird calls a week or so before Alexander arrives. I've stopped worrying about them."

"Or wondering?"

He stripped out the page and stuffed it in an already bulging folder. "I don't think I'll ever get that casual."

She handed back her cup and motioned toward the lead-paned bookshelves. "Do you mind?"

"Not at all." He opened the desk drawer, fished out his key ring, inserted the miniature skeleton key and opened the top set of doors. "These are my most recent purchases."

She slipped on a pair of gold-rimmed reading glasses and began examining the titles. "Is Alexander bringing in a lot of jewelry these days?"

"Just five pieces, but they were all Russian, and all really special, and I didn't know the first thing about them. I've been playing catch-up."

"So I see."

All the books were of the tall, oversized variety favored

by publishers of high-priced, richly photographed volumes. The titles made an impressive list: *The Twilight of the Tsars*; *Russian Art at the Turn of the Century*. Von Solodkoff's *Russian Gold and Silver*. Bennett and Mascetti's *Understanding Jewelry*. Abrams' *Treasures From the Kremlin*. Von Habsburg's *Fabergé*.

She pointed to the book entitled *Das Gold Aus Dem Kreml*. "Do you read German?"

"No, a little French, that's all. But the pictures in that book are the best of the lot, and I can sort of figure out what they are talking about in some of the captions."

"Can you really." She peered over the top of her glasses. "You really must tell me the next time Alexander comes up with one of his little surprises, Jeffrey."

"I thought you dealt only in furniture and paintings."

"I do not intend it for the market." She waved a hand at the other shelves. "Open up and let me see, please."

The books represented an awkward dipping into various wells, spanning centuries and styles and markets with breathtaking speed. There were beginner's guides to identifying the otherwise unseen, such as the well-known *A Fortune in Your Attic*. The remainder were fairly indicative of what Jeffrey faced within Alexander's shop—a need to catch whatever was thrown at him, and speak of it with relative authority.

"Do you mean to tell me you've read all of these?" Betty asked.

"There are a lot of slow days in this business. You ought to know that." Jeffrey found it difficult to describe, even to Betty, how fascinating his study had become. "It gives me something to do while I wait for the bell to ring."

Without turning around, she asked, "Do you ever come across the really singular piece, Jeffrey?"

He thought of the item that had first taken him to Christie's, replied, "Sometimes."

"I was not restricting my question to furniture."

"I know. I wasn't either."

"I'd very much like you to remember me the next time something comes up." Betty reached over and traced her finger along one Moroccan-leather binding that bore the title *Russian Embroidery and Lace*. She kept her voice casual as she said, "I have a number of very rich customers. Very discreet. They would be most willing to pick up a truly singular item and effectively make it disappear." She turned to him. "Do you understand?"

"I'm not sure."

She patted his arm. "How utterly precious. Just promise me that if something comes in that takes your breath away, you won't forget to call me, all right?"

CHAPTER

2

Jeffrey's arrival in London had marked the beginning of changes on every level of his being. From an emotional perspective, it was the first time since a brief fling with faith at an early age that Jeffrey really *felt* anything besides a rising frustration. Before his departure from America, he had recognized his lukewarm attitude toward life and accepted it as the price paid for playing the part. Now, there was an emotional dimension to his life. Everything that registered in his consciousness registered in his heart as well.

His father was the quintessential mild-mannered, soft-spoken man, an electronics engineer turned production administrator and corporate vice-president. Jeffrey had inherited a full dosage of both the emotionless demeanor and the quiet ambition that lurked beneath his father's bland surface. Yet a young life spent witnessing the price his father paid during his corporate rise left Jeffrey wondering what on earth to be ambitious *for.*

Jeffrey adored his parents. It was more than just a bonding of filial love; he truly *liked* them. They were good, genuine people who had struggled through a life of hard knocks, and finally achieved a success they fully deserved. They set about enjoying their definition of the good life with hard-earned determination and their elder son's blessings.

Jeffrey had seldom complained as their lives' course wound through seven states and eleven homes in as many years. He had not felt a need to complain. He was happy with his family. He loved his parents and he trusted them. Early in life he developed a skill at building new friendships and growing new roots deep in strange soils. He fashioned a detachment and a maturity long before most young people were even aware of what the words meant.

As he entered high school, he looked around at his fellow students and saw people who were simply not up to dealing with the torments that life threw their way. They sank into throes of boredom or empty cliques or drugs or casual sex or fanatical devotion to sports. They tried as hard as they could to escape from the fears and pains that kept boiling up inside them.

Jeffrey felt comfortable with himself, and marveled at how seldom that appeared to be the case with others. If his ability to float through turbulent times was a product of being uprooted and replanted every dozen months, so be it. He knew the constant shifting of his life had helped him tap some unseen, ill-defined well inside himself. For this he was truly grateful. He also knew that his father's path was not for him, yet he admired the man for knowing so clearly what he wanted.

Jeffrey was proud of the fact that the furious cross-currents of a life lived without a settled family and familiar surroundings had forged unbreakable bonds between his parents. It had also drawn the three of them more closely together. In the dismal early days of a new home full of boxes and vague smells and other people's histories, they huddled together for warmth and love and comfort.

They learned to laugh at the repetitiveness of problems that drew a sameness into every new city—streets that took them away from where they wanted to go, doctors and electricians and plumbers and bankers who had no time for newcomers, impersonal name-takers who tried to chill their very bones with a total lack of friendliness as they adjusted to new schools and new rules and new lives. The warmth and healing of close friends they found among themselves, and with each move became more intimate, more reliant upon each other.

But not Jeffrey's younger brother. With every move, his brother had fallen a little further away from the safety of their tightly bound trio. And with each new year, his brother

had also fallen a little more apart. His increasingly de-
mented behavior tore at the fabric of Jeffrey's life in ways
that no move, no transition, no earlier trauma had ever prepared him. He found himself faced with the specter of hating
his brother, hating him for the pain he caused to himself and
to their parents. He was unable to respond with the compassion shown by his parents, terrified of having his protective
bland exterior pried away; so he took the only other alter-
native he found open to himself. He decided that he no longer
had a brother. He wiped the slate clean. And in doing so, he
lost the need to hate.

With his move from university into corporate life, Jeffrey
found a new reason to drown in negative emotions. The corporate world clutched at his very existence, calling him to
give his all to some nameless company that offered vague
promises of reward somewhere further down the line. Jeffrey
responded by becoming a consummate actor, playing the ambitious go-getter to all the outside world.

If anyone had ever bothered to ask Jeffrey Allen Sinclair
what it was he wanted most out of life, he probably would
have replied, a calling. But no one ever did. He wore the
yuppie mask far too well for anyone to think he sought more
than just to be on top.

Four years with McKinsey in Atlanta had left him bereft
not of ambition, but of goals. He burned with a desire to
succeed, to achieve, yet he had no idea what to aim for.

The senior partners had one common thread running
through all their lives: they were grimly, determinedly, daily
dissatisfied. He searched their faces with anxiety, just as he
searched his own heart. Why had they spent their lives
struggling for the title and the income and the five-acre colonial spread if all it gained them was ulcers, bad backs,
divorces, kids who hated them, and eyes that lit up only at
the thought of yet another big deal?

Jeffrey was too aggressive and too full of energy to quit
when he saw behind the charade. He would have gone crazy
without some channel, some direction, even if the direction
made no sense. Instead, his life simply became a theater. He
knew the lines and spoke the part well, but in his heart of
hearts there bloomed a yearning desire to be elsewhere. To
do more. To live life with more gusto than was offered by a
padded chair in a carpeted glass-lined cell.

Jeffrey was of slender build. Just over six feet tall, he had a supple strength without appearing overly muscular, and played a number of sports with disinterested ease. He found little on the playing fields that tempted him to give his all, so he played whatever his group played, and only so well as to not draw attention to himself.

Jeffrey's features helped enormously in making the theatrics a success. It was a strong face, full of the sharp angles and long lines of a determined success story. His hair was turning prematurely gray, but only in the most dignified manner. There were brushstrokes of silver at each temple, and faint pewter threads woven through a full and virile crop. To everyone except Jeffrey, it lent him an enviably distinguished note. For him it was the makings of his worst nightmares.

He had dreams of standing in front of his mirror and watching the aging process carry him through all the stages of decrepit decline. He would wake up in an empty-hearted sweat—not because he feared growing old, but because he feared a growing void where life's purpose was supposed to reside.

In his walks to and from the McKinsey offices in downtown high-rise Atlanta, Jeffrey would catch himself staring at the men and women who were barely visible to his fellow high-fliers. He watched their faces, this cadre of underlings, the hordes who trod their way daily through jobs that held little interest and less hope. The older faces chilled him to the bone, their empty exhausted gazes foreshadowing what might befall him if his act were ever uncovered.

Then, fourteen months ago, the invitation to lunch with Alexander Kantor had arrived like a lifeline tossed into a dark and stormy sea. Jeffrey had not seen it as such at first, however; in fact, he had almost avoided the meeting entirely.

They met for lunch at his father's insistence, during one of his infrequent visits back to Jacksonville. A lunch with an unknown relative was positively the last thing he wanted to do on a sunny Saturday afternoon, especially when his friends were headed for the beach. But when he told his father that he was going to skip the meeting, his father shook his head, said, I'm not sure that's a good idea. It wouldn't surprise me to hear that he wanted to talk with you about your future. Jeffrey snorted, said, you mean a job? I've never even met the man before. His father replied, Alexander has his own way of doing things, and he's always seemed to know more about our lives than we have ever known about his.

So Jeffrey went. Angry that he was not at the beach, but he went.

He arrived at the restaurant hoping to find some way of shaking the man's hand and making polite conversation and then leaving. Jeffrey figured a five-minute meeting would be enough to satisfy his father. But Alexander wasn't there. Jeffrey sat in the nicest restaurant in all of north Florida, and smoldered.

The longer he sat there, the more grotesque his picture of the man became. Alexander Kantor. What a name. He probably fit in perfectly with all the interior decorator types an antique dealer had to work with. Jeffrey toyed with the ice in his empty water glass, saw the man take form before his eyes—slender as a beanpole, dressed in skin-tight canvas pants with buttons, liked deck-shoes without socks even though he got seasick at the sight of a boat rocking at anchor. Poorly fitting toupee and a mechanical sunlamp tan that left him looking like an underdone lobster. Yeah, Jeffrey could see him, all right. The black sheep of the family, the one nobody'd even heard from in ten years, the one who'd never married. All they knew was that he had a fancy antique shop in London. Right. That wasn't so easy to check up on from five thousand miles away. The guy probably dealt out of the back of an old van, a battered white one with bald tires—

"My dear boy, I'm terribly sorry to have kept you waiting." A deep, heavily accented voice boomed from beside him, making Jeffrey jerk upright. "I do hope you haven't been here long."

Jeffrey banged both knees in his scramble out of the booth. The gentleman extended a hand, said in his cultured voice, "Alexander Kantor. At your service."

"Ah, nice, that is, Jeffrey Sinclair." His hand was taken in by well-tanned fingers covered with the loose skin of an older man, then squeezed with a strength that made Jeffrey wince.

"You most certainly are. You would not know it, I am sure, but you are the mirror image of your maternal grandfather as a lad. Piotr was my father's brother; you might have heard that from your family. When I was a young boy I positively worshiped the gentleman." He gave a polished, even-toothed smile. "This lunch has already started off well, wouldn't you say?"

He was every inch an aristocrat. His hair was a burnished silver, cut to perfection. His eyebrows bushed upward at an angle that on a lesser man would have looked ridiculous; on him they simply fit. Beneath their jutting arrogance, gray eyes peered at him with frank inspection. His face was fleshy, but held from looking overweight by a ponderous jaw. His nose was a veritable eagle's beak. His dark suit was double-breasted and clearly hand-tailored. His tie was a mellow silk that matched his pocket kerchief, his shirt a crisp gray pin-stripe with white collar and cuffs. His watch, ring, and cuf-flinks were a matching design of woven white and yellow gold.

The waiter appeared at their elbow, beating the maitre d' by half a stride. The two of them hovered about Alexander Kantor and played the roles of imperious restaurant manager and bustling server. The old gentleman paid them no mind, clearly accustomed to this sort of attention. All around the restaurant heads turned, brows furrowing in concentrated effort to remember where they had seen him before. There was no question about it, Alexander Kantor exuded a magnetic presence.

"So." He waved aside the waiter's ministrations, snapped open his napkin. "What is the family saying about me these days?"

"Ah, I don't believe—"

"Come, come. I used to be their favorite topic of gossip; don't tell me I've been forgotten. It never ceased to amaze me how they came up with some of the notions they did."

"All I know is that you have an antiques business in London and live, ah . . ."

"Yes, go on, my boy. This is where it tends to become interesting." At last he deigned to notice the maitre d'. "I'll have what my young guest is having."

"Sir, thus far your young guest has made do with six glasses of water and a dozen breadsticks."

"Is that so? Well then, in that case I should compliment the young gentleman on his graceful manners, don't you agree?" He settled the maitre d' with one frosty glare. "It was most kind of you to wait like this, Jeffrey. It really was."

Jeffrey watched his plans for a quick getaway fade into the distance. "My pleasure."

"We have quite a bit of business to discuss. Perhaps we should dispense with the head-fogging ritual of aperitifs, don't you think?"

"Fine with me."

"Excellent. Now tell me," he said, turning back to the maitre d'. "Does your wine menu extend as far as the fair fields of France?"

"It does indeed, sir."

"Splendid. With this heat, I believe we'd be wise to stay with fish, don't you, Jeffrey?"

"Sure."

"Then let us have a bottle of your finest Pouilly Fuissé," he said, pronouncing it correctly. He waited while the maitre d' made his bowing exit, then turned back to Jeffrey. "American waiters are all either college students with too much smoke between their ears or actors who never made it on stage, don't you agree?"

Jeffrey decided to try a dose of honesty. "You aren't anything like what I expected."

"I'm not the least bit surprised. When the family is not painting me out to be a mock prince sporting around one of his three dozen castles, they have me living off the crumbs from some rich heiress's dining table."

"Something like that."

"Well, there's more than a bit of truth in both of them. I do have several residences, although none of them are quite grand enough to deserve the title of palace. And anyone in the antiques trade lives off the rising and falling fortunes of others. An antique is nothing more than a used bit of life's flotsam and jetsam that someone or another has decided is worth a king's ransom, either because it's old, or because it's pretty, or because it has belonged to someone they deem to be worthy of remembering. Whatever the reason, one thing you may always bank upon—another backside has rested in that chair before you."

As the meal progressed Jeffrey found himself becoming captivated by the gentleman. Alexander's strong Polish accent added an alien burr to his polished speech, and came to represent the two sides of his character—the gracious international businessman on the one hand, and the mysterious relative on the other. Jeffrey sat and ate and listened and slowly came to the decision that he genuinely liked the man, mystery and all.

"Jeffrey. What a positively American-sounding name. I suppose all your friends call you Jeff."

"Not if I can help it."

Alexander Kantor showed genuine alarm. "Don't tell me you've been turned into a Jay."

"Good grief, no."

"Thank heavens. I'm certain I couldn't bear the strain of having a Jay skulking about."

Jeffrey started to ask, skulk about where. Instead he replied, "I don't skulk, and nobody's ever called me Jay twice."

"Do I detect a note of steel beneath that bland American exterior?" Alexander Kantor inspected him frankly. "Well. There might be hope yet. Tell me, Jeffrey. How have you spent your time since university?"

"I've worked with McKinsey Management Consultants out of their Atlanta office for the past six years."

"Really." The jutting eyebrows raised a notch. "In Europe a man hired from university for a consultant position is considered to be one of the best. Is that the case here?"

Jeffrey shrugged. "There were about four hundred applicants for each person hired."

"How interesting. I suppose you must find the work tremendously stimulating."

"Not really."

"Oh? Why is that?"

"Do you prefer honesty or corporate diplomacy?"

"I have always put the highest value on honesty, young man," Alexander replied. "Carry on."

"The pay for the lower grades is lousy. There's an endless back-stabbing battle to see who is going into one of the senior slots. Partners go out to the client companies, make the presentations, and leave us behind to do the trench work. Because of the competition, people on my level spend ridiculous hours doing research, poring over figures, writing out stuff that nobody in his right mind is ever going to read. Justifying the fees charged by the partners, basically."

Jeffrey leaned back, allowed the waiter to collect his plate. "Working there has been like joining a secret order or fraternity, with the partners coming by our cubicles every once in a while to pat us on the back and tell us to keep at it, because look how wonderful it's going to be once we hit the jackpot. But only less than one in ten actually make partner. The rest suffer from severe burnout and drop by the wayside."

"And which are you to be?" Alexander Kantor asked gravely.

"Burnout, most likely. I lack some of the basic ingredients, like an overriding desire to go for the jugular. Sometimes I pull back and wonder what in the world I'm doing there. It all seems so silly, chasing after an ulcer, a heart attack, and an early grave. But every time I put on the brakes I see all the others start pulling ahead, so I dive back down in the trench and keep on digging."

"I take it, then, that your present occupation does not grant you the satisfaction of having found the purpose for which you were placed upon this earth."

Jeffrey laughed a rueful no.

"Let's see. This would put your age at twenty-six, is that right?"

"Twenty-seven. I took a year off to travel before graduating."

"Ah yes. I recall a card or letter to that effect, saying that I should expect to find a bedraggled and no doubt bearded young man on my doorstep, and that I should not set the dogs on him. You were to be fed and allowed to wash your drawers. I believe your dear ones also included a request to have the doctor check you for lice and other horrors before placing you on the plane home—as though there were European strains of bacteria designed to attack visiting American college students."

"I think it was more a fear of where I had been sleeping."

"No doubt with good reason. In any case, I was quite disappointed not to have heard from you."

Jeffrey sipped at his water, recalling the impressions he had carried with him to Europe. Somewhere in his backpack had been a series of three or four addresses, enough to seem as if there was at least one place in each country he had visited belonging to this unknown uncle. Only he wasn't really an uncle, and no one in the family could bring themselves to speak of him without a smirk and a shake of the head.

Jeffrey had dutifully carried the addresses around with him for a year, along with a mental image that kept shifting between a crotchety old man with too much money and something a little more swish. Upon his return, he had made some vague excuse for not having called the mystery relative, and nobody had seemed very concerned.

"Why do they talk about you as they do?" he asked.

"Who, my long-lost American kin?" Kantor made a regal gesture dismissing the waiter's offer of anything further. "That is quite simple. Anything that is not known becomes shrouded with supposition, Jeffrey. It is one of life's unwritten rules. With time, the supposition becomes reality. It is much easier to believe nonsense than to search out the truth, and most people are either too lazy or too comfortable to look for truth any further than their front gardens." He cast a careful glance Jeffrey's way. "I do hope I've not offended you."

"Sounds to me as if you know them perfectly. The family never visited you, did they?"

"Not in years, although I must admit that I have not made an effort to visit your clan since Piotr's untimely departure from this earth. I tried to keep in touch, in my own feeble way, but your own family seemed to hop across the nation at such speeds that I would receive the latest address only to learn that you had already moved elsewhere."

"Yeah, that was Dad's life. When I was a kid I thought for a while that he was paid to move."

"Another of the prices for being an American executive. He was with IBM, I believe."

"Still is."

"Of course. Well, enough about the various kinfolk, as you say. Tell me more about yourself, Jeffrey."

"Like what?"

"Well, perhaps a bit more about your work."

Jeffrey leaned back in his seat and took a moment to gather his thoughts. Alexander Kantor offered a sense of immediate intimacy. He invited a frank discussion by offering the gift of intense listening. Jeffrey found it immensely satisfying to have this chance to speak with someone who *understood*.

"When I started out, the work at the big consulting groups was already shifting—only I didn't know it then. We went from helping companies identify problems and learn better management techniques, to simply growing bigger faster. Mergers and acquisitions became the name of the game in the eighties. Those words alone are enough to start a consultant salivating."

"Change is inevitable," Kantor said. "Why should you be disturbed by an altering of direction within the consulting industry?"

"Mergers tend to wipe people off the map," Jeffrey replied vehemently. "It brings out the worst trait of business, lack of concern for the little person. And even the people who are left after the firing squads have worked their way through the companies—which was one of our jobs—still end up feeling either left out or squashed down. People are so shaken by this change in their working life that they forget about other people. I only see it inside the businesses, but I'll bet it happens in their families, too. They don't have time anymore for other people's feelings, fears, ambitions—anything but their own skin. I hate what it does to people, and I hate the misery it causes for everybody but the handful of top executives who skim off the cream. It's become about seventy percent of our business, the most profitable section. If you're a trench worker like me, the best way to make it to partner is to get yourself attached to an M and A team. You can always tell who they are, too. They're the ones walking around with blood on their hands."

"How remarkable," Kantor murmured. "A businessman with heart. Tell me, Jeffrey. Do you like dealing with people?"

"I've always thought so. That was why I got into management consulting work in the first place, so I could deal with a *lot* of people and a *lot* of issues. Maybe somewhere up the ladder that's the way it is, but right now I spend so much time in my little cubbyhole, I'm not sure I even remember how to be cordial."

"You're doing quite well, I assure you," Kantor said. He reached for an inner pocket, drew out a slender metal tube, and unscrewed the cap. He drew a cigar from a paper-thin screen of wood. "Do you mind?"

"Not at all. My grandfather used to smoke them."

Kantor smiled. "He most certainly did."

"I love the smell; I just can't stand the taste."

"Tell me, Jeffrey." He brought out a polished key chain

and grasped a gold-plated guillotine the size of his thumb, an apparatus with a springblade and circular opening to clip off the cigar tip. "What would you say is your strongest point?"

Jeffrey thought about it, replied, "That I'm hungry."

"I beg your pardon?"

"Not for money. Well, sure, that too. But it's not number one. I want to learn. And do. And expand. I'm not sure that makes any sense."

"On the contrary, it makes very good sense. It is always difficult to put matters of the heart into words. You wish to stretch the limits of your experience."

"That's it exactly."

"A most commendable trait." He rubbed the cigar back and forth between thumb and forefinger, asked with deceptive casualness, "And what would you say is your greatest failing?"

"As far as your business goes? Simple. I don't know the first thing about antiques. Or furniture. Or interior decorating. Nothing."

"It is indeed an issue, but not an insurmountable one. You clearly have the aptitude for learning and have expressed a willingness to adapt." He fastened upon Jeffrey with a gently penetrating gaze. "Besides this, then, where is your greatest weakness?"

He did not need to search very far. Feeling very exposed, Jeffery replied, "I'm so frustrated and impatient with my life I feel as if I'm going to explode sometimes. I get incredibly angry at everyone, at life, especially at the people close to me, because I feel so trapped. I don't know which way to turn to get out of the bind, and that gets me even angrier. I'll start thinking about it sometimes without even realizing it, and then all of a sudden I'm so furious I'm shaking."

Alexander Kantor eyed him for a very long moment. "Your candor is most admirable, young man. You certainly did not need to consider that one very long."

"My girlfriend broke up with me last week because of it, so it's still on my mind a lot. She said she was tired of trying to make a go of it with someone who was never satisfied. I tried to tell her that the problem wasn't with us, but it didn't make any difference. Not to her, anyway."

Kantor released a long thin plume of smoke toward the

ceiling. "If it is any consolation to you, young man, I learned a lesson about dissatisfaction some time ago that has brought me great consolation over the years. Shall I share it with you?"

"Sure."

"It is quite simple really. Dissatisfaction tends to lift one's eyes toward the horizon. Those who are comfortable rarely make the effort to search out something better. They may yearn for more, but they do not often receive it. They are too afraid of losing what they already have, you see, to take the risk. And there is always risk involved, Jeffrey. Always. Every major venture contains a moment when you must step off the cliff and stretch your wings toward the sky."

Jeffrey watched the man across from him and was suddenly struck with a feeling so solid it arrived in his mind already cemented into certainty. *He wanted that job.* There was no question, no need to doubt or consider his possibilities or salary or benefits or anything. Every mundane detail paled into insignificance beside the utter appeal of working with such a man as this. He *wanted* that job.

"A moment ago I mentioned a need to adapt," Kantor went on. "This cannot be stressed too highly, young man. The greatest failure of most intelligent people is a false confidence in what they already know. If you are going to succeed in this game, you must begin by assuming that you know nothing. Nothing at all. It is essential to your success."

Struggling to keep his eagerness from touching his voice, Jeffrey replied, "I understand."

"I am not sure you do," Kantor responded gravely. "I am not speaking solely of your knowledge of antiques and the related businesses. That in itself is only a small part of what is required. You must begin by assuming that you know *nothing.* Not how to dress, nor how to stand, nor how to greet a client, nor what to read, nor in some cases even what to think."

Kantor paused to draw on his cigar and gauge Jeffrey's reaction. He in turn kept his face carefully blank as he felt the words sink deep.

Clearly pleased with this silent response, Kantor went on. "You are about to enter an entirely different world, young man, one totally alien to anything you have ever experienced before. It has rules all its own. To assume that all people everywhere are basically the same, and thus you can get by on what passes for etiquette or correct prejudices or current wisdom here in your American existence, will doom your efforts to abject failure.

"This does not mean that you must affect a false attitude. I personally loathe the catty pettiness that pervades such people's lives. No, what I mean is that you must learn to adapt while remaining true to yourself. Do you understand?"

"I think so," he replied solemnly.

Kantor examined him carefully, and in time appeared to reach a decision. "Splendid. Now tell me, Jeffrey. What would you think of a ninety-day trial period in my London business?"

Resisting the urge to jump up, run screaming around the restaurant, kiss the frowning maitre d', he responded with a simple, "That sounds fine." Then he gave the game away with an enormous face-splitting grin.

Kantor replied with a small smile of his own. "Excellent. Ninety days will grant us ample time to see whether or not you have the ability to learn the required lessons and adapt to the new world, I am sure. Now I think it would be proper to offer you a small gesture of congratulations for this decision. Have you ever flown first class?"

"No, but I'm sure I could adapt to it very quickly."

"No doubt. It doesn't make long flights enjoyable. Nothing could go quite that far. But it does enliven the time considerably. When can you leave?"

The grin would just not stay down. "I have to give a month's notice."

"And I must take care of a few items in Canada before returning to Europe, then travel on the Continent for a week or so before arriving in London. Let us say that I shall expect you on the first day of June. That gives you fifty days to prepare. Is that sufficient?"

"Great. Just great."

"Splendid." He reached back into his coat pocket, extracted two folded sheets of heavily embossed paper, handed them over. "I prepared these in hopes of finding you a worthy candidate. On the first sheet you will find various addresses and telephone numbers for my residences and the London business. I must tell you, however, that when I am on a buying trip I am rarely in a position to be contacted. The second sheet contains a list of books I would like you to commit to memory before your arrival. There are fifteen in all, and should give you a basic overview of some of the more important areas in which my business trades. You will find them quite expensive. They are all extensively illustrated with color plates, which should assist you in understanding the finer points. Bring the receipts with you. At the bottom of the page is the name and address of my New York travel agent. He will be sending you a plane ticket and the address of your temporary London residence."

Jeffrey looked up from the pages, said gravely, "Thanks a lot, Mr. Kantor."

"You are quite welcome, young man." He signaled to the waiter and rose to his feet, extending his hand to Jeffrey. "I shall look forward to seeing you in London. Until then, good afternoon."

CHAPTER
3

As Jeffrey was ushering Betty back through the front door, the phone rang. It was the assistant chief of Christie's furniture section. "Sorry to bother you like this, Jeffrey, but I've had a rather strange call this morning."

A year in the place had not diminished Jeffrey's enjoyment of the fruity way Britain's upper-crust spoke, though it left him feeling the uncouth country cousin. "No problem. What can I do for you?"

"It seems that we have an official from the German government coming in for a bit of a snoop."

"The chest of drawers?" Jeffrey guessed.

"Precisely."

"It sat in our front window for almost a month, you advertised it all over the world and then put it on the front cover of last week's auction brochure. Why do you think he's shown up now?"

"If the German bureaucracy is anything like our own, perhaps because they just heard of its existence," the Christie's man replied. "In any case, I understand you were planning to attend today's auction. I was wondering if you might be willing to pop by afterward."

"Why me? The piece is sold."

"It appears that this chap has the power to block the sale, or at least make trouble for our buyer. You are aware that it is a German industrialist who placed the high bid."

"I was at the auction."

"Of course you were. Well, it appears that our caller intends to apply some rather crude pressure. Tax reviews covering the buyer's previous five generations, or something of the sort. Very nasty, really."

"So where does that leave us?"

"From the sounds of it, this chap intends to claim the high bid as his own. I suppose from our perspective, it's not quite so important as it will be for our industrialist friend. At least somebody will be paying us." He hesitated, then went on. "The gentleman asked some rather pointed questions. I thought it might be nice if you would help me clarify the matter."

"There's not a lot I can say besides the fact that Alexander found the piece and brought it here."

"Yes, your man Kantor does attach a great deal of mystery to most of his pieces, doesn't he? Still, it would be nice if you could come in and meet this chap."

Jeffrey glanced at his watch. "My assistant should be here in about fifteen minutes. I'll need to leave immediately, as my painting is one of the first lots. When is this guy showing up?"

"In about two hours."

"Why don't I meet you upstairs as soon as my item has sold?"

"Splendid. That really is most kind."

He hung up the phone, and reflected that it would not be difficult to keep the antique's origins a secret. Jeffrey knew very little about Alexander Kantor and even less about where his furniture came from. Almost nothing, in fact. Yet the mystery was somehow part of the man, and he liked Kantor intensely.

And the freedom—he liked that too. It was the sort of freedom that he would have dreamed of back when he had been working for McKinsey if only he had been able to imagine it. He had known several friends who had made the major move, risked it all and gone out on their own. They had all spoken of yearning for a freedom they did not have and *could* not have so long as they worked for someone else. Jeffrey had nodded and agreed and secretly envied them.

In the evenings spent watching traffic speed by in endless urgent streams beneath his high-rise Atlanta apartment window, Jeffrey had wished that he too had possessed the money and the ideas and the *desire* to go for broke. But nothing had called to him with an urgent tug of the heartstrings, challenged him sufficiently, or spoken to him with that sense of utter certainty, *this is it.*

Nothing, that is, until now. He did not own the business, but in many respects was already coming to claim it as partially his. Especially when Alexander took off on one of his unexplained tours.

The first such disappearance had occurred nine months before. After three months of working virtually day and night with Alexander, the gentleman had announced that he was leaving the next day on a buying trip.

"For how long?" Jeffrey asked.

"It is terrifically hard to tell about these things," Alexander had replied. "But I would guess about three weeks."

Three weeks alone. Jeffrey looked around the shop. The retail value of their stock at that moment was approaching four million dollars.

Alexander showed his usual perceptiveness. "It's all yours."

"What does that mean?"

"This will not work if I give it to you only halfway," Alexander replied. "Clients will refuse to close a deal with you. They'll assume you won't have the authority to set prices. And three weeks is too long to leave the business without a signatory present."

Jeffrey felt as though he'd been pushed over the cliff-edge. "What if I do something you don't like?"

"If I felt there were even a slim chance, I would not be making this journey," Alexander Kantor replied. "But if the unforeseen does occur, I assure you that it will only happen once."

Jeffrey spent the time waiting for Katya to arrive, going through the morning mail, dusting furniture, doing anything to keep from thinking about the mystery that surrounded this strange young lady.

Katya had begun working at Priceless about a month before, when the regular shop assistant was called away by a family emergency. Jeffrey remained delighted with the arrangement, yet found it to be an exquisite torture. He loved the hours they spent alone together in the shop—she with her classwork, he with his catalogues and books—loved teaching her the rudiments of his newfound passion and profession. But it was so difficult being so close to her for so long, and having to resist the constant desire to hold her, caress her, tell her the thoughts that continually ran through his mind like a never-ending song.

He had met Katya on a bitter-cold November night, in the student's canteen beneath the University of London's central library. He had been granted temporary access through providentially meeting a librarian whose passion for antiques had known no bounds. In return for occasional guided tours of his shop and invitations to all the major antique fairs, Jeffrey had been given a visitor's card—a boon slightly less common than a passkey to the Tower of London's chambers for the Crown Jewels.

Jeffrey was not permitted to check out books, but within the library's confines he had virtually unlimited access to a treasure trove of reference materials. He spent many a happy hour lost in richly pictured tomes, tracing the development of patterns and styles and inlays and jewelry and art.

That particular evening he remained hunched over his book on early Biedermeier furniture for so long that it had taken both hands to unclench the cramp in his neck. His kneading and silent groans were stopped by the realization that two of the most beautiful eyes he had ever seen were holding him fast.

Her face was formed around cheekbones so pronounced and upraised as to give her eyes an almost Oriental slant. Yet the eyes themselves were a startling grayish-violet, with irises whose depths seemed to invite him in, drawing him further and further still, until before he knew what was happening he was on his feet and walking over to her table.

She greeted his approach with neither smile of welcome nor frown of refusal; rather she watched him with a look of utter vulnerability, a helplessly open gaze that had his heart pounding by the time he stopped and looked down and said, "May I join you?"

Her voice was as light as a scented summer breeze. "I was just going back upstairs."

"May I walk with you?"

"To get my things, I mean. I have a bus in fifteen minutes."

"I've been sitting too long anyway. May I accompany you?" He sounded so formal, so silly to his own ears. His usual well of casual banter was sealed off by this unblinking gaze of vulnerability. He had the impression that if he held out his hand, this strange young woman would have been forced to take it, a victim of whatever left her unable to hide her heart. Instead he was content to stand above her, gaze down into the endless depths of two star-flecked eyes, and know that he was lost.

They left the smoky student din behind them, stopped to pick up her coat and books, and entered the startlingly crisp coldness of early November dark. From time to time Jeffrey searched a blank and empty mind for words and came up only with the fear that once they reached the street, this spell would be broken, this moment lost, this woman forever gone. His heart hammered with a fury that left his legs weak and his tongue stilled.

Just as they arrived at the curb a black London taxi rumbled by, its 'vacant' light glowing. Jeffrey's arm shot up automatically, leaving him faced with the dilemma of either telling it to go on or going himself.

Instead he turned to her, and found the same achingly open gaze resting on his face. He said, "You've really got to let me take you home."

She neither replied nor hesitated, but rather gave the driver a Kensington address and climbed in the back.

It was enough to open the gates. "You have an accent I can't place," he said. "Are you British?"

"American." Her voice was so soft he had to lean closer; she did not shy away. "I've lived here since I was nine."

"Here in London?"

"No, Coventry. Do you know it?"

"Not well. I attended an auction there once." Coventry was about an hour from London, one of countless industrial British towns with all the charm of a construction site on a rainy day. Virtually demolished by German bombers in World War II, it had been rebuilt in hasty uniformity as a settlement for factory workers. Its endless rows of semidetached houses looked like products of a second-rate production line.

"What kind of auction?"

"Antiques. I run an antiques business."

"Here in London?"

"Yes."

"Then you're not a student at the university?" She seemed disconcerted.

"No. Why, is that bad?"

"I don't know," she replied. "I don't even know what I'm doing here."

"Sharing a taxi," he replied. The taxi stopped in front of a nondescript row-house in dire need of better care. A long metal plate of buzzers indicated that the three stories had been split into a rabbit-warren of tiny student flats. "Listen, there's a cafe across the street. Can't we go in for a couple of minutes?"

"I really don't think I could stomach another coffee just now."

"The drink is incidental. I just want to talk a little longer."

She gave the tiniest hint of a smile. "All right. But just a few minutes. I have a lot of work still to do tonight."

The place was cramped and cluttered and smoky as only a poorly ventilated London cafe could be. Jeffrey led her to the only free table and went back to the counter for a couple of teas. He said on his return, "You don't have to drink this."

Their conversation flowed more smoothly. She had a way of asking the smallest of questions, and then listening with such absorption that he felt able to tell her anything. He found himself talking at length about his family, Alexander, his departure from America.

"So," she said, absently stirring her cup, "did you leave a lady pining for you back in America?"

"I had a girlfriend in Atlanta," he confessed, wondering what there was in those unfathomable gray-violet eyes that invited an honesty he had not known with some girls even after months together. "But she ditched me, not the other way around."

"And how long have you been separated?"

"Personally about seven months. Now that I look back at it, though, I'd have to say we were emotionally separated since the second day I knew her."

She showed no reaction whatsoever. "Wasn't it hard,

going out with someone you didn't love?"

"As far as I knew at the time, everything was fine. It hadn't occurred to me that there could be something more." He searched those unreadable eyes, said, "Not then, anyway."

"That is so like a man," she said quietly. "So sure the next pretty face is his dream come true, the girl designed to fulfill his every wish and give him perfect happiness."

"I can always hope," he replied, thinking to himself, I've never felt like this before in my entire life. "What about you? Have you been someone's perfect happiness before?"

"You'd have to ask them. I could never tell you that myself."

"So there've been others," he said, hating them all.

"Other what? Other men? Look around you. The world is full of other men."

"You know exactly what I meant," he said sharply.

She turned contrite. "You're right. I should not have said that and I'm sorry. I've always had difficulty talking about myself."

"Does that mean I shouldn't ask?"

The hint of smile returned. She shook her head. "You just need to hide behind something after you do."

He made a motion as to duck behind the table. "So I'm asking."

"About other men?" Her eyes blossomed like petals of a flower made from violet gems and purest smoke, opening and revealing depths that Jeffrey could only wonder at.

"Somebody has hurt you very badly." It was not a question.

A little girl within her eyes cried to his heart. "Yes," she whispered.

"Do you want to tell me about it?"

"It wasn't what you think," she said, her voice a fragile wind blowing words and sadness through the gaping wound in his heart. "It wasn't a lover. I haven't, I've never . . ."

The sorrow filled him with a selfless compassion he had never known before. He reached across the table, took her hand in both of his. She looked down, studied it with eyes that spilled their burden over both of them. "It wasn't a lover," she repeated.

A jangle of boozy laughter from a nearby table shattered

the moment. They both started back, pulling away from the shards of emotion that sprinkled around them. She looked at him and was comforted to find a smile waiting for her.

They left the cafe and walked the short distance to her doorway in silence. She hesitated at the bottom step, reluctant to go inside.

"I'd really like to see you again," Jeffrey said. "Could I invite you to dinner?"

"If you like."

"I'd like very much. How about tomorrow?"

"All right. What is your name?"

"Jeffrey." The openness of her gaze left him aching to hold her. "And yours?"

"Katya."

Then she was up the stairs so fast that his words, that's a beautiful name, were said to empty space. He watched her enter the door without a backward glance, and wondered why his heart suddenly felt such exquisite pain.

Jeffrey heard Katya's gentle tap on the front window only because he was listening for it. He walked toward the front door, where she stood laden down with a half-dozen books. He opened the door, asked, "Are you planning to move in for a week?"

"I thought I would work on my research if there was any free time."

He took the books from her and carried them back to the alcove. "I bet you didn't stop for lunch. I left an extra sandwich in the fridge for when you get hungry."

Katya followed him with solemn eyes. "Thank you, Jeffrey."

"Here, let me take your raincoat." He pointed to the silver serving dish. "Baby's just been fed and changed."

Katya bent over, touched the tiny form with one gentle finger, cooed softly.

Jeffrey watched her, smiling at the way Ling cuddled to her finger. "Who would have thought there could be so much love in a little bundle of fluff?"

"I was thinking about our little bird in church this morning," she told him. "But now I wonder if maybe I wasn't thinking about myself."

"What do you mean?"

"When you're hurt, you think you have to protect yourself against everything."

He set the bowl down on a satinwood side table. "Who hurt you, Katya?"

"Such a little bird," she went on quietly. "He must have been so scared when we tried to help him. He didn't know who we were or what we were doing."

Jeffrey reached up and stroked the silken hairs at the nape of her neck.

"But we made him feel safe, and he's learned to trust us."

"Who hurt you?" he repeated.

"That doesn't matter now. You didn't know who or what hurt this little bird either, but you still helped him."

"I need to know."

She looked at him with desperate appeal. "I can't tell you just now."

"When you trust me enough," he conceded, and wondered if the time would ever come.

There were only three Rolls Royces and one Bentley parked outside Christie's when Jeffrey arrived—it was still a little early. The porter stood as always, dressed in his formal gray uniform, facing the entrance with his back to the street. Within the portals, all was elegant light wood and beige carpet and discreetly armed security guards. Overly thin women wearing too much jewelry spoke in tones of cultured snobbery. They were accompanied by men with fruity voices and diction that made them sound as though they were speaking around a mouthful of marbles. Jeffrey counted seven double-breasted navy-blue blazers in the front foyer alone.

Just prior to Jeffrey's arrival in London, the bottom had dropped from the high-end art and antique markets with a speed and force that left the art world shell-shocked. Although a recovery was currently under way, this instability made Jeffrey's pricing and sales decisions doubly difficult. Alexander left him with such sweeping powers that on some mornings he entered the shop wondering if at the end of the day he would still have a job.

His biggest problem came from the enormous variety of pieces they handled. In-depth study was impossible. There was no predicting from where the next piece would originate—what era, wood, country, or style. Most of their business came from furniture, yet a significant portion covered virtually the entire spectrum of antiques—from jewelry to crystal, plates and watches, boxes and lace and chests. It was easier to predict what the next incoming piece would *not* be.

They handled no guns or weapons of any sort. Alexander viewed such items with a genuine loathing, and referred to weapons specialists as historians of murder and mayhem.

There were few world-renowned painters among the art that they either sold directly or placed under the hammer. Most of the works they handled were from second-level painters, those often found in museums yet not known outside a relatively small circle. Jeffrey either used a professional evaluator for setting the prices of those which he chose to hang in the shop, or passed them on to Christie's.

Occasionally an etching or sketch or watercolor or pastel arrived that took his breath away. The first items he took to Christie's—the first time he had ever entered an auction house in his life, for that matter—were six hand-sized studies of the same woman's face. They were drawn with an astonishing minimum of line and shading, yet were vivid in their portrayal of pensive sadness. The agents at Christie's confirmed that they were by Monet, and treated Jeffrey with the utmost of practiced respect as they pried his reluctant fingers free.

The Priceless shop sold no sculpture at all. There was nothing from genuine antiquity—ancient Greece, Rome, Phoenicia, or Egypt. There were few tapestries, almost no crystal, and nothing at all from the Far East.

In short, Jeffrey had almost nothing upon which to base a valid guess as to where their stock originated.

Other dealers dubbed their shop the West End Jumble Sale, and stopped by often to search and wonder and ask the occasional indirect question. Jeffrey found it easy to offer the dealers a blank face in reply.

Everyone wondered at Alexander Kantor's sources. It was only natural; so did Jeffrey. He had been around enough of the high-end shops and auction houses to know that variety and quantity was almost never combined with quality. An entire estate sold through a single dealer was such a rarity that word spread far and wide long before the last item was sold. Yet Alexander Kantor had continued to handle quality most dealers could only dream of. He had done so for four decades, and no one was the wiser.

Especially not Jeffrey.

On slow days, Jeffrey would find himself cataloging the room and the items he had placed elsewhere, and wonder at their incredible diversity. French Napoleon III vied with Italian Rococo, Russian icons with German Romance paintings, rosewood with oak, satin finishes with gilt—and almost all of it of exceptional quality. There was no possible way that one estate could have contained such a diversity. There was no logical explanation as to how Kantor could disappear for weeks or months at a time, leaving no phone number or forwarding address, and return in total secrecy time after time with such antiques.

The Christie's auction chamber is not particularly impressive—a long high-ceilinged hall with wooden floor and cloth walls of an unremarkable beige. There are padded folding seats for perhaps a hundred and fifty, most of which that day were full. The auctioneer's dais is placed very close to the first row, and raised so high that the auctioneer, a bland gentleman as gray as his suit with a permanently fixed smile and a two-tone voice, has to lean over the ledge in order to focus on the closest patrons. He holds a small handleless wooden stamp with which he smacks the dais smartly to close a sale.

There was a constant silent scurrying behind the dais as Jeffrey entered and seated himself. The lobby-sized back chamber was filled to overflowing by canvases neatly stacked and numbered and turned to face the closest wall. At the rear of this chamber, a door opened to a vault-room used to house paintings not on display. The austere main hall itself was lined with pictures too big to be carried to the bidding table. With the smaller pictures, one of the innumerable red-aproned assistants would hoist the painting onto the baize-covered table set to the right of the auctioneer, and hold it in utter stillness until the bidding ended. Larger pictures were indicated by an assistant standing beneath its place on the wall.

A board set high in the corner beside the auctioneer gave each bid in five different currencies. The moneys listed were determined by those being bid for a particular piece; if a telephone bidder was working with a Danish client, then one listing would be in kroner. If a visiting bidder from Italy made himself known as he entered, then all prices would be listed in lira. A woman at a desk directly beneath the auctioneer's dais typed both the new bids and the currencies required into a computer hooked to the board. When the bidding came fast and furious, the numbers moved in a continual blur.

The hall contained a fairly typical mixture of bidders for a second-level Christie's auction. A first-level, or major auction, was scheduled on an annual or semiannual basis, and attracted museum directors and gallery owners from across the globe; the type of person who would travel only if a ten million dollar-plus purchase was being considered.

Today, several yuppies up on long lunch breaks from the City were looking for bargain investments and eyeing the ladies. The number of yuppies at such auctions had dwindled rapidly as the banking industry had bit the bullet, let them go, and forced them to fill the local used-car market with their Porsches. There was one effeminate Arab with his boyfriend. Beside him was a rock star whose presence anywhere else would have caused a minor riot; here he was just another addition to the scene.

Two contingents of professional agents and gallery owners were present. The ones there for the long haul were seated and reserved and extremely attentive. Some held portable phones and smug expressions, announcing with silent satisfaction that they represented a confidential bidder. The second group congregated at the back of the hall, whispering quietly among themselves and offering cynical comments on the state of the market. They were around to bid on one specific item, or keep tabs on the market, or pretend that they needed to. Their shops were generally second rate, their comments acid, their faces twisted by a determined effort to get the better of everyone.

Jeffrey preferred to sit up front. It gave him the feeling of being at the heart of the fray. He was not comfortable with the clubby atmosphere at the back. The way they offered their single token bid of the day, waving a casual hand and then turning away with a smile and a spiteful word when someone else bid higher, left him certain that they would taint the joy and the thrill and the genuine love he held for this new profession.

Today marked the eleventh time Jeffrey had offered pieces for sale, and the first time he was recognized by a number of the staff as he entered—including the auctioneer. The gentleman gave him a minutely correct smile and bow from the dais as Jeffrey settled himself. He found that just being recognized raised his stock a great deal. The women— and there were many of them, most of them beautiful— watched him with a speculative eye.

Along the side wall, beginning close to the auctioneer's dais, ran a long table holding thirty phones. Telephone sales assistants discreetly came and went, depending on which languages were required by the bidders who had requested calls in advance of a particular sale.

Even after eleven visits it remained incredible to Jeffrey how fast the whole business moved. Bids were entered at the rate of over six a minute. The auctioneer handled the crowd with a surgeon's precision, squeezing the price up at an electric speed, his crisp politeness never slipping.

After several further paintings by artists Jeffrey had never heard of before, his own picture came up—a Musin boat scene. Even before the auctioneer's attention moved from the register where he noted the previous sale, Jeffrey's heart was racing. All fourteen standing telephone assistants were immediately on the phone, some handling two or even three lines and in as many languages.

"And lot fifteen, an exceptional Musin," the auctioneer chanted, looking around and spotting the assistant with his hand in the air. "Ah, thank you very much. Showing at the back wall, being pointed out to you. Lot fifteen. Starting the bidding at fifteen thousand pounds. Fifteen thousand is offered. Seventeen thousand."

After the opening bid was accepted, a price already bid was rarely mentioned. The exception was when the auctioneer chose to identify the bidder and place him or her momentarily in the spotlight. Otherwise attention was immediately drawn on to the next upward move by pointing to the bidder and then stating only the next asking price.

"Sixteen thousand. Seventeen thousand. Eighteen thousand. Twenty thousand. Twenty-two thousand. Twenty-four thousand pounds. It's with you at the very back, madam, at twenty-four thousand. Twenty-six thousand. Thirty thousand."

The next bid increment was set by the auctioneer and offered as a statement, not a question. Never a question. There was no doubt in his voice, no hesitation shown as the size of the jump increased as the bidding price escalated.

"Thirty thousand, thank you. Thirty-two thousand. Thirty-five thousand. Thirty-eight thousand. Thirty-eight thousand pounds. The bidding now stands at thirty-eight thousand pounds."

Initially the bidding was fast and furious and came from all over the room. At thirty thousand pounds the storm abated, and at thirty-five there was a moment's hesitation. The lead bid came from a gallery owner named Sarah, with whom Jeffrey had placed several works. From the light in the woman's eyes, it was clear she knew she was walking away with a steal. Thirty-five thousand pounds for such a painting was a rare bargain, caused by the recession that had wreaked random havoc throughout the art world.

"Thirty-eight thousand. Am I bid thirty-eight thousand. Ah, thank you, bid from the phone for thirty-eight thousand. Forty thousand."

A new opponent had appeared, an invisible bidder whose presence was announced by a heretofore silent telephone operator raising one hand and accepting the thirty-eight thousand bid. Jeffrey watched the gallery owner's excitement turn to brassy defiance. Sarah accepted the forty thousand bid with an angry gesture. The auctioneer recognized the beginning of a battle with a smugly satisfied smile.

"Forty-two thousand. Forty-five thousand. Forty-eight thousand. Fifty thousand. Fifty-five thousand. Sixty thousand. Sixty-five thousand. Seventy thousand pounds."

A light hum rose from the room as the bids began rising at increments of about eight thousand dollars. Sarah continued to make counter-offers with furious jerky gestures of her card. The card had a number, assigned to her prior to the auction's start, and was utilized by habitual buyers to both ensure no confusion over purchases and reduce the need to be identified and fill out forms while the next lot was being offered. The steely grip with which the gallery owner continually thrust her card upward gave her fingers the look of talons locked in a death grip.

The young lady manning the phone read the newly accepted bid-value from the computer board, and relayed it into the telephone with a voice pitched too low for Jeffrey to catch the language she spoke. With each new bid from Sarah and subsequent price-rise offered by the auctioneer, she would whisper, wait, then lift her eyes and nod to the waiting auctioneer.

"Ninety-five thousand." Another pause, this one from the gallery owner. Jeffrey kept his hands still by clenching the auction catalog in his lap. "Ninety-five thousand against you at the back. Thank you, madam. One hundred thousand. Am I bid one hundred thousand pounds. Yes, from the telephone. One hundred and five thousand. At the back one hundred and five thousand pounds is bid. One hundred and ten thousand. One hundred and ten, thank you. One hundred and fifteen, yes, thank you, madam. One hundred and fifteen is bid at the back. One hundred and twenty thousand pounds."

The telephone assistant spoke the bid, waited.

"Am I bid one hundred and twenty thousand pounds."

The girl spoke again, waited, then looked up and shook her head with an apologetic smile. The entire room finally took a breath.

"A valiant try," the auctioneer said to the telephone assistant. Then with a smack of his gavel he said, "Sold for one hundred and fifteen thousand pounds to you, madam. Buyer one-eight," he intoned as he wrote, naming the number on Sarah's card. "Congratulations, madam. A lovely acquisition."

The sale had taken less than three minutes.

Jeffrey raced up the stairs to the larger auction hall, where last week's furniture sale had taken place. The assistant chief of their furniture division was a young man by the name of Trevor with a decidedly Oxbridge accent. He brightened immensely at Jeffrey's arrival.

"Ah excellent, excellent. Mr. Sinclair, may I take this opportunity to introduce Professor Halbmeier from Bonn."

The man did not offer his hand. "I would like to know where you obtained this piece."

"I don't know," Jeffrey replied, bridling at his tone. "And if I did I wouldn't tell you."

"Yes, well, perhaps we might just have a look at it ourselves, shall we?" Trevor exposed a bland peacemaking smile to all and sundry. "The professor was just telling me that he was not familiar with the item."

"How could I be? There was no record of anything from the Kaiser's palace having survived."

"Yes, it must be quite a shock. Shall we?" He drew the professor over, ran a hand along the top, said, "This is actually something we sold last week, as I told you on the phone."

"That remains to be seen," the professor replied ominously.

"Yes, well." Trevor cleared his throat. "In any case, it's by perhaps the greatest German cabinet maker, certainly the greatest neoclassic cabinet maker, a fellow by the name of Johann Gottlieb Fiedler. There are very, *very* few pieces by him still around. Wars and such, you know. Bombs tend to have a rather lasting effect on wood.

"So far as we know, there are three pieces by Fiedler in Berlin, one in the Wallace collection, and this particular piece that literally sprang to life before our very noses. Quite a bit of conjecture about where this one came from. Gave our verifications people quite a time, I don't mind telling you.

"What's most interesting about it is the top, of course," the young man went on. He ran a casual hand across a fitted stone block that had been made to sit on the chest's upper surface as though growing from it. Its face was a geometric mosaic, designed from hundreds of thousands of tiny multi-colored flecks of marble.

"A lot of these are marbles that haven't been known since antiquity. We think many of them were probably carved out of ancient columns, but our people have been able to come up with absolutely nothing certain. Quite frustrating, really. This bit in the center appears to be one piece, perhaps lifted from some early Roman vessel, and the rest was then designed around it. But it's all conjecture."

The mixture of colors on the face was almost psychedelic—rich hues belonging more to semiprecious stones than to modern marble.

"In any case, we do know that it was made around 1780," the young man continued. "Most probably for the Crown Prince of Prussia, Friedrich Wilhelm. The precise date hinges around whether one thinks he was arrogant enough to have it made before his uncle the Kaiser died."

The German official was not taking all this very well. In fact, he appeared to be building up a full head of steam.

"Our man said the fellow positively wouldn't have dared commission it unless he was already the Kaiser," Trevor blithely continued. "It was just so grand, you see. And there was no evidence that his uncle ever owned such a piece. It would have been a real case of one-upmanship, something he certainly couldn't have afforded until the crown was already in his grubby little hands."

Trevor was too caught up in the tale to realize the effect his words were having on the bulbous gentleman beside him, who had begun to take on the shape and rigidity of a beached blowfish.

"At first we actually thought the top might have been put on in England. It was just the sort of thing the early nineteenth-century English grand tourers might have done, you see. They'd been in Italy, we thought, and bought themselves this magnificent top, and then either had this bottom handy or puttered around the Continent until they came upon a piece that would fit it. But then we decided the two pieces were set together too snugly to have been made separately, and also the top's thickness suggests that it was actually designed by a German craftsman."

The man made a sound like a strangled bulldog. Trevor missed it, having bent over to roll out one of the drawers, and went on. "As you can see, there are three central concave-fronted drawers set on the most remarkable roller system. Feels light as a feather, but I would imagine each must weigh close on a hundred pounds. Solid as a rock. Immaculate construction, really. The frieze here is in walnut, but so heavily inlaid it is difficult to tell in places. The waved apron here is also heavily gilded, remarkable work. Scrolled legs, all hand carved. The gilded bronze flanking the corners here was a way of framing the work, of course. Must have been spectacular when it was new. These lion-faced handles here are a bit of a mystery, I must say. The only parts that we don't think were actually made in Prussia. In fact, they were probably bought by mail order, such as it was at the time, from England. The English were masters at the art of making these lion masks."

Despite the gentleman's growing fury, Jeffrey could not help but become caught up in the specialist's enthusiasm. "How can you be so sure that it was not done by the duke?"

"Simply because it is the grandest of its type." In contrast to many of his fellow antique specialists, Trevor clearly relished having someone around who shared his fascination. "He was a real style leader, this chap the crown prince. And the king, you see, his uncle, was never really interested in the whole subject. When Crown Prince Friedrich then became Kaiser, he carried his involvement along with him. Stayed right at the center of the whole style thing throughout his reign. Even retained this fellow Fiedler as his own personal cabinet maker. That of course doesn't mean his furniture was all Fiedler did, but it does make it highly unlikely that he would risk challenging his uncle in such a way before rising to the top of the heap, as it were."

The gentleman demanded, "How did it come to be here?"

"Well, there you are," Trevor replied eagerly. "The thing about all such articles is that with time they become unfashionable. This particular item was eventually given to the Russian ambassador, that much we've been able to piece together from the archives in Germany. It was later sold by his widow, some thirty years after. By then, of course, it had become so unfashionable it was probably used to store dirty laundry in some minor bedroom of their secondary palace."

"Disgraceful," the gentleman rumbled.

"Yes, I suppose so," the young man replied. "Of course, there just is no accounting for taste."

The gentleman rounded on him. "I mean that it is disgraceful for such a piece of German heritage to ever have left German soil."

"My dear fellow," Trevor replied. "This particular piece has never set foot in Germany. When it left the Kaiser's palace for parts unknown, that stretch of earth was still proudly Prussian."

The gentleman ignored him. "And to wind up in a London showroom. Outrageous."

"Yes, well, we have tried our very best not to soil it over much," Trevor replied, winking at Jeffrey.

"It could have been bought by just anyone," the gentleman went on. "Lost to the German people forever."

"Oh, we shouldn't have allowed that, I don't think. Not without a struggle, in any case. As a matter of fact, it appeared that all top five bids were from Germans."

That took the wind from his sails. "They were?"

"Indeed yes. Several museums showed quite a bit of interest as well."

"Which ones?"

"Oh, it wouldn't do for me to pass that on, now, would it? Discretion and all that."

The man gathered himself, said, "I am authorized to offer a substantial amount of money for this piece."

"Yes, well, it would have to be, wouldn't it. The winning bid was the highest price ever paid for a piece of German furniture, which I suppose isn't saying much since the level of prices up to now wasn't particularly staggering."

"You can forget that bid," the man snapped. "He has decided to retract it. Or rather, to grant the German government the right to this property."

"What a pity," Trevor said, not the least put out. "Still, I suppose we'll have to wait and hear that from the gentleman in question, won't we?"

"The final bid was for one hundred and eighty thousand pounds, was it not?"

"That is correct," Trevor replied blandly. "Quite understandable, really. It is a remarkable find."

Jeffrey watched the young man's face, wondering if he would ever reach the point of being able to say the price for a chest of drawers was three hundred thousand dollars without bursting into hysterical laughter.

"You may speak to the former high bidder at your convenience. This article now belongs to the German people. A check from my ministry will be in your hands tomorrow." The professor wheeled around to face Jeffrey. "It is a disgrace that a piece of national heritage has been treated in such a manner. You, sir, will be hearing from my solicitors."

When he had stormed out of the hall, Trevor smiled and

said, "I think that went rather well after all, don't you?"

"I guess so. Do you think there's anything to his threat of legal action?"

"Not unless it was stolen." Trevor eyed him carefully. "It wasn't, was it?"

"I hope not."

"Alexander keeps you in the dark about his sources, then, does he?"

"Sorry, I can't answer that."

"No, of course not. Still, if you're going to keep on digging such treasures out of holes in the ground or wherever it is he comes up with them, you're going to have to expect the odd complaint now and then." Trevor extended his hand. "And do keep us in mind the next time something like this turns up, won't you? We always do enjoy a good mystery. Especially one where there's money to be made."

CHAPTER
4

Jeffrey knew very little about the Polish side of his background. His mother, an only child, seldom spoke of her father's homeland. Jeffrey's own father came from a large family of good Scotch-Irish stock who proudly referred to themselves as hybrid American mongrels. There was a vague sense of uneasiness among his parents and uncles and aunts whenever the topic of his grandfather's birthplace arose.

Once he had asked his grandmother why her daughter, his mother, did not know more about her father's heritage. She had shown a rare moment of regret and said, "Your mother was tutored in Polish by a neighbor starting at the age of six. At thirteen she refused to take further lessons and promptly forgot everything she had learned. All she wanted was to fit in, to be a part of her own little world. A Polish father and a pride in a country other than this one simply did not fit. Her father and I did not have the heart to insist."

"Did it bother you when Mom married so young?" Jeffrey's mother was seventeen when she married and eighteen when Jeffrey was born.

"Of course it did. I was immensely distressed. But your grandfather felt otherwise. He said when he met me he could not have waited another week to be wed, and sensed that same urgency in the way your mother felt about your father."

She smiled in fond remembrance. "I argued with him until he told me that his greatest regret was that we had not met earlier. Let them marry, he said. Give them the joy of the twenty extra years together that we shall not have."

Jeffrey's grandmother looked at him, and went on, "Someday when you have children of your own you will also be faced with problems that will leave you wondering for the rest of your life if you did the right thing. It is the way of the world. All you can do is hope that you tried and acted in their best interests, not in your own."

An immigrant from an Eastern European country that most of his relatives could not even place on a map simply did not fit in with their proper scheme of things. So everyone referred to that Polish aspect of his heritage with a shrug, a wink, a smirk, a glance at the heavens. Only his grandmother's reaction differed from the family norm. Whenever anyone asked, she would reply, yes, my husband was a true Pole. There was so much pride and love in her voice, even after living as a widow for twenty years, that Jeffrey never ceased to wonder at why no one else showed his grandfather's heritage some of the same esteem.

His grandmother was a doddering old lady now, shrunken to teacup size and bent to match the old rocking chair that was her permanent daytime residence. But her eyes were still bright, and she loved to talk of the man who was no longer.

She had been a career secretary, working for the United States Embassy in London on a five-year contract toward the end of World War II. Approaching thirty, facing a worldwide shortage of available men, she had consoled her move to spinsterhood by taking the battery of exams and winning the coveted London post. Her second month there, the impossible had occurred and she had fallen in love.

Piotr, or Peter as he soon came to be known, was penniless, almost homeless, and twenty-three years her senior. To her co-workers and few friends, he was just one of the countless thousands of displaced people who flooded every government office in Western Europe, all with tragic tales of wrongs unrighted and estates lost forever. Some of these stories were even true.

At the time of their meeting, Piotr had barely a nodding acquaintance with the English language. His rough speech, his formal old-world manners and travel-worn clothes, all were a source of endless amusement to the other embassy staff. They called Piotr a clown. But even then, at the very early stages of their blossoming relationship, she knew better. Love granted her the power to see beyond the shabby exterior and realize that this graying man with his strong face and handlebar moustache and weary eyes truly held a heart of gold.

So they were married, and while she worked at the embassy Piotr studied English and continued his profession as a watchmaker and jeweller. When her five-year stint was completed they returned to the United States with their baby daughter, where the first of Peter Kantor's three jewelry and watch stores was soon up and running.

The year Jeffrey graduated from university, his grandmother fell and broke her hip. While she was lying immobilized, her only child—Jeffrey's mother—finally convinced her that the days of living alone were over. By the time she was released from the hospital, her home had been sold and her most treasured possessions had been moved into his brother's old room—the same brother who for Jeffrey was no more.

After that, going home took on a new meaning for Jeffrey. His first year with McKinsey, he logged more trips from Atlanta to Jacksonville than he had during his entire four years at university. His grandmother loved to talk, but few in the family were interested in hearing about the past. In all honesty, Jeffrey cared little for the old days, but he loved this sense of connection with a family that had been shattered beyond all recognition by time and events.

Although her hip was pronounced fully healed, it bothered her to move. She preferred to spend her days in the rocker set by the room's large window. Jeffrey found it immensely reassuring to just come and sit with her. Evenings when his parents were out, grateful for the freedom his presence gave them to take a deserved break alone, he would often bring in his weekend workload, spread it out on her vanity, and sit and work. They spoke little in those times, content to enjoy the silent company. It also helped him enormously to gradually replace the memories of what the room once had been to what it was now.

The Saturday afternoon following his acceptance of Alexander Kantor's offer, he returned to find her resting where she always was this time of day, her rocker set so that sunlight fell on her lap and not her face. His mother had recently redone the room in new wallpaper, one with tiny rosebuds blooming in perpetual profusion. The old lace bedspread covering her miniature four-poster bed was matched with new lace curtains and lace doilies over the two side tables. The whole effect was cozy and feminine and very fitting to the old lady.

"I wanted you to be the first to know," Jeffrey told her, pulling up a chair and sitting down, "I'm going to London to work for Alexander Kantor."

The crystal-clear gray eyes showed a momentary glimpse of deep pain, then returned to their normal calm. "You have certainly been unhappy at work."

"How did you know?"

"I may be old, but I still have eyes. Sometimes I see things more clearly now than I ever did before." Her voice had the toneless quality of the truly ancient. "I shall miss your visits, Jeffrey."

"I'll miss you too," he replied, and realized that he might be seeing her for the last time. The awareness seared him; before him sat the strongest link he had to the family of his youth.

"One thing you should do before you go," she told him.

That was enough to draw him back from the brink of real sorrow. "Don't say it," he replied coldly.

"Make peace with your brother."

"No."

"Please. For me."

"I don't have a brother. Not anymore."

"So much like your grandfather," she said softly. "Stubborn as an ox."

"I wish I'd known him better," he said, relieved to be back on more comfortable ground.

"He would have been very proud of you," she said. "And he would tell you the same thing."

"I can't," Jeffrey said simply. "Can we please talk about something else?"

She nodded her head, a single tiny motion, and said, "Your grandfather thought the world of Alexander. He would be pleased to know the family was staying together in this way. Very pleased."

He had not thought of that. "Is that why he offered me this job?"

"Who knows what Alexander thinks?" she said. "He is a bachelor, always has been. There has always been a little touch of the mysterious about Alexander. And a bit of the mystical about his cousin Gregor. You have never met Gregor, have you?"

Jeffrey shook his head. "I really don't know much about him. He's the one who escaped to England and then went back to Poland, isn't he?"

"That's correct. Gregor was always a religious person. A very gentle man with a wonderful sense of humor. I always felt good around him. He had a way of cheering everyone up, no matter how troubled they might be. He called it his spiritual gift." She looked at him. "You mustn't be concerned about the whys behind Alexander offering you this job."

"Your vision is perfect," Jeffrey admitted.

"Rest assured, if Alexander keeps you, it will be for one reason, and one reason only—because you are good." The old eyes rested gently on him. "Which you are."

"Thank you."

"One thing I know for certain. Alexander Kantor cannot abide mediocrity. Not in antiques, not in houses, not in clothes, and certainly not in people."

Jeffrey settled back. "Tell me about him."

"Well, with a man like Alexander it is sometimes difficult to separate truth from legend."

"I've noticed. What I've heard about him sounds almost like fairy tales from a children's storybook."

"Yes, the family has certainly done him an injustice. But this is the way people often deal with a character who is larger than life. And Alexander certainly is that."

"Why do you let them talk about him like they do?"

Fragile shoulders bounced in a single silent laugh. "Since when does anybody listen to what I have to say?"

"I do."

"Yes. You have been a great comfort. I will certainly miss you."

He pushed the renewed pain away. "So what was he really like?"

"When your grandfather first began courting me, Alexander was a sort of ghost around the apartment. They call them flats in London, don't ask me why. His family all lived there, or rather all of those who had escaped with him. There was your grandfather Piotr, which is Polish for Peter—I soon had him change it to something I could pronounce, I assure you. Then there were Alexander's parents—your great-uncle and aunt. Then there was his cousin Gregor and Gregor's wife. She died soon after their arrival in London; perhaps you knew that."

"I didn't even know he was married."

"He's not now. That is, he never remarried. They were clearly very much in love, and apparently he was able to love only one person in all his life. But you asked me about Alexander. Well, as I said, he was rarely there in those early days of our courtship."

"I love that word," Jeffrey told her. "Courtship. It sounds so formal."

"That's why I use it. Your grandfather was a very formal, courtly person. He had the finest manners of any person I have ever met, except perhaps Alexander. But where Alexander acted with such polish, my Peter acted with heart."

She wiped at the wet spot in the corner of her mouth with a handkerchief as delicate as the hand that held it. "Whenever I visited Peter's flat—which was a ghastly, crowded affair, I assure you—Alexander was never there. His things were on the bed beside Peter's, and next to his in the closet. But the man himself was never around. Never. I did not actually meet him until after Peter and I became engaged. I don't know what I expected, but I was shocked at what I found."

"I can imagine."

She looked at him. "He still cuts a handsome figure, does he?"

"Very."

"I'm so glad. Our heroes should have the right to age gracefully. Back then, Alexander was undoubtedly the most dashing man I had ever met."

"Why did you call him a hero?"

"Well, first of all because of their escape. From what I

recall it was quite an adventure. I'm afraid I don't remember the details. But there was much more than that. Much more. He financed your grandfather's first jewelry store here in America. Ah, I see you did not know that. Yes, and a home for us. And Gregor's education in London—that is, until he decided that he was called back to Poland. That was the way Gregor always described it, that he was *called*. Alexander never accepted a penny in return from anyone. He refused to even discuss it. He called such talk a dishonor." She smiled into the distance, repeated, "Your grandfather thought the world of that gentleman."

"Why was Alexander never home? I mean, when you used to go over there."

Her eyes twinkled mischievously. "Because he was out gambling."

"What?"

"I only learned the truth after Peter and I returned to America. In London they simply wouldn't discuss it. Such a thing was horribly incorrect. His family were old aristocrats, you see, and had a lot of trouble accepting the fact that the war had left them penniless. You cannot imagine how destitute they were when we first met. Your grandfather had one jacket, two pair of trousers, and two shirts to his name. That was all. Still, the idea of Alexander earning the money to pay for the lion's share of their living expenses with cards was simply not to be discussed with anyone. But he was so successful at it that they dared not complain. They couldn't afford to, you see."

Jeffrey leaned forward in his chair. "Successful."

"Incredibly. So successful that he was eventually banned from some of the gambling clubs. Gambling is legal in Britain, you see, but only inside licensed clubs. Yes, Alexander only played blackjack and poker and bridge, games where his amazing ability with numbers gave him an advantage." She was clearly enjoying herself. "You didn't know that either, did you?"

Jeffrey made do with a slow shake of his head.

"He trained as a mathematician in Poland. No, I take that back. Something else. Something to do with calculating odds."

"Statistics?"

"Thank you. He had just started his studies, I seem to

recall something about being quite young, so young that he could not enter university and was being tutored privately. Then the war broke out and everyone's life changed for the worse."

"Amazing," Jeffrey said. "A professional gambler."

"Not just, young man. Not by any means. He took courses at the university and worked a daytime job loading trucks."

"And gambled."

"Almost every night, sometimes until dawn if he was in a private game. Peter was very envious of Alexander's ability to live on two or three hours of sleep a night, rarely more."

"I bet I can guess what he did with the money," Jeffrey said.

"London was full of refugees, or displaced persons as they were known then. Many were quite wealthy, or had been. Most had something to sell—jewelry or silver or rare boxes, perhaps a small painting, anything that could be easily carried as they made their escape from wherever they had come.

"They were terrified of the London dealers, and rightly so. They were offered pennies for treasures that had been in their families for generations. There was so much being sold, you see, and so few people with money to spend. So Alexander began seeking these people out, and when he found something he liked, he would buy it for twice, three times, sometimes as much as ten times what the dealers were offering.

"He bought only the best and tried to pay a fair price. An honorable price, was the way he put it. He was building friends as well as a collection, you see. That has always been his way. And these friends remember him still, him and his honesty and the respect he gave them when they had nothing and were no one. Those who are still alive come to him even today, to buy or to sell. And their children. That, Jeffrey, is the measure of Alexander Kantor."

"So what did he do with those first pieces?"

"Alexander was a man with vision. He knew that prices would eventually rise, especially if he dealt only in the very finest. So he rented a bank box and placed all his purchases in there for safekeeping. Then the box was replaced with a larger drawer, then two, then three, and so on." Her eyes shone with remembered pride. "I can still recall the first time he showed me his collection. It was the day before my wedding. He took Peter and me to Claridge's for lunch—you must go there once for me, Jeffrey. Promise me you will."

"All right."

"Thank you. Yes, then after lunch he took us down into the bank vault and opened up all five of these great drawers that he and a guard pulled out of a wall of locked boxes. He opened them up and said that we were to pick out whatever piece we liked the most as a wedding present.

"You should have seen the treasure. When I collected myself, I told him I couldn't possibly do such a thing. So he gave me an emerald necklace, pressed it into Peter's hand because I refused to touch it, it was all too much for me, I had only met him once before. I still have it over there in the rosewood box on my vanity. I intend to give it to whichever of you boys marries first. I do so hope I'm still around to see that day."

Jeffrey leaned back in his seat and said softly, "Incredible."

"Yes, that is the perfect way to describe Alexander. He is an incredible man. Always a gentleman, always generous and gallant. Yet always a loner, preferring to go his own way. All his life he has held who he is and what he does out of sight from the rest of us. I truly believe that is why he decided to remain in London and set up his business there. Because he preferred to be alone."

"I have to go." Jeffrey rose his feet, leaned over to kiss the withered cheek. As he raised back up he asked, "Why doesn't he ever come to see you?"

"Because it is his nature," she replied simply. "You will discover with time, Jeffrey, that people do not always act in a logical manner. Alexander loved my husband. He has not been to see me since the funeral. Period. I could become angry and destroy the affection I hold for him, or I can accept what is beyond my power to control. He writes me with unfailing regularity, at Christmas, on my birthday, and again at Easter. He never fails to mention how he misses my husband. I do not agree with how he chooses to deal with Peter's absence, but I will not allow this to come between me and the memories of a man my husband adored. I simply will not allow it."

As he was leaving, his grandmother called after him, "Jeffrey, please. Do it for me."

He stopped, felt the old familiar tug-of-war begin inside himself. His hand gripped the doorknob with white-knuckled intensity.

"Think of it as a last request from one who has loved you all your life," she pleaded. "Go and see your brother."

He nodded, not trusting his voice, and left.

Jeffrey's Tuesday morning began as usual. The trash men and the builders arrived at half-past seven, banging dustbins and racing heavy diesels and trading curses in broadest Cockney. Jeffrey swung out of bed, checked the weather by craning and locating the one patch of sky visible in the corner of his bedroom window. He decided to skip his morning run through Hyde Park and instead take breakfast in Shepherd Market.

Even in early June there were mornings when low-lying clouds clamped themselves firmly over the city, a lingering reminder of winter's steel-gray cold. But if the air was dry, as it often was, by midmorning the clouds would lift away, leaving an afternoon of breathtaking beauty. On such days lunch hours were stretched to include lazy strolls through Mayfair's numerous parks and squares. Every bench was full, ties were cast aside, blouses opened another notch. Every possible square inch of sun-starved skin was exposed to spring's gift.

Scattered among these weeks came days when the air took on a jewel-like clarity. Heavy winds and heavier showers scrubbed the air to a newborn brightness. London's buildings and parks and monuments positively sparkled. Dawn runs through Hyde Park became mystical exercises, each breath a perfume-laden draught.

South Audley Street, where Jeffrey's minuscule apartment was located, ran from Grosvenor Square and the United States Embassy to Curzon Street. It was by London standards a broad and smooth-running thoroughfare, one long block removed from Park Lane and Hyde Park. So many films and television programs had used its thoroughly Victorian facades as backdrops that the equipment required for a full-scale shoot caused more irritation than excitement.

His neighborhood was flanked on all sides by the lore of centuries and filled to the brim with wealth. South Audley Street was a ridiculously posh address, made affordable only because the American who owned the flat was a friend and client of Alexander's. In the late sixties—back before London's property boom had pushed Mayfair prices into the stratosphere—he had purchased it both as an investment and a holiday flat. He let it to Jeffrey half as a favor to Alexander and half as a security measure; in recent years thieves had taken to marking down all flats not regularly occupied and robbing them at their leisure.

According to the agreement, Jeffrey had the flat fully furnished for eleven months a year. In July the owner and his wife flew over from California to spend a month doing the London social scene. For that month Jeffrey moved into rooms at his club. The arrangement was ideal. It brought a tastefully furnished Mayfair flat down to an affordable price, and allowed Jeffrey to savor the experience of making the heart of London his home.

By American standards, the flat was only slightly larger than a moving crate. The living room looked down on a busy city street and was just big enough for a glass-topped dining table, an ultra-modern sofa, two matching chairs, and an unadorned Scandinavian corner cupboard. The bedroom, whose tiny window overlooked an alley, was much too small for its American-size bed. Jeffrey had to do the sideways shuffle to arrive at his clothes cupboard. Dressing took place in the front hall.

The bathroom was down a narrow staircase that was both steep and dangerous, especially after a round of local pubs. The kitchen was an afterthought, an alcove so narrow that two people could not pass each other.

The monthly rent was more than his father's mortgage for a four-bedroom house on one of Jacksonville's main canals. Still, Jeffrey was enormously glad he had followed Alexander's urging to accept the offer. The Grosvenor House Hotel, which was half a block behind his flat, charged four hundred dollars a night for a standard double room. A furnished studio flat two doors down from his was advertised for rent at more per week than he was paying per month. And the location suited him perfectly—two blocks to his shop, one to Hyde Park, and three from the fabulous English breakfasts in legendary Shephard Market.

Shepherd Market was a collection of narrow winding streets and tiny cottages more suited to a quiet country village than the heart of London's West End. Tradition had it as the gathering place for drovers bringing their flocks to market, back seven or eight hundred years ago, when London-Town was still confined to its original walls. In those early days, drovers slaughtered their flocks behind local butcheries, and put themselves up in cramped little rooms above the local pubs.

By the time Queen Victoria began her reign in the nineteenth century, the drovers were no more. Yet Shepherd Market survived the centuries and the transitions, retaining its reputation as a gathering place for the less genteel, and gaining a name as having the largest selection of courtesans and streetwalkers in all England.

Jeffrey's walk to breakfast was for him a stroll through a living museum. At the Hyde Park end, Mayfair was mostly brick and stone festooned with an abundance of Victorian foppery. Queen Anne cottages stood cheek-and-jowl with more recent construction, yet to Jeffrey's unabashedly biased eye, the charm had been preserved. In the relative quiet of his early morning walks, he imagined himself transported back to a time of top hats and morning coats and ballooning skirts and hansom cabs.

Jeffrey was in love with Mayfair. All of London held him enthralled; for that matter, the fact that he slept and ate and worked and played on an island perched at the upper left corner of Europe filled him with sheer explosive delight. But he *loved* Mayfair.

To Jeffrey Allen Sinclair, Mayfair had all the makings of a magical land. There were so many hidden nooks and crannies and tales and characters that he could spend a dozen lifetimes within its confines and never drain the cup of adventure.

Jeffrey crossed over Curzon Street, walked the narrow foot passage, and entered a collection of streets never intended for car traffic. Shepherd Market lanes were fifteen feet wide or less, and lined with tiny cottages housing a variety of cafes and shops and pubs and restaurants. Jeffrey's own favorite was a corner cafe with hand-drawn glass panes, warped as though pebbles had been dropped onto their still surface and then frozen in place. The cafe's ceiling and walls were plaster framed by ancient uneven beams, its tables set so close together that a diner who ate with elbows extended was simply not welcome. Jeffrey had long since learned to fold his morning paper into sixteenths.

Once Jeffrey returned home for Ling and arrived at the shop, he barely had time to settle in before the electronic chime announced his first visitor of the day. From the safety of his office alcove Jeffrey glanced up, smiled, tucked the little bird into its new bedding, put on his professional face, and walked forward.

He swung the door wide with a flourish. "Good morning, Mr. Greenfield. Morning, Ty."

"Hullo, lad," Sydney Greenfield said. "I've always wanted to be your height when I walk into a bar. Isn't that right, Ty."

"Gets him proper switched on, it does."

"Come in, gentlemen. Come in."

Sydney Greenfield, purveyor to the would-be's and has-been's of London's Green Belt, entered with his normal theatrics. Behind him walked Ty, his shadowy parrot. Jeffrey did not know him by any other name, did not even know if he had one. Ty he had been introduced as, and Ty he had remained. Jeffrey truly liked the pair. They were a part of what made the London antiques trade unique in all the world.

The Green Belt was an almost-circle of suburbs and swallowed villages that stretched through four counties. They were linked to central London by an extended train service and road system, allowing those who could afford it to live surrounded by a semblance of green and still make it to work more or less on time.

Sydney Greenfield described himself as a contact broker extraordinaire, and survived from the hand-to-mouth trade of bringing buyer and seller together. He had somehow attached himself to Jeffrey and the shop during Jeffrey's early days. They had actually brought him one sale, albeit for the cheapest article in the shop at the time. Nonetheless, following that maneuver Sydney Greenfield had treated Jeffrey and the shop with a proprietary interest, as though their own success were now inexorably linked with his.

Sydney Greenfield was a florid man with thin strands of gray-black hair plastered haphazardly across an enormous central bald spot. Even at ten in the morning his cheeks and nose positively glowed from the effects of too many three-hour pub lunches and liquid dinners—an integral part of the finder's trade. He wore a tailored pin-stripe three-piece suit made from a broadcloth Jeffrey had long since decided came from the inside of a Sainsbury's chocolate box, it was so shiny. Beneath it bunched a wilted white starched shirt and an over-loud tie. A large belly strained against his waistcoat.

"With regard to the cabinet," Sydney Greenfield said. "We've been broaching the subject with Her Royal Highness the Princess Walrus. How long has it been now, Ty."

"Nigh on seven weeks, it is."

"Yes. Long time to be weathering Her Royal Highness' storm, seven weeks is. And I must tell you, your asking price for that cabinet has created quite a storm, hasn't it, Ty."

"Right stood my hair on end, she did."

Jeffrey fished out the key ring for the glass display case. "I think you'd better sit down," he said.

Sydney Greenfield clutched at his heart. "You're not meaning it."

Jeffrey raised up a crystal decanter, asked, "Perhaps a little brandy?"

Greenfield sat with a low moan. "You promised me first call. Didn't he, Ty."

"Stood right there and gave his solemn word, he did."

Jeffrey handed over a crystal snifter holding an ample portion, replied, "I told you I'd hold it for seven days. Which I did. And that was almost two months ago."

Greenfield downed the snifter with one gulp, breathed, "Details, lad. Mere details."

"I had a buyer who waited through that seven-day period, then paid the price I asked."

"Seventeen thousand quid?" Greenfield waved the goblet for a refill. "Paid up without a quibble?"

"Didn't even blink an eye."

"Tell me who it is, lad. There's a couple of little items I'd like to show a gentleman of means."

Jeffrey shook his head. "Seventeen thousand pounds buys a lot of confidentiality in this shop."

Greenfield drained the second glass, smacked his lips. "Well, it's water under the bridge then, right, Ty."

"No use crying over milk the cat's already drunk."

"Did I ever tell you why I call him Ty, lad?"

"Only every time you come in."

Greenfield ignored him. "It's after the *Titanic*, because the fellow goes down like a bolt at the first sniff of the stuff. Never seen the like, not in this trade."

Sydney Greenfield recovered with the speed of one accustomed to such disappointments. He pointed an overly casual hand toward one of the few English pieces that Jeffrey had kept for their own shop, said, "We've done quite a bit of analyzing the market for that other little item."

It was a chest of drawers made in the William and Mary period, and was constructed in laburnum wood, a tree whose seeds were deadly poisonous. The wood had been cut transversely across the branch, creating a swirl effect in the grain which reminded Jeffrey of the inside of oyster shells. The inlay was of darker holly, which traced its way around the outer edges of each drawer; the carpenter had used the inlay to frame the wood's pattern, rather than smother it. The piece was probably constructed somewhere around 1685, given its similarities to other antiques that Jeffrey had been able to identify and which had more established provenances.

Establishing an antique's provenance—its previous record of ownership—added significantly to an article's price, especially if there were either royalty or unique stories attached. One part of the mysteries attached to Alexander's antiques was that they almost never had any provenance whatsoever. They were therefore sold on the basis of their beauty, condition, and evident age. Jeffrey's own education had shown that the more valuable the antique, the more often there was a fairly clear indication of lineage. To have no provenance whatsoever with antiques of this quality suggested that Alexander was intentionally hiding the records in order to protect his sources.

The cost of the chest of drawers was twenty-six thousand pounds, or about forty-five thousand dollars.

"We are on the verge," Sydney Greenfield announced. "Yes, lad, we might actually be pouncing on that one tomorrow. We don't have her signed, mind you. I'd be lying if I said that, and as you know I'm a man of my word. But we're close enough to see the whites of her eyes, aren't we, Ty."

"Close enough to steal a kiss and bolt."

"Yes, that is, if anyone could actually bring themselves to kiss the old walrus. Mind you, I'd probably take the plunge myself if I thought it'd get the old dear to part with her brass."

Katya chose that moment to arrive at the front door. She leaned up close enough to see through the outside reflection, tapped her fingernails on the glass and waved at him.

At first sight of her, Greenfield sprang from the chair as though electrocuted. "Who's that, lad? Not a customer. Life's unfair, I've known that for years, but it'd be stepping out of bounds to hand money to looks like that."

"My new assistant," Jeffrey replied, opening the door and ushering her in. "Katya Nichols, may I present Sydney Greenfield and his assistant Ty. I'm sorry, Ty, I don't believe I've ever learned your last name."

Sydney Greenfield displayed a massive grace as he sidled up and bowed over Katya's hand. "My dear, if this were my shop, I'd have raised the prices ten percent the instant I signed you on."

Katya had compromised over taking salary from Jeffrey in a way that was uniquely her own; she spent it all on clothes that she wore when she was working at the shop. Today she had on one of his favorite items, a high-collared blouse in gray-violet silk the shade of her eyes. It had little cloth buttons and an Oriental design sewn across the left breast and up both sleeves. It was gathered at the waist with a leather belt of almost the same shade, and worn out and draped over a knee-length skirt of midnight blue. Jeffrey thought the color of the blouse made her eyes look positively enormous.

Katya responded to Sydney's compliment with her unshakable poise. "It's very nice to meet you, Mr. Greenfield, Ty. Has Jeffrey offered you gentlemen coffee?"

"He was obviously waiting for you to arrive, my dear. Knowing as he would that it'll taste twice as good coming from your hand, won't it, Ty."

"Like nectar, it will."

"How do you gentlemen like it?"

"Ty likes his straight up, seeing as how it's the only drink on earth he can stomach in pure form. I'll have mine with a touch more of the amber, if your boss here will relax his death's grip on the bottle."

Sydney watched Katya vanish into the alcove, murmured to Jeffrey, " 'Truth, lad. I wouldn't get a dollop of work done with that in the shop."

"I have the same trouble," Jeffrey replied.

"Where on earth did you find her?"

"In the London University library."

Sydney made round mocking eyes. "You mean she can read, too?"

"She's an honor student in Eastern European studies."

Greenfield rolled his eyes. "Oh, you wouldn't catch me studying them places. Or going there, for that matter. Would you, Ty."

"Rather marry Her Royal Walrus, I would."

"What do you mean?"

"Communists, lad. Communists. Stands to reason, doesn't it. What, you think all them card-carryin' pinkos just up and vanished, poof, in the blink of an eye and all that?"

"From what I've read, the Communist parties have either been banned in those countries or have lost so much support they're not really a factor anymore."

"Wrong, lad. Dead wrong you are." Sydney lowered his voice to a brandy-soaked whisper. "There's Commies everywhere, and this time they're mad."

"I rather doubt that."

"Out for blood, aren't they, Ty."

"Worse than Dracula coming off a diet, far as I see it."

" 'Course they are. Been in power for donkey's years, and all of a sudden they're out on the street, nowhere to go, nothing to do but find a capitalist pig and roast him."

"Thanks for the advice."

"Not to worry, lad. There's always more where that came from." He leaned closer, said, "And here's another morsel for good measure. Latch onto that one, lad. She's one of a kind."

Jeffrey bit off the thought that came to mind and said as Katya came back into view, "I've got to be getting over to the Grosvenor House. You gentlemen will be all right here with Katya, I take it."

"Right you are, lad." Greenfield performed another little bow as he took the proffered cup. "Run along and see to your business. We'll suffer on here without you."

CHAPTER
5

The Grosvenor House Hotel dominated the stretch of Park Lane approaching Marble Arch and Oxford Street. Originally built as the city palace for Sir Richard Grosvenor, the then owner of all West Mayfair, it was a modest red-brick affair of two wings and four hundred rooms.

In 1920, when the palace became a hotel, its downstairs ballroom was converted into an indoor skating rink that could accommodate as many as five hundred people at a time. Those days were long gone, however, and now it was home to some of the largest events of London's social season, including the most exclusive antique show in all England.

Jeffrey entered through the hotel's back doors, passing as he did a taxi rank filled to overflowing with Bentleys and Jaguars and Rolls Royces and stretch Mercedes and several dozen bored drivers. He circled the lobby, showed his dealer's pass to the uniformed attendants, and joined the flow entering the double doors.

There were a number of dealers with whom the Priceless, Ltd antique shop placed pieces. Part of the reason was simply volume—when a major shipment arrived, which took place as often as four or five times a year, there was no way they could stock all the items, much less market them properly. Moreover, there was also the issue of quality and style. They did not handle much English furniture, for example, and did not seek to build a reputation in that area. They turned most

such items over to dealers who had made it their life's work—
as was the case today.

Visiting the fair was a daunting experience for Jeffrey,
though nothing like the year before. He was beginning to
know his way around, and did not feel like such a silent idiot
when talk turned to pieces and dealers.

A hodgepodge of languages greeted him as he stepped
into the fair proper. Around him he saw elegant women kiss-
ing cheeks and laughing over snide asides, languidly flickering jeweled wrists to accent their own verbal thrusts. Jeffrey skirted around them, extremely grateful that his own
shop had never become a gathering place for the overly rich
and overly bored.

"Hello, hello, what do we have here?" A dealer named
Andrew stepped back from a clubbish circle of dealers and
waved Jeffrey over.

"Not half bad, that." This voice belonged to a dealer
named Jackie, a short feisty man with a reputation for pro-
voking fights and accepting goods no one else would touch.
"Take a stroll from the shop, whisper a word in the right ear,
steal an honest bloke's customer, sneak on back, pick up a
few bob. All right for some, I suppose."

"Shut up, Jackie," Andrew said, his gaze still on Jeffrey.
"How are you then, lad? All right?"

"Yes, thanks. I was just—"

"Oh, we know all about that. Never a minute free for a
bit of idle chatter, our lad. What's brought you over, then?"

Trying to match his casual tone, Jeffrey repeated a remark often heard among dealers: "Just wanted to see if you
had anything I could use to dress up the shop."

Andrew shook his head. He was a cheerful, solidly built
man who had worked his way up from extremely poor begin-
nings to the management of a very successful Kensington
High Street antiques shop. Jeffrey had placed pieces with
him on several occasions, and found him to be both honest
and shrewd. "No, nothing for you at the moment. Stop back
in a couple of days, though. I'll let you have whatever's left
for a song, long as you haul it away and save my aching back
the trouble."

"Sounds good, thanks."

"Just give us a shout, we'll have us a look around, all
right?" Andrew turned back to the group, asked, "Everybody

here's met Kantor's whiz-kid, have they?"

There were a few greetings, a couple of genuine smiles, several calculating looks from very hard eyes. Jeffrey replied with a hello and a blank smile, and looked forward to getting away.

"Have you ever been into their shop?" Andrew asked the clan.

"Never had the pleasure," a dealer in old silver replied.

"Generally they have this huge great mixture," Andrew said. "Everything comes in, from the most darling little post-Impressionist etchings to great hairy stuffed baboons."

"I missed the baboon," Jeffrey said.

"Did you really? Probably before your time. Gave me such a fright, that one."

"Must be quite the place," Jackie sneered.

"'Tis, yeah. Sort of a flea market for the Bentley crowd, you might say."

"More like a garage sale put on by the British Museum, from the sounds of it."

"It's all right for some," Jackie said. "We're sure not seeing the like."

"No?"

He shook his head. "We're down forty percent on our takings this year. Watched three of our best customers go under the same week. Left me with this lot of paper and a letter from the bank saying I'll stand in line with the others to get paid. What rot."

Most dealers made complaining about business a singular art form, but there was the ring of truth about what the tough little man said. The recession was hitting the antiques and art trades much harder than anyone expected. According to recent figures, the recession was biting into British business at the rate of nine hundred and seventy bankruptcies every *week*.

"Tough times, Jackie."

"It is, yeah. Might have to pack it in."

"You're joking."

"I'm not, I tell you. Another year like the last one and we'll be back to peddling from a pushcart. I'm glad the old man didn't live to see the day. Wish I hadn't."

"It's tough for all of us," the silver dealer said. "Well, the wolf's at the door. If you'll excuse me, I'm off to make an honest quid."

"Me too," Jeffrey said, nodding to the group.

"Here, lad," Andrew said. "Mind if I join you?"

"Who's tending the store?"

"Got me an old dear, must be eighty if she's a day. Better with the clients than I'll ever be. If they try to talk her down, she grabs her ticker like the shock'll do her in. Shuts them up every time. What's brought you over, then?"

"I've got a chest here with a dealer."

"Want to hear him do his pitch? That was a wise move, lad."

One condition Jeffrey placed on dealers who wished to work with him on a regular basis was that he have the opportunity to hear them describe his piece to a potential buyer. It was one of the best possible learning tools, he had found. Some dealers hated it bitterly, accused him of trying to steal their customers. No one accepted it without a fight, and several had taken it up with Alexander. Jeffrey had been gratified to find the gentleman back him on something so totally unorthodox.

"So why did you complain when I asked you?" Jeffrey demanded.

Andrew gave a casual shrug. "Automatic, wasn't it. Anything to do with negotiations, you don't give in without a struggle. You should know that, lad."

The dealer Jeffrey was to visit today was a leading authority on early Chippendale. He had accepted Jeffrey's condition as he would a dose of castor oil, then compromised by allowing Jeffrey to listen in while he was being interviewed by a magazine reporter. Jeffrey did not object. His goal was simply to hear how someone else described a piece for sale. Who the pitch was made to was immaterial.

The reporter was already there when he arrived. Jeffrey stood just outside the stall, pretending to be a buyer who was simply stopping for a gander. Andrew took the silent hint and stepped back a pace, greeting the stall owner across the way. The pair of them moved up behind Jeffrey, far enough back to be unobtrusive, close enough to hear what was going on.

The dealer ignored them entirely. He was a tall aristocratic man in his late fifties, with ruddy features and a patronizing tone of voice. "It is very difficult, this process of locating the right sort of antiques," the dealer was saying. "One is forced to travel all over the world. There are just so few pieces available of the quality our clients demand."

"He's laying it on over thick, don't you think?" a voice behind Jeffrey muttered.

"Not a bit," Andrew whispered in reply. "The dear's just asked him where his stuff comes from, and he's telling her it's none of her business. Quite right too, if you ask me."

The reporter was a fresh-faced young woman whose interest appeared genuine. She pointed to a tall piece with wood the color of a burnished red sunrise and asked with an American accent, "And what about that piece? Is that a sideboard?"

One of the men behind Jeffrey snickered quietly.

"Ah, no, well, that's a bureau cabinet, really." The man's snootiness inched up another notch. Jeffrey kept his features immobile and recalled the time, three weeks after he had started working with Alexander, when he had asked a dealer with a blessedly short memory if a cherry-wood table wasn't eighteenth-century French. The man had looked at him as though he had just grown a second head, replied that it was a brand-new reproduction of an English Sheraton piece, and asked him if he had ever thought of taking up a different profession—accounting, perhaps.

Jeffrey leaned forward slightly, as the piece under discussion was his. It was also clearly the finest article in the man's collection.

"It was made in England in about 1760," the dealer went on. "George the Third, which makes it of the Chippendale period, of course."

"Of course," the cowed young lady repeated, scribbling furiously.

"It's got a lovely color, I'm sure you'd agree. And wonderful architectural pediments."

"Pediments?" she asked.

"Yes, pediments. Quite rare for a piece of such age, actually."

Jeffrey understood both the reporter's confusion and the dealer's refusal to explain himself further. Like most professions, the world of fine woodworking had a technical vocabulary all its own. And like most such terms, it was difficult to explain one point without referring to other unknown factors. Jeffrey had several times approached the point of giving up and burning his books before it all began to fall into place.

A cabinet's pediment was the ornate carving above the cornice, the molding that framed the top. If the antique rose above the level of simple furniture and sought to be a work of art, as was the case here, the cornice often rested upon a horizontal section, called a frieze, which was either inlaid or carved or both. Thus an elaborate item might be crowned in stages, rising from the upper framework, or carcase, to the frieze, then the cornice, then the pediment.

Jeffrey had spent over a week memorizing the more than two-dozen most common styles of pediments. These were most important to a dealer, as they were oftentimes the first indication of where and when the antique was made.

The Chippendale period was usually identifiable by what was called a broken pediment, which basically looked like the roofline of a house with a chunk bitten out of the middle peak. Ornate articles often had pierced carvings rising from this central gap.

"This item still has vestiges of the maker's label inside the top drawer," the dealer was saying. "Not enough to identify it, unfortunately, but enough to establish in our mind that it was made by a man of importance who prized his work enough to put a label in it."

This, Jeffrey knew, was pure conjecture and would not hold water with a serious collector. For all they knew, it was a fragment of an old map or will or anything else important enough to be varnished into a safe and relatively secret place. But it sounded good, and the young lady ate it up.

"This also has all the original cast brass handles and features. Very nice fitted interior. Newly lined in silk."

"What kind of wood is this?"

"Mahogany. One of about two hundred kinds, actually. Cuban or Honduran, we have decided. It was used quite a lot in that period by the better English cabinetmakers. Excellent quality, I'm sure you'll agree."

"And the price?"

"Thirty-eight thousand pounds."

The young lady gaped. Jeffrey bit back a smile. That was the litmus test of a raw beginner—inability to disguise shock over prices.

"What is very difficult for some people to understand," the dealer said, somewhat testily, "is that this piece is exceptional precisely because of such details. The pediments, the original handles and cleats, all these add tremendously to the value."

"As does a good case of the blarney," muttered the voice behind Jeffrey.

"What happens if a piece comes in that has been refinished?" asked the young lady.

"You buy it for a song and then you lie," the voice offered quietly.

"Ah, well," the dealer replied. "If a piece is ruined, then that is it. Once an article like that has been stripped and repolished, no amount of work will ever restore the color or the surface patina."

"Lucky for us there's a world of fools with money to burn who don't know the first thing about patina," the voice murmured.

"It's very difficult to make a generalization, though," the dealer continued. "It depends on the damage to the article. I mean, some things can be restored and some can't. If you don't know what you're doing, you can spend a lot of money on restoration and have absolutely nothing to show for it."

Jeffrey decided the talk was winding down. He nodded to the dealer, who continued to ignore him, and turned away. Andrew followed him. "There's a few of us gathering at the Audley tonight, lad. You ought to stop by."

"What for?"

Andrew smiled at his directness. "You're getting to be known as a real mystery man. Couldn't hurt to show the face now and then, let people know you're actually human."

"I feel as if I'm under attack every time I meet these people."

"Yes, I suppose you are. No more than the rest of us, though." Andrew patted his shoulder. "Give it a thought, lad. If you're going to make this lot your own, it might be time to widen your circle a little." He gave Jeffrey a friendly nod and wandered off.

The remainder of the afternoon was spent preparing for Alexander's arrival the next morning, dealing with the occasional customer, and knowing the exquisite frustration of

Katya's silent presence. When they were alone like this, they shared the cozy shelter of the little back office. Katya set her work on a small satinwood table beside his bookshelves. He sat at his desk and compiled notes, made calls, carefully went through his accounts for the past month, and rewarded himself with glances at her.

He yearned for the chance to tell her that her silence appealed to him, that somehow it created a tenderness in him that he had never known before, an awareness of her fragility that seemed to cry out for his protection. But he could not speak of it because she would not let him.

At a dinner together two weeks before, Jeffrey had almost admitted defeat. He had sat across from her, and wondered if perhaps it wasn't time to let her go. Six months of futility was enough.

Katya chose that moment to look up. She sensed the change within him, and reacted with a look of real fear before saying, "You've never told me about your family."

"I've tried," he replied. "Several times. You never seemed to care."

"I'm listening now."

He started to tell her, that's not what I said. Instead he replied, "My family revolved around my father's business life. I was what you'd call a product of the American corporate culture. The way my father told it, Old MacDonald was president and chairman of the board of the E.I.E.I.O. Corporation."

"Oh, stop it."

"He had his Moo-Moo Division over here, see. And the Oink-Oink Division over there. And the Quack-Quack Division was stuck out back by the lake because they never could get out of the red."

"Did your family belong to a church?"

"For the last eleven years my family has lived in Jacksonville, Florida. That means I'm Baptist. Back home, either you're a retired Yankee or you're a Baptist or you're dead. And if you're dead, then you're a dead Baptist."

"My mother and I belong to an Anglican church," Katya said. "It's sort of like the Episcopalian church in America."

"I've always thought of Episcopalians as sort of Catholic lights. You know, all the fun but only half the guilt."

"There's a real revival going on within the Anglican

church in this country," Katya persisted. "It's really meant a lot to me, being a part of this upsurge in the Spirit."

Jeffrey nodded, worked at keeping a casual tone. "So when were you saved?"

She looked deep at him. "The same time as you, Jeffrey. About two thousand years ago."

"We used to have this preacher, a professional auctioneer during the week. I never heard anybody talk so fast in my life. He'd take ten minutes to get cranked up, like a jet engine winding up before take-off. His face would get all red and swollen, then he'd blast off, and all we'd see was a trail of fiery smoke in the sky. He'd start in Genesis and fly right on through to the maps. In an hour. Every week."

Her gaze remained steady and searching. "Why do you make a joke out of everything?"

Because I love to see your smile, he thought, but could not bring himself to make such a confession. "Maybe because the truth is so boring."

"Try me."

"You sure?"

"If I wasn't I wouldn't ask."

"Okay." He took a breath. "The truth is, I don't even know where to say my family is from. My dad was with IBM. I remember when I was six years old he came home one day, and he and my mom got all excited because he'd been put on the fast track. I didn't have idea one what they were talking about, but I still remember how happy he was and how proud my mom got. From then on, we never spent two full years in one place.

"I've lived in eleven different cities in seven states. I went to four junior high schools. We finally settled in Jacksonville when I was seventeen, and we've been there ever since." Another deep breath. "We had to stay there. My brother got . . . sick."

"I thought you told me you didn't have any brothers or sisters."

His face was set in rigid lines. "I don't."

Her eyes rested on him in silent watchfulness. "And you want to start a relationship with me."

"This has nothing to do with it."

She slid from her seat, rose to her feet, said, "I think it's time you took me home, Jeffrey."

"Why?" He did not try to remove the harshness from his voice. "Because I won't talk about things that don't matter?"

"Are you going to take me home or should I walk by myself?"

He paid and guided her from the restaurant. On the street he realized that he faced a final farewell, and he found himself unable to raise his hand and flag a taxi and open the door and say the words and watch her leave his life. Instead, he took her arm and led her across the street to where the thinnest tip of Hyde Park separated them from a pair of monstrously modern hotels, the Hilton and the Inn on the Park, which in turn backed up onto the Shepherd Market corner of Mayfair. He realized he was simply putting off the inevitable, and that as soon as they left behind the park's leafy confines and reentered the rushing nighttime traffic, she would step into a waiting taxi and be gone. No matter how ready he was to end the futile struggle, the thought left him helplessly wounded.

She appeared to enjoy the evening's cool mist, and walked beside him in a silence of her own. Then she gave a little cry, slipped off the path, bent down and crooned at something he could not see. Jeffrey started to make some comment about the elves of Mayfair when she straightened and lifted cupped hands toward him. He leaned forward and saw it was a baby bird.

Because it was the closest refuge, they took the bird back to his apartment, a five-minute walk. It was the first time Katya had ever agreed to come up.

She gave a cursory glance to the apartment's pastel carpets and glass-topped dining table and light-stained Scandinavian furniture and garishly expensive mirror mural on the living-room wall. "This is not at all what I expected."

"I rented it furnished." He pointed toward the kitchen. "Bring the bird in here."

"Do you think it will live?"

"I don't have a lot of experience with baby birds," he replied, looking down at the shivering little form and the wide-open upthrust beak. "What do we feed it?"

"Maybe just a little warm milk to start." She rubbed one finger along the blind little body. "He can't be more than a day or so old."

Jeffrey lit the stove and set down a pot with a smidgen

of milk. He thundered down the stairs to his bathroom, reappearing a moment later bearing a eyedropper. He washed it thoroughly, filled it with warm milk, and dropped a bit on his wrist. "Feels okay."

"You do that like a real professional."

The baby bird liked it immensely. Jeffrey dropped the milk in as carefully as he could, but the body did not have strength to keep the head steady. He chased the tiny weaving body around and in the process painted its entire form with a warm white covering. Finally he managed to get three drops on target, enough to turn the gaping little mouth into a tiny white lake. The bird took the milk with a swallow that shook its entire frame. There was a moment's pause; then the head raised back up and again begged for more.

The baby was gray and covered with a dusting of scraggly hairs over wrinkled yellowish skin. Its wings were mere nubs of featherless quills, its head a skull covered with translucent skin, its beak bigger than its head. Its claws were feathery wisps that could not close. It trembled continually, even after it accepted the last convulsive swallow, then curled up in Katya's palm and breathed in little gasps that shook its entire meager form.

Jeffrey went out and returned with a pair of clean dish towels. He lined a cereal bowl, then guided Katya's hands over and helped settle the tiny body. He watched her coo and caress the form for a moment. "Katya, I'm not sure it's going to last the night."

She replied with a nod, refusing to take her eyes off the baby. "We have to try," she said. "What will we do with him? I can't take him to classes, and I can't get back home to feed him every hour."

"I'll keep it with me here and take it to the office," he said, and amended silently, if it survives. "You can take care of it there."

She raised her head and gave him her vulnerable look. "You still want me to come in and work with you?"

"I wasn't so sure earlier." He fought to keep his voice calm. "Katya, I care too much for you to be able to go on like this."

"You've got to be honest with me," she replied.

He nodded. "But I need the same in return."

She lifted one hand up from the bird and stroked his

cheek with a feather-soft touch. "It's been difficult for you, hasn't it?"

"Horrible."

Her gaze turned inward. "I wish I knew what to do," she murmured. "It's all so confusing."

"What is?"

She focused on him, real fear in her eyes. "I'm trying, Jeffrey. I really am."

"What is it that makes it so hard for you to open up with me?"

She started to say something, then changed her mind and dropped her eyes back to the little bird. "If I tell you, it won't work."

"I don't understand, Katya." He refrained the urge to pull out his hair by the roots. "If you don't tell me, how am I supposed to figure it out?"

"I don't know," she said to the sleeping little bundle. "But I pray that you will, Jeffrey. Every night I pray."

The Audley Pub stood on the corner of South Audley and Mount Street and maintained a charm reminiscent of a Victorian gentleman's library. Leather-lined booths ringed both the bar and the smaller, more stately saloon. Windows with diamond-shaped panes were set in the polished-wood walls. A trio of crystal chandeliers reflected the cheery light from the saloon fireplace. The clientele came from every walk of society; taxi drivers rubbed shoulders with city gents and foreign tourists avoiding the scalper's prices of West End hotel bars.

The first person Jeffrey spotted upon entering that night was Sarah, the gallery owner who had acquired his Musin boat scene the day before. He sidled up next to her, said, "That was a nice painting you picked up yesterday. I'll miss having it around."

She turned around. "Oh, hullo, Jeffrey. That was yours, then, was it? Pity about the masked bandit on the phone. Thought I had myself the buy of the century."

"So did I."

Her gaze turned penetrating. "That wasn't just a bit of fancy footwork on your part, was it?"

Jeffrey's shock was genuine. "I'd never do that."

She searched his face a moment longer before permitting herself a hard smile. "No," she replied. "You wouldn't, would you?"

"I don't even know who that other bidder was. Honest."

"Honest, yes, that's such a pleasant word." She patted his hand. "The world needs a few more like you, young Jeffrey. Come on then, you can use a bit of your honest killing and buy me a drink."

When Jeffrey entered the circle of dealers, Andrew gave him a smile of approval and the words, "You must be celebrating something special to be out on the prowl like this."

"He most certainly is," Sarah replied for him. "He made an extra eighty thousand pounds off me yesterday by the skin of his teeth."

"Sounds like a good story, that," Andrew said.

The venomous little trader named Jackie slid from the booth, "I don't have time for such rubbish. Some of us have to work for our living."

"Don't be daft, Jackie. It could have just as easily been you."

"What rot." He tossed off the last of his drink, gestured angrily at Jeffrey with the empty glass. "He's got a handle to the royal family, gets them coming and going, buying and selling the royal seat warmers. By rights it ought to stay in British hands."

Sarah turned to Jeffrey. "Seen much of the Queen Mother lately, dear?"

"Not since I stopped by the palace for tea last week," Jeffrey replied.

She turned back to Jackie. "That eliminates your little theory, Jackie."

"Rubbish. You don't think he'd tell us, do you? Nobody's that daft. Not even a Yank." Jackie wheeled around and stormed from the bar.

"Rude, if you ask me," Sarah said. "Sorry, Jeffrey. Guess I'll have to apologize for him."

"It's okay."

"He's right in a way," Andrew said mildly. "That's basically how all Mount Street got its start, you know. Catering to the carriage trade during the social season. Word was, a visit to the Kensington High Street shops would mean too long a time between martinis."

"Jackie's losing his shop," grumbled a dealer Jeffrey knew only by sight. "You can't expect him to pat this successful young lad on the head and say, 'Well done.'"

"He's dug his own grave, Tim," Andrew replied. "I'm sorry to say."

"No you're not," Sarah said. "Sorry, I mean. You positively loathe the man and always have."

"That may well be, but it's beside the point. If he'd had the slightest shred of business acumen, he'd have spent more time building allies and less ripping off anyone who came within arm's length."

"And I suppose you've always handled your affairs with white gloves."

"Don't be silly. Of course not. But what I mean to say is with Jackie you were positively certain that he'd do his level best to turn a dirty trick whenever possible."

"At least you knew where you stood with him," Tim replied.

Sarah set down her glass. "I didn't see you leaping up to help him in his hour of need."

"I don't deal in his sort of goods, though, do I."

"Jackie's problem," Andrew persisted, "is that he's like a chess player who can't see but one move ahead. He's only interested in making an extra quid, honest or dishonest, regardless of who might be hurt. I told him that, too. Quite a few times, actually."

That raised eyebrows around the table. "I never thought Jackie would allow anyone to tell him anything," Sarah said.

"Oh, he always denied it."

"He would."

Jeffrey asked, "Why did you bother?"

"Because, lad, Jackie and his kind hurt us all. It serves no one in the end, especially not Jackie."

"What did he do?" Jeffrey asked.

"Yes, Andrew," the stranger drawled. "Do be so kind as to give the boy a few pointers."

"We'd have to turn him over to you for that," Sarah replied acidly.

"Nothing that a thousand other dealers haven't done," Andrew replied. "Passing rubbish off as authentic antiques, disguising repairs with a new coat of varnish, calling it a genuine article and pricing it accordingly."

"Buffing new silver and stamping it with an old mark," Sarah added.

"Jackie's problem was that he did it too much and too openly," someone else offered.

"He cut his own throat," another agreed. "Drove off all the good dealers, and couldn't get his hands on any decent wares."

"A visit to Jackie's store was like a trip to Alice in Wonderland," Sarah added. "You were certain that nothing you saw was real, and everything Jackie said was utter nonsense."

"And all the while he'd be doing his level best to convince you it was a steal."

"That reminds me of a good one I heard the other day," Andrew said. "Seems a chap read in the local paper up in Glasgow that there was a genuine Louis XIV commode going for a quid."

That brought a laugh. A commode was a sort of ornate chest on legs, much like what in America would be called a dining room sideboard. The going rate for an authentic Louis XIV commode would have been at least thirty thousand pounds.

"The local dealers had quite a good chuckle over that one," Andrew went on. "Strange thing, though. Nobody actually bothered to check up on it but this one chap I know."

"You're not expecting us to believe this," someone said.

"This is the truth, I tell you. No one even bothered to ring up the number."

"I'm not the least bit surprised," Sarah told him. "I can just hear it now. You give them a ring and find yourself chatting with a fellow recently imported from Sicily. At no extra charge the lucky buyer finds, stuffed inside the commode, a body in perfectly good working order, save for quite a small hole in the middle of his chest."

"That wasn't it at all," Andrew replied. "Anyway, this chap I know called and the woman on the other end said, yes, she had this commode for sale, and yes, the price was one pound. So he figured it was worth at least driving by. Which he did. And the lady was quite correct. The article was both authentic and in mint condition."

"Someone's putting you on."

"They're not, I tell you. It was exactly what she said it was."

"For a quid."

"One pound exactly," Andrew agreed.

"Go on, then. What's the catch?"

"There wasn't one. Well, not for the buyer. It turned out her husband had recently passed on, and left instructions in his will for the commode to be sold and all proceeds to go to his secretary. The trouble was, you see, his wife knew all about the little affair he and his secretary had been having."

"You're putting us on," someone breathed.

"So she sold it for a quid," Andrew continued. "And passed the money over, just as the will instructed."

"I still don't believe it."

"Stop by the shop sometime," Andrew replied with a grin. "I'll be happy to make you a special offer."

Jeffrey spoke up. "The other day I had a French client tell me how she'd visited an auction house in Paris. She was leafing through the catalog and saw a marble-topped Empire table just like her own. She thought it would be wonderful to have a matched pair, so she spoke to the dealer, who gave her a really attractive price. She examined the page more closely, just to make sure there were no visible flaws in the piece, and recognized the painting on the wall above the commode. It was the painting from her own living-room wall."

"So what did she do?"

"She immediately placed an order for the table, paid a cash deposit, gave a friend's name for her own, and pressed the dealer for an early delivery date. Then she went straight to the police. They staked out her house, and tapped the dealer's lines. The woman went around making noisy plans for a big trip. The night she left, the thieves arrived and the police busted a ring. Turned out they were working all over France, paying a photographer to break in and photograph pieces, then not stealing anything until a buyer had been found. Kept them from needing to have the stolen goods around for long."

"Is that how your Kantor gets his hands on all those goods?" Tim's voice was taunting. "You telling stories on your own boss?"

"Oh, do be quiet, Tim."

"Absolutely," Andrew agreed cheerfully. "Even if you

were right, our lad here wouldn't let on, now, would he?"

Tim subsided behind his drink. "All I know is, it's uncommon strange how he keeps turning up with these little gems nobody's ever heard of before."

"It's because Alexander keeps his nose to the grindstone and not to his glass," Sarah countered. "Isn't that right, Jeffrey?"

"It sure is," he replied, rising to his feet. "And you'll have to excuse me. His plane arrives first thing tomorrow morning, and I've got to go out to Heathrow to meet it."

"Where'd you say he was coming in from, lad?" Andrew asked.

"I didn't," Jeffrey replied. "Good-night, everybody."

CHAPTER

6

Jeffrey arrived at Heathrow Airport half an hour before the flight was scheduled to land. He sat in the Rolls' front seat, somewhat embarrassed by the stares of passersby. The driver was new, but he came from their traditional car-hire firm, and had clearly been warned in advance of Alexander's abhorrence for small talk.

The chauffeur eased the massive car in front of the arrivals gate, then spoke for the first time since greeting Jeffrey at the shop, "I'll be in the VIP lot at the terminal side, sir. I'll have to ask you to come out to let me know if the plane's been delayed. I can't sit there but a few minutes."

"Right." The door shut behind him with a satisfactory thunk. It was one of the Rolls' trademarks; all the pieces fit together as though designed to last several generations.

Jeffrey stood by the doors to baggage claim and found himself growing excited. He had not seen his boss in almost a month, had not spoken with him for over three weeks. The distances between Alexander Kantor's visits to London were growing longer, the periods when he was lost and gone and out of contact easier to bear.

Large metal doors pulled back and permitted a slightly dazed Alexander Kantor to walk through, followed by a porter carrying three Louis Vuitton cases. Jeffrey stepped forward and took the matching briefcase from Alexander's limp hand. Flying always left his boss exhausted.

"Ah, Jeffrey. You received my fax."

"Over this way," he said, grasping Alexander's elbow and pointing toward the far doors with his free hand. "I confirmed the fax the day it arrived."

"Did you? When was that?"

"Last Friday. Are you sure you want to talk about this right now?"

"Quite right." He rubbed a weary brow. "Why on earth did they do away with shipping liners? Allow a body to arrive in proper style."

"You can't get to London from Geneva by liner, Alexander. The Alps are in the way." Kantor now had his only residence in Geneva. All the others—London, Monte Carlo, Sicily, Montreal, a flat on Copacabana in Rio—had been gradually sold off over the previous twelve months. The only explanation he had given Jeffrey was that the cost of keeping servants on three continents was becoming ridiculous.

Kantor shot his assistant a peeved look. "You are positively enjoying yourself. I had no idea you had sadistic tendencies."

"It's just that you are so seldom in less than top form." Jeffrey allowed Kantor to pass through the exit before him. "Did you have a good trip?"

"Don't be ridiculous. There is no such thing as a good trip on an airplane."

"I've always thought flying was great," Jeffrey replied, signaling to their driver.

"Flying is never great. You can have a ten-course meal, watch the finest film since *The Maltese Falcon,* be served by a matched pair of angelic hostesses, and your flight would still not be great. Interesting, perhaps, but never great."

"You're slurring."

"Of course I'm slurring. I always try to nap on a plane, which makes me more tired than I was before I started, and I always slur. Where is Roger?"

Roger was Kantor's driver of choice in London. As far as Jeffrey could tell, his entire vocabulary consisted of three words: very good, sir. "With a trio of golfers in Scotland. Gone all week."

Alexander replied to the driver's murmured greeting with a nod and allowed himself to be guided into the Rolls' leather backseat. Jeffrey supervised the loading of the cases, tipped the porter, and climbed in beside Kantor.

"Claridge's, driver," Kantor said.

"Sorry, Alexander," Jeffrey said. "We don't have time."

"What on earth are you talking about?"

"Count di Garibaldi is waiting for us at the shop. He is on his way overseas, and he insists on speaking to you personally about a certain item."

Kantor let out a groan. "I positively do not have the strength to deal with that man."

"You always say that when you arrive, and in fifteen minutes you're always fine."

"Am I really?"

"Always." Jeffrey reached over to the front seat, retrieved his briefcase, extracted a thermos and a pair of embossed mugs, said, "Would you care for a cup?"

"My dear boy, how thoughtful. I have no idea what they serve on those planes, but it is most certainly not coffee."

He handed over a steaming mug, sweetened as Kantor preferred. "You always say that, too."

"Am I becoming so predictable in my old age?" He took another sip and color began returning to his features. "Your coffee is improving."

"Betty accused me the other day of trying to dissolve the roof of her mouth."

"Americans declare anything stronger than old dishwater to be dangerous." He took another sip. "Yes, I do believe I will survive after all."

They sped down the M4 until the morning traffic backed up and reduced their progress to a crawl. It took them over an hour to arrive in Mayfair, by which time the thermos was empty, most of the papers in Jeffrey's briefcase had been covered, and Alexander's traditionally alert good nature had been fully restored.

He rewarded his assistant with an approving look. "You have done well, Jeffrey. Remarkably well."

"Thanks. It's getting to be a lot of fun."

"I'm so glad to hear it. A business like ours requires that sort of attitude. Otherwise it is next to impossible to close a sale." He studied Jeffrey a moment longer. "And you are weathering my absences well?"

"Easier each time. I do have the odd moment, though, usually late at night after you've been out of touch for a couple of weeks. I wake up in a sweat, wondering what I'd do if you didn't show up again."

Alexander Kantor turned toward the window streaked with misting rain. "There has been a method to the madness, I assure you."

"I figured there was."

"Yes?" He turned back around. "And what did you suppose was the purpose?"

"To test me."

"Obviously. But in what way?"

"To see if I could be trusted when there was no way you could be looking." Jeffrey took a breath. "To leave me with no set rules, no real parachute, a lot of opportunities to sell at one price and record another, buy and sell on the sly, that sort of thing."

"Quite right. You've done very well, I might add."

"I thought you had some of the customers in there, you know, watching and reporting back to you."

"Of course I did." He reached to the burl table which folded out from the driver's seat-back and lifted the sheaf of ledger pages. "But the real evidence is right here, Jeffrey. Not only are you scrupulous in your record-keeping, you have done an exceptional job in researching our pieces, presenting them in the best possible light, placing them at auction houses when appropriate—basically, in coming to master the various facets of your new profession. I am indeed pleased."

Jeffrey felt his face flush with pleasure. "I've tried to be careful."

"You've been meticulous. I shall return to these compliments under more conducive circumstances. Now tell me—" He leafed through them to the section labeled *Miscellaneous Expenses*. "You have several items here for salary. I take it this is not for a raise you have given yourself."

"No." Jeffrey tugged at his ear. He had thought this over several times, was still not sure how to handle it. "It was one of those judgment calls I had to make myself."

"Go on."

"I needed someone who could help in the shop when I was out at auctions or seeing out-of-town buyers or visiting another business. Somebody pretty much available to work only when I needed them."

The smoky gray eyes gave away nothing. "And how long has this person been employed, may I ask?"

"About four weeks."

"Since just after my trip began, then. And why did we not discuss this on the phone?"

Yes. That was the clincher. Jeffrey swallowed. "It's a little hard to explain."

The Rolls turned onto South Audley one block up from Mount Street. Alexander leaned forward, said, "Find some place to pull over and park, please, driver."

"Right you are, sir."

"Go on, Jeffrey. I'm all ears."

He took a breath. "She is more than just a shop assistant."

"Ah." Kantor was visibly relieved. "I understand. You did not wish to discuss your personal situation on the phone with me, and you did not want to discuss hiring her without telling me everything."

He nodded, immensely glad to have it out in the open. "If I knew what our personal situation really was, maybe I wouldn't have such a tough time talking about it."

"We can leave that for later. Perhaps I shall be able to help you see the situation more clearly. For now we shall focus on the business aspect. And I must say, Jeffrey, your judgment call, as you describe it, was not the optimum one. You should have felt obliged to tell me about this young lady immediately. You have entrusted the shop and all its contents to an unknown. That simply will not do."

Jeffrey nodded miserably. "It started off as an emergency. I had to go out to Sussex to see the Countess Drake. You know what she's like. She called up and said it was now or never, and it was that Florentine dresser you've been talking about with her for as long as I've been with the shop. I had a buyer from Spain who had telephoned for an appointment that same afternoon. And Mrs. Grayson had been called out of town the day before. Her daughter went into labor with Mrs. Grayson's first grandchild."

Mrs. Grayson was a mild-mannered old dear who had been with Kantor's shop for years. She did little more than mind the store when everyone else was away, but she did this with honest diligence. Her courtesy and genuine friendliness ensured that customers returned to learn more details or conclude a transaction with Alexander or Jeffrey.

It had taken several months before Mrs. Grayson would give Jeffrey her approval, for she was fiercely loyal to her oft-absent director. Yet once it was granted, it was done with the wholehearted warmth of a proud mother. She made no bones over her dislike of the previous three assistants Alexander had brought in, none of whom had lasted a year. Jeffrey had known an inordinate amount of pride over his acceptance into Mrs. Grayson's fold. During his boss's long and silent absences, it was the only signal he had received of a job well done.

"So I asked Katya to come over and cover for me," Jeffrey finished, mightily worried.

"Katya," Alexander murmured. "A lovely name."

"Yes, sir." He swiped at his brow. "Anyway, the next week I had this group over from New York, fourteen people in the shop at once, and Mrs. Grayson let me know that even if I threatened her with dismissal she was not coming back. It seems there's been some kind of health problem with her daughter. Mrs. Grayson is staying in the Midlands until everything is okay. Anyway, with the tour and a lot of other things going on right then, Katya came over and worked three more afternoons. And then there was something the week after that—I don't remember what. I had a terrible time just getting her to accept a salary; we had a real argument over that one."

"Did you really. How remarkable."

"By then it was already sort of a done deal. I started to try and call and tell you, if I could track you down. But like I said, I honestly didn't know how to describe our own situation. So I left it. I'm sorry. I realize I messed up."

"Indeed you did. So. Consider yourself chastised, Jeffrey. And see that it does not happen again."

He realized that it was over. "Thanks, Mr. Kantor. It won't."

"Alexander, please. Fine. Now that's behind us. So tell me about this Katya. Is she as lovely as her name?"

Jeffrey nodded. "It fits her perfectly."

"An attractive woman who works well with customers is quite an asset. You obviously trust her; I do hope it is not based solely upon your emotions."

"No, sir. She's very religious, and her honesty is something that I've never had to concern myself about. She's one of the most honorable people I've ever met. I don't think it would even occur to her to steal."

"Is she English?"

"American. Her father was from the States. But she's lived here in England for over ten years."

"Her mother is not American?"

Jeffrey's brow furrowed in concentration. "Katya doesn't like to talk about her past all that much. Her mother is from the western part of Poland—I've forgotten the name. She told me only once."

A new light entered Kantor's eyes. "Silesia perhaps?"

"That's it. Silesia. Her mother came from there to the West some time after the war."

Kantor nodded slowly. "And what does the young lady do with the remainder of her time?"

"She's a third-year student at the University of London. She's in East European studies, specializing in the German and Polish languages."

"How remarkable." He straightened and spoke to the front seat. "Thank you, driver. You may proceed now."

Kantor remained silent and pensive as the Rolls cruised up the block, waited at the light, turned down Mount Street. Jeffrey let himself out as the driver held Alexander's door, then followed his boss into the shop.

"Ah, at last." Count Garibaldi rose from the chair that he had pulled up close to Katya's. "My good friend Alexander, you have saved me from disaster. If you had arrived just two minutes later, I would have been swept away by this lovely face and proposed. You know my heart. It leaps forward with little concern to this frail body. I would have lost our wager for sure."

"But what is the value of a wager in comparison to a new love?" Alexander extended his hand, said, "It is wonderful to see you again, Ricardo."

Count Ricardo Bastinado Grupello di Garibaldi prided himself on being a man of few illusions. He had grown from an unknown immigrant of doubtful heritage into one of London's leading property developers, and his title and courtly manners were as false as his teeth. He did not care who knew it, did not care what was said about him behind his back. He considered the manners and the title and the polish all a part of the game of being rich. Count di Garibaldi had been both rich and poor, and anyone who believed it was better to be poor was a certifiable fruitcake in the count's book.

The count was a dried-up old prune who was so sure he would outlive his friend Alexander that he had insisted they wager on it. His nose was the only feature that had withstood the ravages of time. It was an aristocrat's beak, a craggy mountain that could nest eagles in each nostril. It was a very useful nose. He could raise his chin about one millimeter and snub the world down its double-barreled length. It gave a deceptive sense of strength to an otherwise shriveled frame.

All the count had to live for was his collection of antiques and his seventeen children. His five ex-wives no longer spoke to him. All seventeen children idolized him. They had to. The count demanded it. But he could not control his ex-wives because of what he considered to be the most pestilent of modern inventions—alimony. They had more than they would ever need, so they delighted in scorning him and calling him foul names. His children, however, were a different matter.

In return for seventeen most generous monthly payments, he demanded peace with him and peace with each other. Anyone who let a spoiled nature run wild within the family was swiftly stripped to a bread and water diet. A couple of months without petrol money for the Ferrari, and the worst of them learned to stew in silence. The count did not demand love; he was too realistic to insist on the impossible. He was quite happy to settle for peace.

The count stretched his bloodless lips in a smile of genuine pleasure. "You are well, Alexander?"

"Perfectly."

"No morning aches and pains?"

"I would never permit myself such an indulgence."

The count's smile broadened as he clapped his more virile friend on the shoulder. "You don't stand a chance, Alexander. I'll beat you by ten years."

"This is one wager I do not look forward to winning," Kantor replied. "Which I shall."

The bet was for fifty thousand pounds. On the day the other died, the lawyers for their estates were instructed to issue a check—providing the survivor still had the strength to drink a glass of single-malt whiskey neat, then dance a jig on the other's grave.

"I must compliment you on your choice of assistants," the count said.

Kantor turned to where Katya stood toward the back of the shop. In the soft lighting reflected from the highly polished surfaces, her features glowed. "I confess this arrangement was not of my choosing," Alexander replied. "But she certainly meets with my approval. How do you do, my dear. I am Alexander Kantor."

She walked forward and presented her hand with a poise Jeffrey found remarkable. She stood so erect as to appear regally aloof, a dark-haired vision with eyes the color of heavens seen through the smoke of a winter's fire. "Katya Nichols. Jeffrey has told me so much about you, Mr. Kantor."

"Has he really." Kantor did a stiff-backed bow over her hand, then said something in a tongue Jeffrey assumed was Polish. Katya responded with cool grace in the same language. Her remark caused Kantor's eyes to broaden momentarily. They exchanged more words; then Alexander repeated his formal bow. He returned to English, saying, "This is indeed an unexpected pleasure, Miss Nichols."

Jeffrey thought his heart would burst with pride.

"My dear Alexander, if you would kindly return your attention to the business at hand," the count said sharply. "You may be interested to know that I was not referring to the young lady. I have already been informed as to how she came to grace your establishment. I was speaking of your young man here. I am not sure you realize what a find you have under your roof."

Kantor's eyes lighted upon Jeffrey. "I am well aware how fortunate I am."

"Nonsense," the count snorted. "How could you, since you are scarcely ever here? Now listen to your good friend, Alexander. The only passion left to me is my collection. I would not joke over something as important to me as my passion, you know that. There are few dealers with whom I consider it a genuine pleasure to do business. If you know what is good for you, you will do everything in your power to hold on to him."

"I intend to," Kantor replied. "And now that you have thoroughly embarrassed the young man, shall we get down to business?"

"Very well." The tone turned lofty. "I had thought to purchase that rather poor example of a writing desk you have propped up there against the back wall. But your young man must have misplaced the proper price tag, and I therefore wanted to take it up directly with you."

"The price is correct."

"You have not even asked him what he quoted me."

"I don't need to. You have just told me what an exceptional find he is. I am quite prepared to stand on whatever price he quoted."

The piece in question was a seventeenth-century *escritorio,* a narrow cabinet with a fold-down face used for writing and fronted by as many as two dozen small drawers. In this case there were twelve, forming an upside-down *U* above and around a central door. When opened, the door revealed yet another door, this one opening only when a tiny switch elegantly concealed inside one of the drawers was pressed in just the right manner. The drawers and central door were inlaid with a mosaic of mother-of-pearl, brought in at enormous cost from some mysterious island on the other side of the globe by a wooden ship flying flags and as many as thirty-six sails. Jeffrey had spent long hours fantasizing about what the world had been like when pieces such as this had been created, and the stories connected to their centuries-long journeys to Mount Street.

The price on that particular work of art was seventy thousand pounds.

"Preposterous," the count complained. "No writing table on earth is worth that much money, especially not one which made its debut in the back room of some second-rate counting house."

Jeffrey cleared his throat. "Perhaps I should mention that we've received another offer."

The count paled. "When?"

"Yesterday. A gentleman from Canada. I told him I would have to wait until this morning, as you had been granted first refusal."

The count's bluster dropped immediately to weak relief. "Bless you, young man. That was truly kind."

Jeffrey ignored the fact that Alexander's approving gaze rested upon him. "I knew you were interested in it, Count. It would have been incorrect not to allow you a chance to make a counter offer."

The count glanced at Alexander, then turned to Jeffrey, "Shall we say seventy-five?"

"Perfect," Jeffrey replied. "When shall I have it delivered?"

Since selling his Belgravia flat, Alexander had made Claridge's his London residence whenever he was in town. That evening he and Jeffrey departed the hotel for the *Ognisko,* the Polish club on Prince's Gate, one block off Hyde Park. It was a holdover from the time when post-war Polish refugees with money and status all gathered and lived in the vicinity. With the passing of time, rents in that area grew from high to vicious and on to levels that were affordable only by the super-rich and by corporations seeking headquarter addresses. Yet the Polish club lingered on, secure in its distinguished position because it was a freehold property.

The Polish club had a simple brass plaque on the pillar outside the entrance, announcing in a most understated way that the entire building belonged to the *Ognisko,* the Polish word for hearth. In days gone by, it was a haven for strangers forced by war's uncaring hand to leave behind home and beloved country, and begin again in a strange new world.

The club was open to all who wished to enter, and served excellent Polish dishes at what for London were extremely reasonable prices. In the seventies and eighties, however, as families had moved on and others had died out, attendance slowly dwindled to a handful of old faithfuls.

"Thank you, driver," Kantor said as he allowed the chauffeur to hold his door. "We shall be several hours, if you would care to dine and come back."

"Very good, sir."

Jeffrey waited until Kantor had started up the stairs before turning back to the driver and saying in a low voice, "It'd be a good idea if you'd stick around for half an hour before taking off. We might not be staying as long as he thinks."

"Half an hour it is, sir."

"Thanks."

They stepped through the wide double doors and were immediately awash in a flood of noise. Alexander Kantor hesitated, then stepped into the foyer and bade the two ladies staffing the front desk a good evening. One immediately went into the bar and returned with the club manager, a crusty old gentleman. His features were a series of jagged lines and caverns, carried on a body held stiffly erect despite the weight of seventy-some years.

"Welcome, Mr. Kantor, welcome." The man grasped Alexander's hand and gave a formal bow. "It is always an honor to have you join us."

Alexander glanced over the man's shoulder into the bar. It was wall-to-wall people, loud music, and thundering noise. "Sigmund, what on earth is happening?"

"Ah, Mr. Kantor, it's just awful." The man showed tragic concern. "We've been discovered!"

"I beg your pardon?" As was his habit, Kantor continued to speak in English so long as Jeffrey was in listening range. Even with clients who stubbornly insisted on remaining in the old tongue, Kantor would politely continue to respond in English. If furrows appeared around the client's brow, Jeffrey would normally get up and leave the room. The only exception was when Alexander was dealing with someone whose English was not good; he then went to great pains to translate and include Jeffrey in even the most mundane of discussions.

"It was the Sunday *Times*," the old man said, his voice almost a wail. "Their restaurant writer was brought here by Polish friends, or so the article said. Then some awful magazine called the *Tatler* came by, and since then it's been non-stop."

"It's like this every night?"

The old man nodded. "You should see it on the weekends, Mr. Kantor. Simply dreadful."

"I see. Any chance of a table?"

"Oh, Mr. Kantor." It was clearly what the old man had feared hearing. "If only you had called ahead."

"Of course, Sigmund." Kantor gave the old man's shoulder a conciliatory pat. "Don't let it trouble you."

"I could perhaps have something around midnight if you'd care to wait."

"I think not." Kantor grasped the old man's hand in both of his, gave it a warm shake. "We shall return another night, old friend. Rest assured of that."

"Early is best, Mr. Kantor. It's not so bad before seven."

The driver sprang from the car as soon as they appeared. Alexander asked Jeffrey, "You told him to wait?"

Jeffrey nodded. "I thought maybe it would be better for you to see that for yourself."

"Quite right. I suppose we should travel on to Daquise, then, don't you?"

"Fine with me."

"Number Twenty Thurloe Street, driver," Alexander instructed. "Near the South Kensington Tube Station."

"Very good, sir."

Daquise was another holdover, but from a decidedly different strata of transferred Polish society. It was a single long room set in a block of other small, slightly seedy shops.

South Kensington was a district in perpetual transition. Daquise was located in an area at the scale's lower end; the Rolls' arrival stopped traffic and turned heads a half block away. The restaurant's tables were linoleum-topped, its vinyl-covered booths and seats too old to be truly comfortable. But the food was excellent, and its clientele immensely loyal.

"The old menus looked like choir hymnals from a bankrupt church," Kantor said once the manager had greeted them, led them to a choice seat, discussed the menu, and left to give their order to the kitchen. Kantor's good humor had revived considerably. "They were enormous padded red-leather affairs, and battered as a third-rate French hotel bed."

"You've told me," Jeffrey said, nodding his thanks to the waitress who set down their fluted glasses of steaming tea.

"I realize that," Kantor replied. "Now you will wipe that long-suffering look off your face and play the politely interested employee."

Jeffrey cocked his head to one side, made round eyes, asked, "How's that?"

"Ridiculous. It's not often I indulge in reminiscing."

"Just every time you come over," Jeffrey replied, thoroughly enjoying himself.

"Which is not often enough by the look of things."

"This is the best quarter the shop has ever had."

Kantor waved a casual dismissal. "I dread to think what we could have accomplished were I daily at the helm."

"Bankruptcy?" Jeffrey kept his smile hidden. "Public

shame? Fire-sale signs on Mount Street?"

Their evenings together became times of ever-deeper discussions and ever-greater pleasure for the young man. It was only recently, one evening after receiving Kantor's arrival fax, that Jeffrey had wondered if perhaps the old gentleman was lonely.

Kantor gave him a frosty glance. "Remind me why I put up with your over-active tongue."

"Because it doesn't detach. And because I'm good at my job. And because I'm honest."

"Are you now."

"Totally."

"Yes." Kantor's eyes creased upward. "I suppose you are at that. So where was I?"

"Goodness only knows."

"The menus. Thank you. Yes, the prices were all written by hand and in a shaky Polish script, then rubbed out and redone so often no one could read them."

"Which is why they finally purchased these awful plastic things," Jeffrey finished for him.

"Do I truly bore you that badly with my little stories?"

"Truly?"

"I would not ask if I did not mean it."

"Then truly, I look forward to your visits more than I like to admit even to myself."

Carefully the old gentleman sipped his tea, his face immobile. "Why is that, do you suppose?"

"The truth again." Jeffrey took a breath. "I have never met anyone like you. Never. You are a genuine individual in a carbon-copy world. Neither age nor success nor wealth has ground you to grayness."

"You've obviously given this quite a lot of thought."

Jeffrey nodded. "I've wondered if I'd ever have the chance to tell you. Or the nerve."

"I see." Kantor seemed momentarily nonplussed.

"You're one of the few people I've ever met who is never boring. And with all the changes you've pushed me toward, there's always been a perfectly good reason. I've never felt as if I'm being forced to fit some egotistical role."

"I'd rather try to reform the Rock of Gibraltar."

"You don't know how rare that is," Jeffrey replied. "And

I'm more grateful than I'll ever be able to say for your giving me a job that I love. Truly."

"Well." Kantor was clearly at a loss. "I say, Jeffrey, I do believe you're blushing."

"It comes with the confession."

"No doubt, no doubt."

They were saved from further embarrassment by the arrival of their dinner. They ate in comfortable silence until Jeffrey laid down his fork, pushed his plate back, said, "I come here a lot."

That brought another start. "When I'm not in town? Do you really?"

"I like the food."

"How fascinating."

"A lot. And the people." He motioned toward an old crone nodding in the corner. She was nursing a glass of tea, drawing out a nightly ritual, staving away the loneliness of an empty flat. She wore a blue velvet turban and an ancient diamond tiara. Her face was a mask of sagging folds, her nose a beak. "Everybody in here has jumped from the pages of a Tolstoy novel."

"Mmmm." The old woman noticed their eyes. Alexander gave her a grave seated bow, murmured a greeting in Polish. She responded with a regal nod, replied with a voice made ragged from disuse, and returned to her own internal musing.

"The correct term is *staruszka*. It means little old lady, but only in the nicest of terms. The word for old in Polish is *stary*, a term I'm coming to know on a too-intimate basis."

"I've never thought of you as old."

"How kind. Yes, if truth is to be the evening's main course, then I must confess that my years have become a burden. You must experience the weight of years for yourself, Jeffrey, before you can really understand."

"You've had a good life."

"That I have, in part at least. Too good to leave it willingly behind. But for the first time since the war, I feel as though I can look ahead and see death's door. It's not that far away anymore. Just around the next bend."

Jeffrey felt the room grow chill. "You've seen a doctor?"

"Many doctors. They all say the same thing. I am fine. I have some good years ahead of me. There is nothing wrong.

They have leeched more money from me than even I thought possible, and tortured me with so many machines and needles I have begun to cringe every time I pass a hospital. They with all their modern wisdom have found nothing. But I know, young man. My body does not lie. We have passed more than sixty-five years in each other's company, and come to like one another quite a lot. I heed its voice as often as I can, gracing it with comfortable beds and sensible foods and adequate rest. It in turn permits me the foibles of an occasional cigar and a third brandy on a cold night. In all the years since the war, it has punished me with nothing more serious than a stuffy nose."

"And now?"

"And now. And now it says it is growing tired. It no longer willingly rises when I ask, nor responds to simple pleasures. Food has begun to taste flat, wine bitter, cigars stale. Worse still are the whispers of what is yet to come. Lingering illness. Pain. Embarrassing moments. Lapses of memory. The prospect of growing old distresses me more than anything has since the war."

"I would really like to hear about your escape from Poland if you ever feel like talking."

"Another time, dear boy. I couldn't discuss the escape without referring to what came before it, and to speak of that and the loss of my faculties all in the same night would simply be too much. I will tell you of this, I assure you. I can see your interest is genuine, and I will honor it. There is no need for barriers between us. Honesty becomes a lie if it is doled out in half measures. But not tonight."

Jeffrey nodded, hurting without knowing why. "You look great to me."

"Thank you. I feel it, too. This small dose of truth between friends has done me a world of good, more than all the doctors I have visited over the past months. But the whispers I hear are not vague, and my time on this earth no longer appears as endless as it once did. What's worse, I have begun to question my life. A most uncomfortable pasttime, I assure you. But with this unmarked door up ahead, it suddenly becomes much more appealing to turn around and look back. Only I cannot do this with the same comforting blindness with which I lived the moment. I am finding my own innate honesty has become a finger pointing at flaws and errors I have managed to ignore for a lifetime."

Jeffrey hoped his voice would not betray him as he said, "I think you're one of the finest men I've ever met, Alexander."

"Thank you, dear boy. That means more to me than you will ever know. But I fear my own selfish blindness can protect me no longer from the failings of this life I have been privileged to call my own. Not, that is, if I am going to continue to find solace from the future by looking back. There are few things that I shall be able to change, I recognize that. Age and my own disposition makes change at this late date most unappealing. But there are a few wrongs that I shall attempt to right in my remaining days. And a few of my better actions that I must endeavor to anchor against the unforeseen. Which brings us to the matter of our trip."

Jeffrey sat up straight. "Our?"

"Not in here. I may have been lured into a public confession, but I shall not discuss confidential business in a public place." He signaled to the waitress. "Come along. It's time for a quiet glass at your club."

Jeffrey's club was around the corner from Berkley Square, where the nightingale sang no more—and even if it did, no one situated farther away than the next tree limb would be able to hear the melody. Nowadays the square was awash with an unending toneless symphony of blares, hoots, revving motors, angry shouts, jackhammers, squealing brakes, snarled traffic, and construction turmoil. Berkley Square had been transformed from a relatively quiet alcove to a focal point for Piccadilly-directed traffic, compliments of London's one-way road network. The constant man-made storm had not affected rents, however. People paid staggering sums for the Berkley Square address, long after all charm had evaporated in a cloud of diesel fumes.

The club was a short half block up a street as nondescript as the club's entrance; a gray portal opened in a gray building on a gray street that shrugged its way around a corner and ended quietly in an alleyway. Inside, uniformed porters guarded the entrance with respectful vigilance, offering members a properly subdued greeting.

Jeffrey had chosen the Landsdowne Club because it was close to his home and to the shop, had an excellent sports hall, and because it was available. Many of the London clubs granted membership only to those with title or wealth or renown, and very rarely at all to foreigners. Admission to the Landsdowne had been Alexander's gift at the end of Jeffrey's probation. As far as he was concerned, it was the perfect fit.

Jeffrey had once seen an etching, made in 1811, which vividly displayed the rural atmosphere of the region. At that time, the Landsdowne mansion had stood within several walled acres of garden, and had been surrounded on three sides by open fields.

By the onset of the twentieth century, the gardens were long gone, the fields no more. A road expansion decreed by the London government in the thirties rudely demolished the Landsdowne manor's front forty feet, taking with it a good many of the most beautiful chambers. But as far as Jeffrey was concerned, those that remained were more than adequate.

In a sitting room by the bar, Lord Shelburne, Prime Minister under King George III, had signed the declaration that ended the Revolutionary War and granted the United States its independence. The main hall, a vast affair with a seventy-foot arched and gilded ceiling, was once a central locale in the busy London social season. Jeffrey loved to dine on the club's traditional fare of roast lamb or beef, stare out over the heads of nodding elderly members, and strain to hear the echoes of violins fill a room lit by vast candelabras.

Nowadays the room was seldom more than a third full, and was a most comfortable place to come and sit by the roaring fire and read undisturbed, the chamber's huge dimensions a welcome change from his cramped apartment.

Jeffrey allowed Alexander to lead them to a set of comfortable chairs near the fire and well removed from the few other occupied tables.

"You know the basis for these clubs is to duplicate the atmosphere of the British school system," Alexander said as they took their seats. "The surroundings are grandiose, the food inedible, the furniture tacky, and the rooms frigid even in summer."

Jeffrey saw no need to tell him how impressed he was by

his surroundings. "What was the first club you ever went to?"

"Let's see. Ah yes, that would be the Carlton. Every Conservative prime minister since Peel has belonged."

"Even Margaret Thatcher?"

"Oh, most definitely. They made her an honorary man. Some of those members who put her name forward said she was the only member of her cabinet who deserved to wear trousers, so in their eyes it was not breaking with the all-male tradition."

A waiter appeared at his elbow; Alexander ordered brandy for them both. When they were again alone, he said, "I must tell you, Jeffrey, that I am vastly impressed with your young lady."

"I'm not sure she's my anything."

Alexander waved the comment aside. "What you have not seen is the way she looks at you when you are not watching."

"You're kidding."

"About matters of the heart I never, as you say, kid. Although I do not know her yet, I am coming to know you and trust your judgment. You have chosen well, Jeffrey."

"And if she doesn't choose me?"

"Give it time."

"That's easy for you to say."

"Yes, it is indeed easier to view such matters from a painless distance." He gave Jeffrey a comradely smile. "But if an outsider may be permitted to add his ten pence worth, I think your chances are perhaps better than you think. The tenderness in her gaze touches even this crusty old heart of mine."

Jeffrey gave him a sidelong glance. "Are you sure we're talking about the same girl?"

"It is a good thing to find someone with whom you can share your work, Jeffrey. The antique trade has clearly become a passion with you, and this pleases me enormously. It is one of the essential ingredients of success in our profession. Yet a passion is either the strongest bonding force possible within a relationship, or a barrier you will fight against for all your days."

Jeffrey nodded his understanding. "Is that why you never married? You never found someone to share your passion?"

Kantor took a long time to reply. "I lost my love in the war."

"Oh. I'm really sorry." Jeffrey hesitated, then added, "Nobody back in the States ever said anything about you losing somebody before coming to the West."

"That is not what I said," Kantor replied solemnly. "My love died in the war. What happens to the bodies after such an event is inconsequential."

After a moment's silence, Alexander went on. "As a matter of fact, Jeffrey, there may be a way of my assisting your own affairs. It has to do with the purpose of this little discussion. You don't speak German, as I recall."

"No. Some French, that's all."

"But Katya does."

"Fluently, so she says."

The waiter approached their isolated corner, set down two linen napkins and upon them a pair of heavy crystal snifters containing ample portions of aged amber. Kantor paused to swirl the brandy under his nose, sipped, breathed out that first heady aroma, and said, "For a shop like ours, to sell well is only half the game. Some would say even less. I do not mean to belittle your responsibilities, however."

"But we've got to have something to sell," Jeffrey agreed. The excitement of possibly being partner to one of the antique trade's best-kept secrets added its own flavor to the evening. "Finding the right product at the right price is what separates the men from the boys."

"Precisely. We have no guaranteed source of supply in this game, you see. Nor do we know from whence our next piece will come. There is only a limited number of quality antiques available, and a veritable fury of sharks seeking them out. All the major auction houses right the world around, shops who compete with ours from Tokyo to New York, many of our own customers who seek to lower their purchase price with a direct buy; they hunt for the same items as we do."

Kantor lowered his silver-gray mane, and sought answers from the swirling brandy. He said to his goblet, "There are times when a risk must be taken in order for life to progress. But knowing that the time has arrived and actually taking the step can be two quite different matters."

Jeffrey sipped from his own glass and held back on the

dozens of answers that came to mind. No amount of pushing would help here.

"There are a few things which I have shared with almost no one. Were I to include you in this very small group, Jeffrey, the only gratitude I wish to receive from you, the only thanks, the only show of respect, is that you would keep my secret and guard it well."

"I understand."

"Excellent. It so happens that I have a supplier who has disappeared, leaving me with several unsold pieces—some quite remarkable antiques, really. All on consignment. Besides that, there is the matter of the money I owe him for those which have already been sold."

Alexander paused as a pair of slow-moving elderly gentlemen ambled by their table, then said quietly, "Something over eight hundred thousand pounds."

One and a half million dollars. Jeffrey gave a low whistle.

"This sum has been collecting in a special account for over a year," Alexander said. "I have heard nothing from him since the one and only shipment was received."

Jeffrey waited, decided it was time to ask the one impossible question. "Where did it come from?"

Alexander eyed him over the rim of his goblet. "You are aware of what you are asking."

"Yes."

"I see that you are. Very well, I agree. It is time to tell you." Alexander sipped his brandy, then went on. "About two years ago I was approached at an auction in Geneva by a man I had never seen before. Which is a surprise, I assure you, especially considering the quality and the number of articles he had to offer. Were we speaking of only one or two antiques, it could be entirely possible that I was meeting a dealer new to the realm in which we operate. But he showed me photographs of over thirty antiques. Thirty, Jeffrey. All of them absolutely first rate, I assure you. It was an astonishing collection."

Jeffrey understood Alexander's surprise. The number of dealers at such levels was quite small. It was part of any professional's job to know all the major players. Thirty world-class antiques was for any house an immense number; coming from a total unknown it was unheard of.

"The man told me he was an arts and antiques dealer

from Schwerin," Alexander said. "Have you ever heard of the place?"

"No."

"It is the capital of Mecklenburg-Vorpommern, the northernmost state in what previously was East Germany. This contact came about two months before the Wall collapsed. Already there were rumblings, with street demonstrations and so forth, but no one imagined it would all move as swiftly as it did. In any case, I found it astonishing that a perfect stranger from such an unstable region would approach me with such an offer."

Jeffrey snapped his fingers. "King Freddy's drawers!"

"I beg your pardon?"

"The Kaiser's chest of drawers. That's how I always thought of it. Putting a nickname on a piece like that helps me not to get overawed by how much money we're talking about."

"How remarkable. Well, it so happens you are correct. That was indeed one of the pieces included in this little collection."

"We had a little trouble with the sale," Jeffrey said, and related the story of the professor's arrival at Christie's.

"I am most sorry to hear of the hue and cry," Alexander said when Jeffrey was finished. "Although I suppose it is not overly important who in the end acquires the piece, I thoroughly detest strong-arm tactics of any form. You must find me the name and address of the industrialist, Jeffrey."

"You're going to offer him something at cost, aren't you?"

"I must seek to make amends. It is the least I can do." Alexander eyed his assistant. "Why are you smiling?"

"No reason. You were saying about the East German dealer."

"Precisely. I was most concerned that I not become involved with a thief. But his documents were impeccable, Jeffrey. Flawless. He had papers declaring him to be the director of Schwerin's official antiques store, which of course would make him a member of the Communist Party, but I have managed to do business with such people in the past. Never from East Germany, however. I had no contacts there whatsoever."

"Which made it all the more suspicious," Jeffrey added.

"Indeed. But he said that I had come highly recommended

as a man whom they could trust. Honesty in these matters was essential, I was informed. In any case, he also had official export documents, and permitted me to telephone both the East German Embassy in Berne and the Department of Arts and Antiques in East Berlin to confirm who he was."

Alexander waved his empty snifter in the direction of an attentive waiter. "What was more, the antiques were already in a bonded warehouse in Hamburg, waiting for me to pick them up."

"Did he tell you how he had obtained them?"

"An excellent question. One, I might add, which is not always possible to ask. However, in this case I positively insisted on being informed. It appeared that a number of very senior officials within the East German Communist Party had read the writing on the wall, and were seeking to unload items that they hoped would help ease their own personal transition to a new capitalist empire."

"Amazing," Jeffrey breathed.

"Indeed so, but also most believable. And an explanation which could not be checked up on, I might add. My calls resulted in nothing but confirmation of everything that the man had told me—everything, I hasten to add, which could be confirmed."

"And you want me to go find him."

"Or find out what has happened," Alexander replied. "There is always the risk that our gentleman has been swept away in the tide of change. If that is the case, then we must try to find which of the actual sellers is still around and seeking his due.

"You should not need to stay for more than two days," Alexander continued. "If it requires more time than this, you will need to return later. There are some pressing matters that cannot wait, a shipment which must be seen to. Do you think Katya could mind the shop for a week by herself?"

"Without a doubt. There's a lot she doesn't know, but she is very honest with the clients, and is careful to write down their questions for me to answer. Sometimes it actually works out better that way, because we then have their addresses on file, and the clients like her a lot. Her classes are over for the summer, so I don't think it'll be a problem, but I'll have to ask." Jeffrey felt like dancing on the table. A shipment. He was going to be taken along on a buying trip.

"Then I want you to pack for a week's voyage," Alexander instructed him. "Longer, perhaps, It is hard to know before we arrive. I will meet you at the airport in Hamburg after you have checked on this, and we will continue on from there. But you must not under any circumstances take more than two days for this Schwerin business."

He nodded, resisted the urge to ask where they were going. It was Alexander's secret, and he would have to choose the time. "Why won't you go yourself to East Germany?"

"You are no doubt aware that World War II began with the Nazi invasion of Poland. After five years of Nazi occupation, Poland then suffered the tragedy of the Warsaw Uprising, where the Soviets stood across the Vistula River and watched almost eight hundred thousand Poles be massacred by the Nazi forces. Once our own forces were decimated, the Soviets then rolled into Warsaw and took up where the retreating Nazis left off. We suffered under their iron grip for over forty years." Kantor paused while the waiter returned with a new drink. "Wild horses could not drag me to Schwerin. A land that is both Communist and German is a land with one devil too many."

"They're not Communist anymore."

"The shadow still lingers across the land, I assure you. No illness that grave can vanish overnight after having been around for forty years."

Jeffrey waited, and when nothing more was forthcoming, said, "I'm not sure I understand."

"No," Alexander Kantor sighed. "I suppose not."

He reached into his coat, extracted his wallet, and drew out a yellowed black and white photograph. He handed it over. "This was my sister."

Jeffrey examined a lively smiling face who missed being truly beautiful by having a little too much of Alexander's strength. There was no doubt of their being related. "I didn't know you had a sister."

"Svetlana was much older than I. In 1939, after the Germans invaded Poland, she and her husband started a clandestine anti-Nazi newspaper. They were caught." His voice took on a toneless drone. "He died in a concentration camp. She was imprisoned. Unfortunately she was three months pregnant, and the prison guards beat her badly. Svetlana gave birth in her prison cell to a crippled baby boy. She died nine months later, spending her time until then trying to keep her baby alive within the prison."

Alexander reached over and extracted the photograph from Jeffrey's numb fingers. With slow, deliberate motions, he inserted the picture back into his wallet. "To travel to a Germany frozen for five decades, occupied by the same Russian invaders who have stifled my homeland since 1945—" He shook his head. "No, my good man, that combination is simply too much. This trip you and your young lady will have to take on your own."

CHAPTER
7

Katya asked, "So the two of us would be traveling to Schwerin together?"

Late afternoon sunlight spilled through the shop's front window, turning the gauze curtains surrounding the dais to burnished gold. Alexander had left to take care of some personal business, and to let Jeffrey broach the issue with Katya in solitude.

"Alexander will take care of the shop. He doesn't want . . ." Jeffrey hesitated, then decided it was Alexander's secret. "He can't come with us. It's not possible."

"So you're saying you want me to go off with you for a sort of long weekend?" She shook her head. "I don't think so."

"I need you, Katya," he insisted. "Alexander says almost nobody speaks English over there. The second language is Russian, the third Polish or Czech. And I have to take somebody we can trust." He softened his voice. "I trust you."

"It just wouldn't be proper."

"What is there to be proper or improper about? We really need your help on this. I need it."

"Just a business trip?"

"Well, yes and no," Jeffrey was flustered. "I wouldn't be honest if I didn't say how much I'd like to do this with you."

"So this is a business trip and you want to enjoy my company."

"This is a special time in Germany, especially in the East. You're studying about it. I'd have thought you'd leap at the chance to take an all-expense-paid trip over there."

"It's not the trip."

"I want to understand what's going on over there," he persisted. "I can't do that without you."

She was silent for a long moment. "For how long?"

"Two days. We leave together, have one night in Schwerin, then you come back to mind the shop while I travel on with Alexander."

"When?"

He took a breath. "Tomorrow. Alexander says there is another trip which he and I have to make immediately afterward."

"What about Ling? Who will take care of him?" Then she answered it and gave her assent at the same time. "I'll ask Mama. Will you come with me this evening?"

He was already up and moving. "Let's go. I just closed up."

Coventry was a charmless town located about an hour from London. Katya's mother lived there because of the company that bought her ceramics. Katya refused to discuss the ceramics, which left Jeffrey to imagine that her mother made bowls and sold them on the sly, supplementing what was probably a meager monthly relief check.

Magda lived in a run-down council house attached on both sides to two equally drab tenements. Her neighbors were a rainbow coalition of Indians and Pakistanis and Africans and Arabs, with the odd white face thrown in for good measure. The view from her front porch revealed block after oppressive block of red-brick council houses, whose crumbling facades and dirty windows and peeling woodwork exuded an air of tired resignation.

Magda had the face of a shrew and looked twice her age, which Jeffrey guessed to be something over fifty. A long bony nose thrust from an overly pointed face. Her thin lips sagged under the weight of pasty-colored cheeks. The first time he met her, Jeffrey had the impression of a spoiled child grown into a perpetually unhappy adult. The only color to her face was in her eyes, which peered from sunken burrows with surprising light. Her gray hair was perpetually unkempt and looked hacked with garden shears. It was only partially trapped in place by dozens of bobby pins.

She was always suffering, and each pain had its own signal. When her arthritis flared, she kept her hands close to her stomach and rubbed them constantly, one with the other. When it was her back, she walked bent at what Jeffrey thought a ridiculous angle, teetering from one chair or other support to another. When it was her shoulder, she stooped inward, as though only one side of her body were whole.

Her expression was one of silent suffering. Jeffrey would sit across from her, searching for something benign to say, imagining her doing a quick check in the mirror before opening the door to greet her daughter. Then he would look up and catch those piercing eyes watching him steadily, and wonder if she could also read minds.

Katya always responded with loving sympathy and heartfelt concern. Always. This transformation from cool and distant beauty to attentive daughter never failed to give him a severe pang of jealousy.

Jeffrey had continued to go with Katya on her regular weekly visits because he had little choice. It was either that or miss seeing her on Saturdays. As it was, he held his breath through the two-hour ordeal, and was rewarded with the pleasure of her company during the train rides and with an evening together afterward.

During his first visit, Jeffrey had been severely stung by Magda's total indifference to his presence. She had inspected him briefly, ignored his smile and outstretched hand, and turned back to her daughter with a painful grimace. He had stood there, as hurt by Katya's silent acceptance of her mother's rudeness as he was by Magda's actions, then turned away. Two could play at that game.

He opened his briefcase and brought out a book he had taken along for the voyage, a text on identifying types of wood. Within a few minutes of sitting down in the farthest corner from Magda's padded chair, he was lost in his work. He registered the musical tone of Katya's voice and Magda's querulous replies, but they did not intrude on his concentration. It was more than half an hour before he felt eyes on him, looked up, and found Magda watching him with a measuring gaze, as though she were seeing him for the first time.

Today it was her feet. Jeffrey watched her open the door and greet them with a little teary-eyed smile that never slipped, never changed, always crying for attention better than words ever could. Jeffrey pasted on what he hoped was an expression of concern, entered the cramped and cluttered living room behind Katya, watched Magda walk forward with little steps that swayed her body from side to side like a ship at anchor. Every chair, every stool, every low table wore a cushion for a hat.

He stood in the middle of the cluttered room and watched Katya settle her mother back in her customary chair and set the baby's box in her mother's lap. She left Magda crooning over the bird while she went around picking up and setting the room in order with swift little motions. She returned and plucked the shopping bags from Jeffrey's arms and carried them into the kitchen. He started after her, then decided against it. There was barely room in there for one.

Magda finally greeted him with a very tired, "How are you, Jeffrey?"

"Excited," he said, refusing to play the false sympathy game.

"Ah, how nice." She settled down farther into the thick padding, raised her legs one at a time with her hands underneath the calves, handling them like hand-blown glass. When both feet were safely on the cushion, she pulled up her cheeks in a long-suffering smile. "And what do you have to celebrate, young man?"

"The director of my store is increasing my responsibilities."

"A promotion." She picked up the lace prayer shawl she always wore when Katya took her to church, and laid it across her lap. "How nice for you."

"It's not a promotion," Jeffrey said, mentally gripping his teeth to keep his voice casual. She barely seemed to be listening to him. "Well, not in the sense of a raise or anything. I am going to start traveling for him as a buyer."

"All young people like so much to travel," she said, her

eyes following Katya's movement in the kitchen. "And where will you be going?"

"East Germany. And perhaps Poland."

Her eyes snapped around. "Is that so."

Katya's voice called out from the kitchen. "Jeffrey's boss is Polish, Mama."

"Is he now. And why haven't I heard of this before?"

Katya returned from the kitchen, drying her hands on a towel. "Why should you be interested in who Jeffrey's boss is?"

Her gaze held a strength that belied her ailments. "Because he is your young man, is he not?"

Katya gave her mother a startled glance and vanished back into the kitchen.

"It is remarkable that your little bird has survived this long," Magda went on. Her speech had a rough-edged quality. "Why did you bring it here?"

"I have a chance to go to Schwerin," Katya said from the kitchen alcove.

"With Jeffrey?"

"On business. Just for two days."

Jeffrey held his breath, wondered if Katya was mentioning it in hopes that her mother would object.

"Some questions have come up about a supplier," Katya went on. "Jeffrey needs me as an interpreter."

"That sounds like a wonderful idea," Magda replied. "I traveled there once after the war. There are some truly beautiful lakes in that city."

Katya reappeared in the kitchen doorway. Her face mirrored Jeffrey's astonishment. "You want me to go?"

"You have to see if the old Strand Hotel is still there. It was quite a place in my day."

"That's where the travel agent has placed us," Jeffrey said, and added hastily, "in separate rooms."

"It's such a romantic place," Magda said, looking at her daughter. "At least it was."

"Then you don't mind me going?" Katya asked.

"Oh, Katya. You're a big girl now. It's a wonderful opportunity to apply your studies. I always told you the German would come in handy, didn't I?"

Katya entered the room and pulled up a straight-backed chair beside her mother. "Sometimes you surprise me,

Mama. I thought it would worry you."

"Katya Maria, you are an adult woman. You must make your own decisions. I can tell by your eyes that you really want to go." Her tone sharpened. "Were you hoping that I would say no and give you an excuse?"

Katya remained silent.

"Go," her mother said. "Have a good time. Be sure to take an extra sweater. It gets quite cold at night by the sea. Don't worry about your little bird. What do you call him?"

"Ling," Jeffrey offered.

"I've had tougher assignments than this in my life." She turned to Jeffrey. "You will be sure that she takes her extra sweater along."

"All right."

Her wrinkled features took on a hint of a smile. "You think I am acting out of character, young man?"

He started to nod, checked himself just in time.

"The fact is, young man, you don't know my character. Not at all. To you, I am an old sick woman living out her days in a little English town. But I have lived in many places, and lived through many things, that have made me what I am."

Magda's eyes remained on him. She demanded, "Are you my daughter's boyfriend?"

"I wish I were," he replied bluntly. "I'm not so sure about what she thinks."

"Ah, an honest answer."

"It's what I feel most comfortable with."

The gaze sparked. "Do you, indeed?"

"Leave him alone, Mama," Katya said quietly.

"It's all right." He then said to Magda, "I've never met anybody like you before."

"And what is it that makes me so special, may I ask?"

"Mama," Katya stood and resumed her activities. "That's enough."

Your eyes and your illnesses, Jeffrey thought. They don't match. "I haven't decided."

"I see. And will you tell me when you do?"

If I'm still around, and feel like committing hari-kari with our relationship. "I don't know."

Magda seemed pleased with the response. She turned toward the kitchen. "Why don't you show your young man my workshop."

"He's not interested in your ceramics, Mama."

That stung him. "Why don't you have the courtesy to ask me before you say what I do and don't like?"

Both their reactions surprised him. Katya immediately turned sheepishly apologetic; her mother clearly approved. Magda repeated calmly, "Show him the workshop, daughter."

With the motion of a little girl, Katya gestured for him to join her in the kitchen. Mystified, Jeffrey stood and walked over, and was surprised to see that the house did not end with the kitchen as he supposed. Through the window of the back door he saw a glass-walled addition, one originally intended as a greenhouse.

"That atelier is why I chose this house," Magda said from the front room.

Katya led him forward and opened the door but refused to meet his eyes. Jeffrey stepped into an artist's atelier. Shelves lined both side walls and contained an immense variety of ceramic shapes. Very few of them were exactly the same. All wore the bone-white coloring of once-fired clay. Beneath the shelves stretched thick wooden slabs, standing on legs about waist-high—tables set either for standing or sitting on a stool. A number of flexible lights stood at varying degrees, and beneath them rested paints, jars, pallets, rags, cans, magnifying glasses, several unfinished works, and some of the thinnest brushes Jeffrey had ever seen.

He bent over one work, a double handled loving cup. It stood perhaps ten inches high, and had a delicate peaked cap set to one side. The cup's base was formed like the foundations of a Doric column and was gilded a shimmering gold. The cup's background began as a delicate cream coloring at the bottom and rose to deep sky-blue. At the center-point of the transition, a gathering of clouds was back-lit by a sun whose light burst forth in a radiant circle. Set in the center of the clouds was a lamb bleeding from a wound in its side.

"You may pick it up if you like." Jeffrey turned to find Magda leaning heavily against the doorjamb. Her expression was lacking all the pain he had come to think of as permanent. "It is all right. Just use the handles."

"You did this?"

She nodded and said simply, "It is my life. This and my daughter and my faith. It is all I have." She smiled for the very first time, a bare flickering that did not register below her eyes. "Sometimes it is almost enough."

Jeffrey examined the cup more closely. "This is fantastic."

"Thank you, young man." She searched his face with a gaze that bit deep. "This is to be your first visit to the East?"

"Yes."

"Perhaps when you return you'll understand better." She thought it over a moment, gave a decisive nod. "Perhaps."

They sat across from each other on the train ride back to London, a linoleum-topped table between them. Jeffrey watched the final remnants of a glorious cloud-flecked sunset beyond the train window and thought about what Magda had said.

At last he turned to Katya. "You've never told me anything about your father."

"That's because I don't remember a lot about him. He left home when I was seven."

"I'm sorry." Subdued, he still did not want to let the moment of rare candor go. "Was the divorce tough on you?"

Her eyes remained fastened on the train window. "I didn't say they were divorced, Jeffrey. I said he left. And yes, it was hard."

"You mean he just walked out on you?"

"Can we please talk about something else?" Katya asked the window.

"Sure, we can. Only I really would like to know more about your past."

She faced him then, her gaze steady, the distance between them vast. "Why?"

What came to mind surprised even him. "Because I want to share the hurt with you, Katya. Not just the good times."

The look of utter defenselessness that had pulled him close their very first night returned, and he yearned for something stronger between them, something that would allow him to say what he felt and feel what he dreamed.

Katya said, "My father was an American soldier in Germany after the war. A private. He was in the Occupying

Forces. Germany was split up into different zones, each one with a different military government."

"I knew that."

"My mother and her older sister were raised in Poland, but wound up in Germany at the end of the war." She gave him a helpless look. "This is a very difficult story, Jeffrey. And complicated. I'm not sure I can tell it."

"Try," he urged.

She was silent for a moment, then said, "My grandmother was Polish and her husband was German. They lived in a village in Upper Silesia, not far from the German border. My grandfather became active in anti-Nazi activities. Towards the end of the war he was caught and shot. My grandmother feared that the family would be arrested, so she sent my mother and her sister to my grandfather's family. They lived in a town in Germany about a hundred and fifty miles away. I am sure they expected to be re-united soon, but it never happened.

"At the end of the war, the town where my mother and her sister lived was declared part of the Russian Zone, what later became East Germany." Katya's soft voice carried a determined note. "The border with the American Zone was only twelve kilometers to the west, but it might as well have been on the other side of the world. There wasn't any hope for returning to Poland, or going anywhere else. Travel was very tightly controlled, even between cities within the same zone.

"My mother was very good at languages, and even though she was still just a teenager, she went to work in an American military base called a *Kaserne*. She crossed the border between the two zones every day with a special pass.

"The American Zone was better off than the other areas, and because of her job on the base she and her sister always had enough to eat. But there were enormous problems everywhere in Germany, and every morning more old people would be found dead from cold and hunger and no medicines for their illnesses. A lot of people became sick and died because there was no treatment. My mother's sister was one of them.

"Soon after her sister passed away, Joseph Stalin died. His death sparked off riots all over Eastern Europe, as the people he had oppressed began fighting against the occupying forces and demanding their freedom. The Russian soldiers guarding the border with the American Zone started harassing people who were passing through every day. One night after work she saw a group of Russian soldiers club a man with their rifles. She suddenly turned and fled back towards the American Zone. It must have been a very frightening experience for her. She could hear the Russian guard-dogs snarling and barking to be released as the soldiers yelled for her to come back. But the American patrol came to her aid. The Russian soldiers got into a big shouting match with them, but the Americans would not send her back. My father was one of those American soldiers.

"They got married a couple of months later. It was a big problem, because the American military didn't like soldiers to marry local girls. They called these local women gold diggers, the ones who tried to get an American boyfriend. A lot of them were, I suppose. Anyway, when my father's tour of duty ended, my parents went back together to the United States."

Jeffrey waited, and when he was sure nothing more was coming he asked quietly, "Where, Katya?"

"Baltimore."

"And that was where you were born?"

She gave the window a small nod.

"And you lived there until your father left?"

" 'Put it in park, sport,' " Katya said softly. "I can remember my father saying that a lot. 'Put it in park while you still can.' "

She looked at him, her eyes two pools of sadness. "Isn't that a strange thing to remember about your father?"

"Do you remember what he looked like?"

Her forehead creased with concentration. "He was big, I remember that. And his hair was dark. He had big hands, strong hands. He was a mechanic in a factory, and his hands were hard and strong. When he would come home, I would run to him and he would swoop me up and over his head. I would squeal, and he would give me this big booming laugh. Sometimes he would make a muscle for me, and I would try to push it down. It was like trying to crush a stone with my hands. He liked to roll his shirt sleeves up so you could see his muscles, I remember that." Her face had the look of a little girl's, wide-eyed and open and yearning to be sheltered.

"And then he was gone," Jeffrey said, aching for her.

"I didn't understand it. Why would he leave like that? I spent *days* looking all over the house for a letter, a note, anything. How could my daddy have left me without saying goodbye? What had I done that upset him so badly?"

"Nothing," Jeffrey said quietly.

She came awake with a start, spent a moment faltering over what she had said. Then she turned back to the window. "I don't want to talk about it anymore."

He reached across and took a small warm hand in both of his, then held it the rest of the way to London.

CHAPTER
8

From the outside, Claridge's was easy to mistake as just another row of expensive apartment buildings. There was no sign with flashing lights, no ornate marquee announcing its presence, no break in the turn-of-the-century red-brick decor. Claridge's did not advertise. It did not need to.

Claridge's, like its sister hotels the Connaught and the Berkley, did not accept groups. Even visiting kings and presidents were requested to arrive without a large entourage. There was no check-in desk at Claridge's; instead, an arriving guest was ushered into a small sitting room to one side of the main foyer. Quietly efficient staff in starched white shirts and dark formal wear filled out the various details before personally escorting guests to their rooms.

The style throughout the hotel was Art Deco, the fittings worth a fortune. The entrance hall was tiled in marble, the chandeliers all gilt and silver, the furniture antiques that Jeffrey would have been delighted to display in his front window. Passages from one room to the next were tall and arched and flanked by marble pillars, with liveried footmen stationed at discreet intervals. One suite that Alexander had previously used held a Regency display case filled with silver-framed photographs of royalty who had stayed there, including Czar Nicholas and Queen Victoria. Another had a sitting room large enough to contain the grand piano used by Sir Arthur Sullivan to compose the Savoy Operas. All the suites enjoyed working fireplaces, which a butler would stoke at the press of a button.

Jeffrey's favorite room, however, was the main restaurant. Even at breakfast it was an artistry of massive floral arrangements. Cream silk wall coverings and beautiful Art-Deco mirrors lined the chamber. It was laid out on two levels, with an upper terrace where Jeffrey enjoyed sitting and watching the arriving guests and scuttling waiters. Alexander vastly preferred having breakfast in his room, but knew from experience that Jeffrey would put up a struggle to be able to sit downstairs and watch six waiters serve his table. Six. For a dawn breakfast.

It was the morning of their departure for East Germany, and as instructed, Jeffrey had packed for a longer voyage. To where, he still did not know.

"It is vital that you do not take more than two days in Schwerin, Jeffrey," Alexander began, once their breakfast dishes were cleared away and coffee cups refilled. "These other matters simply will not wait."

He nodded. "But why send me now? I mean, it's waited this long, if this other stuff is so urgent, why not put it off until later?"

"An excellent question." Alexander Kantor paused to sip from his cup, went on. "Last week I received a telegram to my Geneva address asking me to call a number in Schwerin. It took me a surprisingly short time to place the call. I suppose the West Germans are managing to improve things after all. In any case, a woman answered—someone I've never heard of before. A lawyer—at least that's what she said she was. She did not speak English, and I speak no German, but I had anticipated the difficulty and had an interpreter available. Through this individual she told me that she had heard I was an honest man."

"Just like the dealer."

"The exact same words," Alexander agreed. "But if it was meant to be a code, someone failed to tell me about it."

"So what did you say?"

"In all my years I've never known how to reply to something like that. I asked her how the weather was."

"She must have loved that."

"It did give her pause. Eventually she came back and said she had a most urgent matter to discuss with me. Something to do with several of her clients."

"Plural?"

"Yes, that disturbed me too. I asked if she referred to the dealer, and she said only indirectly. He was not the client to whom she referred. On that point she was most clear." Alexander Kantor toyed with his coffee spoon. "She said it was absolutely crucial that we speak together immediately, before the matter was brought before the courts."

"What matter?"

"I haven't the faintest idea." Alexander Kantor replied. "But the idea of being taken to court in East Germany is most appalling, I assure you."

"That stuffed shirt from Bonn, the one who made all the trouble at Christie's over the chest of drawers, threatened us with the same thing."

"I want you to go and find out what has happened to this dealer," Alexander instructed, "and what on earth this lawyer is concerned about."

"I won't let you down," Jeffrey said.

"Of course you won't." Alexander reached to an inner pocket, drew out a neatly printed page, went on. "The dealer's name is Götz. He runs the official antique store on the central market square."

"Can you describe how he looks?"

"Mind you, I only met him once, and that was two years ago. He was a smallish man, certainly no higher than your shoulder. Pale features. I don't recall the eyes save that they were most unfriendly. Bad teeth, yes, I recall that vividly. You will no doubt see a great deal of that in your travels, but his were exceptional. My impression when he smiled was of looking at more cavities than teeth."

"Strange for a man who's got eight hundred thousand pounds waiting in a London bank."

"Perhaps, perhaps not. Many a village child in Poland after the war had his or her teeth worked on without the benefit of a painkiller, simply because there was none available. I have no doubt that such a memory would keep many people from returning to the dentist chair for a lifetime."

Jeffrey scanned the page, mispronounced the name.

"Götz is pronounced Gertz, because of the umlaut. Gertz."

"I thought you didn't speak German."

"There was a time in my past when a little German was

forced upon me, but we shall not go into that just now. His shop is part of the National Antique Association, and like most shops in the East, it has no further name than that."

Jeffrey read down the page, tried the lawyer's name on for size. "Renate Reining."

"Almost there. The last name should rhyme with the river Rhine. Reining."

His eyes still on the page, Jeffrey asked, "May I ask where it is we're going after this?"

"It is almost time for your departure, so if you will permit me I will wait and give you the details upon meeting you in the Hamburg airport. Is that acceptable?"

"I suppose I can wait," Jeffrey replied. Barely.

"Splendid. There is no harm, I suppose, in telling you our destination. It is Cracow, the medieval capital of the Polish Empire."

"Our family is from there."

"Indeed they are. We will be speaking of all these things in greater length, as I have said. But from the very outset I wish to impress upon you how vital it is that you do not discuss any of this with others."

"I understand."

"Whenever you make travel arrangements from London, you must always have as your destination a city in Western Europe. There is a travel agent I use in Zurich, a most confidential sort of individual. I will give you his name. Use him for booking everything in the East."

Jeffrey took the information as it was intended, an assurance that he would be told everything, and that this was not to be his only trip. "Thanks, Alexander."

"I thank you. This affair is long overdue for a conclusion, and it is good that you will be representing us. As I said, it is one trip I would avoid like the grave."

"I mean, thanks for trusting me."

"You have earned it, I assure you." He pushed back his chair. "And here comes your lovely young lady."

Jeffrey felt only relief as Katya entered the restaurant. Alexander noticed his expression. "You look as though you didn't expect her to appear."

Jeffrey waved her over. "With Katya I'm never sure about anything."

"In my youth we would have called that a woman's prerogative," Alexander said, rising to his feet.

"Nowadays we call it infuriating."

"That, my boy, is both universal and constant. Unless you intend to make a life for yourself as a celibate, you must accept the burden of patience."

Katya approached their table, said breathlessly, "Good morning Mr. Kantor, Jeffrey. Are we ready?"

"You look positively splendid this morning, my dear." Alexander glanced at his watch. "I suppose you had best be off. You have a plane to catch, and I a store to open."

He extended his hand first to Katya and then to Jeffrey. "You will take care, and you will call me."

"This evening, as we agreed," Jeffrey replied.

"Excellent. I wish you both a splendid trip, and all success."

Jeffrey's nerves pushed to the surface. "What if—"

Alexander stopped him with an upraised hand. "There is no need to anticipate trouble. I know you will do well, Jeffrey. I am sure of it. We will discuss what you find as you find it. Have the same confidence in your abilities that I do." He patted his assistant on the shoulder and repeated, "I know you will do well."

The flight from London to Hamburg took just under an hour. Continuous turbulence made it seem like five. They arrived to the darkness of a heavy thunderstorm, rented a car, and worked their way through snarled traffic to the autobahn for Berlin.

After an hour and a half of monotonous highway driving, the shadow of a tall brick tower appeared through the pouring rain.

"The weather certainly is appropriate," Katya said.

"It looks ghostly," Jeffrey agreed.

Vague skeletal shapes rose from the gloom and took on the form of high metal watchtowers, barbed-wire fences, and concrete-lined trenches. The autobahn went through a violent burst of bumps and uneven strippings, then the former East German border was upon them.

A vast expanse of asphalt stretched out to either side of the highway, now cordoned off with makeshift fencing. Beyond the inspection area loomed multistory brick and glass buildings. Structures with mirrored glass walls rose from their roofs, reminding Jeffrey of airport control towers.

All around this compound, and down the barbed-wire fencing as far in each direction as they could see, rose tall prison watchtowers.

The border-control buildings were thoroughly trashed. The lower windows were all smashed in with a violence that had torn many of their frames from the walls. Huge chunks of the buildings themselves had been hewn out, leaving gaping holes and corners that looked gnawed by a raging giant.

The entire border area was gripped in a deathlike stillness. Nothing moved. Nothing at all. There must have been a dozen buildings in all, with no sign of life anywhere.

"Where is everybody?" Jeffrey asked.

"Trying to convince anybody they can find that they had nothing to do with anything," Katya said, her voice very small.

He glanced over. "Are you all right?"

"Drive on, Jeffrey. I don't want to stay here any longer than I have to."

By the time they reached the turn-off for Schwerin, the worst of the storm had passed and the sky was clearing. It was a good thing; the road leading to the capital city of Mecklenburg-Vorpommern was little more than a rutted country lane. Ancient cobblestones vied with sloppily poured asphalt, and the covering of rain hid potholes of bone-jarring depth. The road passed through tiny villages of unkempt houses, their front doors just inches away from the stumbling traffic and clouds of diesel fumes. Trucks loomed up from time to time, slowing for no one, demanding most of the road as their right; Jeffrey reduced his speed to a crawl, hugged the curb, and hoped for a safe passage.

They passed a sign identifying the Schwerin industrial estate, a series of factories with dirt-clouded windows and filthy facades. Then they became thoroughly lost in a Schwerin housing development—scruffy multicolored highrise buildings that dominated a hill on the edge of town. Three sets of directions finally took them through a tiny forest and down to the edge of one of the city's lakes.

The sun was forcing its way through the scuttling clouds as Jeffrey turned onto a narrow road that ran alongside a dirty sand beach. A number of heavyset people in shapeless sweaters and rolled-up trousers were making their way down to the lakeside, eager to soak up whatever meager good weather they were granted. Jeffrey pulled up in front of an attractive white-stucco three-story building with yellow trim, bearing a small sign announcing itself to be the Strand Hotel.

The woman staffing the reception desk was as heavyset as the beach-goers, and gave them a dubious look when Katya confirmed that they wanted two single rooms. She led them upstairs and showed him cramped chambers barely large enough to hold the narrow bed and small corner desk. He dropped Katya's bags off, went to his own room, opened the window, and spent a few moments looking out over the lake to the distant skyline of Schwerin.

When he came back downstairs, Katya was on the hotel's only phone, speaking in what he assumed was German. He walked out and sat down on the hotel veranda.

Now that the sun was out, the weather was balmy. Every veranda table was taken, the people talking softly and gazing out at the lake. The body of sparkling water was wide enough for its farthest shore to be beyond the horizon. Its border was mostly forest, except for where Schwerin rose to his left. The people walking along the narrow beach and seated on the veranda seemed all cut from the same mold—overweight and pasty-skinned, older than their years, wearing clothes of muted colors and clunky shoes.

"I tried to call the numbers you gave me," Katya said as she appeared on the veranda. "There wasn't any answer. They must be taking a late lunch."

Jeffrey had a fleeting sensation that at the sound of Katya's English every face turned their way, then just as swiftly ignored them. A lifetime habit, he supposed. "Why don't we have a bite to eat here?"

The waitress watched with half-hidden curiosity as Katya explained the German menu to him, took their orders, gave Jeffrey another of those fleeting glances, and left. He turned back and found Katya watching the other tables.

"Why are you smiling?"

"This is a holdover from another era," she replied.

He reached over and took her hand. "Tell me what you see."

She looked down at his fingers covering hers. "This is supposed to be a business trip, remember?"

He left his hand where it was. "Tell me, Katya."

She looked back out at the veranda. "Those ladies over there have been coming here for forty years. They come to breathe the good sea air—that's what they would call a lake this big, an inland sea. Their doctor once told them it was good for the lungs, and they still believe it. Their husbands all died during the war. And the one real pleasure left in life is to get in a bus and come to the Strand Hotel once every summer."

"And the rest of the year?"

"Life in a little gray village, somewhere unmarked on any map."

The waitress returned with their food. Jeffrey waited awkwardly while Katya bowed her head for a moment. No matter how often she did that in public, it did not become easier for him to endure. When she lifted her eyes he pointed toward a distant table and said, "My grandmother used to have a hat like that one. A straw boater lacquered with white enamel and a couple of fake flowers on one side."

"Don't point."

"Why not? Nobody's looked our way since they heard us talking English."

"Yes, they have. They've seen we're foreigners and that's all they need to know. They have a lifetime's practice of not appearing to look where they're not supposed to."

"But that's all gone."

"The reasons for it might be," Katya agreed. "But it's one thing to say it and another to relearn habits so ingrained they are instinctive."

Jeffrey looked around, said, "There's more gray hair here than I've ever seen in one place."

"Clairol's campaign for youth in a bottle didn't reach to the East," Katya said. "People look a lot older here than Westerners of the same age. They don't think about looking chic. They can't. They struggle too hard just to arrive at being comfortable—or at least as close to comfortable as they can ever come."

She tasted her food, then went on. "They wear orthopedic shoes and use canes when they're in their fifties, twenty years earlier than in the West. They'll never think it strange or embarrassing, though. Look at the people on the street when we go out today. You'll find eyes that slide over to one side of their head and bad scars and worse teeth. All products of a system that lifts the welfare of the state above all else."

"I thought the state was for the people."

"Don't be sarcastic. Many of these older people believed that with all their hearts. It has been extremely difficult for them to accept that the basis for a Communist society was nothing more than a lie."

When they had finished eating, Katya went to try the two numbers again. A few minutes later she returned and reported, "There isn't any answer at the antique shop. But I did reach the lawyer, Frau Reining. She will meet us at the Café Prague in one hour. Do you want to leave now and go by the shop first?"

The city of Schwerin was a jarring mixture of old and new. Jeffrey's progress was slowed to a crawl by the surrounding traffic; plastic-looking cars bearing names like Trabant and Moskovite and Lada puttered by in clouds of blue smoke, smelling and sounding like poorly tuned outboard motors.

Their way took them back by the new section—the apartments were nicknamed *Arbeitersschliessfächer*, Katya said, or filing cabinets for workers. From a distance they loomed in irregular patterns of multicolored brick and pastel concrete. Up close Jeffrey saw that the yellows and blues and pinks were gutted and peeling and shabby. The roads were scarred and potholed, the sidewalks pitted. Weeds grew everywhere in unruly clumps, giving the entire area an atmosphere of abandonment.

Forty thousand families lived in the housing project, Katya said, reading from a pamphlet she had picked up at the hotel. The buildings stood like tired bastions to a forgotten dream. They were crammed one against the other, balconies strung with laundry and old flowerpots and frayed curtains.

"This looks like the punishment block to an inner-city housing project," Jeffrey decided, looking around as he drove.

"In East Germany," Katya told him, "the average waiting time for an apartment in these developments is five years."

"You've got to be joking."

"At least they have a bathroom for each family," Katya said. "And indoor plumbing. And running water in the kitchens. Most of the time, anyway."

Farther along, the road leading to the city center was lined on one side by the Russian military compound and on the other with the dilapidated Russian officers' apartments. Both were encased within concrete walls and razor-wire and metal gates topped with bright red stars. The stars were the only recently painted item along the entire mile-long stretch.

They parked their car at the outskirts of the city's old section and walked, soon coming upon a vast eight-story palace—the former residence, according to Katya, of the Dukes of Mecklenburg. The castle dominated an island situated in one of the city's lakes. The island was connected to the city proper by a narrow bridge, its surface paved with cobblestones and its sides decorated with ancient sculptures and gas-lit lamps. Everything, from the street to the carvings to the palace itself, suffered from a severe case of neglect.

The city was no different. All but the main streets were laid in uneven cobblestones. All but the tourist areas were lined with buildings buried under decades of soot. Ornate facades protruded at odd intervals from beneath layers of filth.

The antique store stood on the central square. According to a small card taped to the door, it was owned by the central East German Ministry for Art, Subsection for Paintings and Antiques. A fly-blown sign tilted against the front window announced that it was closed, and from the looks of the dust blanketing every surface, Jeffrey could see through the window it had been for some time.

He stepped back from the window and scanned the square and connecting streets. The shop was a couple of businesses removed from what appeared to be the newest and gaudiest store in town; flashing lights surrounded a sign announcing that it sold pornography. A line of customers waited patiently by the door, gawking at the relatively conservative display in the windows.

Many of the stores were undergoing radical innovation, with bright new displays gracing the windows of tired gray buildings. Katya followed his eyes. "Under socialism," she said, " all the shops had names given to them by the department that ran their section. They were all generic names, like grocery, watch repair, and so on. These buildings you see around here, the old ones with the sort of shadow writing above the store, are all left over from before the war. They probably haven't been painted in forty years, since they were all nationalized and placed under central control."

Jeffrey nodded distractedly, then pressed his face to the antique shop's window and spent several minutes carefully scanning the room.

Katya watched his expression, asked, "What's wrong?"

"Something doesn't add up," he said, using his hands to shade his eyes from the sun's reflection. "I can see almost the whole shop."

"So?"

"There's nothing in there that I would even think of having in our shop. It's all second-rate stuff. Worse. Some of it's barely above junk. Not even antiques at all, just used furniture."

Katya moved up closer. "It stands to reason that a shop like this would hold its best pieces and send them out where they can get better prices. And Western currency."

But Jeffrey wasn't satisfied. "This is a state-run store. The guy who spoke to Alexander had all sorts of documents saying it was official state business. Nowadays they could get Western currency selling goods directly from the store, couldn't they? I mean, they're using the German mark here now. So why isn't there at least one piece like the stuff he sent us? It's a completely different collection. Worlds away."

"What are you suggesting?"

He turned away. "I don't know. It doesn't add up, that's all. Come on, let's go meet the lawyer."

The Café Prague was a recently remodeled little gem across the street from one of the central ministries. The ceilings were thirty-five feet high and supported by a series of pillars. The upper windows were arched and set with lead-lined stained glass; the lower windows were broad and high and cast a lovely light through the interior.

They had been at their table only a few minutes when a bird-like woman came up, inspected them with sharp nervous eyes, then leaned over and said something in German.

"She wants to know if we are the ones from London," Katya said.

"Yes," Jeffrey replied, standing and extending his hand. "Nice to—"

The woman seated herself and spoke again in the same abrupt manner.

"She wants to know if she can trust us."

Jeffrey lowered his hand and sat down. "She should have already decided that before asking us to come all the way here."

"I can't tell her that. And you behave."

"If she can be rude, why can't I?" Jeffrey turned to the woman. "Yes."

"Good," the woman replied in English. She extended her hand. "Frau Renate Reining. Excuse. Few words English only. Russian, yes. German, yes. Czech, some. You speak Russian?"

"No."

"No. Nobody speak Russian. A new world. People speak Russian last year. This year, all forget. World change."

The lawyer was a tired dark-haired woman in her middle forties who clearly gave little concern to her appearance. Her fingernails were chewed to the quick, her gestures nervous and as abrupt as her words. She wore a pair of dusty double-knit pants, an unironed white shirt, and an open sweater with two of the buttons hanging by raveled threads.

She stood and motioned for them to follow her. "You come."

She led them out of the cafe and around the corner to a door whose stone and mortar frame was decorated with half a dozen brass plaques announcing various professional offices. They climbed five flights of circular wooden stairs that bowed and creaked with their passage. The center of each step was worn to a cavity of bare splintered wood.

On the fifth floor, they walked down a long dusty-smelling hall on a strip of moth-eaten carpet. Bare ceiling bulbs illuminated flaking paint and warped wood. Frau Reining produced a set of massive pre-war skeleton keys and opened a door with a cracked plastic sign announcing the law offices of three partners.

The office was one room crowded to absurdity with three desks, a kitchen table for conferences, and floor-to-ceiling wall cabinets. She waved them toward the table, shrugged off her sweater, and spoke to Katya.

"She says this costs nine hundred dollars a month now. Before the Wall came down it cost eighteen. It's all they can afford."

"It's, well, functional," Jeffrey replied.

"Sit, sit," Frau Reining said. "Business."

"Business," Jeffrey agreed, seating himself in an unyielding wood-and-metal chair.

The lawyer lit an unfiltered cigarette, leaned back in her chair, and began speaking rapid-fire German in a low drone. She smoked as she talked, the words rolling out in a cloud of smoke. The longer she talked, the larger grew Katya's eyes, the more pallid her complexion.

"What's she saying?" Jeffrey demanded, alarmed by her expression.

Katya replied with a single upraised finger. Wait.

"Minute," the woman said. "One minute still." She continued on in German, stopped, and gave Katya a hard-eyed inspection.

"Well?"

Slowly Katya turned his way. "Something's gone horribly wrong."

"With the furniture?"

"Not exactly." Katya brushed distractedly at the hair on her forehead. Her hand trembled slightly. Jeffrey shot a glance at the lawyer. For some reason Katya's reaction seemed to please her.

He leaned forward. "Tell me what's wrong."

"The antique store director has been arrested."

The discomfort he had felt on the street before the closed shop solidified, became reality. "Tell me," he repeated.

"They arrested his assistant too. She's agreed to give evidence in return for a lighter sentence—I forget what it's called."

"Plea bargaining."

"Yes." Katya's eyes had a lost look. "According to the assistant, the dealer came to you—Alexander, I mean. They came to him because they heard he was honest. The dealer they used before knew what they were doing and started raising his commissions."

"What they were doing was illegal," Jeffrey said. It was not a question.

"Illegal," the lawyer agreed, nodding her head vigorously. "Everything illegal. That man breathes, it is done illegal."

"Frau Reining represents some of the lawful owners of the furniture. About forty. In one . . . I can't think of the word—"

"Consolidated claims," Jeffrey suggested.

"Yes. Thank you." Katya took a breath. "She says most of them are out of prison now."

"Prison," Jeffrey repeated.

Katya nodded. "Those they can find. Some have disappeared. She's representing their families."

"Poof," the lawyer said, blowing her fingertips open. "Dust in wind. Story of Communist life."

"Jeffrey, they were finding people with antiques and just putting the owners away." Katya's expression mirrored the pain in her voice. "Stealing all they had, forcing them to sign documents saying they were sold for money the people never received. If they complained they were just locked up. No trial, no rights, no word to their families. Nothing."

"I don't understand," Jeffrey said, struggling to hold on. "The antique dealer was doing this?"

"Stasi," the lawyer corrected. "Secret police."

"He was a front," Katya said. "There were people involved right up through the Party hierarchy. They don't even know how high it went."

"High," Frau Reining confirmed. "This much money, maybe top."

"It was millions, Jeffrey. Millions. They still don't know how much, or how many people were hurt. Frau Reining says all but two of her clients were imprisoned, some with their families, even little children. Some were tortured." Katya pleaded with him. "Why did this happen? How could they do this to people just for pieces of furniture?"

"Not furniture," the lawyer interrupted. "Money. Much money. In East, before Wall, one dollar like one hundred dollars in West. People do much for millions here. Anything."

Alexander didn't know anything about this, Jeffrey kept repeating to himself. For the old man to be caught up in something like this went against everything he stood for.

Still, the niggling doubt remained; had he been sent over in Alexander's place to sniff the wind? Had the story of his sister been a lie?

"Jeffrey?" Katya asked softly.

"I—" He felt the lawyer's eyes on him. "Tell her I'm sorry. We didn't know. Nothing." His words sounded feeble in his ears. "All the documents, everything, it was all correct."

The lawyer searched his face, then nodded abruptly and reached forward to grind out her cigarette. "I believe."

"Alexander even called Berlin to verify." The whispers of doubt laced painfully across his mind. It couldn't be. Alexander wasn't involved. Jeffrey shook his head to clear the fears away.

The lawyer misunderstood his gesture. "No. Means nothing. Documents all correct, but all false. Correct for law, false for man. Old Communist story. Big lie."

She started rushing through another flood of German. Katya nodded in time to the words, then turned to Jeffrey and said, "Frau Reining says that she believes you knew nothing about all this. You and Alexander. The dealer's assistant was very clear. She says you mustn't blame yourself.

"She has studied the law," Katya went on. "There is no redress permitted them, since the export documents and the sales were all done legally, and were done in another country. She will give you a notarized letter to that effect. But she would like to know if you can give them an idea of how many pieces you handled."

"Alexander said something like thirty, I don't know the exact number."

"She would like to know if you can give them either a picture or a description of the pieces you sold. It would help a lot in the court cases."

"We photograph every piece we sell," Jeffrey replied. His voice sounded dead in his ears.

The lawyer smiled for the first time, showing crooked and yellowed teeth. "She says that is excellent," Katya translated. "Could they please have copies?"

"I'll ask. I think so."

"She wants to know if any are still unsold."

"A few. Not many."

"She doesn't think the people will want them back." Katya's voice gave a slight tremble. She cleared it, went on.

"She says they would probably be too much of a reminder of things they will want to forget. If Alexander could send pictures of them also, she will try to track down the owner and see what they say."

Katya surveyed him with wounded eyes. "This is horrible, Jeffrey."

"A nightmare." He had difficulty bringing his thoughts together. "Tell her I'm not sure how long we can keep pieces that aren't for sale. Our shop is really small. We can put them in storage, though."

"She understands. She'll come back within the week with instructions. Is that okay?"

He nodded. What would Alexander say? He pushed himself to his feet. "I have to call Alexander." His body weighed a ton.

"We meet tomorrow," the lawyer said. "Have more talk." She turned to Katya, fired off a rapid flow of words.

Katya translated. "There are a couple of important things she wants to discuss with you. Alexander explained the time limitation to her in their conversation. But she really has to speak with you again tomorrow early." Katya looked at him. "Are you all right?"

"Not really."

The lawyer went to her desk and started rummaging in a drawer, talking all the while. Katya said, "She has something she wants to give us. She was invited to a piano concert at the castle tonight. She has to meet with a client and can't go. She wants to know if we would like the tickets."

Jeffrey struggled to focus his thoughts. "I don't know."

Katya's expression held concern for him. "Maybe it would be a good idea, Jeffrey."

"Yes. All right." To the lawyer he said, "Thank you. That's very kind."

She nodded in her short, sharp way and handed over the tickets. "No blame," she said.

CHAPTER
9

The telephone line hissed and popped as though Jeffrey were speaking with darkest Africa. "I have some bad news and some incredibly worse news. Which do you want first?"

"A trip of extremes, I take it." Alexander paused, asked, "Is the very bad truly so earth-shaking?"

"Worse. What's stronger than awful?" Jeffrey spoke from within the hotel manager's office, where he had been permitted to pull their phone after Katya had pleaded with her for almost twenty minutes.

"I'm sure I don't know. Perhaps you'd best ease me into it before plummeting over the cliff."

"The dealer Götz has been arrested." Jeffrey worked at keeping his voice level. "We are not implicated in any way, however. In fact, it appears from his assistant's testimony that he came to you specifically because we have a name for honesty."

"So our integrity remains intact. Good. That is very good. I am sorry to hear about Götz, but I cannot say that I am all that surprised. Tell me the details."

"That's part of the plummet."

"I see." The voice turned brisk. "Very well, Jeffrey. You may now deliver the blow."

Jeffrey told him the story in its entirety, from finding the shop closed to what the lawyer said. When he finished he sat listening to the line hiss and sputter, his heart hammering a frantic beat.

"Alexander?"

The line emitted a hoarse groan. "Blood money."

"Alexander, are you all right?"

"I've dealt in blood money." The man sounded totally spent, broken in body and spirit.

Jeffrey felt a flood of relief sweep away every last vestige of doubt. "She knows we were not aware of what we dealt in," he said, sinking into a nearby chair, his body trembling slightly. "She's giving us a notarized letter tomorrow saying that her clients will not seek reparations. She asks if we would be willing to give her photographs of the pieces we handled from Götz, and store the unsold pieces until she identifies the rightful owners and learns what they want to have done with them."

Jeffrey waited, strained, heard what sounded like a series of low moans in the distant hissing background. "Alexander? Do you mind us giving her copies of our pictures?"

"Do what you think best." The voice was so feeble as to be almost inaudible over the constant crackling.

"I'm sure she'll wait until I'm back, then if you'll tell me which ones, I'll make the duplicates and mail—"

"Give it back to her," Alexander said, his voice low.

"What? Give back the unsold antiques? She doesn't want—"

"The money. Give it back. All of it. Tell her she can have every cent."

"The eight hundred thousand pounds?"

"More. She is to have all the interest and my commissions as well. I refuse to taint myself by living from blood money."

Jeffrey's heart surged with pride and affection for the old gentleman. "What about setting up a fund to help all those who have suffered, maybe to help with legal costs or something?"

"Do what you think best. I'm sorry. I . . . I must go. We will speak at the airport tomorrow. I . . . Do what you think—"

The line went dead.

When he appeared on the veranda, he found Katya sitting in the far corner, reading intently from a small book in her lap. He walked forward and looked over her shoulder. It was a New Testament. She raised her head at the sight of his shadow, studied him intently.

"You're feeling better," she decided.

"Much."

"Talking to Alexander helped you a lot, didn't it?"

He nodded. "Really took a weight off my shoulders."

She closed the book. "In Polish, you say that a stone has dropped from your heart."

"That's exactly how it feels, too."

She waited a moment, then, "Did you think that Alexander was caught up in all this?"

"I didn't really think it. Nothing that strong. Just afraid that it might be true." Terrified was a better word, he decided.

"And now you're not."

"He didn't know. I'm sure of it now."

"I never doubted you," she said solemnly. "Not at all."

He felt himself falling into the violet depths of her eyes. "Thank you, Katya."

"I couldn't," she replied. "There wasn't room in my life at that moment for doubt."

The Schwerin Castle was a six-story behemoth crowned on one corner with a knight riding rampant on a two-story steed, and on the other three angles with eighteen spires and turrets. As Jeffrey and Katya joined the crowds passing through the palace's main gates for the concert, they watched a variety of punts and rowboats and paddle skiffs flow in the slow-moving water that surrounded them.

The throne room, where the piano concert took place, was extravagantly gilded. Scenes were painted in the shape of shields around the ceiling, each depicting with timeless clarity the nation-state ruled from this one room for over three hundred years. Marble pillars supported an ornate fresco of smiling gold cherubs and detailed scrollwork. The throne, gold-over-precious wood, sat empty and regal beneath a royal blue and gold canopy.

The sound of Mozart lilted in harmony with the room's elegance. Jeffrey sat and listened and looked out through the tall windows that flanked the polished grand piano. The windows were open to permit the gentle breeze entry. He was borne on the music out to the water that flowed in constant peaceful silence just beyond the palace grounds. The melody, soft and coaxing, carried him away from the questions and the problems and the issues and the worries. Its purity spoke to something deeper, beyond the turmoil that had buffeted his world. He closed his eyes and saw the furniture he had studied so carefully, not as items to be evaluated and sold, but as works of art. In that moment, the price tags and the buyers' greed and the dealers' cynicism and the business competition were all swept away.

He listened, and visualized the pieces that had come to be his own personal favorites, savoring the artistry and the loving craftsmanship that had gone into their creation. He listened, and felt the world to be split in two—the creation and the craftsmanship on one hand, the greed and the material desire to have and to hold and to possess on the other. He listened, and saw himself balanced on the fulcrum, teetering to either side, not knowing where he belonged.

Jeffrey reached over, slipped his hand into Katya's, and waited. Sometimes when he did that she reacted as one trained to be polite even when faced with something repulsive. She would sit and let her hand rest there with the cold limpness of a dead fish, then a few moments later extract it softly and pull her body slightly away. It always left Jeffrey tremendously hurt and afraid to try again.

But this time she *enfolded* it in both of hers with the calm movement of one giving him his rightful place. She too was caught up in the music and the mood and the flowing waters and the evening's perfumed breeze. Jeffrey felt his heart grow wings as she drew his hand farther into her lap, where she could better nestle it with one hand and softly stroke the hairs of his wrist with the other.

At intermission she sat for a long time, not looking his way, not letting his hand go. Finally she stirred and sighed gently. "Shall we stretch our legs?"

They joined the crowd drifting through the adjoining rooms, inspected paintings and gilded adornments in silence, too shy over this newfound closeness to face each other directly.

At the sound of the bell, Jeffrey followed the crowd back

into the throne room, only to realize upon his arrival at their seats that Katya was no longer with him. He returned back through chamber after interconnecting chamber, and breathed a silent sigh when he found her in the very back room, what once had been a formal library. He walked toward her, then faltered when he saw the tears on her face.

She stood before a statue of a young woman, a girl probably a year or so beyond puberty. She was nude save for a long shawl draped over her head. Her arms were tied behind her back with the same rough cord used to bind her ankles. She remained on her feet, yet crouched down so that she could cover much of her naked body with the shawl. There was an air of tragic submission, of utter fear, of helpless fragility about the girl.

"Katya?"

She turned and looked at him with brimming eyes. "She's going to be put on the block and sold into slavery. Did you know that was the story? It's written here in German. It happened all the time in the Eastern lands, Jeffrey. All the time. The Tartars or the Cossacks or the Mongols or the Turks would come marching through, and all the girls young enough and pretty enough were stripped and shackled and counted as loot. This wasn't a thousand years ago, and it wasn't on the other side of the earth. This was yesterday. And today, somewhere else on this earth. Some girl is trapped and scared and helpless, some father has been taken away without reason, some mother is no longer there to take care of her. This is what they've done to these people, Jeffrey. Enormous evil for the sake of greed."

Jeffrey swept her into an embrace. He stroked her hair, and shushed her gently, feeling for her own pain, wondering if this was what it meant to be in love.

"Why is the world so cruel, Jeffrey? Can you tell me that? When will it ever end?"

CHAPTER
10

The next morning Jeffrey and Katya returned to the lawyer's cluttered office. "She wants to know if you were able to speak with Mr. Kantor," Katya translated.

"Yes. He was very upset by the news. Extremely upset."

Frau Reining nodded as though expecting nothing less. She spoke in a torrent of German, which Katya translated as, "Not half as upset as the people I am representing. I would like to hope that such horrors are behind us completely, but the times have taught me nothing if not caution."

Jeffrey took a breath, then announced, "We have decided to give back the income from the sales of Götz's antiques."

The words were greeted with silence. Frau Reining turned to Katya and demanded a translation. Reluctantly Katya turned her eyes from Jeffrey, told her what he had said, then asked him, "Is it true? That's what you and Alexander discussed?"

He nodded, keeping his eyes on the lawyer. "All of it."

Frau Reining said sharply, "You no must."

"We're going to do it anyway."

She appeared not to hear him. She stood and went to her desk and returned to the table with a letter which she handed to Katya.

"This is a notarized document," Katya translated, pointing to the official seal and signature at the bottom. "It says that they are relinquishing all rights to prosecute or request restitution."

"You no must," the lawyer repeated.

"Yes, we do," Jeffrey replied. "Tell her that there is a difference between what the law says we must do and what is right. We are giving it all back. Commissions included."

The lawyer's sharp gaze bore into him as she listened to Katya's translation. Then she asked, "How much?"

"I don't know the exact commission we charged, but I would guess the total to be around nine hundred and seventy thousand pounds."

The gaze continued to rake him for a long moment. Then she reached for her pack of cigarettes and lit one with trembling hands. She said with the first gulp of smoke, "Million pounds."

"Give or take some change," Jeffrey agreed, and told her what he had spent sleepless hours mulling over. "We want you to set up a trust to help cover the damages caused to everyone you can find. We will draft a letter of instruction, but it is important that you offer us any suggestions you may have as to how the money should be spent."

He was startled to find Katya's hand slide over his. He glanced her way, but found the gaze too inviting to pay it any mind just then. He went on. "We want to remain very flexible about how the money is to be used, so that it can be matched to individual needs. Since this is not legally required as repayment, I think we would prefer not to have it all go back to the people who owned these particular antiques. You can give them something; we'll work out a figure. But not all of it. There are too many others in need."

When Katya had translated, the lawyer nodded agreement. She said with Katya translating, "It now looks like the German government will provide compensation to the victims of these crimes if we can successfully prove our case in the courts. But this will of course take much time. Your money will help a great deal to cover their needs in the meantime."

"Much needs, much help," the lawyer said in English, approval shining in her gaze. "Thank you. For all families. Thank you."

"You're welcome."

She stubbed out her cigarette and stood. "Come. We go."

They followed her down the stairs and out of the building. She set a brisk pace over the cobblestone passages. Katya walked between Jeffrey and the lawyer, never letting go of his hand for an instant.

She paused before a block-long building topped with the watch-walk of an imitation medieval castle. Miniature turrets rose at each corner, far too small to be more than pillars intended to hold up the sky. Despite its finery and broad windows and fresh white paint, there was an air of isolation to the place. No one walked along that side of the road—all crossed over to the opposite side, all refused to look at it. No one entered or left through the high central portals.

"Stasi," the lawyer announced. "Secret police. Before, not now."

"The place of children's nightmares," Katya said quietly.

The woman spoke rapidly. Katya translated. "When the protest marches began the week before the Wall toppled, there were forty thousand the first night, and eighty thousand the second. Out of a population in Schwerin of one hundred and twenty thousand. That left the Communists, the grandfathers, and the babies at home. We all walked down to this building, and set eighty thousand candles into the stonework at the building's base. Then we stood and held hands and sang. Toward dawn we went home smiling, because that night we knew we had won."

She set off once more at her brisk pace, talking all the while. Katya translated in breathless snatches. "When we all marched on the streets, we were truly one Volk. One people. It was this spirit of community we had to build up in order to survive. If it had not been there, the Wall would never have come down.

"It's all gone now, put to sleep by greed. Nowadays everybody hears that they can have everything they want, buy all they desire, if only they go out and work and earn more money and don't give it to anyone else, just keep it for themselves. This new greed isolates us. It makes us more conscious of being alone. And overnight the feeling of pulling together was lost.

"People are diving headfirst into consumerism, and don't understand that there are rocks beneath the surface. Nothing in their lives has prepared them for the shock of this change. Everything tells them to buy now, the signs on the street and the new fancy shop windows and the television and the radio and the newspapers and the magazines. Everything. Buy, buy, and nowhere is anything teaching them the principle of self-discipline.

"They have never learned the first basic lesson of debt, that whatever they borrow they have to pay back. Under the Communists, debt was not allowed to a private citizen. Many people do not even know what the word *interest* means. So they are given this enormous freedom which they don't understand, and they buy everything immediately. The strain on these people, and their families, is tremendous."

She turned into a worn-out building with stone stairs beaten by countless feet into scrabbles of crumbling granite. She fished in her purse for yet another set of massive keys, led them downstairs into a dank and grimy cellar, and stopped before a solid-looking door.

Through Katya she said, "This is from a client. An honest man. Someone who is not part of any plot or secret action. He received these two pieces from a relative before the war."

A heavy skeleton key was inserted and twisted with both hands. She stopped with the door only half ajar and looked back at Jeffrey.

"There are questions everywhere. Questions from everyone, East and West. Too many evil men have hurt too many innocent people, so now there are questions about all hoards of private wealth."

Katya rushed to keep up with the woman's hurried speech. "This is an honest man whose family must have money now. There is a person in the West who claims their home. It is a historical right, granted to people who can show that they were forced out of their holdings by the Communists. Those who can prove this can have their holdings back. She doesn't have any quarrel with the law, just with the pain it is causing to innocent people.

"The person in the West is going to sell the house, and this family will lose the place they have lived in for more than thirty years unless they can come up with the money. There is an enormous housing shortage, and if they can't buy it they don't know where they will live."

The lawyer waited until Katya was finished, then said directly to Jeffrey, "I trust you. You trust me. This not bad man. Good man. Honest. Not many, but this one yes. Honest. You take?"

"I don't even know what it is yet," Jeffrey replied. "But if it is an antique and I think we can sell it, yes, I'll take it."

She nodded her satisfaction when Katya had translated, then opened the door and flipped on the light. Jeffrey stepped into the doorway and breathed a long sigh.

The room's single bare bulb shone down on two articles so fine that even the bare concrete walls with their covering of mold and dust could not alter their impact. Jeffrey stepped forward, feeling the thrill of discovery.

The first was an Italian work, probably Florentine, certainly from the seventeenth century or earlier. It was designed as a cabinet and rested on four graceful mahogany legs connected by a crisscrossing centerpiece. The cabinet itself was modeled after a single-story villa with a tiny roof terrace lined by an even smaller, intricately carved banister. The villa was flanked by four Grecian columns, and paneled with gracefully inlaid floral and fountain scenes. It was in immaculate condition.

The more valuable of the two items was at first glance the less impressive. Jeffrey had never seen one in person before, but he had inspected enough pictures to be almost positive what lay within the blank dark exterior.

From the outside, it was a simple hardwood cabinet, standing on short sturdy legs, rising up to about chest height. The exterior wood had been darkened by time and by its original finish to the point that it was impossible to detect either the grain or the type of wood. It was unadorned save for brass handles on each door, a keyhole designed for a ten-inch skeleton key, and a small wooden lockbox on the chest's top. But from the side Jeffrey could see the cleverly imbedded hinges and the three-inch thick solid wood from which the box was constructed; these two clues gave the cabinet away.

He stepped forward, swung open the doors, and felt a tingling up his spine. It was a royal family's jewelry chest. Date uncertain, but without doubt prior to seventeen hundred. Probably central European.

The interiors of the three-foot-high doors were a pair of solid ivory frames. Within these frames, birds had been designed from thin slices of semiprecious stone and set against a backdrop of onyx. The cabinet itself held ten drawers, five on each side of a larger central chamber. Each drawer was inlaid with a repeated pattern done in ivory and semiprecious stones. The central chamber door was framed by solid ivory pillars and faced with gemstone flowers in a vase of hammered silver.

The lawyer's roughly accented English brought him awake. "You can sell?"

Jeffrey eased himself from his crouch. He nodded. "Without a doubt."

The lawyer was genuinely relieved. "How much?"

"I can't say anything for certain without further evaluation."

When Katya had translated, the woman waved it aside impatiently. "Guess. This important for family."

He rubbed a hand across the side of his face. "This looks to be of what we would call museum quality. Both of them. We would sell it to a serious collector or to a house seeking to build up a selection of Renaissance works."

This time she did not even allow Katya to finish. "Words, words," she barked. "Family must know. How much?"

He took a breath. "At least fifty thousand pounds."

The lawyer made round eyes. She asked through Katya, "Fifty thousand pounds is one hundred and fifty thousand marks, is that right? Yes. I am not used to this new money yet. You will give us that for the two?"

"No. Fifty thousand pounds each. Mind you, they have to be evaluated. We must be absolutely certain they are genuine."

She listened to Katya's translation, then said directly, "But you think yes."

He feasted his eyes on the two works a moment longer, nodded. "I think yes."

"And if genuine, maybe worth more?"

"If the finishes are original, and if they are dated as I think they will be, then the right buyer could pay a lot more."

The cellar was very quiet. "How much more?"

Jeffrey shook his head. "I can't begin to say. Possibly . . . well, I wouldn't even want to guess what the possibility might be."

"Maybe twice, three times?"

He bent back over, traced a gentle hand across the safe's interior. "Possibly."

The lawyer spoke through Katya, who said, "There are

other people who will need to sell family treasures in the days and weeks to come. This is not the only family with problems and things to sell. There are too many dishonest people seeking more than is their fair share. They will be happy to know I have found an honest man. Will you come back and do business here again?"

"Of course," Jeffrey replied. He allowed himself to be ushered from the room. "But you have to realize that there is a very big difference between the price paid for a good imitation and the value of an original antique. A world of difference. And I won't know for sure what these pieces are until I have completed a full evaluation."

"This is clear," she replied through Katya. "But I believe you will tell me the truth. You gave back money when you did not need to. You did not try to first tell me that the antiques were fake. The quality of honesty is very rare when such sums are involved. You must come back again. There will be other opportunities for business."

"I'd like that very much," he said, trying to keep his voice calm. "Thank you."

She flipped off the cellar lights, started up the stairwell, and continued to talk over her shoulder. Katya translated. "The next time you come the new autobahn to Schwerin will be open, and the power lines will loom like metal giants over the land. And with the coming of all that wealth and ease and comfort, something will be lost. I am not sorry to see communism go. It had to be. But with this blind rush to join to the West, I tell you that something truly will be lost."

Jeffrey strode back toward Schwerin's old town as though he were walking on air. His first find. His first buy. He filled his lungs to bursting, feeling as though he were breathing champagne.

The family would receive an initial sum sufficient to cover the downpayment on their house—the safe's facades were worth that much alone. Once the pieces arrived in London and authentication was completed, another fifty percent of the minimum estimated value would be sent via the lawyer. Upon sale, the remainder minus commissions.

As they strolled back toward the center of town Katya

said softly, "I am very proud of you."

"For what?"

"For the offer of help."

He shook his head. "It was Alexander's idea and Alexander's money."

"I think maybe you had a little to do with it."

"Well, with the arrangement, yes. A little."

She pointed to where a red-brick spire rose above the old city's rooftops. "I'd like to go in there and pray for the people before we leave. Do we have time?"

"If we hurry."

The church was erected around the year eleven hundred, a vast structure of red brick and stone and floored with colored tile. The forty-meter-high domed ceiling took a tour-guide's voice and bounced it back in rolling echoes; the guide paused with practiced cadence to allow the reverberated tones to silence between his phrases.

Jeffrey sat beside Katya as she knelt and prayed. He was content to spend his time looking about the chamber, happy to have the trip behind him, enormously pleased to be at peace with Katya.

The former Communist masters had stripped the churches of their finery and painted the ornate interiors a blank-faced white. All that was left were two wooden crosses, the altar panels, the empty bishop's chair, and a painting of Christ on the cross. All the stained-glass windows had been blown out during the war, replaced with simple translucent glass panels. Stripped of its multicolored lighting, the vast whitewashed chamber held all the warmth and hope of a tomb.

"I love these old churches," Katya said as they left. "It's as though I can feel in my heart the centuries of prayer."

Jeffrey pointed over his shoulder at the church entryway. "Did you see that kid there by the doors?"

"Which one?"

"He was standing at the announcement board when we went out. He was looking at that poster, the big one. It was a Bible verse, wasn't it?"

Katya nodded. "John 3:16. I saw it."

"He was just *standing* there. I'm pretty sure he was the same one I saw when we went in. I noticed him because of the expression on his face. A kid of fifteen, maybe sixteen years old, standing in front of a church reading and rereading a Bible verse."

Katya pulled Jeffrey to a stop, gave him a very tender look. "What was his expression?"

"Total confusion," Jeffrey replied. "Can you imagine? He had no idea what it meant. His face was all furrowed up as if he was trying to figure it out."

The light in her eyes reached out, caressed him, drew him to look both without and within.

"What does that mean, Katya? That he'd never even *heard* the concept of salvation before? Is that really the truth?"

"All but two of the city's churches have been closed for the past fifty years," Katya told him. "Two churches in a provincial capital of over one hundred thousand inhabitants."

He shook his head. "It's one thing to hear about it, another thing to see it."

"You couldn't belong to both a church and the Party," Katya went on. "You couldn't be seen in church, not even for a friend's wedding, and hold a government job. You couldn't go to church and apply for a government pension. To be a practicing Christian meant that at retirement age you received no social security, no payments of any kind.

"If you joined a church in spite of all this, your children were ostracized. Your home was threatened—remember, there was a terrible housing shortage. Some church members were simply tossed out on the street with nowhere to go. There was no social safety net for a believer. Your requests for anything—a new home, a passport, sometimes even a driver's license—were automatically turned down. You couldn't teach. You couldn't study at a university. You couldn't hold a management job or be an engineer or work at a sensitive position. You were always suspect. You were liable to be arrested at any time, charged with sedition and sentenced to long terms in prisons too horrible to describe. You were persecuted, Jeffrey. You and your family. You weren't wanted. The Communists did their best to grind the church and all believers into dust."

"This really happened," he said quietly.

"Just because it wasn't your family or your backyard doesn't make it any less real, Jeffrey. These are real people with real needs who have never even heard that Jesus Christ is the Son of God."

CHAPTER

11

Their plane to Poland was delayed, a common occurrence according to Alexander. Jeffrey had ample time to see Katya off. When they arrived at her departure gate, she lifted her face for a kiss. "I've really enjoyed the trip, Jeffrey. It was very difficult at times, but I'm glad I came."

"Too short, though."

"Anything that is not for forever is too short," she replied.

"I wish you really meant that."

Katya enfolded him in a fierce embrace, mumbling into his chest, "I wish . . ."

"You wish what?"

"Sometimes I wish for too much," she said, releasing him and turning swiftly away. "Goodbye, Jeffrey. Have a safe trip. I will wait for your return."

When he returned to the Hamburg airport's first-class lounge, Alexander said, "You must forgive me this morning. I do not feel quite myself."

"You've had a pretty bad shock," Jeffrey replied.

"More than you perhaps will ever understand," he agreed. "It appears that some things one is not ever able to completely leave behind."

"I don't understand."

"No matter." Alexander cleared the air with a weary wave. "Let us change the subject, shall we?"

"Fine with me." Jeffrey allowed the smile to break loose. "I have some good news."

"Excellent. I cannot recall a time in recent years when good news would have been more welcome." Alexander made a visible effort to pull himself together. "I take it that this beaming visage of yours is not due solely to your departing lady friend."

Jeffrey shook his head. "I made a buy." He related the story of the two pieces.

Alexander listened in silence, then replied, "And on your first trip. Remarkable."

"I couldn't say for sure if they were genuine articles."

"Of course not. There is always the risk that the safe is decorated with stones of paste and tinsel. But you explained this and hinged payment upon authentication." He gave Jeffrey a respectful look. "I am surprised. There is very little these days that surprises me. And I am most pleased."

"Thank you."

"It is I who must offer the thanks. And I believe it is now time for me to divulge some matters of my own." Alexander sipped at a glass of water. "I am indeed grateful for the patience you have shown. It is most unusual for a man of your years to be willing to wait for a explanation about mystery trips to unknown lands."

"I figured you would tell me when it was time."

"Indeed. And that time has now arrived." Alexander inspected him solemnly. "I do not need to tell you how confidential these matters must remain."

"No," Jeffrey replied, his voice rock-steady. "You do not."

Alexander gave his head a single nod. "Very well." He looked around the almost-empty room, removed a silver tube from his pocket, unscrewed the cap, drew out a slender Davidoff cigar. "I hope you don't mind."

"You know I don't."

The lounge steward bustled over and lit the cigar with a long wooden match. Alexander nodded his thanks, waited for the man to depart, then said, "Approximately one third of our purchases come from the open market—auctions or public sales or through other dealers, usually in this latter instance from other countries. One third come from my own acquaintances and friends, built up over the years. And the final third, the source upon which we rely the most, is the East."

"The East?"

"Several places, but all channeled through one man. A relative of mine—ours, I should say. He escaped with me to London, then decided to return to Poland."

"Uncle Gregor?" Jeffrey made round eyes. "The priest?"

"He is not a priest, nor has he ever been. He is what is known as a lay brother, which means that while he does not reside in a monastery, he has made a formal commitment to live a life of service and poverty. Gregor is a most remarkable man, as you will soon discover. He lives according to rules which I have never fathomed. Yet I admire him tremendously, and rely on him completely. You should as well, Jeffrey. You may trust him with anything."

"Uncle Gregor deals in antiques?" This did not fit with what little the family had told of his long-lost relative. "I don't understand."

"I don't expect you to. Not yet. I will ask you to wait until we arrive in Cracow, and see for yourself how our arrangement operates. It would take too long to explain here, and even if I did, you would still not understand until you had seen it for yourself."

Jeffrey nodded. "So these long trips you make are to Poland?"

"Some of them, yes. I choose to cloak all of my trips under the same veil of secrecy, so that none draws more attention than any other. But yes, I do spend a considerable amount of time in Poland and some of the neighboring lands." Alexander smiled. "You have recently spoken with Gregor, by the way."

"When—" He made round eyes. "The blessing?"

"I beg your pardon?"

"The man I told you about, the one who knew my name and left the message that the shipment was ready." Jeffrey smiled at the memory. "He blessed me before he hung up."

"Yes, well, Gregor is known to do such things." Alexander drew on his cigar and emitted a long plume of smoke before continuing. "It is important for you to understand that while there, I wear two entirely different labels. Or have, so long as the Communist regime was in power. So much has changed in recent months that my new roles have not yet been defined. But my former status I must take time to explain now, if you would please be so kind as to bear with me."

Kantor paused to sip from his glass. "First of all, it is important for you to know that under the Communists it was illegal to export anything from Poland that was more than forty years old. To be precise, the law read that nothing made before 1947 could leave the country. But as with any totalitarian government—and believe me, young man, no matter what guise the Communists may have operated under, they were true totalitarians—the concentration of power within a few hands meant that *any* law could be circumvented if it suited the power-holders. The question was, how to make the power-holders see that my interests coincided with their own.

"By establishing this export law, Poland sought to preserve its historical heritage, or what was left after both the Nazis and the Soviets had ransacked the country from end to end. The problem was, only so many items of furniture or paintings or jewelry could be purchased and housed in a museum. And since there was no access to the outside markets, the prices for Polish antiques was set by the internal market. And this market, young man, was barely above starvation level.

"The summer before the Communist regime was toppled, a doctor in the capital city of Warsaw earned the equivalent of forty dollars a month. He or she survived by receiving gifts of food and services from clients who sought preferential treatment and medicines that were not out-of-date. That small example illustrates how close to collapse the occupying forces had brought my homeland. I could give you a thousand others, but you will see these for yourself soon enough. Forty years of Soviet oppression is not going to be wiped out in just a few months.

"As for antiques, the market barely existed at all. Pieces that caught the government's eye—which meant anyone from a museum director to a greedy official—were sometimes purchased. But just as likely the owner would be questioned as to how he or she came to own such an item of capitalist wealth, and then it would be requisitioned. End of story.

"The result was that few pieces ever made it to the open market, and when they did they were available at prices that to our eyes would scarcely be believed. As recently as three years ago, I walked through an antique store in Cracow and spotted items that were selling for less than *one-fiftieth* of the price they would bring in the West. A nineteenth-century Biedermeier cabinet for one hundred dollars. An eighteenth-century Florentine writing desk for about twice that.

"Again, you must remember, prices were so low because most people were so poor, and the nation repeatedly suffered from economic turmoil. Money was set aside for purchasing food when shop shelves were empty, not luxuries like antiques. And the fortunate few with extra money usually desired something new, something manufactured, something that appeared vaguely Western. There was simply no market for old furniture. None."

Alexander rolled his cigar around the ashtray until its tip was a brightly smoldering cone. "More than twenty years ago, I began advising the Polish government on items of national and cultural heritage. I will not bandy words with you, young man. I despise the Communists and their Soviet masters for what they have done to my homeland. But I am a Pole, and as you will soon discover, the Poles are some of the most patriotic folk on earth. They love their country, and it is only with great agony and despair that they will break with the land of their birth. I began this work as a means of maintaining some contact with Poland, and to help preserve a few of the remaining historically important antiques. Five years later Gregor developed his brilliant scheme. Not me, you see. Gregor.

"For over two decades now I have sought both inside and outside Poland to discover items that are closely linked to our history. Jewelry, paintings, ceramics, porcelain, amber, drawings, and furniture. Limited funds were placed at my disposal. I refused to either requisition pieces or identify my sources inside or outside of Poland. Inside the country I paid a fair price—what to the seller no doubt was a fortune. Outside Poland I bought on behalf of the Polish nation, if necessary using my own funds.

"In return for this, the Polish government began granting me export licenses for high quality pieces that I felt would fetch handsome prices in the West. I have been scrupulous in my dealings with the government. Absolutely scrupulous. I take out nothing that could even vaguely be described as a part of our heritage."

He puffed a few times on his cigar before continuing. "But there is so much that remains in our land from the centuries of invading armies and occupying forces. So very much. The history of our nation is not a happy one, and for a long and tragic time Poland even ceased to exist as an independent country. It is these items in which I deal, foreign-made goods if you will, and with which I have managed to create this little empire."

It was long after dark by the time their plane touched down in Cracow, yet even so the transition was very harsh, very sudden. In the space of less than an hour, the Lufthansa plane had transported them from the efficient glitz of a new West German terminal to the dusty haphazard grayness of Socialism. The Cracow Airport was little more than a dilapidated warehouse with ugly appendages and gave no concern whatsoever to artistic appeal or passenger comfort.

Alexander was in his usual querulous bad humor upon their arrival. He passed through customs in utter silence, allowing Jeffrey to assist with his baggage. He then proceeded through the terminal and past the unshaven men offering taxis and hotels, and walked out into the night without saying a word.

A slender young man with jet-black hair stepped from the shadows, gave a formal half bow toward Alexander, and said something Jeffrey could not understand. Alexander replied with a brief word, then said to Jeffrey, "Our driver. His name is Tomek. Almost no English, I'm afraid."

Tomek met Jeffrey's gaze, solemnly shook his hand, motioned for them to remain where they were, and disappeared into the darkness. Beyond the airport's perimeter there were almost no lights.

"Things are certainly much simpler now since the Communists have been removed," Alexander murmured, staring out at nothing.

"What things?"

"Oh, logistics for one. Visas took a month to obtain without connections or bribes or both. Airport arrival formalities took two hours, departures up to five." He wiped a shaky hand across his forehead. "Waiting for taxis that never arrived. Being thrown out of hotels because a powerful Party official arrived unannounced with forty of his closest friends. Changing money illegally because the black market paid ten times the official rate. Waiting in line half a day to purchase a train ticket, only to find once boarding that your place had been sold to three other people as well. Standing in crowded train gangways choked with smoke, having your journey extended by hours because your train had been sidetracked to allow a freight train right-of-way. Shortages of everything and lines everywhere. Public drunkenness wherever you looked."

Car headlights appeared out of the gloom and stopped. Tomek led them over to a relatively new, boxy-looking car called a Polonez. Alexander allowed himself to be settled into the backseat, then leaned his head against the neckrest and closed his eyes with a sigh.

Once the luggage was stowed and Jeffrey was seated beside Alexander, he asked, "Are you all right?"

"I'm afraid not." Under the passing streetlights his skin held a sickly pallor. "This trip appears to have affected me more than usual."

The driver asked a question. Alexander answered curtly. To Jeffrey he said, "We must stop by my cousin's for a few moments."

"Shouldn't we be getting you to bed?"

"Perhaps, but Gregor is expecting us, and I was unable to reach him prior to my departure. It will be a short visit, I assure you."

Jeffrey could make out little of the city. Once the airport complex was left behind, the distance between streetlights lengthened until they became glowing islands in a sea of black.

After a long stretch of silent travel, Alexander stirred himself, lifted his head and said to Jeffrey, "One word of warning. Gregor's health is not the best, as you will soon see. He suffers from some ailment of the joints—my guess is severe arthritis. You must be careful not to overtire him."

"All right."

"The truth is, I don't know what it is exactly that ails my iron-willed cousin. He refuses to tell me, no doubt for fear that I would make a fuss. Quite rightly, I might add. I am fairly positive that his condition would be treatable in the

West, but has not received proper attention here. He went in for an operation some ten years ago and came out with the most wretched limp."

"He won't leave to get medical care?"

"Gregor will not leave Poland for any reason whatsoever. You will find, if you work with him awhile, that my cousin can be the most exasperatingly stubborn old goat on earth." The car slowed and stopped at the curb. "Perhaps that is why I care for him as I do."

Gregor lived in a building that Jeffrey put down at first glance as an upscale slum. Even under the cloak of darkness, large bare patches of molding concrete lay exposed where the plaster had flaked off. Wires crawled up the building, held at intervals by twisted metal bands nailed into the wall.

Gregor buzzed them through the front entrance and was waiting on the second-floor landing when they arrived. "Welcome, my dear cousin, welcome."

"Hello, Gregor," Alexander replied, making no effort to mask his fatigue. "I hope you are well."

Gregor took Alexander's hand, grasped his other shoulder, and kissed him soundly on both cheeks. "You had your usual flight, I take it."

"Horrible," Alexander agreed, and turned toward where Jeffrey waited two steps behind him. "May I introduce you to Piotr's grandson. Jeffrey, this is Gregor Kantor."

"A pleasure I have waited a lifetime to realize," Gregor said, his English perfect yet heavily accented. He grasped Jeffrey's hand in a firm grip.

Gregor possessed the same regal features and strong gray eyes as his cousin. Yet his gaze held a gentler light, and his mouth a greater tendency to smile. "Come in, both of you."

"Thank you," Alexander replied, motioning Jeffrey forward. "I believe I shall remain standing."

Gregor lived in the smallest apartment Jeffrey had ever seen. But after a few days in Cracow—after seeing entire families eating and sleeping and living in one room, after seeing buildings with one single stinking toilet for an entire hall of overcrowded apartments, after visiting complexes with a thousand families housed per building and twenty buildings lined up in rows like giant concrete monoliths—Jeffrey changed his mind. At least Gregor had his own toilet and heat and a window that shut and a gas stove and electricity. But Jeffrey did not know about all these things his first night in Cracow. When he walked into what he thought was the apartment's front hall and then realized it was the entire place he thought, I'd go crazy in here.

Gregor read his expression and replied with a smile. "I would invite you to make yourself at home, but as you can see I don't have the room. All I can offer you is a chair and a cup of coffee."

Alexander refused to move beyond the entryway. "Your phone isn't working again."

"Yes, that is true." His gentle smile urged Jeffrey toward the room's only comfortable chair. "But I do have hot water. If I have to choose between the two, I believe I would rather have a nice bath and meet personally with whomever I can't call in a clean skin."

Alexander said to Jeffrey, "My cousin remains in this apartment in order to embarrass me."

"Nonsense. I stay here because it is central and meets my needs." He moved around so as to stand and look down on Jeffrey. With each of his right steps his body listed heavily, throwing his left hip out and arching his entire frame. He straightened, smiled down at Jeffrey, said, "I have long since learned never to expect a civil word from Alexander after a flight."

Gregor was a frail replica of his cousin. He was as heavy as Alexander, and as tall, yet gave the impression of being scarcely contained within his frame. Jeffrey had a fleeting image of a strong breeze blowing him from his body, taking him to a place where those glowing eyes and warm look and gentle smile better belonged.

He remained standing over Jeffrey for a long moment, said, "He is the mirror image of his grandfather, don't you think?"

"My memory fails me at the moment."

"You must have noticed it. Did you have an opportunity to know your grandfather, Jeffrey?"

"Not so well. He died when I was still a kid."

"There. His voice even sounds like Piotr's."

"Perhaps."

"It is most certain. My dear boy, your grandfather was one of the finest men I have ever known, and I have known many people." He smiled down at him. "I am sure he would be most proud of you. Would you like a cup of coffee?"

"If it's no trouble."

"None at all. I was just preparing one for myself." He moved behind a ragged-edged curtain to what Jeffrey realized must be the kitchen alcove and pantry and, by the looks of things, a very cramped bathroom.

Alexander said, "You booked us into the Holiday Inn, I hope."

"Certainly not. I booked you into the Cracovia, which is just around the block, as you well know."

"It is also a testament to the Communist doctrine of minimizing taste and maximizing discomfort in their hotels."

"You weren't so choosy when they first opened it twenty years ago."

"At the time it was the only hotel approaching decency south of Warsaw. And they have not changed a thing since. Not even the sheets."

"Don't be absurd. How do you take your coffee, Jeffrey?"

"Black is fine, thanks."

"Such nice manners." Gregor limped back into the main room bearing a steaming glass with no handle. He carried it by wrapping his fingers around the upper edge, above the level of the coffee. Gingerly Jeffrey accepted it, holding it as Gregor had. He started to raise it to his mouth, then stopped when he saw a quarter-inch of coffee grounds floating on the surface.

Gregor, who had already turned to draw up a straight-backed chair, did not see Jeffrey lower the glass. "Next time upon your arrival I shall ask you to come visit me by yourself while my cousin keeps his ill temper downstairs in the car. He won't even allow me to meet him at the airport."

"I won't allow it because you make a scene when I refuse to submit to a ride in that deathtrap you call an automobile."

"There are a dozen better ways to spend money than paying Tomek to act as driver for the entire time of your stay."

"I have long since stopped trying to tell you what to do with your earnings. I suggest you do the same." Alexander pushed himself away from the doorjamb. "Come, Jeffrey. I am tired. We mustn't keep my cousin from his mole-like existence."

Gregor was not the least bit put out by their abrupt departure. "Yes, go on, my dear boy. We can become acquainted another time, when my cousin is not such a bother."

"Sorry about the coffee."

"Nonsense. I was just about to make a cup for myself."

He took Jeffrey's hand, leaned closer, and peered at him with bright gray eyes. "Alexander has told me quite a bit about you, and now that I meet you I see that he was not exaggerating. I am indeed glad that you have inherited more than just your grandfather's fine looks. I am even happier that my cousin has finally managed to find an assistant he can trust."

A voice called up from the front door. "Coming, Jeffrey?"

Gregor patted Jeffrey's shoulder. "Go on, dear boy. We shall have ample time to come to know each other. Of that I am sure."

The Hotel Cracovia took up an entire block. It faced the National Museum—the hotel's only redeeming feature, according to Alexander. In too soft an undertone to be heard by the sullenly inattentive staff, he described the hotel as typical of Communist hospitality. Jeffrey thought it was just plain tacky.

The lobby walls were one shade off blood red. The carpets were a mishmash of squares and floral patterns. The ceiling was water-stained and peeling. Light was supplied by military-like rows of hanging orange glass-and-brass globes, about the same size and aesthetic quality as a beer keg.

The guest rooms had beds nailed to one wall and a long table that served as both desk and television stand attached to the other. The bathrooms were narrow enough, as Alexander put it before closing his door on the world, to do everything at once. The mirror was set at the perfect height for Jeffrey to inspect his navel.

As Jeffrey unpacked his single valise, he wondered about calling Katya. He placed a call through the hotel operator, who warned it might take as long as two days for a connection, then fell asleep waiting for the phone to ring.

CHAPTER

12

Breakfast took place in a cheerless, institutional-style room. Alexander was already nibbling absently at a piece of bread. He waved Jeffrey to the seat across from him. "I hope you slept well."

"Okay, thanks. How about you?"

"I have found that as I grow older, sleep becomes a rare comfort at times," Alexander replied. "I spent most of the night chasing that most elusive prey, then found myself being chased in turn by ghosts I could not see, only hear."

Jeffrey inspected his boss, not pleased with what he saw. The man looked positively haggard. "Maybe you'd be better off spending the day in bed."

"Perhaps you are right. It shall certainly be no easier to find by the light of day what eluded me all last night. But at least I can rest." As the waiter approached their table, he asked, "What will you have?"

Once breakfast was ordered, Alexander said, "So. Tell me what you thought of my cousin Gregor."

"I don't think I've ever met anybody like him before."

"That is most certainly the case."

"He sure is enthusiastic."

Alexander smiled for the first time that morning. "My thoughts exactly. As a matter of fact, I once accused him of being overly enthusiastic about a life that had little to delight in. Do you know what my dear cousin said?"

"I can't imagine."

"He replied that the word enthusiastic came from two Greek words, *en* and *theos*. Together the words mean to be one with the Divine. He then thanked me for the nicest compliment anyone had ever paid him."

"Which meant, mind your own business."

"In so many words. But my cousin did not stop there. He went on to say that I lived on the basis that comfort was essential to a good life. He, on the other hand, only needed something to be enthusiastic about. Something that would draw him closer to his Maker."

Jeffrey thought it over. "Did he find it?"

"Something to be enthusiastic about? That, my young friend, you must decide for yourself."

"I can't thank you enough for this opportunity," Jeffrey said. "All the opportunities, for that matter."

"The first opportunity—the job itself—I suppose was in part a gift, and for that you are most welcome," Alexander replied. "But you have earned all the others, and for this I too am grateful."

"Would you mind telling me why I was hired?"

"When so many local antique specialists would have given their best dozen years on this earth to become an associate in a Mount Street salon?" Alexander nodded. "Because before such a person arrived on my doorstep, their own self-interests would have already been cast in the fires of greed and ambition, and then honed to a killing edge."

"I think I see."

"They would have had ample time to learn the lessons followed by most people in this trade, concepts such as loyalty to no one but themselves. Or the belief that honesty is a commodity to be traded just like that slow-moving chair in the back room. Or that duty is a word that went out with sabers and cavalry charges."

"And with me you could start out fresh."

"At least so far as the antiques trade was concerned, yes. My primary wish was to obtain the services of an intelligent, honest, trainable assistant. So long as most of the actual purchasing fell into my hands, you would have ample time to study and to learn. Time that you have used well, I must say. I am most pleased with the manner in which you have filled your idle hours."

"I wouldn't call them idle."

"Just as I said. You came to know each piece in the shop so well that you fooled even the best of them. I have heard some rather dreadful comments about you from the vultures that frequent auctions, Jeffrey. There could be no greater praise than to have them see you as a threat sufficient to make them take notice." He examined Jeffrey from beneath his lofty eyebrows. "Most certainly you've been approached about how to line your own pockets while stabbing me and my shop in the back."

"I'd never do that."

"Of course you wouldn't. That is precisely my point. No doubt you've also received your share of offers in the meantime. Perhaps even a senior associate position in a major auction house?"

"A few," Jeffrey admitted.

"Don't take them. You're not ready yet. When you are, when you can buy as well as you now sell, there is a certain shop on Mount Street that awaits you."

"That's what I'm hoping," he confessed.

"I won't tell you not to get your hopes up, Jeffrey. I am too practical to waste precious time on such nonsense. And I will not describe this as a test, for if I were not already sure of the outcome I would not be inviting you along. No, I want you to simply keep in mind that this is first and foremost a learning experience."

"I understand."

Alexander leaned over the table. "You will need to come up to the room with me before you go. I want you to carry my money belt. It contains ten thousand dollars. You are to carry that much every time you go for a buy. Many people will demand a cash advance, and it is important that you be able to acquire something valuable without delay, to ensure that it is not sold to someone else before you can return. Before you go in for a buy, slip a couple of thousand into your pocket. If you need additional funds, go back out to the car. Don't let them know you are carrying more than what you have in your pocket. Remember, a thousand dollars is still a small fortune in Poland—more than many people earn in a year. And keep the money in your belt around to your back in case thieves search you."

"Things are that bad here?"

"Most of the people we deal with are repeat clients, and Gregor knows almost all of the others. But don't take chances. If they think you have money and are vulnerable, they may decide honesty is too expensive a virtue."

"I meant, things in general."

"Things in general, as you say, are disastrous. The police are increasingly ineffective, and thieves know this. Poland is becoming a lawless land. The last time I was here, I decided to take a walk around my Warsaw hotel. On the first corner were addicts moaning for their drug. On the next, Rumanian refugees begging for pennies. On the next, two men beating each other's faces in. On the next was a police station with the men lounging out front. On the opposite corner was a church with its door locked and windows barred. At four o'clock in the afternoon."

He glanced at his watch. "Gregor will be expecting you in about a half an hour. He'll have been up since the crack of dawn, as always. You are sure you will be all right without me today?"

"I suppose so. I'd rather have you come, but you really don't look up to it."

"Which is exactly how I feel. This trip is not going as I had intended, but life seldom does." Alexander pushed himself from his chair with a visible effort. Jeffrey hurried over and steadied him with a hand on his shoulder. "Thank you. I shall rely on your young strength today. Give Gregor my regards, and tell him to teach you well."

"He is not ill, is he?" Gregor asked when Jeffrey explained Alexander's absence.

"Not really. Just exhausted." He related the happenings of the previous two days. "I have the feeling that it might have something to do with it."

"Ah." Gregor nodded his agreement. "I am so sorry to hear this. And on your very first trip as well."

"Why is he like this?"

"The reasons are for him to say, my dear boy. They are his memories, not mine. All I can say is that your experiences in Schwerin have brought his worst nightmares to life." Gregor began briskly preparing for departure. "That is enough on that, I should think. Shall we be off? We have much to do today.

"Despite what Alexander refers to as my apartment's minuscule proportions," Gregor said as they left the apartment, "it has several major advantages. It is a fifteen-minute walk to the old town, and the building has only five floors and thirty-seven apartments. That is nothing compared to the monstrosities that the Communists have erected. You will be visiting a few of them."

"I can hardly wait," Jeffrey said, casting a backward glance at the building. He took in the dull gray exterior, the flaking windowpanes, the crumbling front steps, the dusty strip of unadorned earth fronting the curb, and wondered what a disadvantaged place must look like.

"My building was erected in the fifties," Gregor went on, making his rolling way down the sidewalk. "At that time, buildings were still being made from brick and concrete rather than mortar blocks and steel. As a result this building is insulated, you see. My walls do not sweat in the cold. Nor do they freeze in the dead of winter, as happens in some of the newer buildings—the interior walls, I am speaking of. Sometimes I feel a little guilty not residing as most people do here, but as you can see my health is unfortunately not the best. One winter in such a place and I would be immobilized for life."

He stopped in front of a stubby car the color of old mustard. Jeffrey looked it over, tapped the plastic hood. It was a square cigar box on skinny tires, designed to grow old swiftly and fall apart. Gingerly he pushed down on his side; the car rocked like a boat in high seas. No shocks at all.

"Don't you think we would be better off having Alexander's driver take us around?"

"I wouldn't dream of such a thing," Gregor replied, climbing in and shutting his door. It bounced back open. He reached out with both hands and slammed it into submission. He inserted the key and ground the ignition. Jeffrey sighed in defeat, slid onto the narrow seat. The car sounded like a motorized sewing machine. "This is an East German car, a Trabant," Gregor said above the engine's whining putter. "In Poland they call them Hoennecker's Revenge. Hoennecker was the former ruler of East Germany."

"Back in the U.S., people put quarters in motel beds and

don't get as good a ride as this," Jeffrey replied. He hung on to the door strap with both hands, tried to lift himself over the worst of the bumps. He turned his head as a bus coughed out a vast cloud of black smoke that engulfed their car. "Do they have a nick-name for buses?"

Gregor nodded. "Skunks."

They left Cracow, turned onto a small secondary road, and began making their way through open farmland. The fields were verdant green, the sky a baked blue. Jeffrey rolled down his window and inhaled the fresh air.

They passed a smattering of run-down houses that gradually condensed and formed a small village. Jeffrey remarked, "It seems as if the main color of communism wasn't red. It was gray."

"The hardest lie to accept is one told time and time again," Gregor replied. "I would hear the Communists lie on the evening news, and some evenings I would just cry out for my country's pain."

Jeffrey eyed row after row of sagging sad-faced houses. "Why didn't they ever paint anything?"

"Ask a thousand people, my boy, and you'll receive a thousand reasons, all of them true. For the larger housing projects, there was no need to keep up appearances because all the property was state-owned. Resources went to new projects, not maintaining old ones. Buildings erected after the war with one bathroom for ten or eleven apartments—which was a vast improvement on no indoor plumbing at all—have remained exactly as they were built.

"Those families who wanted to improve their apartments had to fight against a system that controlled all supplies of *everything*. Paint and brushes, for example, had to be ordered through requisition, and could take *years* to obtain. What was received was used indoors on their apartment. No one but the state laid claim to the building as a whole, and the state's attention was always elsewhere. So the buildings were usually left to rot.

"Most village homes remained privately owned in Poland, but here again the supply problems remained catastrophic. Added to that was the lack of money, the people's sense of resignation over their plight, and a desire to blend in with their surroundings. A well-maintained private dwelling would attract the worst type of attention—thieves or tax inspectors."

Cobblestone streets and gray buildings gave way to a small central plaza. Two carts piled high with vegetables and pulled by bony horses with drooping necks stood in front of the only store whose sign Jeffrey could understand—Bar. They continued to the village's other side and halted in front of an old farmhouse.

Gregor stared through the front windshield at the house's dilapidated condition. "The Communists did not choose to give up power in Poland. They were *forced* to leave because they led the nation to economic ruin. Worse than that. They led the nation by an economic lie, and generations of Poles have paid the price for this lie."

From the front, the farmhouse was almost smothered by a veritable forest of dahlias. They began around ankle-height up by the gate, and mounted steadily until arriving at the low-sloping roof.

As Jeffrey started to climb from the car, he was stopped by a hand on his shoulder. "Before we go in, I need to know how much Alexander has told you of the way we work."

"Just the bare bones." When they had returned upstairs after breakfast that morning, Alexander had outlined their purchase strategy. Gregor was responsible for both locating the items and making the initial check; he knew enough about antiques by now for him to be trusted to weed out any obvious fakes. Any purchases that had to be made immediately, in order to keep them from falling into other buyers' hands, he also took care of and stored for Alexander's arrival.

Purchases were concluded immediately on the basis of paying a fair price by Polish standards. Once the piece was sold, the full sales price less commissions—often a fortune by Polish standards—was passed on through Gregor. Gregor received half of the commission less expenses, plus an unidentified sum from the shop's total profit.

"Prices here are still excellent by Western standards, but nothing compared to what we found in the past. This is especially true with the smaller items."

"Because they can be smuggled easier," Jeffrey guessed.

"Exactly. The border guards are daily becoming more lax and open to bribery. People are taking their heirlooms out of closets and into the antique stores, and receiving prices that mount daily. The price that was unthinkable yesterday would not buy a bent spoon tomorrow.

"Nowadays people with something to sell are being approached by strangers from all over," Gregor continued. "The Italians are busy buying up everything they can get their hands on at rock-bottom prices. Meanwhile, they have lawyers who are lobbying the new parliament to change the export laws."

"We have new competition, then," Jeffrey said.

"Yes and no. Most of these strangers are sharks. They look to pay pennies for what they can sell for fortunes. The Polish people know this. Still, their families are hungry, their children are sick and needing medicine, many have lost their jobs. They hold and they hold and they hold, because this precious item is often the only real savings they have, the only security against trouble, the only hope for their old age. But in times as bad as these, sometimes it only takes one more small problem, one more calamity for them to give up and sell. When that happens, they may act out of panic and sell to whomever gets there first."

"Things are that bad right now?"

"Horrible. You will see that in your travels, I am sorry to say."

"So I should make an initial payment equal to what the Italians would pay as a total, is that right?"

Gregor gave him an approving look. "Alexander said that you were quick to catch on. Yes, that is exactly what I want you to do. And if it is something we can fit in the car, we carry it away with us. If not, I arrange to have a truck come by the same evening that we make our visit. These people are hungry, Jeffrey. They may decide to sell the item twice. It is best to remove such temptations as swiftly as possible."

"So where do we store it until it's time for shipment? A warehouse?"

Gregor shook his head. "Warehouses have become the favorite target of gangs. No, we have worked out a safer and a quieter place than a warehouse, Alexander and I. Someplace where we can keep whatever pieces I find and purchase before his arrival. Tomek works for me when Alexander is not here. He owns a truck that he and his son use to transport all the articles we purchase."

Gregor led the way around back to a swept yard made muddy by the morning's heavy dew. A host of tame ducks greeted their arrival with apprehensive glances and worried quacks. A truly ancient dog made do with a couple of wheezy barks, then watched in silence as they progressed through the ducks and chickens and mud.

An old woman pushed aside the draped cloth that served as her screen door, spoke what clearly was a greeting to Gregor, and led them inside. The house was built for people of her height; Jeffrey had to remain in a perpetual stoop. The ceiling beams were about five and a half feet high; the woman passed under them easily.

She was very heavy, standing almost as wide as she was tall. Her face had taken on the shape of a featureless circle and the color of unbaked dough. Her arms were thick and wobbled as she walked, her legs massive and encased in several layers of socks and flesh-tone support hose. She wore three sweaters and an apron over her faded housedress.

"I am so very sorry," she said through Gregor. "The house is too small, I am too poor; you must be used to so much nicer things than what I am able to offer."

"Everything is just fine," he said, wondering what on earth there might be of interest. The house was furnished with either rough-hewn pieces made from lumber scraps or just plain junk.

She ushered them into her minuscule sitting room, where Jeffrey found a table loaded with food—sliced ham, roast chicken, devilled eggs, fresh rolls, homemade pickles, vegetable salad, and two cakes. She said through Gregor, "Won't you have a little tea?"

Jeffrey whispered, "This is for us?"

"This is Polish hospitality," Gregor replied.

"We just had breakfast."

"It doesn't matter. We are her guests, and in Poland you offer your guests the very best of what you have."

The old woman stood with hands crossed in front of her stomach and watched them sit and begin loading their plates. She poured them tea and said through Gregor, "It's nothing, really. Just a second breakfast."

Gregor smiled. "The fact is, she has been preparing for several days for our arrival. She is not a wealthy person, as you can see. But whatever she has, she will devote to hospitality. It is the Polish way."

"Please tell her the food is great."

"Nothing would thrill her more than to see her American

guest take seconds," Gregor said.

Jeffrey ate and examined the cramped surroundings. The walls were covered with a continual design that had been painted over the cracked limewash and decorated with religious prints—saints, crucifixes, photographs of icons. The floor was ragged carpet laid on ancient linoleum. Each room had a single bulb for illumination. The light filtering through handmade windowpanes was cloudy and vague. The entire house was neat as a pin and gave the impression of a snug little cave, saved from being claustrophobic only by its cleanliness and the woman's genuine smile.

When they could eat no more and refused her offer of yet another piece of cake or another glass of tea, reluctantly she allowed them to stand and follow her back into the narrow hall. She stopped at the entrance to the cottage's other room and said, "My husband was hit by a truck and killed last year. He was a victim of Poland's greatest killer—vodka. It was the driver who had been drinking, not my husband. He had never given in to the temptation, may the good Lord bless his soul. It was so strange to hear of his death from the official, when the house still smelled from his morning coffee and his shirts still hung from the line. Now I am alone, and my daughter has three babies and a husband who has been laid off. I have hoarded things I never needed for far too long."

Jeffrey followed Gregor's lead and stood patiently, nodding to her words, wondering why she continued to smile as she spoke, feeling the onset of a serious crick in his bent-over neck.

With a theatrical flourish she swept the curtain door aside and said through Gregor, "My daughter's room."

Jeffrey stepped through the doorway, looked around, and laughed out loud.

Gregor stepped up beside him. "She wants to know if anything is the matter."

"No, nothing. It was just a little unexpected, that's all."

Opposite the doorway stood a cabinet, so heavily carved as to make the exterior appear like a pile of unsorted sculptures—vases and grapes and bas-relief statues and hanging flowers and gods' faces and framed designs—all jumbled into something only a museum curator could love.

Gregor moved up beside him, said, "In the late seventeenth century, one quarter of the students at the major Italian universities were the children of Polish gentry. That particular generation transformed the country's tastes, as you can see. They drew it toward the ornate foppery of early Italian Renaissance style. This is a perfect example of the result."

"Horrible," Jeffrey decided.

"Perhaps. Alexander would certainly agree with you. But the last time we came upon such a piece, he said he knew of a dozen curators who would positively drool at the news."

Beyond the cabinet was a bed. It rested on a simple wooden frame, but around this was a second frame the likes of which Jeffrey had never seen. The floorposts were a foot square at the base, rising to carved Grecian urns that sprouted tall flowering plants. Each of the posts appeared to have been carved from one solid log, and supported an upper bedframe carved and gilded to appear like golden grapes hanging from a leafy vine. The carving on the headboard alternated between pastoral scenes and royal coats-of-arms.

"A young prince's bed," Gregor guessed, coming up beside him. "Remarkable."

"How did it get here?" Jeffrey ran a hand across the headboard, could not find any trace of a seam.

"That, my dear boy, is a story we shall most probably never know." Gregor turned back to where the lady waited in the doorway. "I'll tell her that you are interested in taking it, then, shall I?"

"This belongs in a museum," Jeffrey said, then corrected himself. "If it's real, that is."

"Oh, I imagine it is. Thankfully, most of the items I locate are authentic, especially ones of this size. Although the Communists had visions of making themselves the new royal class, with all sorts of special privileges, they had few resources for making replicas of anything. What was available usually went for massive statues of Lenin."

After leaving the farmhouse they drove slowly on past the village. The roads were narrow and in terrible condition. Jeffrey maintained his death's grip on the door strap and enjoyed his tour of the countryside.

The evidence of poverty was starkly vivid. No one he saw

wore well-fitting clothes, much less anything new. The people themselves looked worn down to the point of absolute exhaustion. Even the children they passed had pinched, chiseled features and dark shadows under their eyes.

Almost all the farm work he saw was done by stoop labor. Women tilled fields with hand hoes, wearing headkerchiefs and high rubber boots. Men walked beside horse-drawn plows or wagons filled with produce or manure or wood.

There was very little car traffic on the roads. Trucks and buses wobbled along on uneven axles and belched deep clouds of smoke. People rode bicycles or walked along the road's edge.

It appeared that everyone he passed had some physical ailment—a pronounced limp, a disjointed shoulder, a bent spine, a missing limb, a scar. When they passed a group of people standing together or stopped for a traffic light, he watched intently but saw no smiles. All the faces looked closed to him, screwed down and clamped shut against a world that was always hostile, always a risk, never open or friendly or helpful or safe. All the voices drifting in through his open window sounded tired. Tragic. Resigned.

The village where their second meeting was scheduled was much like the first—a series of winding streets that led nowhere.

"I keep looking for a center of town," Jeffrey said.

"The war destroyed many towns' central structures," Gregor explained. "The Communists then came in and built endless rows of functional housing. This was vastly cheaper than restoring the grand old structures. The Communists were very big on functionalism. Beautification was not a word in their vocabulary."

He pulled up in front of a split-beamed log cabin, the spaces between the wood chinked with spattered concrete.

Jeffrey did not open his door. "They have an antique?"

"I have done business with them several times," Gregor replied. "Perhaps the pieces came from a friend or a relative or someone else who did not want to risk having his face seen."

Gregor opened his door and stood. When Jeffrey joined him, he said, "At the same time, it could very well have come from a midnight raid on the local manor. Flaming torches carried by a mob attacking in rage and panic against an official who had sold his soul to the Nazis, with the sound of the Soviet tanks rumbling in the distance. Quite a bit of that happened as well. If the booty was small, it might have been buried in the cowshed. If large, it may have spent the past forty years as one wall of the chicken coop.

"Even if the family was better off, the antique was always hidden," Gregor went on, making his limping way along the roadside. "Valuables may not have been dumped into a hole in the ground, but they were never on display. The room with the desk or the painting or the silver was never open to non-family. If the owners were fortunate enough to have a small garden plot, they might build the piece into the wall of their shed, or stack it behind all their tools. But the antiques were never there to decorate. They were held as the family's last resort, the item to sell when all was bleak and the crisis was life-threatening. Never for show."

Gregor walked with his swinging gait across the dusty street. "Never ask where the article came from, my boy. It's tempting, I know, especially when you want to establish provenance. But trust here is very fragile and very carefully given. Everyone fears questions. Questions may lead to suspicions, and suspicions to some sort of harm. Let them offer the information if they care to, but never ask." He looked up at Jeffrey. "They just might tell you."

As they approached the farmhouse gate, they were hailed from behind. They turned to see a short, slight man hustle across the gravel road on very bowed legs, his progress slowed by the water yoke suspended across his shoulders. The buckets hung from two metal chains and water sloshed on his pantlegs as he hastened to join them. With a practiced motion he swung open the gate, walked into the miniature yard, lowered the buckets to the ground, dropped the yoke, and motioned them inside. His neck and shoulders remained bent in the same posture they had while wearing the yoke.

He offered Jeffrey his hand, but could not manage to unfurl his fingers. Jeffrey fitted his hand inside the man's; it felt as if he were grasping an animal's horn.

The man's age fell somewhere between thirty and seventy, and he barely reached Jeffrey's rib cage. He and Gregor spoke a few words, enough for Jeffrey to see that the man had only two teeth in his mouth. Then he led them inside.

A narrow hall opened on one side into the cow stalls and

on the other into the cottage's single room. The room's floor was hard-packed earth covered with layers of cardboard boxes opened and trampled flat. The ceiling was even lower than in the other farmhouse. Heat was supplied from a tiled wood-burning stove, along whose upper surface stood several pots left to simmer all day. The air was full of scents—cabbage and pork and potatoes and nearby animals and stale sweat.

In the center of the room an ancient woman half sat, half leaned on a tree-limb carved into a cane. Despite the day's heat she wore multiple layers of sweaters, a headkerchief, and bright yellow boots with the toes cut out. A pair of gray woolen socks peeked through the toe holes.

She eyed Jeffrey with a friendly glance and spoke a few words at Gregor.

"Babcha—that means grandmother, or old dear in Polish—says that if she had a couple of men as big as you to carry her, she'd be all over the village," Gregor translated.

Jeffrey grinned from his bent-over stance. "If I see anyone my size looking for work, I'll send him over."

The old woman cawed, showing a few lonely teeth, and said something that made Gregor laugh. "That was the first time she'd ever heard a language other than Polish. She asks if you'd talk some more."

"You mean, give a speech?"

The old woman laughed once more. "You've made her day," Gregor said.

The old woman waved her cane at the man, who rummaged in a rag pile by the stove and came up with a rotting burlap sack. He handed it over to Jeffrey, said something that Gregor translated as, "Their grandson is getting married and wants to buy a farm. Prices are very cheap now for anyone with cash. There is a real crisis in the farming industry because the government has retracted all subsidies, and market prices often do not cover their spiraling costs. A lot of farmers have gone under."

Jeffrey hefted the article and guessed its weight at more than ten pounds. He tried to match Gregor's casual tone. "Farmland wasn't ... what do you call it when the state takes it over?"

"Collectivized. No, they started to, but the Poles in the government urged the Soviets not to insist. They feared a civil war. Land remained in the hands of the farmers who owned it already, with only the big estates being taken over by the government. Some of that land was also given out in small plots in an attempt to win the farmers over to their side."

Jeffrey nodded. He decided he had been polite long enough. Gingerly he unfolded the covering, stopped short when the article came into view. It was an eighteenth-century Meissen porcelain *brule-parfum,* an ornate container used to burn perfume—a sort of royal air-freshener. The central burner was square, each face decorated with delicate paintings of a young lady standing in her garden. The large base was of *ormolu,* or gilded bronze, as were the flower stems that wove a delicate pattern up each side of the burner. The flowers themselves were layer upon petalled layer of porcelain, some of the finest work Jeffrey had ever seen.

"This is a treasure," Gregor said softly.

Jeffrey nodded. Intertwined within the flowers were two cherubs, peeking out in timeless gaiety at a world of poverty and grime. "How on earth did it get here?"

"That is a tale we shall never know." Gregor drew himself upright and turned to the smiling old woman. "I shall tell her that we are interested, yes?"

"Gregor was quite right not to ask where it came from," Alexander told him that evening. They walked beneath a sky turned into a crowning glory of brilliant hues by a slow-motion summer sunset. "We are here to buy antiques, not tales."

Jeffrey allowed himself to be guided by the gentleman's silent directions, unsure if there was a destination, but glad to at least have Alexander up and about. "Don't you ever wonder?"

"Of course I do. And I am extremely grateful when someone trusts me enough to share a story or two."

His color was still not good, and his interest in the pieces was not as great as Jeffrey had expected. Alexander's attention remained caught by something only he could see, with only a small part of his mind given over to the matter at hand. "After a while you learn enough to make a few guesses.

That first woman's house may once have been the servant's quarters to a manor that was bombed out of existence during the war. Perhaps the lord of the manor gave her husband those pieces when they went out of fashion, a gift to an able servant. But about that second item, one can only speculate."

Alexander indicated with a motion of his chin that they should cross the street and take a course that appeared to follow the first line of old buildings. The contrast between old and new Cracow could not have been greater, especially at this border area. New Cracow consisted mostly of unadorned and unpainted multistory structures of concrete; they had been streaked and darkened by decades of pollution and neglect. Old Cracow cried to every passerby of a distant royal past. Palatial residences crowded close to one another, a living museum of structures whose designs spanned more than nine hundred years.

"In December of 1981," Alexander said, "all of Warsaw talked about the possibility of starvation. All of Poland, for that matter." He led them onto a thin strip of green, beyond which rose remnants of an ancient city wall. "After months of protest marches and labor unrest, the Polish government had declared martial law. The Russians, everyone believed, were diverting food in order to discredit the Solidarity movement. The situation was growing more desperate by the day."

Alexander shook his head. "One day I went to the countryside near Lublin, and in a pub that night I heard one old farmer talking to another. He was using this loud voice that you would never have heard in Warsaw. He said, beating the table as he spoke, 'In 1943 there were three entire Nazi divisions in Lublin province. And there were the partisans. And all the refugees from the bombed cities. Besides that, because the Russians were approaching, Lublin was the only province supplying food to Warsaw! The only province, feeding three Panzer divisions and the partisans and its folk and a city of a million and a half.'

"At that point I noticed that the entire pub had grown silent. It was not just a listening silence, it was an agreement. This old man with one foot in the grave and nothing to lose was speaking for all of them. Even the chefs and dishwashers came out of the kitchen to listen and agree. I sat and watched, and I felt that here in this rotting little pub on the edge of a backward farming region, I had been brought face-to-face with the heart of Poland.

"So this man, who all the while totally ignored the effect his words were having on the people around him, continued to clump his fist on the table with the regularity of a heartbeat. He went on, 'So what does that tell you? That Poland is poor? That Poland cannot feed itself? No! It is the Russians who have done this to us, who have robbed and impoverished us! People don't need to fear starvation, and what's more they know it. They fear hunger because they're afraid to fear the real enemy. The people need to wake up and fear Russia! They need to open their eyes and see that here is a beast that will eat them whole! They need to recognize that the menace to the east does not care for them or their families or their land or their history, only for what they can take. They need to see it as a parasite that will suck all the blood from this great Polish nation, then cast the remains aside. There will be no tombstone for our nation, no marker in history, no more notice made than to any poor soul passing on in a Siberian labor camp. We will be gone, and that is that. Unless we wake up and know fear.'

"The man went on for over an hour to a completely silent group. Nobody said a word the entire time. When he stopped, he became just another trembling old gentleman in dirty farming clothes, and the pub became just another roadside hut selling simple food and watery beer and vodka. Mind you, in Warsaw the man would have quietly disappeared. That, my friend, is the power of a farmer in hard times. No one but a man supplying food could have spoken those words and lived to see another sunrise."

Through the trees up ahead, the dimming light illuminated a shadow-structure of towers and turrets all clustered tightly together. Jeffrey pointed. "What on earth is that?"

At first Alexander did not reply. They left the trees behind and stopped at the edge of a plaza that ringed the structure. His voice was none too steady when he finally said, "That is Florian's Gate."

In the foreground of Florian's Gate stood a sturdy circular barbican, a sort of mini-castle built as a first line of defense. It was constructed of brick and crowned by numerous peaked towers. The barbican fronted the gate itself, an older square tower connected to the medieval town wall. Both wall and gate were of stone, with upper reaches notched for bowmen and crowned by a tall wood-slat roof.

"In olden times each guild was assigned a gate," Alexander said, working to keep his voice steady as they walked around the barbican. "They had to both maintain the structure and arm it. St. Florian was the patron saint of fire fighters. You'll find his statue in the tower's recesses. He's always shown suited in shining armor, pouring water from his helmet over a flame."

As they approached the tower's arched portal, Alexander took a firm grip on Jeffrey's arm. "If you would please allow, I will rely on your strength for just a moment."

Jeffrey slowed his pace to match Alexander's, feeling the fingers digging into his arm. They stopped fifty feet or so before the entrance; it was clear that Alexander was going no farther. Jeffrey searched the fading sunlight beyond the portal but found only crowds strolling down cobblestone ways.

"I haven't visited this part of Cracow in fifty years," Alexander said, still maintaining his clenched grip on Jeffrey's arm.

"Why not?"

"Centuries of history have passed through this gate," Alexander replied. "But for me it holds only one memory. It was here that I was arrested and dragged off as a sixteen-year-old boy."

"What for?"

"Reasons were not always given at that time. Events simply occurred. Survival was such a difficult matter that questions of any sort became luxuries one could not afford."

Jeffrey felt the chill of horror. "You were arrested by the Nazis?"

"I cannot imagine passing through that gate ever again," Alexander murmured. "Not ever. Even standing here, I am filled with dread and hopelessness." He pointed a shaking hand toward the portal's recesses. "Do you see the candles flickering there?"

"Yes."

"In the center of the tower gate is an altar. There is a brass frame imbedded in the stone, and in it is a sacred painting. Still today travelers stop and pray for a good journey, as they have done for almost a thousand years." He allowed his arm to fall back. "There were lilacs in the altar vase that day, and candles flickering where someone had come to pray earlier that morning. It was the last thing I saw before they loaded me in the truck and drove me away."

Alexander steered Jeffrey around and began walking away. "Where was mercy when I needed it? Why were my prayers not answered?"

Jeffrey fought against his rising sense of dread. "Where did they take you?"

"I have a favor to ask," Alexander said in reply.

Jeffrey turned to face him. "Anything."

His discomfort was plainly visible. "This is a most difficult matter, but I need your help, I'm afraid."

"All you have to do is ask, Alexander."

"Ah, but you do not know what it is that I wish to request."

"It doesn't matter," Jeffrey replied flatly.

Alexander inspected him, said, "You are indeed a friend."

"I'd like to be."

"Very well." He took a shaky breath. "I am called to face my past. And because I know no other way to say it, I shall confess to being afraid to face it alone."

"You want me to go somewhere with you?"

"If you would."

"Sure. When do we leave?"

"Tomorrow at first light. I wish to have this done and behind me."

Jeffrey nodded. "I'll go over and leave a note for Gregor."

"Thank you, my young friend. Your strength will be most needed."

"May I ask where we're going?"

Alexander gave him a haunted, empty look. "Auschwitz."

CHAPTER

13

The two-lane road to Oswiecim, as the town was called in Polish, had neither lane markers nor road-signs. They passed through village after small cluttered village, the stretches in between lined with chestnut and oak and silver-leafed birch. At times their branches reached up and over the road, weaving a green canopy through which golden sunlight flickered and streamed.

The slow-moving traffic held their speed to less than forty miles an hour for most of the way. Dark-fumed trucks thundered around horse-drawn carts, old men pushing wheelbarrows, sedately bouncing buses, and boxy East European cars. The only transport refusing to obey the unmarked speed limit were the newer Western cars, which powered around other vehicles and blind corners with aggressive madness.

Signals of newly planted capitalism sprouted alongside the way in the form of dilapidated buses converted into roadside cafes. Only the multitude of *Kapliczki*—shrines with a Christ or Madonna and child—bore fresh paint. Often someone was kneeling in prayer before them; always they were encircled by wreaths of newly planted flowers.

Alexander said nothing from the moment he seated himself in the car to the point when they arrived in Oswiecim, the village where the Auschwitz concentration camp memorial was located. He sat with shoulders hunched and face pointed slightly to the right, seeking to keep himself hidden from the driver beside him and from Jeffrey behind.

They passed the city-limits sign for Oswiecim. Kantor stirred and sighed the words, "It is indeed a heavy day."

Their way took them along two sides of a mile-long wall constructed from concrete blocks framed with steel girders and railroad sidings. It was topped by rusted steel pylons and coiled strands of barbed wire. Every fifty meters or so, a guard tower's peaked roof and blank windows stared down at them from beyond the wall.

They pulled into a vast parking lot where several dozen buses vied for space with taxis and private cars and minivans. Hundreds of people, most of them teenagers, milled about under the leafy shade trees.

Alexander seemed blind to all but his own internal world. He rose from the car with the slow trembling of an ancient man, blinked at the sky, murmured, "Why is there sun?"

Jeffrey moved up next to him. "I'm sorry, I didn't—"

"There should be no sun here. From this place the light should be forced to hide its face."

Jeffrey touched Alexander's arm. "Are you sure you want to do this?"

Alexander drew himself erect with an effort. "Come along, Jeffrey. My past is calling."

As they passed into the reception hall, a sign covering the entire left wall announced in seventeen languages that no child under the age of thirteen was allowed past this point. Alexander stood before it for a time before saying, "The Nazis were not so considerate."

The hall was lined with broad-framed photographs: multiple barbed-wire fences; a nighttime view of the infamous entrance gates; an Orthodox Jew in prayer robes and tefflin saying Kaddish; flowers strewn in great piles on and around the ovens used for cooking down the bodies; a snowy winter dawn casting gloomy light over the central prison square; a black-and-white sea of forks and spoons that at first glance appeared to be a pile of glinting bones.

Jeffrey halted before a poem posted at the door leading out to the camp. It read:

Electric wires, high and double
Won't let you see your daughter
So don't believe the censored letter of mine

Since truth is different,
But don't cry, Mother
And if you would like to seek your child
Look for the ashes in the fields of Birkenau
They'll be there, so look for the ashes
In the fields of Auschwitz,
In the woods of Birkenau,
Mama, look for the ashes, I'll be there!

Monika Domlke
Born 1920

As they walked into the green park bordering the camp, Alexander began, "In the morning of August 12, 1940, about a year after the German invasion, I walked down to Florian's Gate. The plaza there held a sort of unofficial market, a place where people gathered with things to buy or sell. I was looking for a pair of pants and a pair of shoes. Things were getting steadily worse, especially with respect to supplies. It was becoming harder and harder to find food and simple things like clothes. So that particular morning I went by myself on the streetcar to Florian's Gate.

"It was not a licensed market, so many sharp city people would wait there to take advantage of people coming in from the countryside, looking for wares they could not find in their villages. For example, a man would stand with one shoe held high up over his head until someone came by and asked how much for it. He would perhaps reply, two hundred zloty. They would bargain, and settle on maybe one hundred and fifty, the man would ask for the money, then hand over the one shoe. The country fellow would ask for the other shoe, and the man would say, ah, you want to buy *two*? Why didn't you say so? That will be another hundred and fifty zloty. A lot of small-time shysters like that operated around the gate. I suppose that was why the Nazis chose this place to make one of their sweeps."

They arrived at the looming metal gates. Jeffrey paused to look down the gravel path running between double rows of fencing and concrete pylons. He stood there a moment, willing himself to turn to steel, harden himself against whatever awaited him inside. Then they entered.

To his left were several red-brick barracks. To his right was the wood and brick camp kitchen. The camp itself was neat and orderly and incredibly silent given the number of people walking the paths. The loudest sound was that of wind rustling in the tall trees. Jeffrey walked the rock-lined path and felt grateful for Alexander's droning voice. Otherwise the silence might have smothered him.

"That particular morning, as the trams approached that side of town, they were being stopped by the German police— the *Schutzpolizei,* not the Gestapo. It was the first time this had happened in the city, the very first time. Eventually the Polish people came to call such sweeps by the name of *Lapanka,* the trap. But that morning it was too new, and there was no name. All we knew was that the tram was stopped and we were forced to get off."

The renovated prison blocks were red-brick two-story, utterly featureless constructions. Jeffrey followed Alexander's lead and stopped in front of one labeled *Block 4—Extermination Exhibit.* As he climbed the stairs with Alexander, he imagined the walls to be weeping blood.

"They started checking documents," Alexander continued, leading them down a bare whitewashed corridor. "I had documents, not real documents, saying that I was a gardener's helper. Documents saying one had work were most important. They looked at them and told me to step aside, along with several dozen other men. A few minutes later these covered trucks arrived and we were loaded up. We were not told anything, nothing at all. Not where we were going, or why we were selected, or how long we would be away. Nothing."

The first room showed wall-sized black-and-white photographs of the transport story, remarkably clear in their frozen portrayal of agony on one side and stiff military indifference on the other. Trains expelled masses of people; children stared with frozen fear at the camera, or were hustled through barbed-wire gates, or clung to their mothers' skirts, or wailed in timeless terror.

Alexander walked beside him, viewing everything, seeing nothing. "I cannot say I was particularly scared. Age certainly had something to do with it. I was sixteen at the time, you see, and at that age your own death is something quite difficult to imagine. It is very hard to look further than that day, or that week, to what might lie beyond, or what might be on other people's minds."

The next barracks greeted them with a sign that said in

French, Russian, Polish and English: *This barracks houses all that remained of the victims' belongings and was found after the camp's liberation.* Jeffrey entered the first room, and found himself facing a wall of glass. Beyond it stretched forty feet of brushes. Shaving brushes. Hairbrushes. Shoebrushes. Toothbrushes.

"We were first taken to old Polish military barracks near the city," Alexander went on in his ceaseless drone. "On the way, I wrote a note to my mother on a scrap of paper, putting down her address and saying what had happened, that I was taken by the Germans and I didn't know where I was going or why, but that I would try to let her know. I threw three or four of them out from beneath the canvas covering on the truck, and the remarkable thing is that my mother received every one of them. I learned later that people picked them up, read the address I had scribbled, and took them to my mother. Every single one. When we left the barracks and were taken by trucks to the railroad station, I wrote several more, just dropping them outside the truck on the road. Again she got every single one."

In the next room was another glass wall with yet another pile, this one of metal bowls. Thousands and thousands and thousands of bowls.

Another room, another glass wall, another display—this one of crutches and prosthetic limbs and back braces. A wooden hand made for a child, with fingers perhaps two inches long, reached out to Jeffrey across the years.

"At the station they put sixty or seventy of us into a cattle car. At that time they weren't taking women to Auschwitz, only men. We had one container with water, and another for waste, with straw on the floor. It was a most unpleasant voyage. It was extremely crowded, and it stank horribly. There were Germans with machine-gun placements on the roofs of each car, and every time we came to a crossing where the train stopped, some people would try to escape. The Germans would machine-gun them, then go out and pick up their bodies and throw them back into the cattle cars with the rest of us."

Upstairs there were no rooms, just one long hall with glass walls to either side. Half of the entire floor was filled with shoes. Men's, women's, children's, babies' shoes—piled to the ceiling in a broken array of lost possessions and lost lives.

"We arrived at Auschwitz on August 15, 1940," Alexander continued. "They divided us up into rows of five and began marching us toward the camp. At that time there was only the one camp. Birkenau had not even been started yet. So we were marched across to the main camp, and through this big iron gate. Above the gate was written in big iron letters the words *Arbeit Macht Frei*—'Work makes you free.' So all of us thought we had been conscripted for a labor camp. It was still early enough that the truth about Auschwitz was not yet publicly known, you see. Perhaps there were rumors floating around, but they had not made their way down to the ears of a sixteen-year-old boy. Or to my fellows, for that matter. It did not even occur to us that we were being brought into an extermination camp."

The second floor's other half was given over to suitcases, turned upward to shout the names of those unable to claim them. Frank of Holland. Birmann of Hamburg. Ludwig of Baruch, Israel. Eva Pander of Recklinghausen. Gescheit of Berlin. Else Meier of Cologne. Helene Lewandowski of Poland.

"So they brought us into this central square. I suppose our transport held fifteen or sixteen hundred people. It took a very long time for them to process us. We had to go to one place where we had to leave all our clothing. Everything. Then to another place where they shaved us completely. Our heads, our bodies, everything. Then we were forced to bathe, and then given these Auschwitz pajamas. That is what I thought of them, those striped camp suits. We were left barefoot."

At the end of the chamber, diagonal to the suitcases, was a deep narrow display of baby clothing. Jeffrey simply had to turn away.

"Already some pretty terrible things were happening right there and then on the square. It appeared that the Germans wanted to see how people reacted to various situations. We had not eaten for twenty-four hours. So what they did was set out twenty or thirty large loaves of bread, heavy Polish bread, and then tell the people to come forward and take some. But every time people stepped forward, the Germans with their heavy boots and guns would beat them. The soldiers were laughing and joking as they did so, treating it as great sport. Still, because the people were so hungry, some would try to grab a handful, and they were beaten very badly."

Another downstairs room had two glass walls. One displayed Jewish prayer shawls hung from wooden frames whose outstretched fabric cried for attention. The second held a cobwebbed mass of eyeglasses, their thousands of lenses gathered in the case's forefront to peer silently into Jeffrey's aching heart.

"The water inside the train car had been used up in the first two hours, and afterward we had nothing more. While we were out there on the square, an elderly man was coughing very badly. Somehow he managed to get a soldier to bring him a full bucket of water, and for this he gave the German his gold pocket watch—this was before he had been stripped, of course. When we were stripped all valuables were taken from us. So the old man drank his fill, and then turned to us and said, anyone who wants can have some. But when we looked we saw that the old man, who had TB, had left the water scummy with coughed-up blood. Even so, many drank from that bucket—that is how thirsty they had become."

Upon their exit from the building, Jeffrey turned to read the name above the door. It said: *Block 5—Evidence of Crimes.*

"While the processing was taking place, the Germans brought forward a prisoner who had arrived earlier," Alexander continued as they walked toward the next barrack. "I suppose there were already thirteen or fourteen hundred prisoners there when we arrived. They had been there three or four months, from what I gathered later. Auschwitz had formerly been a Polish army camp, and when the Germans arrived they began gathering people from prisons around Cracow and sending them there. The soldiers brought out this prisoner with his harmonica, and from our group they brought out a Catholic priest and a Jewish rabbi. These men were tired, and hungry, and the rabbi with his long beard could barely stand up. They gave them a sheet of paper and told them to sing the words while the prisoner played the harmonica. The words were very obscene; these holy men stood there, forced to sing obscenities, while the guards listened and laughed."

Block 6 was titled *Prisoners' Life.* In the first hall, black-and-white etchings by former inmates loomed over display cases of passports and family photographs and personal documents. The pictures required no explanation—S.S. soldiers stripping newly arrived inmates of rings, Kapo guards pulling an inmate from line for a beating, new prisoners adding to a mountain of suitcases outside their barrack, prisoners being selected for experimentation.

"At the end of the processing they gave us each a number. My number was one-nine-one-four, *neunzehn-vierzehn*. We were told that if a German or a Kapo came up, we were to stand at attention and recite, *Politische Schutzhäftling, Pole, neunzehn-vierzehn, meldet heir zur Stelle*."

Across from the etchings, against a backdrop of barbed wire, a wall display shouted in red letters a foot high the command: *A Jew is permitted one week to live, a priest two, anyone else a maximum of three months.*

Alexander examined the display with eyes blind to all but his memories. "There were already a hundred or so Jews here when we arrived. The Germans put them into what was called the *Straff* company. The penalty company. These people had it very, very bad. They were forced to haul this enormous roller around and around the square, while the Germans continually beat them. It was a horrible thing to watch. Horrible."

The barrack's central hallway was about seventy feet long and lined on both sides with three rows of photographs. Men were to the right, women the left. Beneath the pictures were written their number, their name, their date of birth, their former profession. Jeffrey made out the words for tour guide, teacher, sailor, waiter, lawyer, priest, religious brother, chemist. Beneath the profession was their date of arrival and their date of death.

Their eyes. Their eyes. Jeffrey felt their eyes searching him even when he walked the hall with his own gaze remaining on his feet.

"Every day we were gathered on the central square where they made us go through these extremely difficult, pointless physical exercises. We were already growing weak, and whenever anyone stumbled the Germans would immediately begin beating him. One Kapo hit me over the head with his stick, here, I can still feel the place. The Kapos at that time were all German. We were told that they were criminal prisoners, and under them the men in charge of the barracks rooms were Polish criminals. I can still remember the man in charge of my barracks, a big man, very big, of perhaps forty-five years and completely bald. His number was four hundred. He carried this great stick with him always, and beat on us constantly."

At the back of the central hall stood a tall sculpture. It showed six women whose rags covered their heads and little else. They were nothing more than taut skin and staring eyes and jutting bones. The sculpture was entitled *Hunger*.

Alexander remained before the statue for quite a long while. "Our normal ration was a soup called *Avo* for lunch, a blackish mixture with perhaps a couple of rotten potatoes. Nothing for breakfast. At night there was so-called tea, water boiled with some unknown leaves, and hard, moldy bread. Bread was the common currency at Auschwitz, bread and cigarettes. The exchange rate was three or four cigarettes for a hunk of bread. People who really craved tobacco would exchange it, knowing full well that they couldn't last without food, and not really caring all that much. For some, the hunger for cigarettes was stronger than for food, especially as life lost its meaning. Then, when someone smoked a cigarette, they would inhale and then blow the smoke into the mouth of a friend. He would in turn blow it into the mouth of a third man."

One room was dedicated to children. Jeffrey refused to enter. Alexander stopped a few paces inside, turned back with a look of addled confusion, then shrugged his accord and led them down the hall, out of the building, and on to the next barrack. The sign above the door announced that it held a display of how prisoners lived.

"In our barracks room there were one hundred and seventy men," Alexander told him as they entered. "It was so tight that we were forced to sleep on our sides, and when one turned, all were forced to turn with him. No beds. We were sleeping on the floor, with only straw between us and the concrete floor. In the mornings we were kicked and beaten outside to the hand pump, where we were supposed to have our only wash of the day. One hundred and seventy men around a hand pump, with the Kapos beating us to make us hurry.

"One time I was late, maybe five minutes late coming out of the barracks. The Kapo marked my number, and about two weeks later a Gestapo soldier came up and called out five or six numbers, mine being one of them. We were penalized because we had been late coming out of the barracks. The punishment was something terrible. He stood there in the concrete corridor inside our barracks with a horsewhip and ordered us through truly horrible gymnastics for over two hours. Whenever we stumbled we were kicked and whipped until we were unconscious. One of the five men punished with me was killed, murdered, beaten to death right there before our eyes. I received one kick in the small of my back, on my kidneys, that I truly thought had killed me too."

Inside the barracks the central hall held two more walls of eyes. Jeffrey checked the professions in an attempt to escape the stares—seamstress, mayor, bureaucrat, blacksmith, activist. The wall opened for a doorway that framed a brick-sided barracks room as it was in 1944. Straw was laid beneath blanket rags. Three tiers of wooden beds rose like animal stalls in a room less than six feet high. The stalls were perhaps four feet wide. A sign by the doorway said that eight women slept in each of the four-foot-wide tiers. A thousand women to a barrack.

"After a time," Alexander said beside him, "they began marching us a mile or so every morning to the building site of Birkenau. This was the second stage of the Auschwitz death camp, and the larger one. I was ordered up on top of very steep roofs—I don't know what they had been before they were turned into Birkenau—and I cleaned them with a stiff wire brush. It was extremely steep, very dangerous work. One day a man working beside me fell to his death."

Block 10 was closed and the door barred. Beside the door a sign read: *In this block the German physician, Professor Clauberg M.D., conducted experiments dealing with the sterilization of women*. Three women knelt on the steps and prayed, candles lit before them.

"One morning while at work at Birkenau I happened upon some rotten potatoes. You must understand that by that time hunger was a ruling force in my life. It dominated my daily existence. Several of us there together swiftly gathered them up. It was approaching winter by that time, so we took these potatoes and put them on a fire there at the work site. While we were watching them, a German came up. All the others fled, but I was caught, and the German demanded to know who they were, these others who had been cooking potatoes instead of working. When I refused to tell him, he sent a Kapo to fetch him a special stick. It was very heavy, almost as thick as my forearm, and had nails hammered into it to give it extra weight. He ordered the Kapo to take my head between his legs, and then he began to beat me on my back and thighs. I was supposed to get twenty-five blows. On the eighth stroke he hit me on the kidneys, and I lost consciousness."

Beside Block 10, metal gates opened to a graveled courtyard. At its end was a bullet-ridden concrete wall, the Death Wall. Row after row of flowers and candles and wreaths and cards were set at its base.

"Every day, sometimes several times a day, they would tie a man's hands behind his back, and pull him upward on a tall post until his feet left the ground, suspended with his arms pulled back and up from behind. They were left hanging for two, sometimes three hours. The pain was indescribable. People who went through it told me afterward that they would rather die than endure it again."

The neighboring block contained a large room with a line of simple wooden tables. A sign described it as the camp court, and said that almost all who were tried here were executed. Immediately.

Two opposing rooms were assigned for male and female prisoners to strip naked before being led outside to be shot. The sign above the men's chamber said that most had their hands bound with barbed wire.

"One day a pair of prisoners escaped, and we were forced to stand in the square until they were found. Eighteen hours we stood there, in the dead of winter. Any time anyone fell, he was beaten and kicked to the point of death. Eventually the guards found the fugitives, and they were punished with the Standing Cells."

In the cellar were the Standing Cells, arrived at through a barred crawl-space perhaps two feet square. Four prisoners were crammed into a space three feet wide, three feet long, and four feet high. Those placed there for trying to escape, according to the sign above the first cell, were left to starve to death.

"They had a crematorium already in operation. The prisoners knew about it, of course. Even I, as a sixteen-year-old boy, learned what was happening there beyond the wires. But many were already seeking a way to commit suicide. Many men threw themselves against the barbed-wire fence so the Germans would shoot and kill them. For many of the prisoners, death was preferable to an endless stay in this living hell."

Across from the Standing Cells was the first experimental gas chamber. Another chamber at the end of the cellar hall was the Death Cell, where prisoners were held before being placed inside the gas chamber. On one wall of this room, a prisoner awaiting death had carved the figure of Christ. Alexander stood there for a long time before turning and leading Jeffrey back upstairs.

At the turning that led away from Block 10, the walkways and window ledges were filled with modern-day casualties of Auschwitz; men and women, boys and girls, knelt and wept and prayed or just stared with blank-faced blindness at the passers-by whose legs would still carry them. The eyes of those crippled by what they had witnessed resembled those of the prisoners whose photographs hung within.

Alexander led him through the barracks dedicated to the Poles who died in Auschwitz and to the Polish war effort. He then turned down the path and led them out the gates to the main gas chamber and crematorium. They were located beyond the camp's perimeter fences in a smaller enclosure all their own. The entrance was a stone-walled path leading into the side of an earth-walled bunker.

The death chamber was a tomb of concrete, where 800 prisoners were gassed at a time. The next chamber held row after row of curved brick furnaces. Candles and flowers were strewn in the long metal trays used to pass in the bodies and bring out the ashes.

A guide standing beside Jeffrey told his group that the Nazis would notify the families of Poles who had been killed, saying that the relative had passed on of a heart attack, and that his or her remains could be collected upon making a payment. Whenever anyone appeared with the money, they would shovel up a boxful of ashes from whomever had just been incinerated.

Alexander led Jeffrey out into the bright sunlight and back to where their car and driver waited. The narrative continued as his softly droning voice kept them company on the journey back to Cracow.

"As soon as my mother learned of my arrest, she began seeking my release. My father was one of the commanders of the Polish forces fighting under General Anders, in the Polish Second Corps under British command, and my mother remained in Cracow all alone. Someone told her to go to the Gestapo headquarters, and time and again she went and pleaded with anyone who would listen to tell her news of her son. She was repeatedly thrown out on the street, just tossed out the door and down the stairs like refuse. But she kept returning.

"Then someone else told her that there was a German lawyer with connections. If she could get her hands on a thousand zloty, he would help her. So my mother sold her rings and went to this German; he took my name and promised he would do what he could. To this day, I don't know exactly who it was that in the end worked out my release. I don't know how many people my mother spoke to and pleaded with. But I do know that there was a commandant of the Polish police, a good friend of my father's from before the war. He had the responsibility of supervising Polish police in all of Poland under German military command. My mother went to him and pleaded for his help. But whoever helped her never admitted it, and so I have never been able to thank the one responsible for my release. But somehow, somehow, toward the end of January 1941, I was released from Auschwitz.

"That morning, as we gathered in the square, a German called out several numbers, mine being one of them. We were ordered to report to the *Schreibstube,* some kind of office. The head Gestapo, the chief Auschwitz commandant, made a little speech to us, which was translated by a Polish count who was also a prisoner there with us. It was a patriotic German speech, saying how lucky we were to live in these days and watch the rise of the German empire. Then we were ordered never to tell anyone anything of what we had witnessed inside the camp. If we ever did speak of it, we were told, we would be returned to Auschwitz immediately, and there would be no release for us except death. Then he ordered us to go, and to do well in the great new empire of Adolf Hitler.

"Five of us were released, and with typical German efficiency, they gave us back the very same clothes we had arrived in. Upon my capture in August I had been wearing a thin shirt, no jacket, white pants and sandals. Now it was mid-winter, with snow on the ground, and very, very cold. I was allowed nothing but these same summer clothes.

"Two Gestapo men took us to the Auschwitz train station and bought us our tickets. While we were waiting for the train to leave, a girl of perhaps eighteen or nineteen came up and took off her beret and said to me, 'Please take this so that your head won't grow cold.' We were still shaved, you know, and from our starved looks everyone could see we had just come from the camp.

"So the Gestapo put us in a third-class train compartment and stood there waiting for the train to leave. Then up came another attractive young lady. She spoke to the Gestapo in a very sweet voice, taking the button of one of their long leather coats and twisting it as she tried to persuade them. Finally he snapped, *aber schnell,* make it fast, and she rushed away. Five minutes later she came back with a huge package and shoved it through the train window to us, then turned and walked away. In this package were sausages and fresh bread and butter, everything.

"Eventually the train departed, and as we were sitting there and eating, a German officer came walking by our compartment. He opened the door and asked where we were coming from. He was a soldier, so we did as he ordered and told him that we had just left the Auschwitz camp. He stood there a moment, then asked if we would like to have a pack of cigarettes. He just handed them over, this German officer in uniform.

"We had to change trains soon after that, at the border between Germany and the General Government, or GG as it was known then. The German officer went into the waiting room and chased out the Germans—this was in Silesia, so the people there were mostly German. He came back and told us to go inside and lie down and rest. While we were lying there, he went inside and brought back big glasses of beer.

"By that time we had finished the food the lady had given us, and in the train restaurant there was a display of some really appetizing sausages. We were still extremely hungry. We searched our pockets and came up with forty-eight pfennigs between us. The price of a sausage was four marks and something. But we were moving into the GG area, where the zloty was the official currency, so I took the money and went to ask if we could get maybe a little slice with it while we could still spend it. An old lady was tending the counter. I laid down my small coppers and asked if I could please have a little something for this money. She stood there and looked at me, and looked at me. Finally she said, 'Yes, sir, right away.' And she gave me four kilos of sausage. Mind you, this was during wartime rationing. That was how bad my appearance was after leaving Auschwitz."

The car pulled up in front of their hotel. Jeffrey got out, rushed around, and helped his friend get out. Alexander stood very slowly, raised his eyes to the heavens, and blinked several times.

"Can I help you to your room?"

Alexander lowered his gaze to the pavement at his feet. "No thank you, my boy. It is time to face the fact that I am alone. It cannot be put off any longer."

With that he turned and climbed the stairs and disappeared through the doors.

CHAPTER

14

Jeffrey was already awake when Alexander called him shortly after six the next morning. "I am sorry, Jeffrey. My attack of memories has become most severe. I fear staying here in Poland just now would only make matters worse."

"I understand."

"Yes, I thought you would. I am catching a flight in two hours and leaving you here in charge. I shall return to London and assist your young lady in running our shop. Please call when you can. Until later, then. Goodbye."

When Jeffrey climbed to the second floor landing, Gregor was waiting for him with a bulky sweater wrapped around his shoulders, his eyes full of concern. "My dear boy, are you all right?"

Jeffrey rubbed a tired hand down his face. "I didn't sleep so well last night. I think I've inherited Alexander's voices."

"Yes, we all have the night whispers from time to time. It is the price of being human."

Jeffrey nodded. "It was some day."

"I am sure it was. Alexander stopped by this morning and explained his departure. I told him that it was no doubt the best thing to do, and that we would get along fine here together." Gregor turned and limped heavily into his apartment. His movements were much stiffer than usual. "Where are my manners? Come in, Jeffrey. Come in."

"Are you feeling all right?"

He waved a dismissive hand. "It is simply another attack. I have long since learned to accept the complaints of this cantankerous body. I will be fine in a day or so. Sit down here and tell me everything."

Jeffrey did as he was told. Gregor stood above him, silent and still, save for occasionally pulling the sweater closer around his chest, consumed by the act of listening.

"Poor Alexander," Gregor sighed, once Jeffrey was finished. "If only he would not insist on carrying that burden alone."

Jeffrey nodded. "I keep wishing I had known what to say."

"In cases such as this, it is sometimes best to say nothing at all. To listen from the heart, without judgment, without impatience, is sometimes the greatest gift one can give." He turned toward the alcove and winced at the sudden movement. "Would you like a glass of coffee before we go?"

"Okay, thanks. Are you sure you're all right?"

"As I said, I have these attacks from time to time. The nicest thing about them is that they pass. I don't suppose you would object to using Alexander's car and driver this morning? I don't believe I would be able to drive."

"That would be great."

"I thought you would approve. Tomek has promised to come by as soon as he sees Alexander off. It shouldn't be too much longer."

Gregor moved into his alcove. "In times like this, I often find that words of my own can do nothing at all. What Alexander needs more than my words in his ear is the Holy Spirit speaking to his heart. Perhaps sympathetic listening will help him to quieten enough to hear that stiller voice speaking deep within. I can hope, at least. And pray."

Jeffrey thought back over the day. "It was incredible how caught up Alexander was in remembering," he said. "All his life he's tried to put the Auschwitz experience behind him, but when he was walking around with me, it was the most real thing in his entire existence."

Gregor pushed the curtain aside. "These experiences were so great, so powerful, that at times other aspects of life dim to unimportance. For some poor souls, the experience leaves the rest of life caught in shadows. All life carries the grayness caused by that which they can not overcome."

Jeffrey shook his head. "I don't see how anybody could ever leave something like that behind."

"Perhaps you can't," Gregor agreed. "I resent these people who rest in the comfort of their faith and say with smug glibness that if only a person in pain would believe a bit more strongly, or pray a little more, the Lord would heal their every wound. I know too many devout believers who remain crippled by their pasts to ever agree with such nonsense. No, all I can say for certain is that the Lord has promised us a peace that surpasses all understanding. Even in the midst of our suffering, this peace is promised us. Peace for now, salvation forever."

Jeffrey felt the rising up of his own old shadows. "How can you have peace in the middle of suffering?"

Gregor set a glass of coffee down at Jeffrey's elbow. "Better you should ask how a man might have peace at all in this world, my boy. Now you let that sit until the grounds have settled to the bottom of the glass."

"I don't think I understand."

"About how to find peace? Of course not. Such understanding can only come through experience, not an exercise of the mind." Gregor pulled over a straight-backed chair, settled himself, went on. "There was another survivor of Auschwitz, a man by the name of Father Bloknicki. Before the Nazi invasion, Bloknicki was an atheist, a philosophy professor. Like a lot of Polish intelligentsia, he was declared a threat to the new German state and shipped off to a concentration camp. Once in Auschwitz, Bloknicki looked around himself and realized that intelligence or education made no difference whatsoever as to the presence or lack of evil in a man. He spoke German, and he discovered that many of the officers and even some of the enlisted men were intelligent, well-educated people. And yet here they were, making it their life's work to foster evil.

"Bloknicki decided that there had to be an underlying concept of morality. There had to be something *behind* life, something that granted man a choice and gave him both strength and purpose. There had to be a God. Then and there, in the horrors of a factory of death, he gave his life to Christ.

"By a clerical error—or miracle, whichever you prefer—

Bloknicki was released long before the end of the war. He did the only thing a man of God knew to do in the Poland of that time—he became a priest. He first started working with alcoholics, and was imprisoned once again, this time by the Communists, because of his success in both curing and converting the addicted men.

"While in prison this second time, he received a vision from God as to how to work with young people. He was to involve lay people, utilize the Scriptures, and foster an atmosphere of communal prayer and Bible study. He began as soon as he was released, and enlisted the help and the support of many other local priests. Then he came into contact with several Protestant mission groups and asked them to help as well. This was a most unusual request. The government, some of the Protestant mission boards in the West, and the Polish church hierarchy began to oppose him. But still he went on.

"By the seventies, this little group of believers had become what is now known as the Oasis, the largest mission organization operating in all Poland. They would arrange to come into a medium-sized village for a fifteen-day revival and prayer retreat, and literally take over every square inch of available space. They would usually have with them thirty or forty thousand students. They slept in primitive farmhouses or makeshift tents, and held their classes in barns. By the time martial law was declared in the eighties, over a million young people had taken part in these revivals."

Gregor sipped at his coffee. "Even in the darkest of hours, people have a choice. They can turn toward self, or they can turn toward God. They can turn toward hate, or they can turn toward forgiveness and love."

Jeffrey shook his head. "I just don't understand how you can have such confidence in your faith after all you and your family have been through. Where is the assurance for Alexander when he comes out of the concentration camp and finds his sister imprisoned and beaten to death? Where is God when your country has been occupied and your people imprisoned and tortured and murdered?"

Jeffrey ran half-clenched fingers through his hair. "I don't see how you can praise God and then turn around and see the misery and the poverty and the pain that surrounds you everywhere."

Gregor's kind, tired, patient eyes shone with an other-worldly light. "Has there been such pain in your own life, Jeffrey?"

"Not like this. What has happened here is a lot worse than anything I've ever gone through. But it doesn't make what I've known any less real for me."

"No, of course it doesn't. That was not what I asked."

"I know. It's just that I feel a little silly talking about my own problems when I'm surrounded by things I couldn't even imagine before coming to Poland."

"Pain is pain," Gregor replied simply.

"It seems to me you're trying to avoid my question by talking about something inside my life."

"The world is such a big place," Gregor replied in his own mild way. "Greater men than I have spent lifetimes discussing your questions. I'm afraid my little mind is only able to deal with such things one person at a time. I only asked you, my young friend, because I hoped to help you find an answer for your own life, if such an answer is indeed needed. I will leave it to you to find answers for the rest of the world."

Defeated by the man's calm honesty, Jeffrey stretched back in his chair and replied, "Then the answer is yes."

"I see. And did you turn to God and ask Him to end the pain?"

Jeffrey nodded glumly.

"And He did not reply."

"Not a word," he replied bitterly.

"You and Alexander have more in common than you realize," Gregor said.

The door buzzer sounded. Gregor cast aside his blanket, reached for a well-patched sweater hanging by the door, slipped it on, and pocketed a small book from his shelf. "That will be our driver. We have an appointment in less than an hour. We can discuss this as we drive."

Gregor said nothing more until he had made his way to the car, walking like a boat passing through heavy seas. The effort of motion required all of his attention. Tomek helped him settle in the backseat, nodded a solemn greeting to Jeffrey, started the car and headed them out of town.

Once they were surrounded by dusty shades of summer greens Gregor said, "Before I begin, Jeffrey, I must warn you of one very grave danger. Only you can say whether or not the warning applies, of course. I only ask that you search your heart very carefully before setting it aside.

"Sometimes in our selfish attempts to keep God out, we develop questions to which we believe there are no answers. Then we set them up as barriers between ourselves and God, and we never seek an answer. If a response is offered us, we either cast it aside with embittered anger over someone daring to challenge our defenses, or we immediately throw up another unanswerable question. The truth, you see, is that no answer is desired.

"Doubt can be a most valuable instrument of growth, if it is seen as a challenge. If it is a fuel used to search for *more* answers and a *deeper* understanding, then you who are poor and hungry in spirit shall inherit both profound answers and the kingdom of heaven. Believe me, my boy, if your search for answers is truly open-hearted, the Lord will reward you richly. But beware the blindness you are causing yourself if your questions are nothing more than defenses to keep Him out."

Jeffrey pondered the question. "I guess that's partly true. But I really did need God and He really wasn't there. Maybe all I'm trying to do is keep from getting burned a second time."

Gregor gave him an approving glance. "Your honesty is most admirable and most rare, Jeffrey. Very well. Let us look at the fact of your own suffering. And make no mistake, I do not question your pain. This matter of relativity is mere nonsense. Whatever it was that caused you pain was clearly something profound, and it carried a lasting effect. You have suffered. That is enough.

"For just a moment, I would like to ask that you remember whatever it was that caused you pain. Go back in your mind to that moment when you decided that God was not listening, and you turned away from Him."

"I remember," Jeffrey replied grimly.

"I know this is difficult for you, my young friend. I truly do. But try to see if one fact was not true for you right then. When you were in the midst of your suffering, did you not become more aware of how other people were living in pain?

Did you find that barriers within yourself were crumbling?"

Jeffrey felt wracked by memories and by remembered pains and by a truth he had never recognized before. "Yes."

"Yes. You felt it. The barriers fall as all lies must fall, if we are to remain honest with ourselves. The veil is ripped away, and you find yourself able to walk the valley that others know. This is a basic truth that we seek to flee from all our lives, my dear young friend, that no one can minister to a suffering soul except one who has passed through these flames and retained an open heart.

"Emotional, spiritual, physical pain—it doesn't matter. Pain of any kind reduces the highest of us, even the great King David himself, to the lowest level of loneliness. We flee from it. We rage against it. We battle it with every weapon we have.

"You yourself know the desperation of searching for an end to your misery. And if the heart is awake, as yours surely is, you wish there could be a cure for *every* sufferer. You wish you could touch them, and cure them *all*.

"But you cannot. You can't even keep your own puny self from knowing this horror called pain. You can't even lock the door to your own life and tell this nightmare called suffering to stay out. It breaks down the door and *forces* itself upon you.

"So what do we do? Well, it is certainly possible to blame God. 'You didn't listen to me,' we say to Him. 'You forced me to endure this horrible pain! You crippled me, or at least allowed it to happen.' This is the way it begins, you see. And the next step is of course very clear. We then turn our backs on God. We seek to punish Him as He has appeared to punish us. And once that is done, we continue our walk into darkness by *hating* God. By *cursing* God.

"What we do not ever want to see is that sometimes there is no earthly cure, no earthly solution. The stronger we are, the more we wish to see every problem in our life as temporary. To realize that something must simply be accepted and borne is to acknowledge that our own strength is not sufficient, that the world is not always under our control. This realization is such a hard task. So very, very hard."

Gregor reached into the pocket of his voluminous sweater and emerged with a tiny pocket New Testament. "I brought my English version along." He handed it to Jeffrey. "Would you please be so kind as to read from Second Corinthians, chapter twelve, verses seven through ten?"

It took quite some time for Jeffrey to find the passage. He squinted and braced the book with both hands against the car's jouncing journey, and read:

> "To keep me from becoming conceited because of these surpassingly great revelations, there was given me a thorn in my flesh, a messenger of Satan, to torment me. Three times I pleaded with the Lord to take it away from me. But he said to me, 'My grace is sufficient for you, for my power is made perfect in weakness.' Therefore I will boast all the more gladly about my weaknesses, so that Christ's power may rest on me. That is why, for Christ's sake, I delight in weaknesses, in insults, in hardships, in persecutions, in difficulties. For when I am weak, then I am strong."

Gregor nodded. "Even the great St. Paul has a painful thorn thrust deep into his side, and the agony has crippled him. He has *great* suffering. Three times the man who spoke with God begged Him to grant a cure. God refused to give a complete healing. Do you hear what I am saying, my young friend? God said that He *knew* of Paul's suffering, yet refused to end it. He said *no,* I will *not* heal you. Not because you are a sinner and should be punished. Not because you have been found guilty. No. God recognizes Paul as a true disciple of Christ. So why does the divine Healer not heal? How can this be?

"It happens, my dear young friend, because God has something *even better* in store. Yet what can be better than a cure? What? The answer is, *the presence of God.* He gave Paul the grace to *bear* this suffering, and in so doing, to bear witness to His glory.

"In times of suffering, if we resist the temptation to blame God and curse God and hate God, He will strengthen us, deepen our faith, and *see us through.* It is not what we may want, it is not the end of our pain coming at the time and in the way of our choosing. But He in His own perfect way will *use* our imperfections and our weaknesses to the glory of His name. And in so doing, He will enrich us beyond all measure.

"He will deepen our life, our wisdom, and our faith, through the act of suffering. He can and will use the sufferer to reach those who might otherwise never know the glory that awaits them were they to only open their hearts to His call. He will help us to stretch out our hand, and give light to those who are entering into their own dark night."

CHAPTER
15

The building had one entrance and two elevators for five hundred apartments set on nineteen floors. It was one of several dozen identical concrete monoliths grouped together on the outskirts of Cracow. The entrance doors, cracked wire-mesh glass and rusting frames, flapped noisily on their hinges.

The entrance hall was unpainted concrete—floors, walls, low-slung ceiling. Bent and scarred postboxes wept rust down the damp side wall. Meager light filtered through two fly-blown overhead globes. Mildew painted gray and green streaks in the corners. The air stank of refuse.

"We see fewer small items nowadays," Gregor said, all business now that they were approaching a sale. "But as I said the other day, most buyers are out to spend as little as possible and will happily lie to the seller if it means paying a few dollars less. Others follow the person home and steal whatever is there. We, Alexander and I, are still approached by those who have done business with us in the past or heard of us from people who have, especially those with something truly valuable to sell."

"Like today?"

Gregor tugged sharply at the elevator door and motioned Jeffrey to enter. "That, my dear boy, we shall soon see."

The elevator complained like a cranky old man as it clanged past each floor. It stopped on the seventh; Gregor pushed the door open with his shoulder. In the concrete-lined hallway squalling babies competed with echoing televisions and punk-rock music. Refuse littered the passage.

Gregor paused outside a battered door and said to Jeffrey, "As I have said before, it is best not to ask too many questions."

His knock was answered by a balding man in unkempt clothes who greeted Gregor with a gap-toothed grin, a handshake, a clap on the shoulders, and words with the permanently slurred, coarsened quality of a vodka-and-cigarette fanatic. Gregor replied, turned and introduced Jeffrey. The man gave him a long, hard-eyed inspection before nodding a greeting.

He led them into the cluttered apartment of a dedicated bachelor. Empty vodka bottles and dirty plates littered every flat surface. Newspapers were scattered across the threadbare sofa and much of the floor.

A younger man, slighter and darker than their host, rose at their entry and stared at them with feverish eyes. Their host waved a hand toward the younger man and said something to Gregor, who translated. "This man is from the Ukraine, a section of the former Soviet Union which borders Poland. I have done business with our host several times before. He is Ukrainian himself, and keeps contact through his family with smugglers crossing the border. He will translate for us."

The host bustled off to the kitchen alcove. Jeffrey seated himself at Gregor's nod and gave the Ukrainian visitor a frank examination. He had black red-rimmed eyes, and skin the color of old leather. He was very slight, standing no more than five-three and weighing perhaps a hundred pounds. Despite the man's twenty-odd years, his full beard was going gray.

When their host had returned and handed around tulip-shaped glasses of heavily sweetened tea, Gregor began a three-way discussion with the pair. He would ask a question to the host, who would then translate to the Ukrainian, who replied with a hoarse whispery voice. This was then translated back to Polish for Gregor.

Eventually Gregor turned to Jeffrey and said, "I asked him what the wait at the Polish border was like before passing through customs. He said this trip it was twelve days. It gets a little worse each time—I already knew this from the news reports. There are so many Soviets on the brink of starvation, you see. Anyone with something to sell is desperate to make it to Poland or Czechoslovakia. Polish currency is now freely convertible—you can change it for dollars or marks or whatever. The ruble is not. The Soviets have no faith in their monetary system, and are fearing the possibility of a total collapse. They are very keen to lay their hands on hard currency.

"This man also said that only the very small items are getting through these days. For months now the Polish border guards are trying to stop the smuggling of alcohol and cheap wares, and each car is searched carefully. You cannot bribe your way through, because the guards would then know you have something valuable and just confiscate it.

"Many people use the waiting time at the Soviet-Polish border as an indication of the state of the Soviet economy. They say it is a much more honest evaluation than anything the government puts out."

"He must have something very valuable to make a trip like that," Jeffrey ventured.

The Ukrainian waited through the laborious translation process and sipped at his glass of tea with fingers that trembled from fatigue. "He hopes so," Gregor eventually replied. "He says the worst part of waiting at the border was the fear of bandits. He hasn't slept very much for twelve days. He dared not travel with another man, because two men seen together was an automatic signal both to the border guards and the thieves that there was something of great value somewhere in the car.

"The Russian mafia has taken over the border area, according to this young man. He actually used the word mafia. They charge five dollars for a liter of water—one tenth of the average Russian's monthly wage. Anyone who pays too quickly or buys too much has his car broken into at night. Keep in mind, there are no camping parks or hotels. They eat and sleep and live in their cars throughout the twelve-day wait. When the thieves pick their prey, he is beaten, maybe killed, and the car driven off somewhere to be searched at leisure."

"What about the police or the border guards?" Jeffrey asked.

The man paused from his tea to give Jeffrey a look of bitter humor. "He says the line is over thirty miles long," Gregor replied. "At night the guards never go farther from their hut than the circle cast by their lights, no matter how bad the screams. Every day or so there is another body to be brought out, identified, and buried."

"Then why do people do it?"

"To trade," Gregor replied, not bothering to translate.

"Seems like an awful risk," Jeffrey said.

"That depends on how hungry you are, wouldn't you say?"

Without preamble the small man stood, unbuckled his belt, and dropped his baggy trousers to the floor. With a grimace of pain he peeled black tape from either thigh and brought out two small packets wrapped in grimy rags. He fastened his trousers, sat back, motioned toward Jeffrey, and demanded something in a tense voice.

"He wants to know if you will offer him an honest price."

"Honesty is the only thing I have to offer," Jeffrey replied. "Ask him if he has any idea what he wants for the items."

The smuggler gave a grin that split his dirty face and exposed teeth the color of aged teak. He said one word. "Valuta."

"It's a term you hear all through the Eastern Bloc," Gregor explained. "It means Western cash. Transferable currency."

The older man spoke. Gregor nodded and said to Jeffrey, "He says to tell you that valuta means cash that you can buy something with. Money with a purpose."

The smuggler began speaking, the older man nodding and translating. Gregor passed it on. "You stand in line for everything today in Russia. A fistful of rubles won't buy you bread. His sister has a sick baby, and last month waited three days in line for condensed milk. Each night the people in line would mark their place on one another's palms, agree to a certain time to be back the next morning, and return and check carefully to make sure no one had broken into place. It's been like that since early last winter. Sugar, milk, bread, meat, paper, soap—everything is either hard to find or just not available."

"So how do they survive?"

When the translations were made, the man took his rag-covered bundle, set it firmly into Jeffrey's hands, looked him hard in the eyes, said hoarsely, "Valuta."

Jeffrey unfolded the rags from the smaller of the two parcels. It was a tiny case, no larger than his palm, of aged cedarwood. He had seen enough of these, and of the seal embossed on the top, to know that it was an original case from the House of Fabergé, court jewelers to the Czars of Russia. At least, that was what it appeared to be. He willed his hands to remain steady, and opened the box.

Inside rested a crystal *flacon à sels*. He recognized it immediately from the pictures he had studied. Almost every book on Fabergé contained an example, as it had been a favorite Christmas gift of the Empress Alexandra. It was designed as a container for either smelling salts or special healing salts brought in from some distant land, but as with many Fabergé items, it was probably rarely used. Such an item, even when originally acquired, was seen as a work of art to be enjoyed as such, rather than something that required a function.

The crystal jar was slender as a lady's finger and octagonally shaped, the tiny dividing ridges chased with gold laurel bands. The cap was hand-fashioned from red gold in the form of an Eastern crown, and topped with a cabochon sapphire. It rested on a silk lining stamped with the Imperial Russian Eagle and the words *Fabergé, London, Paris, St. Petersburg* in Cyrillic, the Russian alphabet. Jeffrey had seen the words often enough in his reference books to identify them immediately.

The object within the second bundle was equally impressive: a slender gold box, perhaps twice the size of a pack of cigarettes. On its underside was scripted *Jean Fremin, Paris, 1759*. Jeffrey did not recognize the jeweler's name, but traditionally only artists with better-known houses signed their work. The sides were decorated with carefully etched desert scenes done with royal blue enamel, or *basse taille*. Jeffrey opened the lid to find that the inner lining contained a miniature painting done on ceramic. It showed a young woman seated in her drawing room. The colors, preserved by second-firing the ceramic once the portrait was completed, were as vivid as the day they were painted. The miniature was held in place by an intricately scrolled bezel of gold.

Another round of translation ended with Gregor asking, "How much do you think they are worth?"

He was accustomed enough to the question now not to cringe. "Please tell them that I cannot give a true figure until they have been evaluated by experts. Which I am not." He waited until this had been translated, and saw the small man nod his understanding. He went on. "But if they are real, which I think they are, they will be worth quite a bit."

The tension was palpable as Gregor translated and returned with, "How much is that?"

"At least ten thousand dollars. Minimum. Per item."

Gregor took out a pen and a piece of paper. As he wrote down the figures, he said to Jeffrey, "My insistence on this little act almost cost us the first deal with the gentleman seated to my right. He had clearly intended to use his mastery of Ukrainian as a means of exacting a larger commission. But I stood my ground, and he has come to see that my insistence on honesty has earned us more new business, and therefore more profits, than he would ever have gained from one large killing."

He picked up the paper, held it over one piece and then the other, and said each time the single word, "Dollar."

The Ukrainian's eyes grew round, then he nodded and spoke sharply. The translation was, "It is agreed."

"Make sure he understands that we won't know anything about their real worth until the evaluation is completed."

The translation came back, "He wants two thousand dollars now for both pieces. He needs that to buy essential things for his family. The rest he will receive later by means that we have already worked out. And two hundred dollars more for our friend here."

"All right." Jeffrey brought out the money. The man watched him count, scooped up the money, shook hands swiftly all around, and headed for the door.

"Wait," Jeffrey called out. "Ask him what it's like over there."

The small man turned from the door long enough to give him a haunted look. Through Gregor he replied, "Hell."

Gregor was visibly in pain by the time they returned to the car. "All this movement has aggravated my condition. I fear that I must take a few days off and rest. I am indeed sorry for having let you down."

"You haven't let anyone down."

"Perhaps, perhaps not." Gregor spoke to the driver, who nodded and started off. "Would you please allow me to make one stop on the way home? It is personal business, some medicines I must drop off, and which must be done today."

"Sure."

"Thank you." He gave instructions to Tomek, then continued, "The problem we face with my being ill, you see, is that I have arranged our buys to a rather precise timetable. Many of these people face extremely dire needs. For us to postpone our visits raises the risk that they will seek other buyers, even if they know they may well be cheated." Gregor shifted in his seat, searching for a more comfortable position. "I shall endeavor to heal as fast as possible."

Their way took them out beyond the rows of high-rise concrete tenements that ringed the city, into the verdant green countryside. The roads became increasingly narrow and potholed. They turned into a small grouping of nondescript houses, stopping before what appeared to be a Victorian manor. Its pale yellow paint had long surrendered to the march of winds and rains and winters, its fenced-in yard equally neglected.

"Where are we?"

"This is what I do with my income from the antiques," Gregor replied. "That is, here is one such project. Would you like to come along?"

"Sure."

"Splendid. It won't take long."

A set of new swings and slides on one side of the entrance gate stood in glaring opposition to the house's general state of disrepair. To the other side of the path leading toward the front door was a massive pile of coal.

Gregor noted the coal spill as they walked toward the entrance. "Ah, it arrived. Excellent. Only nine months late. Just in time for next winter, I suppose."

"What is this place?" Jeffrey asked.

"A state-run home for young orphans," Gregor said, pushing open the door and shouting into the dark interior. "I work with the very young and the very old, you see. I seek out the ones who are least able to work for themselves."

A slatternly woman in a filthy apron and gray-grimed

dress waddled out on dilapidated slippers, dried her hand, and offered it stiffly to Gregor. He bowed over it as though greeting royalty, turned and pointed to Jeffrey. The woman gave him an indifferent nod and pointed back down the murky hallway.

"She is now alone, at least as far as the state is concerned. Her two assistants were let go, as the state no longer had money to pay them. She is responsible for cleaning, cooking, and tending to the needs of sixty-one children."

"That's impossible."

"I have hired two young village girls to come in and help her. But all the state orphanages are suffering from funding cut-backs, and I can only do so much." He turned and walked down the hall. "Come. Let me show you something."

They entered what had once been a formal sitting parlor, and was now a sort of holding pen for young children. There was not a stick of furniture in the room. Some of the children held ragged toys, others blankets, but they were not doing anything. Five- and six-year-old children just sat and rocked constantly, hugging themselves and humming a single note. Their blank faces yearned for what they had never known.

Gregor stepped through the doorway, and immediately they *surged* toward him, gluing themselves to him, reaching for any part possible to touch, to hold, to hug. Their little voices keened a wordless cry.

"They have food and clothing, these children," Gregor explained over the clamor. "But they have no love. If you are feeling brave, I dare you to smile."

Jeffrey did. Gregor bent over, shook a child loose from his sleeve, and turned the boy around. He pointed toward Jeffrey and said something. Immediately several children turned and searched his face, then *flung* themselves on him.

"Alcoholic parents, unwed mothers, families who cannot afford another child," Gregor said above the loud keening. "Most are not the victims of disaster, but of neglect—which of course is a disaster all its own, as far as these children are concerned."

Uplifted faces searched Jeffrey's face with a yearning that threatened to pull his heart from his chest. He stroked a little face, found his wrist held with a ferocity born of lonely panic.

"The children here are neglected," Gregor said. "They are

intellectually and emotionally starved. Their parents are either dead or too tired, too worried, too beaten down, or too drunk to give them the love and the attention they need. We—myself and the people with whom I work—try to set up visiting schedules using people with a good heart and a strong faith. We have book-lending trucks for the older children. We arrange for doctors to make regular visits. We set up groups small enough to give each child some personal attention, and take them out to show them a bit of the outside world. We try to awaken hope, to stimulate thought. It is so much more important than giving them a piece of candy or another bit of clothing."

As they were leaving the house, with a dozen-dozen little faces pressed to the windows, Gregor told him, "It is far worse in the handicapped children's homes. I would not dare to take you there on your first visit. Under the Communists, these little people were simply written off. They spend their time lying in bed for lack of wheelchairs and people to push them. They need everything, my dear boy. Everything from toys to baths to hands who will bathe them with love."

Jeffrey was immensely relieved that the first call to come through that evening was the one to Alexander. He shouted over the static, "How are you feeling?"

"Not well, I'm afraid. It seems that I am powerless to silence voices I have no desire to hear. It makes me wonder if perhaps there is not some message which I should heed. Much as I detest the notion, it is not one that I am able to shake."

Jeffrey resisted the urge to tell of his conversation with Gregor. Now was not the time. "Gregor has been taken ill."

"Ah," Alexander sighed. "This trip has proven to be a veritable deluge for you, Jeffrey. Perhaps you should return home and wait for a more opportune moment to make your debut."

"I'm doing okay, really. I've found some good pieces, and Gregor says there are some other things that we'll lose if we don't move swiftly."

"Gregor tends to know best about such things." Alexander's voice gathered a bit of strength. "I take it you have a plan."

"I really need an interpreter, someone I can trust. I was wondering if I might ask Katya to join me."

Alexander was silent a moment. "I have had a most delightful time coming to know your young lady. The more we talk, the more I am reassured with your choice." There was another pause, then he said, "I find myself unable to face the prospect of returning to Poland at this moment. I must therefore agree with your idea. You will impress upon her the need for secrecy."

"As hard as I can."

"Very well. Do as you see fit. I would be grateful if you would try to call from time to time. I realize that it is sometimes harder to find a telephone line to the outside world than it is to find the crown jewels of Russia, but nonetheless I would like to hear from you when it is possible. Your calls do me more good than I shall ever be able to convey."

"I'll try every night," Jeffrey replied. "Take care of yourself."

"I shall do my utmost, although I must say that my efforts seem of little avail just now. Perhaps you might ask my cousin to remember me in his prayers."

"I'll tell him," Jeffrey replied. "But I imagine it's going to be superfluous. I don't think he's ever stopped."

The call to Katya took another four hours. After apologizing his way around an extremely irate roommate who answered the phone, he said, "I need you."

"Where are you?" The voice sounded totally asleep.

"Don't you want to know who this is first? Katya, wake up. This is the real world calling."

"Jeffrey?"

"Katya, come on. I can't give you time for coffee. It took three bribes and two shouting matches to get through to you once."

"Aren't you supposed to be in Poland?" She worked the words out around a yawn.

"Where do you think I'm calling from? Of course, the way these phones operate I might as well be on the dark side of the moon. Katya, are you awake yet?"

"Sort of."

"I need you. My world is unraveling here. I can't even talk to my driver."

"You have a driver?"

"It's part of my inheritance from Alexander."

"He's dead?"

"Come on, wake up, Katya. No. You spent this afternoon with him in the shop."

"Oh yeah," she said around an enormous yawn. "I remember now."

"I've had to take over for him."

"He wouldn't tell me why you had to stay there all alone." Katya yawned again. "Can't this wait until morning?"

"No!"

"There's no need to shout, Jeffrey."

"Take a deep breath, Katya. You have *got* to wake up." There was a long pause. "Katya?"

"I'm here, Jeffrey." Her voice sounded more focused.

"I need you. Can you come tomorrow?"

"You want me to fly to Poland? Really?"

"Desperately really. Can you meet me here in Cracow?"

"I've never been to Cracow."

"I sure hope you're awake. Can you come?"

"Yes, I'm awake." There was another pause, then, "Yes, all right. I'll come. If you really need me."

The pleasure he felt at her words bordered on pain. He had not even wanted to admit how much he had been missing her. "I do. In more ways than one."

"What is that supposed to mean?"

"Let's leave the discussions for your arrival. You need to call Alexander at Claridge's first thing tomorrow morning. He will make your travel arrangements and fax me your arrival details. And, Katya, it's very important that you don't discuss this with anyone besides your mother."

"You've explained the need for secrecy. I haven't forgotten." Her voice took on the tone of a little girl's. "It will be nice to see you again, Jeffrey. Especially in Cracow."

CHAPTER
16

Greeting Jeffrey with a fierce hug upon her arrival, Katya allowed him to take her first by the hotel and then into the center of town. She made no attempt to hide her excitement. "I've always wanted to come here."

"Gregor suggested we walk to the central square and have lunch there," Jeffrey said. "Then we meet with him, and afterward get back to work."

Following the hotel receptionist's directions, Jeffrey led her the seven blocks to where entry into the city's old town was announced by a return to cobblestone streets. Katya walked slowly, her eyes bright with discovery, her gaze touching everything.

She pulled him over to one side. "Look at this old state-run store. That's how drab everything looked the last time I was in Poland. You can't believe how startling it is to come back and find so many new signs of capitalism springing up. Let's go inside, so you can see for yourself how it used to be."

The lamp store fully retained it's stodgy socialist style. Wares were displayed on unpainted plywood shelves. "This is everything the shop has," Katya whispered. "There isn't any back room for extra stock, and there's no need to ask the shopkeeper anything. She's here just to take your money. And don't expect her to thank you or ask you to come again."

The glass globes were dusty, the wares outdated, the bulbs packed in little gray cardboard boxes stamped with smeared Russian Cyrillic. The shop was empty save for a bored young woman camped behind her magazine, the air dusty and undisturbed by change. Katya picked up a hand-blown ceiling light and read the tag. "This translates into thirty-seven cents. They set the price before the government changed, and they never bothered to alter it. They'll just sit here and wait for the government to get around to selling the shop and putting them out of business. It's called Communist initiative."

Next door was a new store, its window set in a shiny copper frame on a marble base. Its wares suggested the shop was still so new that the owners were not yet sure what would sell—women's high-heeled shoes competed for space with Japanese watches, cordless telephones, electronic pocket games, pressure bandages, and bras.

No one on the street smiled. People stared at shop windows, darted their eyes everywhere, or stared at nothing. Everyone they passed seemed to give him one swift glance, recognize in an instant that he was foreign and Western, then turn determinedly away.

An old woman in a filthy woolen shawl came by, begging with a tear in her eye and a crack in her voice. She shuffled from one passerby to the next, never raising her steps from the stones, her feet encased in men's work shoes that slapped softly against her feet. Jeffrey gave her the equivalent of twenty cents, and was rewarded with a sign of the cross made by hands knotted with arthritis.

When they entered Cracow's vast central square, Katya pointed to the tall age-blackened church with its two spires of totally different designs. "It's called the *Mariacki,* and it's over a thousand years old. Part of it, anyway. There's a living legend attached to it, as there is to a lot of this city. Most of the stories are based on fact. So much has happened here that they don't need to make anything up."

"I thought you told me you hadn't ever been here before."

"When did I say that?"

"On the phone last night."

"I don't remember."

"I'm surprised you remembered which city to go to, you were so asleep."

"I was awake by then. It's true, though. This is my first visit to Cracow."

"So how do you know about all this?"

"I read, Jeffrey. They have books about Poland. It's not the middle of darkest Africa or anything."

"So tell me the living legend."

"Legend isn't right. Legend has to be fiction. Living history is better." She pointed at the left-hand spire. "Every hour a trumpeter comes out and plays the *Hejnal,* which is an old Hungarian word for revelry. He plays it to the four corners of the globe. The trumpet call always cuts off in the middle of a note. It symbolizes the time the Tartars invaded Cracow—I'm not sure when, I think around six hundred years ago. A Tartar arrow stopped the trumpet call when it pierced his throat."

"That's a pretty grisly story to repeat every hour for six hundred years."

"A study of Polish history is a study of war." She looked up at him. "There's a lot of sadness, but a lot of beauty, too."

Like you, he thought. "I'm really glad you came," he said.

She allowed her gaze to linger a moment longer before pointing to the square's central structure. "Let's go in there."

As they walked toward the massive edifice, she said, "This is called the *Sukiennice,* or Cloth Hall. It was built in the fourteenth century to house the cloth, thread, cotton, wool, silk, and dye merchants who clothed the upper half of Central Europe. At that time, Cracow was the capital of the second largest kingdom in the world after the Holy Roman Empire, and cloth was a very important industry."

Wrought-iron lamps hung down the hall's narrow hundred and fifty-foot length. The merchants' stalls were converted into shops selling crystal and amber and tourist trinkets and silver and hand-knit lace. The vaulted ceiling was lined with the old royal shields from the Polish-Lithuanian Empire, which at its height had stretched from the icy wastelands crowning Europe through modern-day Czechoslovakia, Hungary, Bulgaria, Austria, Rumania, the Ukraine, and parts of Turkey.

"There isn't the danger I used to feel here in Poland," Katya said as they crossed from the Cloth Hall to a large cafe at the edge of the square. "There is still sadness, though. Too much of it."

"You'll be meeting Gregor later," Jeffrey replied. "That's one thing the two of you will certainly agree on."

The Café Kawiarnia Sukiennice was a series of bright white and red chambers. The ceilings were domed, the rooms small and interconnected, the windows decorated with wrought-iron, the atmosphere splendidly foreign.

"Look around these rooms," she said. "Every face is a character, an individual. When I go out in London, I feel as if everybody has spent hours polishing off all their individuality. They wear stylish clothes, they fix their hair just so. Then they sit somewhere and pretend that everything in their life is perfect.

"Here they can't, Jeffrey. It's a luxury they can't afford. They come as they are, they sit here because they want to be with a friend or talk with family or just have an ice cream. They don't seem to have on the false facade. They sit without the lies which wealth creates. You look around here and you see a roomful of extremes. Every face is a story. I *love* that. I am sorry for the hardship that created it, but that does not make me love the result any less."

As they waited for Gregor to buzz them into his apartment building, Jeffrey warned her, "As far as Gregor is concerned, you are something of a risk. I imagine he's going to test you a little."

"Of course he will," Katya replied, and pushed on the door as the latch sounded.

By the time they made their way up the two flights of stairs, Gregor had returned to his bed. He sat propped up by a half dozen pillows, wrapped within a voluminous shawl. Still he greeted them with a genuine smile. "You must excuse me for not rising any more than absolutely necessary. When my joints become inflamed, there is no better healing salve than rest."

"Can we do anything to help you?" Katya asked.

"Thank you, my dear. That is most kind. But I have a very sweet old woman who would mother me to death if I let her." He shook Katya's hand, inspecting her frankly. "My cousin was most impressed with you. I can see why. Sit down, my dear. Take the comfortable chair there."

He turned his attention to Jeffrey. "You had your walk around central Cracow? What did you think?"

"I feel as if I've been sent back to school," Jeffrey replied, bringing over one of the straight-backed chairs. "I never realized how little I knew. I think before I came to Poland, my clearest impression of the East was of people standing in line."

"It was quite a true image," Gregor replied. "Before, when people saw other people standing in line, they automatically assumed it was for something worth buying. If they had time, they got in line too."

"It was a favorite way of passing a few idle hours," Katya agreed. "If you got to the head of the line and it was not something you needed, you'd buy it anyway. There was always someone you knew who could use it."

Gregor gave Katya a thoughtful look. "You built up obligations—in a good way, of course. The word is *Rewanz,* a positive revenge."

"Reciprocation," Katya offered. "Returning a favor."

"Exactly. You balanced obligations. You helped out neighbors because you knew they in turn would help you out."

Jeffrey asked, "So what happened if someone always took and never gave in return?"

"That very seldom happened," Katya replied. "Too much was at stake."

"No one would ever remind you," Gregor agreed. "You were simply expected to remember."

"You were always conscious of when it was your turn to give a gift or extend an invitation," Katya explained. "There was a sense of honor and duty involved in not allowing the relationship to get out of balance."

There was a moment of silence, with Gregor smiling

and nodding. "So, so. Tell me, my dear. When were you last in Poland? This is most certainly not your first visit."

"No. It was two years ago, just before the first cracks in the Communist power-structure appeared."

"Things have changed," Gregor said mildly.

"I've noticed."

"Yes, we passed through our period of euphoria, and now we're in a period of worry. Already we are forgetting what we gained, and are spending all our time wanting for more."

"Many of the people I've seen on the street look shell-shocked," Jeffrey said.

"Indeed they do," Gregor agreed. "They have come to realize that with the opportunities of change comes the darkness of uncertainty. That was one thing which the Communist regime stifled, you see. Change. Security for the worker was achieved by imposing iron-bound laws backed by fear."

"I have never seen so many people on shopping streets," Katya said. "Everybody stops and looks at all the windows, standing there for hours."

"The shortages are gone," Gregor said. "Nowadays the only thing that is hard to come by is money. Unemployment is rising daily as more and more obsolete factories are losing their government subsidies and are being forced out of business. The government is in virtual bankruptcy, services are being cut back, and with the West in recession there is little help coming. People are worried over how to make ends meet, and afraid of being hungry."

"Not just for food, from the looks of things," Katya said.

"Exactly. They are hungry for things they have seen in television and magazines and never had the chance to try or taste or wear or drive or own. Their hunger for experimenting in all these new Western wares is immense. Overwhelming is a better word. They are overwhelmed by desire for things they now find in stores, which before were nothing more than wispy visions of a world they weren't sure really existed at all."

"I remember," Katya said. To Jeffrey she explained, "Russia was always sending propaganda throughout Poland about what a great life communism was giving them.

Poles *knew* this was a lie. But when they saw pictures from the West—on television or in a magazine or from a cousin in Chicago—they not only believed that the wealth was there, but also that it was easy to have. *Everybody* in the West was rich, in their eyes. There was this misguided notion that dollars were lying along the American streets just waiting to be picked up. And this has been the great disenchantment. All these fabulous goods are now on display here in Poland, but almost no one can afford them. Simply to be joined with the West does not guarantee immediate wealth."

"The people are exhausted," Gregor went on. "They are stretched to the last possible limit, and this is causing an incredible isolation. Isolation of people, isolation of families, isolation of regions. Dialogue is gone. When I go to a council of regional Protestant and Catholic churches, theological differences are a luxury that no one can afford. The topics are how to feed the children. How to obtain medicine for the sick. How to stop the spread of pornography among the young. How to combat alcoholism."

"The Communist system guaranteed a certain stability," Katya said. "Despite oppression and foreign domination and persecution and fear, it nevertheless offered the common folk security. There was bread. There was heat. There was a roof over everyone's head. These were valuable things to people who had been totally devastated by war after war after war."

"But the cost." Sorrowfully Gregor shook his head. "My goodness, the cost. Look into the eyes of a nation taught not to strive, to hope. There you will find the cost."

There was a moment's silence; then Katya stood and said, "Perhaps you two would like to have a moment alone together. It was very nice meeting you, Gregor."

He extended a hand and a very warm smile. "My dear, the pleasure has truly been my own."

"I'll see you downstairs, Jeffrey."

As her footsteps echoed down the stairway, Gregor said, "That is a remarkable young woman you have found for yourself. Or perhaps that God has found for you. I wondered at Alexander's decision to allow a stranger to work with you, but now I see that he was correct."

"It means a lot to hear you say that."

"Yes, I can also see a bit of the Mongol horde in Katya. It is true for many of Eastern Europe's most beautiful women—the mysterious slant to their eyes, and cheekbones shaped by icy Steppe winds."

Jeffrey couldn't help but smile. "I thought you weren't supposed to notice such things."

"Who on earth told you such nonsense? Not my cousin, I hope."

"No one did."

"My dear young friend, faith does not make one a eunuch. It simply points out the borders of correct thought and action. There is a very great difference between appreciating beauty and *desiring* it."

"I suppose I've never thought of it like that," Jeffrey confessed.

"Human society says so long as the person is not violated, there is no harm in lust. But God says you must draw the line at appreciating, before it hardens into sinful thought." Gregor smiled. "Such beauty is always a joy to appreciate."

Jeffrey felt the familiar ache. "And what if I can't appreciate her without wanting her?"

Gregor turned an understanding gaze on Jeffrey and replied gently, "Then temper your desire with God's love. And want her first as your wife."

Jeffrey looked toward the open door. "For the first time in my life I can think about taking that step without diving for cover. I just wish I knew how she felt about it."

"You are most fortunate, my boy. The girl loves you dearly."

"Alexander said the same thing. I wish I knew how you two could be so certain. She sure doesn't show it."

"In her own way, she makes it perfectly clear, I assure you. She does not tell you what you wish to hear because you are not yet ready to receive it."

"I'm ready all right."

"No, no, listen to what I am saying. The girl loves *you*. Not the man you want to become, and certainly not the man you want the world to see. She loves *you*." He reached to the side table for pen and paper. "The question is whether you are able to make peace with the true Jeffrey Sinclair. She has, you may rest assured of that. She has seen you as you are and she loves you. That should help you quite a bit."

Gregor scribbled busily, said, "Give this to Tomek. He will take you to meet a gentleman in a village less than an hour from here."

Jeffrey accepted the slip. "Do you think I could come by and talk with you some more?"

"Nothing on this earth could give me more pleasure," Gregor replied. "Perhaps you can stop by alone in the mornings before you begin work."

"That would be great. Thanks."

"My dear boy, it is I who thank you." Gregor adjusted his shawl. "And now you should be going. It is best to return before nightfall. Vodka remains the greatest hazard on Poland's roads, and you have more difficulty recognizing who is caught in its clutches after dark."

CHAPTER
17

As they left the main road and made their way through small townships, Jeffrey said, "I wonder what life is like in these villages."

"For most young people with intelligence and ambition, it is an imprisonment for the crime of daring to hope and to dream." Katya shook her head. "It is because of the pressures *against* success that the Communists have so beaten down this people."

"You and Gregor agree on that point."

"I imagine there are a lot of things where Gregor and I agree."

Outlying villages gave way to a concrete forest of high-rise tenements, and they to an unending stream of three-story apartments. The street became hemmed in by gray sameness—without pause, without individuality. Buildings appeared to lean inwards, pressing down on the sidewalks and the streets and the people with a draining force. Here there is no hope of change, they seemed to say. No hope of improvement. No way to escape.

"Even in the poorest villages there was at one time a castle and a cloister," Katya told him. "Wars have done away with one or both in many places. In the villages where the Communists rebuilt, they did not feel a need to spend money on a heart, a town center. The streets have an aimless feel, none of them leading anywhere."

The car stopped a block away from what appeared to be the town's only park—a dusty, unkempt stretch of grass with a few twisted trees. Beyond the park loomed a factory, its trio of smokestacks defiantly dwarfing the park's stunted growth. Jeffrey and Katya left the car and entered a first-floor flat, where a man identified himself as the former factory manager.

"I'm out of a job," he had Katya translate once they were seated on a rock-hard sofa. "I didn't move fast enough."

Jeffrey nodded as though he understood, and practiced patience. The man was overweight as only a once-skinny man could be. A pronounced swayback gave his overhanging belly an even greater bulge. His eyes and hair were grayish brown, his voice equally drab. Katya kept her face blank and nodded in time to his words. She waited until he was finished, then turned back to Jeffrey. "I do not like this place, can we please hurry?"

"What did he say?"

"Nothing of importance." She rushed through the words, blurring them together. "He probably speaks a little of our language. I'm talking just to fill the air. Can you ask me to ask for the furniture?"

Jeffrey nodded solemnly, as though receiving information of great importance. He replied, "May I please see the items for sale?"

The man nodded and led the way down the hall to a door that he unlocked and ushered them inside. The room held a set four Biedermeier pieces, one of the few intact sets Jeffrey had everseen. They were all of ash, another rarity, the grain so fine as to outshine the paintings on the walls above them.

Biedermeier furniture dominated the style houses of central Europe from 1815 to around 1850. Its strict lines and lack of gaudy exterior decoration was intended as an absolute rejection of the overblown carvings and intricate mosaics of earlier periods.

Closest to Jeffrey was an upright secretary-cabinet, the fold-down face flanked by black side pillars. Its straight unyielding lines were made more delicate by the ash's grain. Beside it stood a waist-high chest of drawers, and beside that a sofa table on a center-column and platform base. The real prize sat against the back wall—a settee fully nine feet in length. Rising from the silk upholstery was a long back piece carved from one single massive tree. The circular arms were also entire tree trunks, but scrolled with a waved pattern that gave even their massive breadth a delicate air.

Jeffrey worked to keep his voice calm. "Anything else?"

The man deflated instantly. In broken English he said, "Is not okay?"

"It's excellent. Really first rate."

The room lit up again. "And the price?"

"Equally high. Are there any more pieces for sale?"

With unrestrained eagerness Jeffrey was led to the bedroom, where a suite of garishly modern quasi-Western furniture sidled up to one piece that dominated the room.

"Polish," the man announced proudly.

"It certainly might be," Jeffrey replied, stooping for a closer look.

"No might. Is. Is. Have picture in book."

Polish Biedermeier was called Simmler, after the major factory in Warsaw at the time. It was very rare, as few pieces had survived in this war-torn land. The chest of drawers was of nut burl, and the tree that had sacrificed its roots for the facade must have been massive—the top and each drawer was covered by one solid strip of veneer. Jeffrey felt a keen sense of pleasure; if authentic, it would be a nice piece for Alexander to present to the new regime.

When they were back in the car and under way, Jeffrey asked, "What did that factory manager say that so upset you back there?"

"It wasn't what he said," Katya replied. "He's probably like a lot of others, but it was sort of like having a snake crawl out of the grass when you're not expecting it."

"What do you mean, like the others?"

"Oh," Katya sighed. "He probably started off a staunch Communist, not just a Party member for the sake of his card but a real activist. That was more or less required for somebody in a position like his. But like a lot of them in the late eighties he saw the writing on the wall and started working strong for Solidarity. He was too shrewd to go down with the Communist clunker, too flexible, too awake.

"Then came the time for the government to sell all the state-owned companies. As long as the Communists were in power, all companies were state owned. All of them, Jeffrey, from the local newspaper vendor to the biggest car factory.

Private companies were against the law. So now the new government was to sell these companies. How? By auction. When? At a time to be announced. To whom? Whoever bid the most money."

"Here comes the catch," Jeffrey guessed.

"But of course. The problem was, how was the auction to be announced? Well, if the company director was shrewd and kept his old ties, it might have been with one group of placards that were conveniently misplaced, and one well-timed telephone call."

"So what do you think happened here?"

"Who knows? Maybe a foreign company decided it was a perfect entry into the new capitalistic Poland, and all the attention kept everybody honest. Or he was caught trying a fast one. Or maybe, just maybe, the people in this region responsible for the auctions were intent on being honest. That happened, too—not everywhere, but more often than you might think."

As they passed beyond the high-rise apartment houses and re-entered the countryside, Katya pointed to a small chapel where a crowd was gathering. "Could we please stop for afternoon Mass? It would be lovely to hear one in Polish again."

Sheep grazed in a pasture beside the priory, and blossoming fruit trees gave the enclosure a sweetly perfumed air. Under the shade of a dozen ancient trees stood over two hundred people with hands folded in front of them, facing toward the unseen priest.

"There is no room left inside," Katya whispered as they approached the crowd. "It is the same all over Poland."

Katya stood and listened, and Jeffrey contended himself by watching those around him. The children played quietly or stood and faced the church with their elders. The attitude was prayerful, respectful, peaceful. The contrast to the hopelessness he had felt in the street could not have been greater.

Once they were again under way, Katya asked him, "Why isn't Alexander here with you? He wouldn't tell me anything."

"We went to Auschwitz two days ago," Jeffrey replied simply.

"Alexander went back to London because of seeing Auschwitz? I don't understand."

"It's a little hard to explain."

The driver said something. Katya turned forward and replied briefly.

"What did he say?"

"He said that yes, Alexander looked very pale when you returned from Auschwitz. What happened there, Jeffrey?"

He turned to the driver. "I didn't know you spoke English."

"Not speak," the man replied, his accent most guttural. "Understand few words."

The driver began speaking in Polish. Reluctantly Katya turned her gaze from Jeffrey and listened in silence. When the driver finished, she sat there for a moment, then without turning back she told him, "He says his school was taken to visit Auschwitz when he was sixteen. What he remembers most was that there was one enormous boy, much larger than anyone else in his class, who used to bully everyone horribly. He says the boy was very cruel and liked to hurt people, especially the smaller children. He would take money from them, and if they didn't have money he would beat them up. At Auschwitz their class was first taken into a big hall where they saw a documentary made by the Russians when they liberated the camp. What he remembers most is that the only one who lost control during the film was the bully. He started weeping so hard the whole hall could hear, and then toward the end when they showed some victims of the medical experiments, he fainted."

Katya was silent for a moment, then said, "I think that's horrible."

Jeffrey shrugged. "There are bullies all over the world."

"I wasn't speaking of the boy. I can't believe they brought schoolchildren to see such horrors."

Jeffrey watched the canopy of verdant tree limbs sweep over their car like a translucent tunnel. Eventually he said, "When I arrived there, that's exactly what I thought, too. I couldn't believe there were so many buses in the parking lot—there must have been twenty or thirty of them, mostly Polish but some German and Czech and English. And kids everywhere. Well, not really young kids. Teenagers. Some probably in college, but I guess most were in their last couple of years of high school. And I thought the same thing. How can they allow their own children to come and see such a nightmare. Why keep it alive?

"Afterward, though, when I walked out, I understood. I don't know if I agree with it, but I do understand, I think. There was one of those barracks, one of the camp halls, that had been set up as a Polish museum. And it wasn't to the people lost in the camp—well, not most of it anyway. It showed life under the Nazi occupation. Alexander translated some of it for me; it was all in Polish. Besides the millions of Jews who were slaughtered, four million Polish Christians died during the occupation. Four million, Katya.

"That was about one-eighth of the entire population. And that was just the number *killed*. There was no estimate for those injured. I guess there wasn't any listing. Let's make it conservative and say another quarter of the population. And then on top of that, how many carried emotional scars?

"There was one document talking about the critical situation for children. By the winter of 1943, they were being restricted to a diet of two hundred calories a day. I stood there trying to remember what our daily intake is—something around three thousand, I think. Then beside the document they had a photograph of two little kids, ten or eleven years old. They were dressed pretty nice, ragged but clean-looking, the boy in a little suit with short pants and the girl in a dress with a petticoat. They looked like puppets, Katya. Just painted sticks inside clothes five sizes too big. They had little shoes on with newspapers for socks. Their legs were so thin I could have made a circle with my thumb and forefinger around their *thighs* and still have room left over. Their faces were so shrunken I could see the edges of their skulls jutting out from around their eyes. And their eyes . . . I can't get them out of my mind. I have nightmares about their eyes."

The driver turned onto a four-lane highway and speeded up. The road was almost empty. He glanced at his watch and said something. Katya did not reply. Her eyes were fixed on Jeffrey's face, her attention unwavering. The driver glanced into his rearview mirror, and lapsed into patient silence.

"When I walked out of the camp," Jeffrey went on, "I looked at all these kids visiting the camp in a totally different way. When I went in, I was watching them and half-wondering which one might have had a relative or the relative of a friend who had been here. When I came out, I wondered if any of them came from a family that *didn't* suffer during the war.

"Auschwitz isn't a monument just to a concentration camp. I didn't understand that before I went. It is a monument to a tragedy that covered the whole country. Auschwitz wasn't some isolated island of destruction and death, it was just the eye of the storm. And the storm almost destroyed them.

"Maybe Poland is wrong to show their children this factory of death. There's always the chance that the kids will go away feeling only hate. But maybe they want their children to be able to come back and understand, this is why Auntie Martha walks funny. And why George's father's back is all crooked. And why Grandpa cries whenever he gets drunk and talks about the war. Not because of Auschwitz, but because of what Auschwitz *represents*."

Katya's violet eyes enveloped him. "You've changed, Jeffrey."

He didn't deny it. "These past couple of days, I have been seeing this whole place differently. Before, I couldn't help looking down on them—the Poles, I mean. They're so *sad*. And it's really crazy how much they drink, Katya. After seeing Auschwitz, though, I've been kicking myself for ever feeling superior. This was just one more horror in centuries of occupation and oppression."

"You have learned a lot this trip," she said quietly.

"Back in the camp I was constantly bracing myself. Every time I entered one of those barracks, I felt I had to get ready to face something more horrible than what I'd heard about those places. But it wasn't like that. I didn't see anything new. I just came out feeling different."

"That it was more real for you," Katya suggested.

Jeffrey shook his head. "No, it's always been real. But afterward I saw it in a different way. More personal, not for me, but for the people who had died there. They stopped being this incredible number, four million, five million, and started being individuals. The faces on the walls, the glasses, the names on the suitcases. Each belonged to a person. They shouted out, *I was somebody. Me.*"

He looked out the window. "After it was over I just walked out and returned to the world. I felt such an incredible shock. On one side of the fence is a place of death, and on the other a world of life. I felt as if there should have been a more gradual transition, a no-man's-land, or at least a warning—

beware, beyond this point life starts again."

He was silent for a long while, staring out at the summer scenery, seeing the shadows of other days crowding up around them. Katya waited patiently, her eyes resting upon him with an unblinking steadiness. "Going there brought all the sadness I've found here in Poland into perspective. For the very first time, I'm beginning to understand why so many people walk around wrapped in tragedy. Why so many of the children already look so old."

"It wasn't just the Nazis," Katya said quietly. "You must understand this to understand Poland. Stalin ranks with Hitler as the greatest murderers of modern times. They scarred Poland so deeply that the wounds may never heal. There are no records of how many Poles he shot or sent to Siberia. None. Records were simply not allowed."

"I tell you," Jeffrey said. "These have to be the strongest people on earth, not to be crying all the time."

CHAPTER
18

Rain transformed this world. So long as there was sunshine, it was possible to believe that at least one direction was open to escape. With the rain the sky closed down, a gray ceiling to a wet gray world. The sense of imprisonment was complete.

Jeffrey hurried through the blustery summer rain to Gregor's apartment, climbed the stairs, found him propped up in bed and looking very worried. "What's the matter?"

"There has been a most unfortunate change of plans. Have you ever heard of a place called Wieliczka?"

"No, I don't think so."

"No matter. Poland's most famous salt mine is located in that village. We store our purchased antiques there."

"In a salt mine?"

"It has served us well for over twenty years. Cool salt air is ideal for preserving fine wood." He plucked fitfully at his shawl. "The mine is a labyrinth longer than Poland is wide. During the last war whole airplanes were constructed in its depths. We have handled a number of articles for people of that region, and like miners all over the world, they are experts at keeping secrets."

"They want more money," Jeffrey guessed.

"It seems that they too have been hit by the economic crisis," Gregor agreed. "It is not just that they want more money. I am now concerned at just how long they will remain trustworthy."

"How much do I pay them?"

"They want another five thousand dollars. I would suggest you agree. Otherwise there is the risk that the articles may not stay sold." Gregor reached to his side table, and handed over three sheets of paper covered with a cramped scrawl. "I have prepared an inventory of those items I purchased before your arrival. You should use this as an opportunity to make sure none of the pieces have grown legs."

Gregor leaned back and seemed to melt into his pillows. "Have a successful trip, my boy. I shall be with you in my prayers."

The salt mines' central building was painted a bright pastel, its wrought-iron gate and ornate veranda giving the place a very cheerful look. Children swarmed and laughed and did nothing to hide their excitement. The adults around them, both those with the children's groups and other visitors to the mines, watched their antics with genuine fondness.

Katya returned from calling for their contact. She saw the direction of Jeffrey's gaze as she sat down beside him. "The Polish people truly love their children," she said. "Oh, there are some exceptions, mostly brought on by too much stress and hardship and alcohol. But for the most part children here are really loved. The majority of parents have forced themselves to develop an incredible amount of endurance and patience for the sake of their children." She brushed at a wayward strand of silky black hair and went on, "They remain patient with an impossible life, all for their children. They endure suffering so that their children may have a home and food and learn hope. They imagine a better world for their little ones, and now, God willing, they may see it."

"There is so much to learn here," Jeffrey said.

Katya pointed to a marble plaque alongside the entrance. "It's a line of poetry from a Polish writer. It says, 'You praise what is foreign, and remain blind to the riches at your feet.' "

Jeffrey returned his gaze to the children. "This really is a land of contrasts. Night and day. I've never been in a place where there is so much to hate, but so much to love as well. So much beauty."

"A land of night and day," Katya said, and smiled at him. "I like that very much."

A young man in miners' coverall and torch-lit hat made his way through the children. He gave them a perfunctory greeting, asked about Gregor, shrugged at Katya's reply. He was a short, solidly built man who spoke in quick bursts, which she hurried to translate.

"He says his name is Casimir," Katya said. "We are here for a private tour if anyone asks, and we are going to take the standard route as far as we can."

Casimir pushed his way through the heavy fire door and led them down a sloping narrow tunnel. They came to a square mine shaft lined with wooden stairs. Jeffrey took time to look over the banister and saw a group of teenagers descending far below them; beneath that was nothing save the stairs tunneling into darkness.

"There are 320 kilometers of tunnels," Katya continued to translate. "We'll go down 300 meters today, which is 890 stairs. He says not to worry; we'll take the miners' elevator back to return to the surface.

"This is the oldest working salt mine in the world, and has been in operation for over eight hundred years. The earliest commercial sale document they have is dated 1281, but it speaks of a mine that's been in existence for at least one hundred years before that."

It took them almost fifteen minutes to reach what Casimir said was the first of three stages of descent. Jeffrey flexed his knotted leg muscles and reached over to touch what looked like logs frosted with ancient ice. It was salt.

Cramped halls made for people far shorter than he opened unexpectedly into massive domed caverns. Their guide took evident pride in the mine, and showed no hurry in reaching their goal. They passed cavern after cavern filled with statues, all carved from salt by the miners in their free time.

One cavern showed a salt peasant kneeling before a salt queen and her warriors beneath a hoary salt icicle ceiling. "In 1251," Casimir said through Katya, "Queen Kinga's father gave her a salt mine in Hungary as a wedding present. She threw her engagement ring into the salt pit to commemorate her ownership. The legend is that a miner here in this very mine, some thousand kilometers away, found the ring.

He went to her court, offered the ring, and told her that it was a sign from God for her heart and her wealth to remain in Poland. She went on to become one of Poland's greatest rulers."

In the next cavern, another set of salt men knelt and crawled in narrow passages with salt torches held above their heads. "Ever since a fire in 1740," Casimir told them, "the highest paid miners were the ones who crawled the new passages with torches held to the ceiling. Methane was given off in the mining of salt, and they tried to ignite the little gas bubbles before they gathered. These miners did not usually live long."

They passed down a second long set of stairs to the mine's next level, where the air took on a crisp feeling. It tingled in the throat and left the lungs feeling scrubbed.

They entered the largest of the mine's forty-four underground chapels, where saints, altar, chandelier, walls, chalice and cross were carved from salt. "Construction was started in 1600," he told them. "And it was used by the miners for weddings, baptisms, funerals, masses, and daily prayers until the Austrians conquered Poland about two hundred years ago. Their governors decided that the Poles prayed too much, and closed all the chapels down."

The hall was over two hundred feet long. Light came from six fifteen-foot-high salt-crystal chandeliers. He walked in awed silence across a floor shaped like geometrical flagstone, which was also carved from salt. The walls were decorated with salt crystal bas-reliefs from the Gospels—the stable birth, the flight to Egypt, Christ carrying the cross, the Last Supper, Thomas doubting the resurrected Christ.

The passage from the second to the third levels was through a cavern so vast it was hard to catch its height. It twisted around in a rough-edged spiral, crowned with a roof like a thatched cottage—only here the thatch was made from entire trees, and each of the supporting columns from two dozen logs lashed together with iron bands.

At the cavern's base, Casimir stopped and waited in silence. Jeffrey understood why this place had been chosen; its size gave them the possibility to look both ahead and behind to spot any nearby groups, and the distant walls were perfect reflectors for footsteps and voices. They stood there for about three minutes before Casimir placed a finger to his lips and led them on.

A hundred meters beyond the cavern, Casimir turned off the main corridor into what appeared to be a dead end. He reached inside a box set above the wall's support logs, and switched on a light; instead of a simple indentation in the tunnel, they faced a metal gate. Beyond it a narrow corridor stretched down at least a quarter mile.

Walking the corridor's length was the only moment during the entire passage that Jeffrey felt the weight of stone and salt and earth bearing down above his head. From ahead of him Casimir spoke in a low voice, and Katya translated, "Down here they developed chambers where the entire collections of both the Vavel Castle Museum and the National Museum can be kept in an emergency. Otherwise they aren't used—except by us."

He stopped before a door recessed in the side wall, like hundreds of others they had passed, marked in no way at all.

The overhead bulb came on to display a chamber stuffed with antiques. Jeffrey fumbled for Gregor's list, began checking off items, resisted the urge to hunker and gawk. A set of Louis Phillippe furniture. An early German secretary so inlaid with burl veneer it was hard to tell the original wood. An English commode of mahogany in impeccable condition. A bureau cabinet, possibly of fruitwood, definitely central European, the ornate carving around its edges creating a frame for the grain's natural artistry. A *fin de siècle* glass-fronted cabinet, its sides carved into a bouquet of blooming lilies.

Jeffrey maneuvered his way among the room's treasures through the narrow U-shaped passage. When he returned to the entrance he was sweating. "All there," he reported.

"Of course it is," the man replied through Katya, his eyes turning hard. "For now."

"What's that supposed to mean?"

"Prices of everything are going up faster than anyone can believe," Katya translated. "Storage space especially."

"We were told that you wanted another payment," Jeffrey replied, forcing his voice to remain steady. "I've been authorized to pay you."

The miner's eyes held a greedy light. He spoke again, and Katya said, "There's a lot of wealth here. Somebody is getting very rich from all this."

"You're getting your share."

"That's good to hear." Casimir nodded in the direction of the room. "We have to work day and night to make sure nobody gets in and steals away these riches."

"The furniture has to be moved soon," Alexander told him by phone that evening.

"Gregor agrees with you. He said that if we can't get the export documents and move it out of Poland, he has another place where we can take the items. It's an old folks' home he works with who'll give us part of their cellar."

"Such a move would be expensive," Alexander said. "And risky."

"Gregor wants to know how long you think it will be before the furniture leaves Poland."

"That is hard to say," Alexander replied. "I needed to make new contacts this trip."

"Is there anything I can do?"

"It would be far better to obtain the proper export documents and ship the furniture immediately." Alexander paused. "I am indeed sorry to burden you with all this your first trip, Jeffrey."

"It happens. To tell the truth, I'm really enjoying myself."

"Indeed. Experience is most certainly the best teacher."

"What exactly would you want me to do?"

"There is an expression in Polish that says, 'He walks after things.' It refers to a man who can get things done, especially when dealing with the government. That is what you require. Someone who will walk your export documents through a different labyrinth, this one inside a government ministry."

"So how do I go about finding someone like that?"

Alexander paused, said finally, "Perhaps this should wait until I am feeling better and can come down to help you, Jeffrey."

"Maybe so, but at least let me try."

"Very well. You are looking for someone whose interests coincide with yours. Perhaps it will be someone with whom I dealt in the old government—Gregor knows most of them. This is doubtful, as past services rendered to a disgraced regime will not carry much weight now. No, it will most likely be someone from within the art world who knew of my earlier efforts, who now has a position in the government."

"Any ideas who that might be?"

"Again, Gregor may be able to tell you. It is part of his responsibility to keep track of such things while I am not around. But because you will be working with someone new to our operation, you are going to need some gift, some important favor or service to offer them. He or she will want to make sure that we still have either assistance or articles of value to bring to the table."

"That's not a lot to go on."

"No, but keep your eyes and ears open. Something may turn up. If you can find that hook, obtaining the export documents should not be too difficult. Many of the new administrators have a very real contempt for the laws instituted by the Communists, and rumor has it that regulations governing the export of antiques are soon to be changed in any case."

"So I'm to find both a person who can actually write the documents, and find something that I can offer them, like maybe an antique of Polish importance."

"That would be the best, of course. But such items do not grow on trees. Have you come across anything you might use?"

"A Polish Biedermeier chest of drawers. Not enough on its own to warrant this kind of special treatment."

"No. Well, a service of some kind, something you can offer that no one else can do, this too would be an excellent gift."

"Sounds impossible."

"Yes, it may well be. In that case, we shall simply have to hope that our friends in the salt mine do not decide to sell the merchandise twice."

"And that you get well soon," Jeffrey added.

"Thank you, yes, it would be very nice if we were to be able to seek this new door together. I have often thought in the past that it would be so much nicer to work with another."

"You have Gregor."

"Ah, but Gregor is often ill, as you can see for yourself. Not to mention the fact that his somewhat peculiar attitudes makes him unsuitable for the rough and tumble of business."

"What would you use as leverage if you were here?"

"That, my friend, is what we must apply ourselves to

identifying," Alexander replied. "And with great diligence."

Friend, Alexander had said. "Gregor has somebody he wants me to go see tomorrow. It's a long shot, something he hasn't felt was all that important until this came up."

"He gave you no details?"

"He said he didn't have any to give me, except that the man spoke English, and that I needed to go alone."

"Strange that he would not have mentioned it before."

"It's a long shot at best, like I said." Jeffrey took a breath. "And the meeting has to take place at Florian's Gate."

"Ah. Well." The life drained from Alexander's voice. "It is certainly one that you must handle yourself, then. Call me when you return. And watch your back."

CHAPTER
19

Dawn painted the promise of a beautiful day in heaven-wide hues of gold and blue when Jeffrey left the hotel the next morning. He walked the brief distance to Gregor's apartment and found him moving painfully about his little alcove fixing tea.

Jeffrey took him by the elbow and guided him back to bed. "Let me do that for you."

Gregor did not complain. "I am most grateful, my dear boy. Just be careful that the stove does not singe your fingers as it has mine."

The kitchen was nothing more than a walk-through closet with a cramped little bathroom at the back. On one side wall, a tiny refrigerator clanked and shivered beneath a dripping faucet and battered sink. Set into the wall overhead was a draining rack for all the utensils and plates Gregor owned—none of which matched. On the opposite wall, twin gas pressure tanks supported a plywood board, upon which rested a portable cooker. A safe distance above this were more shelves, containing a bare minimum of canned and boxed food.

Jeffrey filled a pot with water, lit the stove with a kitchen match, set the pot in place, and went back to the main room. "Do you mind if I ask why you returned to Poland after having escaped?"

"Because I was called," Gregor replied simply.

"That's it?"

"That is more than enough, and all I can offer to someone who has never known the experience. But the *how* of my return is perhaps more interesting. Would you like to hear of it?"

"Sure."

"Very well. On March 5, 1946, Sir Winston Churchill gave an address in America, and we heard it on the air the next day. You are too young to remember, but in these times the radio was our lifeline, our source of joy and entertainment and news. That particular talk became famous later, but it was new then. I still recall the words. He said, 'From Stettin in the Baltic to Trieste in the Adriatic, an Iron Curtain has descended across the Continent."

"I know the expression," Jeffrey said. "I suppose everybody does these days."

"An iron curtain. I can't tell you what an impact those words had on me. I felt the iron curtain had come down inside me, and my life's work was waiting on the other side. It was a very wounded time for me. Zosha, my wife, had died—just before Christmas of that first year in London. Her health had never been good, and she had not really recovered from the strain of our escape from Poland. On rare occasions when my anguish would subside, I would catch hold of this feeling, a very clear sensation that I was being called back home.

"By that time, there was a tremendous amount of suspicion and numerous rumors—and a growing body of hard factual evidence as well—about Stalin's death grip upon Poland. We heard ever more horrific stories of mass arrests and executions. Polish patriots, officers, and intellectuals were being denounced as fascists and shot. Stalin's true nature was being shown by wave after wave of oppression and terror. I knew exactly what I was going to find upon my return. It was impossible for a Pole to meet a Pole anywhere—on the street, in a shop, at the club—without hearing of another atrocity. Street-sweeps were being instituted again, just as in the time of the Nazi occupation. The secret police were again arriving in the middle of the night to steal away whole families and relocate them to Siberia. Yes. I knew what awaited me. But I also knew I was called, and that I was going to go.

"There was one main problem, however. No, that is incorrect. There were two. The first was, how on earth was I going to escape back into Poland. The Polish border police mirrored Stalin's growing paranoia and hatred of everything tainted by the West. All arriving Poles were viewed as spies. After all, why would anyone who had managed to escape wish to return, unless it was to overthrow Stalin's puppet government?

"My second problem, and my greatest worry, was Alexander. I realize that in this day and age you will find this difficult to understand, but I did not want to go against his wishes. I loved and admired him very much. I wanted to go back, yes. I *knew* I was going to return. But I also wanted to do so with Alexander's blessings.

"I began by dropping hints, making it as clear as possible to a man who had no faith in God that I felt this same God was calling me back. But I did not tell him directly that I was going, so he did not have a reason to ask me to stay, do you see? I simply let him know of my desire, and I waited. And I prayed."

Jeffrey caught a whiff of steam from the boiling pot. He moved into the alcove, dropped a pinch of tea leaves into two glasses, filled them with water, picked them up gingerly around the rims, and returned.

"Ah, excellent. Thank you so much, my dear boy. This first cup of tea has become a ritual that holds my mornings together." Gregor blew on the tea and sipped it.

"I don't see how you can drink it like that. The water's still almost boiling."

"Practice, my boy. A practice best done on winter mornings when you have passed a night without heat, and when you awaken to an apartment so cold you are not sure that your pipes are still running." He sipped again. "That night in London, I switched off the radio and went down to the *Ognisko*. Do you know it?"

"Sure. The Polish Club in South Kensington. Alexander takes me there whenever he's in town."

"It was quite a place back then, not a club in the sense of being exclusive. Anyone could enter. It was a place where the Poles of London would gather and feel that they *belonged*. It always made me feel better just to go in there, to hear the Polish voices, smell the stuffed cabbage cooking. I am sure many others felt the same. The atmosphere was always lively in the evenings, filled with serious flirtations and mock conspiracies—and laced with good vodka and cheap cigarettes.

"I went upstairs to a room devoted to the most serious of pursuits—bridge. The stakes were by our standards very high. A game had just broken up, and in the corner of the room I saw Alexander talking with Piotr."

Jeffrey straightened up with a jolt. "Piotr my grandfather?"

"Indeed. I don't know how much you know about what your grandfather did during the war—"

"Nothing at all," Jeffrey replied. "I've never even heard anybody mention it before."

"I thought not." There was a mischievous twinkle to Gregor's eyes. "You didn't think he had been a jeweler all his life, did you?"

"I guess I never thought of it."

"The steady hands and the trained eye that made him a good jeweler in America made him a master at the forgery of documents."

"My grandfather?"

"I assure you, my dear boy, I am not exaggerating. A true master forgerer. He had been very active in the Polish Underground Army. He was an artist of sorts. He had a name for creating the best false documents anyone had ever seen."

Jeffrey leaned back. "Incredible."

"Indeed. War has a tendency to bring out the strangest traits in men, the best and the worst. In your grandfather's case, I am happy to say, it was the best. In any case, he and Alexander were talking to a man in uniform that everyone addressed as *Prosze Pana Kapitana,* or Mister Captain Sir. I suppose he had a name, but to me and the others he was an aristocrat and a war hero, someone who bolstered our own feelings of patriotism by simply allowing us to recognize him in this honorable way.

"London was really the center for maintaining the struggle for Poland during and after the war. The Polish government-in-exile was headquartered there. Almost everywhere you went in Polish circles, there was some bit of intrigue, some preparation for rescue or revolution. The

Captain-Sir was talking to Alexander and Piotr about a man who had worked undercover for them just outside of Warsaw. The man knew a tremendous amount about Red Army activities and intentions. The Soviets had almost consolidated both their position and their new political power. To be sure, they often made promises to hold elections, but by the end of 1945, it was clear to almost everyone that any elections which were held would be rigged. Moscow-trained Communists held key posts in the ministries of Justice and the Interior. They completely controlled the police, the courts, the press, and the new government propaganda machine. It was simply a matter of time before they would eliminate the remaining nationalists in the government structure, and consolidate their power.

"It was time, the Captain-Sir declared, for their undercover man to get out. His situation was becoming too dangerous, and they needed his information back in London. Your grandfather was very concerned, because this man was a friend. The Red Army and the Polish government were cracking down quite severely. No Poles were being allowed out—of course, this had been the situation since the Russians had invaded, but it was growing continually worse. Stalin's paranoia was mounting. He had secret police planted everywhere."

Gregor cradled his cooling glass with both hands, his gaze bright with remembering. "The captain and Piotr were discussing a plan to make their man a set of American documents. You see, there were quite a few Americans going in and out of Poland on these inspection-evaluation missions for reconstruction and foreign aid. What concerned them, and what they were trying to work out, was how to get the documents safely into Poland and in his hands.

"I positively jumped forward, as though struck by a lightning bolt. 'Send me,' I said.

" 'Impossible,' Piotr replied. 'There's a slim chance you could get through, but it's very unlikely. The situation is becoming impossibly tough at the borders. They could ransack everything you have, find an American passport among your things in someone else's name, and then what?'

"The captain agreed. 'They would have you drawn and quartered, and our missions both in England and in Poland could collapse.'

" 'Then send me with one set of travel documents,' I replied. They did not understand. 'I will enter on the American passport, then turn it over to your man for him to exit with. We will simply need to have someone on the other side insert his picture where mine had been before. Or place his under mine, so that I can peel mine off. There must be a way to do that.'

"The captain thought it could work. The document would be stamped upon entering Poland, and there would be no problem exiting a few days later.

" 'Impossible,' Piotr repeated. 'Gregor gets in, delivers the documents, and then what? He'd be trapped there.'

"Alexander spoke for the first time, and told them, 'That has been my cousin's plan all along.' He looked at me with an expression of sadness and defeat, because he knew I had found the one way of returning to Poland to which he would never object. Then and there, it was decided that I would be the courier."

Gregor smiled at Jeffrey. "As you know, Piotr by then had a very good connection in the American Embassy."

"My grandmother?"

He nodded. "She was already his wife by that time, your grandmother. She was so much in love, terribly infatuated with Piotr. When he asked for her help, she could not refuse. Her first sense of loyalty was to him and his causes.

"She dug out an American passport from the vaults, one of hundreds that had been returned to the embassy over the years—perhaps stolen, perhaps lost, who knows. It did not matter. She found one for a Mr. Paul W. Mason. Older than I, not as old as the man waiting near Warsaw. A few travel stamps—Mexico, Canada, Italy, some of the places that I had once dreamed of visiting and now never would.

"Your grandmother prepared a lovely letter of introduction on embassy stationery, and once I had used the letter to obtain a Polish visa, she arranged for a Mr. Paul W. Mason to travel to Warsaw with an American engineering delegation. She booked his return for four days later with a different group.

"Then Piotr worked his magic. He substituted my picture on the passport and forged the embassy seal that covered the photograph's right side. He then took a photograph of the man in Warsaw and embossed it with the same quadrant of seal. I hid this photograph in my package of playing cards, glued between the joker and the ace of hearts. Once I was safely in the country, I lifted my photograph off with a razor and glued his into place. The documents were passed on to our man, and he returned to London in my place.

"When I arrived in Cracow, I informed the authorities that we had fled the Nazis and wound up in a small Carpathian village, someplace so remote that they would not bother to check. There my wife fell ill, I explained, and after her death I returned."

Jeffrey asked, "And all this time, you could never tell anyone here you ever went to the West?"

"The world of an oppressed people is a world of secrecy, my boy," Gregor replied. "There were many things no one told anyone, not even their family. It was not discussed, it was not questioned, it was simply done. For myself, I was forced to pretend that the West had never existed for me."

"Did you ever regret coming back?"

"I have only one regret. And that is, when I die I will not be buried next to my beloved Zosha, whom I laid to rest in London. I must leave it to the Lord above to bring us together somehow." Gregor glanced at his watch. "Goodness, look at the time. You must be on your way, my boy. This is one appointment for which you cannot be late."

Florian's Gate was one of the few remaining portals from the fortified medieval city walls. Beyond it ran a street open only to pedestrian traffic and lined with small shops making the transition from dingy government-run outlets to colorful Western-style boutiques.

Just to the right through the archway was a long stone wall where dozens of artists hung their works in hopes of obtaining a few foreign dollars or marks or francs— anything that would help them to buy further art supplies and feed the hungry mouths at home. Most of the art was very bad—amateurish landscapes, gaudy nudes, predictable still-lifes. A few were good, two or three truly exceptional.

Jeffrey strolled along the makeshift outdoor gallery until he came upon a man fitting the description Gregor had given him. The man was of small stature, with a long thick silver moustache and hands with fingers like stubby cigar ends. He wore a pale gray oversized shirt as an artist's smock over navy-blue pants and shoes so scuffed the color had long since disappeared. He was working intently on what appeared to be a Monet landscape, a scene from the artist's garden at Giverny.

"Mr. Henryk?" When the old man turned toward him, Jeffrey continued. "Gregor tells me you speak English. Your work is good. Very good."

The old man turned and bowed his head slightly. "Parlez-vous francais?"

"Some," Jeffrey replied in English. "A few words. From school, one long vacation a few years back, and now I have some business there."

The man switched to English. "I love France. I *adore* France."

"You've lived there?"

"Ah, no. The closest I've ever come to France is copying a Frenchman's brushstrokes," the old man replied. "But it has always been my dream to go to Paris, to see the art. Yes, that has been the lifelong dream of this artist."

"If it's so important, why not go? You have your freedom now. You can take the train."

Henryk faced Jeffrey straight on. "These eyes are still good," he said. "These hands are still steady. But these legs, no; I could not manage on my own. For me the end of communism came ten years too late."

"Perhaps you can find someone to take you."

"My wife, yes, she would go. But her dream of Paris is a dream of luxury. Fine hotels. Famous shops. Wonderful food. Things that would require much money. And once seeing these things, my wife would not wish to ever return to the hardship of life in Poland."

The man went back to his painting. "Yes, I should like to see Paris before I die." He dabbed at his easel, said casually, "I should also like to tell my secret."

"And what secret is that?"

"If I tell you my story, will you make it possible for my wife and me to live in Paris?"

Jeffrey laughed. "That depends on how good your story is."

"I have reason to believe," Henryk said, "that a painting by Peter Paul Rubens hanging in the Vavel Castle Gallery is a forgery."

"And what makes you say that?"

The old man turned slowly around. "Because I painted it."

Jeffrey worked at keeping a straight face. "Maybe we should go somewhere and talk."

"An excellent idea." Swiftly the man packed up his brushes and paints and folded his easel. He walked over and set them down before another artist, exchanged a few words, returned to Jeffrey, said, "I am at your disposal."

At the man's guidance they walked the half block to the Jama Michalika. Once they were seated, the man said, "This is a cafe by day and a cabaret by night. It gained a most positive reputation under the Communists by being closed down many times. They staged very strong political satire. How do you describe the way you clean metals?" he asked, making a dipping motion with his hand.

"An acid bath?" Jeffrey guessed.

"Exactly. They gave the Communists an acid bath. The Communists did not approve."

The room was decorated with dark hues; it had a warm and snug feeling despite its size, an atmosphere of intimacy despite the lofty stained-glass ceiling. The lighting was indirect, the framed drawings along the walls mostly savage caricatures, the numerous showcases full of Punch-and-Judy puppets depicting Communist politicians.

When the waitress appeared, Jeffrey asked, "Coffee?"

"No, a small glass of champagne, if you don't mind. I want to get into the mood for Paris."

When the waitress left, Henryk continued. "Oh, Paris. You can't imagine what magic that name holds for me. When I was a little boy, my father gave me an album filled with prints from the great French masters. I loved that book. I would spend hours studying each page. That book is why I wanted to become an artist. I too wanted to create something so beautiful, so moving. And to go to Paris . . .

well, the dream started then."

"About the Rubens," Jeffrey pressed.

"Ah yes. In the late nineteen-thirties, as a young graduate of the Academy of Fine Arts, I was hired by the curator of the Vavel Castle Museum. It was my job to inventory paintings, clean the frames, do occasional touch-up work. I was very good at that, you see. Very good. So I began to undertake more and more complex restorations for them. There is a real art to that. You can't imagine. You have to be so careful about texture and color and lines and tension and brushstrokes. Your brush must move like the brush of the master."

The waitress returned, set down the two glasses of champagne, and departed. The old man raised his glass, inspected the golden bubbles for a moment, said, "To Paris."

"To a good story," Jeffrey replied.

Henryk sipped, then set down his glass and went on. "I had a very good boss, a fine man whose heart and soul were broken by the war. A man who dreamed of leaving Poland, much as he loved his country. He asked for my help. He knew he could trust me, and I knew in turn that he would take care of me, that my job would be secure, that I could stay with my art, and not be forced into the factories like so many of my generation.

"You cannot imagine the displacement during and after the war. Displacement of everything. People, families, governments, and art. There was a tremendous stockpile of paintings just outside Warsaw in an old warehouse. The Nazis started the collection in their raids throughout much of Europe, and the Soviets inherited the collection when they marched into Warsaw in 1945. What was there in that warehouse, I cannot even begin to imagine. All of the great names. Treasure troves of jewelry. Tons of silver, literally tons. Crystal. Furniture. Eventually the Soviets loaded a convoy of lorries and hauled most of the treasures to Moscow.

"One of the *aparatchiks* came up with the clever propaganda idea of rewarding Stalin's new Polish allies with a few pieces of art from our own warehouse. Plans were made to disperse a portion of the collection to Poland, to Czechoslovakia, and to Hungary. And so one morning, May

19, 1950, a truck pulled into the castle courtyard and started unloading crate after wooden crate of these masterpieces.

"You can imagine how we felt as we opened up these crates, unwrapped bales of tapestries, opened treasure chests, examined the cabinets and chests—so many that we could not even store them in the museum's unused chambers. The mind boggles at what the Soviets must have taken with them back to Russia.

"A few days later, the curator came into my workshop. It was a funny place for an atelier really, deep in the basements with just a little light through a grimy window set at street level. But I was left completely undisturbed, and I had room to work. Such space and freedom was an unknown gift for my generation. I counted myself blessed and rarely spoke about where I worked or what I did. That day, the curator said he had a special assignment for me. And a favor to ask.

"He brought with him a flat wooden crate, about the size of this table. He set it in front of me, and with the tip of a screwdriver slowly loosened the edges and lifted the top. In one sweeping motion he drew out the Rubens. The Portrait of Isabel of Bourbon, painted in 1628. It was absolutely stunning. There was a tiny brass name plaque on the frame in the center, as if a Rubens really needed to be labeled. The curator asked, 'Can you do this kind of work?'

" 'Well, sir,' I said. 'A Rubens. It would be an honor, a challenge. But it does not look in such bad shape to me.'

"The curator was sweating very heavily. 'It is perfectly all right,' he said to me. 'It does not need to be repaired. It needs to be traded for my freedom.'

"And so I began my work. First I had to find an old canvas, which I did by painting over a meaningless portrait that had sat in our cellars for several centuries. Millimeter by millimeter of painstaking effort, and four months later I was ready to bake and oil and smoke and in this way age our new work by the old master. Or so the world would think.

"We placed my work in the original frame, tagged with the little brass plaque that said Rubens, and hung it with great ceremony. The delay was explained by the need for substantial restoration work.

"Things were quite fluid and confused after the war. Our curator had thought it would be a matter of months before he could slip away to the West in some delegation, and there find a buyer for the original. Questions would not have been asked in the West. Even from within our Soviet-made cell we knew that there was such a place as a Swiss bank vault, where buyers could be brought to view a work, with absolute secrecy as to the seller's identity. The forgery in Cracow would immediately be denounced, and the experts would cluck and say they suspected it all along, and would quietly blame the Soviets' artistic judgment for having thought it a true Rubens in the first place.

"But the curator was not permitted to leave. He knew too much about art, about what art the Soviets had stolen and what had been confiscated during the war and never returned. He was also a little too outspoken for the regime's own good. And so they denied his application for a passport, and posted him to the art history museum in Kielce."

"I've never heard of it," Jeffrey said.

"Hardly anyone ever has. It is a small provincial town— for a man such as him, it was a Polish Siberia. He died soon after, never having exchanged the Rubens for his freedom. A few days after his death, I received a visit from my new curator, who warned me that a factory job at the Lenin Steelworks awaited anyone in our section who ever tried to escape."

Jeffrey had trouble getting out the words. "Where is the Rubens now?"

The old man shrugged. "I imagine the curator hid it."

"Where?"

Henryk reached into his pocket and pulled out a coin. "If I wanted to hide this coin, I could put it here, under the sugar bowl. But there is always the risk that someone will come by and move the bowl and find my coin."

He reached back into his pocket, pulled out a handful of change, and placed the single coin in along with the others. "But if I place my coin here, no one would pay it any attention. I would be the only one to know that it had any special value."

"It's still in the museum," Jeffrey breathed. "He put it

in a crate with false markings and stored it somewhere in a cellar."

"It would not be questioned," the old man said.

"And you've found it," Jeffrey pressed.

Henryk looked Jeffrey square in the eye. "I would so very much like to see Paris before I die."

CHAPTER

20

On the way to their first appointment the following day, they stopped at a crossroads where Jeffrey found himself staring at a soot-darkened entrance to an apartment house. A middle-aged man had pried open vast double doors and set down a chair. He had no teeth, so his chin almost met the tip of his nose. One shoulder looked sawn off, leaving a sharp slope that began at his neck and ended with his rib cage. He eyed the passersby with a narrowed squint, showing no re- action, following them in one direction, then taking hold of another with his rheumy eyes and following them back as far as he could see.

When the light changed and they drove on, Jeffrey found he could not leave behind the image of that man's slanted frame, nor the lines that had turned his face old far before his time. "I don't understand how there can be so many peo- ple with such awful health problems. It's like a trip back to the Dark Ages."

Katya's voice took on the tone of the patient teacher. "Will you do something for me?"

"Sure. Anything."

"Think of the times in your life when you had to have surgery."

"Okay. Do you want me to tell you?"

"If you like."

"I had my tonsils and adenoids out when I was a kid. I

broke my leg and it had to be set by surgery when I was fourteen. Let's see, I had problems with my wisdom teeth and they finally decided to put me under to take them out. I think that's all. Oh, and I tore a tendon in my shoulder playing touch football in college and they had to sew it back."

"Okay," Katya said. "Now imagine that each one of these is a major calamity, a life-or-death risk."

"A torn tendon?"

"What if there's no doctor? Worse yet, what if the doctor says your shoulder's not worth worrying about, go home and rest for a week. Or a month. Or six months. Then you can either apply for a pension or go back to work—it's your choice, but whatever you do you're going to have to live with the pain and weakness of a badly healed tendon for the rest of your life."

Katya shook her head. "In a place like this, the smallest splinter in a child's hand can break a mother's health with worry."

The *Komenda Wojewodzka,* or Cracow regional police headquarters, was on the main road running from town to the Nova Huta steelworks. From the gate it appeared to be a single ten-story high-rise. The driver pulled up in front of the main gates, spoke at length to Katya.

"He says that there are three identical buildings erected behind each other, so that from the street they won't seem so imposing," she told Jeffrey. "And the rumor is that they go almost as far underground as they rise up."

"I'm afraid to ask what's down there."

"Prison cells and interrogation rooms," she said, staring out the window at the buildings. "Come on, let's go before I lose my nerve."

Their documents were carefully searched by the guard before calling the name Gregor had printed on a card. They waited under the guard's undisguised suspicion before a small officer with sad eyes and nervous gestures came up, shook hands, and ushered them through.

"This gentleman is responsible for the children's section," Katya explained as they walked past the trio of the high-rises, and came to a vast paved lot filled with armed personnel carriers, riot buses with wire screens for windows, water cannons, bales of barbed wire, and mountains of crowd-control barriers.

"Tell him I hope he won't be offended, but this is the strangest place I've ever been to look at antiques."

The man laughed, and the atmosphere lightened considerably. "He says that they heard of Gregor through the state orphanages where they sometimes take kids."

"I thought it was supposed to be a secret."

"It is," the officer reassured him through Katya. "Not all of them know how Gregor gets his money, and those who do wouldn't dare endanger this income. For many of the village orphanages, Gregor's money is the difference between providing homes to needy children and catastrophe. They told me because they trust me. They know my first concern is for the children."

At the far corner of the back lot stood a yellow cottage. Beside it was a small fenced-in lawn with a rusty slide and swing. He ushered them through the door and into the front office, its desk spilling papers, the air smelling of cheap disinfectant. They sat at the small conference table and accepted his offer of tea. He left and returned swiftly bearing the customary steaming glasses.

The police officer did not mince words. "It is impossible for an outsider to comprehend how crime is increasing," Katya translated. "The criminal mind senses the growing lack of authority and *leaps* at the opportunity."

"A lot of people have talked about this power vacuum," Jeffrey said.

"It is on everybody's mind," the officer agreed. "The new government is trying to rebuild a democratic process and at the same time dismantle the Communist power structure. You cannot imagine the problems this is causing. All laws passed under the Communists are now being questioned, which means that nobody is really sure what the laws will be tomorrow.

"The police situation is even worse. I was originally placed in the children's division, which other policemen call the nursery and say it's not real police work, because I refused to join the Communist party. Now they have to replace most of the officers, all at the same time, with untrained people. Why? Because only party members could rise through the ranks.

"To make matters worse, there is a tremendous budget crisis. The government is basically broke. Our own police budget has been cut thirty percent in two months, while in this same two-month period, prices have almost doubled. And so with an exploding crime problem, our hands are being chained. This week, for example, the Cracow police did not have enough money to buy petrol for their cars. All but the emergency police had to do their beats on foot. No Cracow police car has radio. At the same time, the criminals are driving around in stolen Mercedes with car radios and telephones, and more and more of them are getting away."

"What about the kids?" Jeffrey asked.

The officer blew out his cheeks. "Families are being hit hard by rising prices and unemployment. The pressures are breaking some of them apart. We see a lot of young children being either kicked out or running away. The mafia groups are using young children for a lot of their thefts because sentences are lighter and the children will basically work for food and a place to sleep."

"That's what you call them? Mafia?" Jeffrey interrupted.

The officer smiled and replied through Katya, "Too much American TV. Organized gangs are mafia. Police officers are called Smurfs. Detectives like me are Kojaks."

The smile disappeared. "At the same time that the government has a money crunch, housing and living costs have skyrocketed. This has hit orphanages, hospitals, foster homes, everything that relies on state money. Last month, orphanages in the Cracow area had to cut down on the amount of food each child could have."

He leaned across the table, his eyes boring into Jeffrey. "One thing I want you to understand. There are police, good men, who have gone on the take. I can't blame them anymore. They have families to take care of, and they've seen their salaries cut by thirty, sometimes even fifty percent. But I want you to know that every cent I will get from this is going to our children. They have cut my budget to almost nothing. I don't have enough to buy clothes for the ones in rags, or feed them."

"I believe you," Jeffrey said solemnly.

The detective led them back through a pair of locked doors, down a hall opening into bunk-rooms and a kitchen-lounge. Jeffrey looked through wire-mesh windows and saw a number of children dressed in a variety of oversized, patched clothing. They looked extremely young.

As they walked, the officer continued. "There's a Russian mafia operating in Poland these days. They steal cars mostly—Mercedes, Volkswagens, BMWs, Audis are the favorites. We know some of the tactics now; any racket this big is bound to give some clues away over the months."

He said something further to Katya, who nodded her agreement and then said to Jeffrey, "Every week there is an entire page of the local newspaper where they list in small print the car types, years, and license numbers of those stolen in the past seven days."

"A big business," Jeffrey replied.

"Very big, very organized," the policeman agreed through Katya. "They have two normal ways of taking the cars across the border to Russia—that is, two we know of. Sometimes they pack the car in a wooden crate, put it in a big truck, and fill the remainder of the truck with potatoes. The border patrol can't empty every potato truck—there are dozens every day this time of year.

"The second way is to make copies of the customs seals used to close containers that have been checked and made ready for shipment. Then the day the ship leaves Gdansk for Russia, they load twenty or thirty last-minute containers, each with anywhere from one to three cars."

Jeffrey asked, "Can't you get help from the Russian police?"

The man shrugged. "Interpol doesn't operate in Russia, and even if they did they wouldn't bother with such a small matter as a car. Not now. Not when the rates of crimes involving bodily harm and death are rising like rockets. The thieves know they are relatively safe, and it is making them bolder. They have border guards between Germany and Poland who are now operating on the mafia payroll. When a nice car comes driving through, the guards ask the driver where he is going and where he plans to stay, and then they sell the information. The car is tracked until a good time and place arises for it to be stolen. Nowadays, however, the thieves swiftly become impatient. We're getting reports that they follow the car to a filling station or cafe, kill the driver and the family and anyone else in the car, rob the bodies, and drive away."

He opened another pair of steel-rimmed doors and led them through the unkempt playground toward a metal shed.

"Every week we are uncovering new scams. Last week, we learned that a group was repackaging used motor oil in false brand-name cans. This week it is a major Swedish company selling frozen fish. The market has been slow because not so many people can afford their prices. So when the expiration date was reached, they repackaged the fish into boxes and bags with new expiration dates and shipped it out as fresh caught."

He unlocked the shed door. "My men busted a ring of children used to steal household items. This was never a problem before—probably because so few houses had anything worth stealing. We were led to a warehouse full of radios, televisions, everything. We also found this."

The officer swung open the door, reached to an upper ledge and switched on a flashlight. The yellow beam hit upon a drinking horn. Jeffrey took the light, stooped over, and entered the shed.

The horn itself came from a truly giant bull; it was well over two feet long if the curve were straightened. The horn was not chased in silver, it was *sealed* in the metal, inside and out. Three royal emblems were stamped around the horn's mouth. A miniature knight knelt beneath the horn upon a rocky ground of solid silver, and with his back and both hands offered the horn cup to his master. From the knight's dress and the ornate hand-carved battle scenes along the horn's silvered sides, Jeffrey guessed it to be from the early sixteenth century. Gingerly he hefted the piece, guessed its weight at thirty pounds, most of it silver.

From behind him the police officer said through Katya, "I have fought with myself over this for five days. I cannot answer the questions of right and wrong. I can see no further than the needs we have. I must feed these children. I must clothe them. I must give the sick ones medicine. I must heat the building at night. Some are criminals, yes, but they still are children, not animals. The government cannot help me, so I must do it myself. No one anywhere in Poland has declared such a piece missing, I have checked. So you must sell it. But not for me. For my children."

The outer walls of the Vavel Castle were built of massive

red brick, and crowned a hill of summer greens. Beneath the castle's lofty visage flowed the calm waters of the River Vistula. A broad paved walk wound its gradual way up the rise to the first castle gates. Jeffrey and Katya joined the throngs of strollers and walked past the statue of St. George, who according to tradition did battle on that very site to make the world safe from dragons.

Pavement gave way to brick cobblestones as they drew nearer to the first ramparts. The central church's six domes were gold-plated, the acres of gardens bearing ancient gnarled trees, the inner towers imposing.

The palace proper was reached through yet another set of ramparts. The innermost keep was a paved yard of perhaps two acres, and surrounded on all four sides by buildings five stories high. The palace was in dreadful condition, with very little paint and even less of the original murals remaining. Limestone stucco had been washed away by decades of wind and rain to reveal the raw stone, and in places the stone itself was crumbling. Yet despite the rust-covered ironwork and crudely reinforced pillars and a quiltwork of patches over the worst cracks, the palace remained enormously impressive— redolent of history, age, and tragedy.

The castle museum had one room given over to paintings by the workshop of Rubens. It was dark and lofty, floored in geometric marble, windowed with tiny hexagons of glass still bearing the center mark of handwork.

"There's not much light," Katya said.

Jeffrey nodded. "Harder to detect a forgery. If it's good."

The walls had probably once been gaudy with gold and silver gilt arranged in a series of intricate designs; now the gilt had faded to match the dull background hues. The ceiling paintings had long been lost to water stains and mold. Only the paintings hung from the walls kept a fragile hold to the breath of artistic life, and most of them were in dire need of restoration.

Katya signaled to him from across the room. Jeffrey joined her and recognized the Rubens from the guidebook he had purchased downstairs. It was the smallest painting in the room, an oval portrait barely three feet high. It depicted an attractive young woman whose delicate face was almost overwhelmed by the stiff circular collar of her dress.

The painting was a series of frames. An ornate gilded

square framed an equally extravagant passe-partout, also gilded. This gave way to a dark background and dark clothing that framed a pale face, which in turn framed a pair of brilliant dark eyes. It was a masterful interpretation of a somewhat lackluster lady.

Katya whispered, "What do you think?"

"That I wish I knew more of what to look for," he replied. "If this is an original and we take it any further, we're going to look like proper fools."

"It's very dark," she said, moving up closer. "I can see little flecks of dust and stuff."

"If somebody was going to copy a major piece, this would be a perfect one to choose and a perfect place to hang the fake," he agreed quietly. "Come on, we won't learn any more here."

"I may have found us a way out," he reported to Alexander that evening. "Emphasis on the word may."

Jeffrey related the meeting and his visit to the museum. "There's no way I can tell whether or not the painting is real, though. None at all."

"But your Mr. Henryk does not expect to be paid until the original has been found?"

"He's not my anything, and no, he doesn't want a cent up front."

Alexander's voice took on a touch of its old strength. "Then there is at least a slight chance that he is telling the truth."

"So what do we do?"

"What we are most certainly *not* going to do is call in an independent expert. The fewer who know of this, the better chance we have of gaining our own goals."

"If this guy is for real."

"As I said, for the moment let us assume that there is at least a chance. At the same time, you must be very honest about your own lack of knowledge when you speak of it."

"Speak with whom?"

"Yes, that is indeed the question." Alexander was silent for a moment. "Several years ago I helped the central Warsaw museum gather together a collection of paintings. It was not supported at all by the Communist regime, because we sought pictures of the royal city of Warsaw. We searched after quality pieces that depicted an era of our almost-lost heritage. There is now an entire wall in the Warsaw museum of some two dozen paintings hung tightly together, forming a collage of what our capital was like some three hundred years ago. One may look briefly and see a city of palaces and gardens and light, or linger and walk its streets, greet its people, enter royal residences and stand awed by their riches."

"It sounds beautiful," Jeffrey said, relieved to hear the renewed life in his friend's voice.

"It was a most satisfying work. History has not been kind to Warsaw. The second World War reduced much of it to rubble. The pleasure we knew from bringing this collection together was immense. It was a silent call to all our people to look, to study, and to imagine."

"How it once was?"

"No," Alexander replied. "How they might make it yet again."

"So you think maybe one of those people you worked with is still around?"

"There is a very good chance," Alexander agreed. "I was brought into contact with a number of museum officials and painting experts who had no love for the Communists. You leave this with me, Jeffrey. With any luck, a few of them might have resurfaced in the Ministry of Culture."

CHAPTER

21

Jeffrey arrived at Gregor's apartment the next morning to find him up and about. "You look a lot better."

"Yes, thank you, my boy. My body has decided once again to be agreeable." Gregor smiled warmly. "Life takes on a very special joy on such days. I feel more grateful than I know how to put into words. I was just boiling water for tea; would you care for a glass?"

"Sure. Thanks."

"I see no reason to interrupt the excellent work you and your young lady are accomplishing," he said, moving behind his alcove. "There are a thousand other things for me to see to, and so if you agree we shall continue to meet in the mornings, and then go our separate ways."

"If you like. It's been really nice working with Katya."

"I am sure it has." Gregor reappeared and deposited a steaming glass on the narrow table. "Sit down, my boy. Make yourself as comfortable as my little dwelling will allow."

"I spoke with Alexander again this morning," Jeffrey announced, pulling out a chair. "He may have found us a contact inside the Ministry of Culture."

"Excellent. I had no doubt that Alexander would locate a connection for us. He is positively brilliant when it comes to solving such puzzles. Did he say how he was feeling?"

"I asked, but all he would say was that he felt he should return to Cracow. It sure would help me a lot."

"Whether or not Alexander returns," Gregor said, "I don't think you should count on his direct assistance just now."

"Why not?"

"Sooner or later he is going to have to face his past. If this is the case, there will be little room left in Alexander's world for anything else. Call on him in emergencies, but otherwise try to give him the space and the solitude he requires." Gregor brought over his own glass and eased himself down. "If only I can remember to pace myself for the next day or so, I shall hopefully not suffer another attack until the first frost. That is not always easy, however. I tend to be much harder on my own weaknesses than on anyone else's."

"I don't know, you were pretty tough on mine," Jeffrey confessed.

"Ah. You have been thinking about our little discussions, then."

"A lot. Especially at night. I don't seem to be able to sleep. I think too much."

"The difficulty, my dear boy, is that you are trying to understand my actions from a perception based within this world. Why, you may as well try to understand Polish simply because you have learned English. The languages are so totally different that even the *sounds* you think you recognize represent different letters.

"No, there must be a return to your life's most basic building blocks. You have to start right at the foundation." His eyes sparked with joy. "Which means you must begin by tearing down."

"You don't make it sound very appealing."

"Of course I don't. And it never will be, so long as you look at it from an earthly perspective." He blew the steam from his tea and took a noisy sip. "The world says there is no greater tribute you can grant yourself than to say, I can make it on my own. *My* perspective says there is no greater deception.

"The power within our own will and our own body and our own confined little world is comfortable, and it is tempting. It gives us a wonderful sensation of self-importance. Thus most of us will try to live outside of God until our own strength is not enough. Yet the way of the cross is the way of inadequacy. We need what we do not have, and therefore we seek what is beyond both us and this world.

"Here, let us try this. Would you take a question away and think on it for a day or so, then come back and let us talk again?"

"I guess so."

"Excellent. I will give it to you in two parts. The first question is, what would happen to your life and your world if you were somehow able to erase from your mind, your heart, and your memory—from your very existence, in fact—the motivation, 'What is in it for me?' "

Jeffrey snorted. "That's impossible."

"We are not talking possibilities here, my boy. We are talking *challenges*. So. Will you do it?"

"You want me to go out and ask myself, how would it be if I never considered what I might gain from a particular course of action, is that it?"

"Precisely."

He shrugged acceptance. "And what's the second question?"

"The second, is, who deserves to be served in selfless devotion and total love?"

Jeffrey waited. "That's it?"

"That's it? That's it? What do you expect from an old man, the keys to the universe?"

"I guess you were right about it being a different language."

"Indeed I was. Will you think on these questions?"

He nodded. "I can't say I feel very optimistic about ever solving them."

This did not trouble Gregor in the least. "The asking is what is most important, my boy. Who knows, you may even find the answer there waiting for you."

Jeffrey shrugged on his jacket. "We're supposed to be at our first buy in less than an hour. It's time I was going."

"Yes, I suppose it is. Here, let me offer you one little clue to help you in your search. You will find it possible to not just find the answers but also understand the questions only if you are willing to turn your back on this world. A single life does not have room for both worlds, my dear boy. You will eventually learn to hate one and love the other." Gregor's gaze left traces of light as he searched Jeffrey's face. "Now, which world will you choose?"

The actress sat enthroned upon the splendor of a brocade sofa, surrounded by the lore of days gone by. Her apartment was a high-ceilinged collection of rooms in one of the beautiful old town buildings. The floors were of inlaid parquet, the silk wallpaper bore an oriental design. High arched windows were covered with plush velvet drapes.

"When martial law was imposed on Poland in the eighties," she said through Katya, her voice a throaty purr, "the militia filled the streets, breaking heads with their batons and making the world cry with their tear gas. In the *Stary Teatr*, we would make the nation weep with joy, and strive to fill hearts with the same hope the police wanted to beat to death. It was a sad time, yes. But for an actress with work, it was a grand time."

The passing years had honored the actress. Her formerly beautiful features bore the marks of age and too many parts played for too many people, on and off the stage. Yet her eyes were as clear as dark green emeralds, and her voice caressed and sang words that lost nothing by being in a language Jeffrey could not understand. Her hair was piled in an auburn wealth that filtered down in teasing wisps around her ears.

"When the shops were empty," she went on through Katya, "when the lines were growing daily longer, we fed their spirits. Our lives had purpose then. We were the voice of a people who were afraid to speak for themselves. We reminded them of who they were. The theater was filled every night, with people standing along the back and down the sides. We worked to keep our people alive, playing the classic Polish pieces, stories of patriotism and pride and endurance with success at the end. When we performed the plays of Mickiewicz, the audience would stand and *shout* the lines back at us, crying from their hearts the words which were forbidden to them in the outside world, but tolerated here as part of the play. We granted them a determination to survive the enemies of the night and the morrow."

The animation left her face with the departure of her memories. "Now the world is changed, and people struggle to put the past behind them. And the crowds do not come anymore. The theater has been saved by the new government, but there are few positions open to an actress who has committed the crime of growing old."

She waved a languid hand toward a glass-fronted display case. "These are gifts from people whose faces I cannot remember. Take what you can sell. I will use the money to spend a few more days reliving the time when my life had meaning, when I knew how to give the people what they needed."

They left the actress's apartment and continued on to a stretch of green which Katya called *planty,* lined on one side by the medieval town wall. Katya pointed out graffiti from student demonstrations against the Communist regime which translated as, Don't kill us unarmed children.

They sat on a park bench, the afternoon sunlight making playful golden streamers through the breeze-tousled trees. A trio of beautiful young girls walked by arm-in-arm, giggling over some private gossip. Jeffrey turned his face upward, closed his eyes, and thought back over the past several days.

He had begun to see things in the people's faces that had not been visible before, things he had missed in his concentration on their sadness and their injuries. He was finding a strength, a silent power of endurance, bearing weights no one else knew about. He saw the wisdom of pain in their faces, and determination tested by fires he dared not even imagine.

Another transformation was tied to this first one, a change as startling as it was revealing. As he learned to understand and love these people, he came to know and accept Katya's reserve. Her own stillness mirrored the strength he found in so many of these people, the ones who had not given in to the bottle or the hopelessness or the fury. She had her own sorrows, her own battles to conquer, and in growing through them she had equipped herself with a faith and a strength that remained unshakable. Jeffrey marveled at the power that this slight young woman held in her heart.

He opened his eyes to find Katya staring at an old woman on the next bench. The woman was watching a group of children playing with bright-eyed eagerness. The old woman's gaze was the only part of her with life—her body looked little more than a shell.

When the last child had left and the *planty* was empty, the crone edged her way up from the bench by degrees. When erect she was just over four feet tall and dressed entirely in black—kerchief, sweater, blouse, skirt, stockings, lace-up shoes. She listed to one side and leaned heavily on her black cane as she walked. She moved one foot forward eight inches or so, then the other sort of fell forward to meet the rest of her body, another tiny step, and on she went.

"Look at her," Katya said. "She was born when her country didn't even exist, except in people's hearts. When she was a teenager, Poland gained independence for the first time in over a hundred and fifty years. Her children were still in school when Hitler invaded and wiped out one-fifth of the country. She survived, but she probably saw her own relatives killed right before her eyes. Almost everyone did."

Jeffrey slid his hand into hers. She looked down at it uncomprehendingly, then turned back to the slow-moving crone and continued with her story. "When Hitler was finally defeated, Stalin and his hordes took the Nazis' place. No doubt she struggled to keep what remained of her family strong and together through forty nightmarish years of Communist occupation. Her children and grandchildren are now either grown or dead, and today Poland is independent again. If she has any thoughts on it at all, I bet it is for those children she was watching. What flicker of hope she still has, she has willed to the children of this nation."

That afternoon Katya accompanied Jeffrey to the Ministry of Culture. It was located down Ulica Grodzka, a street leading from the main market square. The building probably dated from the early eighteen hundreds, which meant that sometime at the beginning of that century either a new structure had been erected on the site or an older one restored—there had been a structure on that spot for over twelve hundred years.

The building was again newly renovated, painted a pastel peach on the outside, with large wood-framed windows and a massive oak door taken from an earlier medieval structure.

Inside, it still smelled of fresh paint. There was no receptionist to direct newcomers, no plaques or directions on the walls, no signs by the doors. Jeffrey hesitated a moment in the utterly bare foyer, then started down the central hallway, calling out if anyone was there.

A voice called down from the galleried landing above. "Ah, Mr. Sinclair! Please come up! Welcome! Welcome!"

Jeffrey followed Katya up the winding staircase and met the man's outstretched hand at the top. He was in his late forties and wore a Western-cut double-breasted suit and silk tie, rather than the standard gray Communist garb. Beneath the well-trimmed gray hair was a rounded pasty-colored face and gold-rimmed glasses over alert brown eyes. More than anything else, the eager friendliness marked him as a member of the new regime.

"I'm sorry, we are still housecleaning," he said, leading them down the hall and stopping before his office. "Come in, please." He waited until they had entered, closed the door, and stuck out his hand once more. "I am Dr. Pavel Rokovski."

"Jeffrey Sinclair," he replied, growing accustomed to the traditional formality. "This is my associate, Katya Nichols. She speaks Polish, if you require it."

"*Bardzo mi milo,*" Dr. Rokovski said, taking her outstretched hand and bowing down as though to kiss it. He stopped when her hand was about ten inches from his face, and rose back in a formal, practiced motion. Katya stood with graceful inattention.

"*Prosze, prosze.* Please, sit down. I speak some English. It is good to practice. Maybe some coffee?"

"Coffee would be fine, thanks."

"I also have some very good cognac," he said, returning to his door. He hurried across the hall, said something in the tone of one used to giving orders, hurried back, closed the door behind him.

"I think it's a little early in the day for cognac," Jeffrey said. "But you feel free to go ahead."

"No, I wait too." He seated himself behind his desk. "I am so very pleased to meet you, Mr. Sinclair. Mr. Kantor's advice has been very helpful in the past. When he called me last night to say you wanted an appointment, I was very happy to rearrange my schedule. I understand you have some information."

"Yes, sir. I have to say, though, I don't know how reliable it is." He hesitated, went on, "And it's important that you understand that I have to keep our sources absolutely confidential."

Dr. Rokovski waved his hand toward himself, urging Jeffrey on. "Of course, of course."

"Research on antiques, as you know, is the reason for my visit here." Jeffrey leaned forward. "And of course you know that we have several applications pending here in your ministry for export permits."

Dr. Rokovski was giving nothing away. "Mr. Kantor would certainly have something very interesting to discuss if he were to call me at night and say it is urgent for us to meet."

"We think it is, yes."

"Well, then. In that case we would certainly owe you and Mr. Kantor a favor."

The coffee arrived; Dr. Rokovski leaped from his seat, took the tray from his assistant, and with formal bows poured and served the coffee. He then returned to his seat, said, "Among trusted allies of the new Polish government, such export documents are just formalities. I'll see that your applications are expedited."

"You realize that we intend to export nothing that might be even remotely considered as a part of the Polish heritage."

Dr. Rokovski nodded. "We have the greatest respect for Mr. Kantor's honorable name."

"Thank you." Jeffrey took a breath. "About this other matter, as they say in America, I have some bad news and some good news. The bad news, Dr. Rokovski, is that we believe one of the Old Master paintings exhibited at your Vavel Castle Museum is a forgery."

Dr. Rokovski turned even paler than before. "This is always possible. May I ask which one?"

"The Rubens portrait."

"The one of Isabel of Bourbon?"

"I'm afraid so."

Rokovski bent toward his desk, picked up a paper clip and began unbending it. After a moment he looked up and said in a resigned voice, "And the good news?"

"The good news," Jeffrey replied, "is that we also have reason to believe that the original is in Cracow. Probably in one of the museum's underground vaults."

Rokovski leaned back. "A Rubens lost in our own vaults? But everything is carefully inventoried."

"Yes, but if a certain painting was packaged and mislabeled, it might go unnoticed for a very long time."

"I see," he murmured. "May I ask how long?"

Jeffrey hesitated. "A few decades."

"So long." The head slowly nodded. "And who else knows?"

"The three of us, and of course Mr. Kantor."

"No one else?"

"You need not concern yourself with it going any further," Jeffrey replied firmly.

"And do you think you could identify this mislabeled carton in the museum vaults?"

"I would need to do a little more research, but yes, I think I could."

Rokovski glanced at his calendar. "Tomorrow I am scheduled to be in Warsaw. Could you complete this research by the day after tomorrow?"

"I think so, yes."

"Then meet me here at three o'clock that afternoon. We will go together to the museum." Dr. Rokovski rose to his feet. "And of course you understand, in a matter of this delicacy, everything must remain between us."

CHAPTER

22

Their morning appointment was only a few blocks from the hotel—a priests' residence attached to a church-run children's hospital. As they strolled through the morning sunlight, Katya talked about the Catholic church in Poland. "To be Catholic does not necessarily mean to be religious in Poland. From 1772 to 1918, Poland was partitioned between Russia, Prussia, and the Austro-Hungarian empire. For a good deal of this time, Poland ceased to exist as a country. Patriotism to the Polish nation was a crime punishable by death. You could not call yourself a Pole without being arrested. Your language was outlawed and could not be spoken in public. You could not be seen to own a book on Polish heritage or literature. The Austro-Hungarian empire swore to erase Poland's memory off the face of the earth."

"But you could be Catholic," Jeffrey guessed.

"A *Polish* Catholic," Katya emphasized. "The Catholic church became the only legal haven for Poles. The only place where people could defy the occupying forces and be Polish. All the hymns were Polish. All the prayers were in Polish. All the confessions were in Polish. Christian instruction was given to the children in Polish, so that when the language was outlawed in the schools, they were still able to learn."

"Which meant every family would send their children to church," Jeffrey said. "Whether or not they were religious. Smart."

"*Every* family," Katya agreed. "It was the only way for their children to remain their children."

"And then history repeated itself under communism," Jeffrey said.

"In a way it did. Under Communist rule, church activities were restricted to the church buildings themselves. The church was too powerful to outlaw entirely, which was of course what the Communists wanted to do, and did accomplish in other Eastern Bloc nations. Here, they had to be satisfied with cutting off all outside charitable and evangelical efforts.

"Their ruling allowed churches to be seen as totally separate. They became totally isolated from the regime and its oppression. They became havens, islands of safety and peace to which the people could turn and find a renewal of hope."

"Just like before," Jeffrey said.

"All the nuns were thrown out of hospitals and schools, so that there was no threat of evangelism in state-controlled operations. The church used these experienced women to set up religious schools and local church clinics. Because this could take place only inside the churches, children at the age of five or six were introduced to the church and religion, even by families who otherwise would not be seen within these walls."

"What about other denominations here in Poland?" Jeffrey asked.

"Today, there are less then forty thousand Baptists in Poland, out of a population of just under forty million," Katya replied. "The other Protestant denominations are somewhat smaller. At the same time, we are seeing an interesting phenomenon, something unique in all the world, as far as I can tell. Many of the people who have either lost their faith as Catholics or never had any faith at all are finding it in Protestant-run Bible studies. But they do not leave the Catholic church. The Catholic church is history, culture, and heritage. For many, to leave the church would mean to break with an important part of their past, and they do not wish to make such a break."

"They are forcing an internal revival," Jeffrey guessed.

"Exactly. Even in some of the small villages you can find spiritual renewal. Home churches and evening Bible studies are springing up all over the country. Not only that, but they are maintaining their very close ties with the Protestant churches. These new believers have no time for those who wish to quarrel across established lines of doctrine. They have found faith, and it is too precious to allow somebody else's arguments to stand in their way."

"A strong Polish nationalism is emerging," the priest told them through Katya. "It is wedding itself to the Polish church. A number of priests are becoming involved in what is called 'black power.' It means church involvement in politics, named so because of the color of priestly robes. It does not usually signify running for office. More often it is a priest who takes an active interest in local or national politics, backing certain candidates, weaving politics into his sermons."

He was an intelligent-looking man in his mid-forties, his face seamed by years of hard work and worry. In the background could be heard faint cries and shrills of laughter as children thundered down unseen halls. Here in this room, however, all was at peace. They sat in a small entrance chamber, the only furniture being a simple crucifix on the wall, five straight-backed chairs, a small center table, and a large item in one corner—the piece they had come to acquire.

"Although I do not agree with those who are so politically oriented," the priest continued, "I can understand their concern. Many parish priests work with under-educated people who are totally confused by these new earth-shaking transitions. In the last election, *seventy-eight* political parties fielded candidates. How is a sixty-year-old man who has never been allowed to vote for anyone but the appointed Communist official going to understand what to do? Naturally, he will turn to his local priest, as he has done on numerous occasions in the past when faced with problems and an uncaring, too-distant government."

Jeffrey forced himself to concentrate on what the priest was saying, although his eyes were continually being pulled back toward the article in the far corner. The priest had waved at it as they entered, said a parishioner had given it after a miraculous cure of his son, and they were going to use the proceeds to equip a modern surgical clinic. After that he had dismissed it as of no consequence, and Jeffrey had been forced to sit on his hands and wait for a chance to examine it.

It was a medieval chest, most probably intended for a palace chapel. It was perhaps four feet high, three feet deep, and seven feet long. Its curved roof and sides were carved with a variety of royal shields. The front was embossed with a painting of ladies-in-waiting serving men-at-arms. All but the painting had been covered with a layer of fine gold flake, then lacquered for protection.

"There is another group within the Polish church, however," the priest went on, intruding into Jeffrey's thoughts. "And this group is growing in strength every day. Their first concern is the Kingdom of God, and this is what they are called. They are a charismatic renewal group, who see a very real need to return to the basic elements of faith in Christ.

"This group is pushing hard for contact with Protestant mission groups," the priest continued. "Their concern is not church membership, but faith renewal. They fear that what communism has not done, secularism and capitalism may achieve. Now that our enemy of the past forty years is defeated, another more silent and pervasive enemy may gradually erode church attendance. These priests and their followers believe that there must be a vocal declaration made of the importance of salvation, a concentration on this very first point above all else.

"There is a problem, however. If the evangelical arm manages to dominate, and if political involvement is limited, a vacuum may appear. This is a very real fear within the church just now. Democracy requires pressure to operate, as you in the West well know. Here in Poland, you must remember, there is *no other organized moral voice*. There are no groups to push the government to remember the sick, the infirm, the needy—you have a word for this in the West, I believe."

"Lobbyists," Jeffrey offered.

"Exactly. There is no one here to apply this pressure in the name of God and service except the church. Two months before the last election, for example, in the midst of massive price rises on everything from bread to milk to bus tickets, the government decided they had to cut social security payments—the same payments that had not risen since the Communists were defeated. Retired people who were unable to fight for themselves had seen their purchasing power reduced by over half when the new regime deregulated prices. And now what was to happen but a second reduction of over thirty percent. There was only one voice organized to fight against this measure. The Polish Catholic Church."

The priest stripped off his glasses and began polishing them with a pocket handkerchief. "The evangelists point to another area where the church has tried to apply pressure, and failed miserably. I refer to abortion. Because this is very important to many of us, we have studied what is happening in your country, and we have made a very important discovery. In America, opposition has come from a groundswell of individuals, all joined together to combat it. In Poland, it was very different. Here the church tried to *order* the government to outlaw this. The result was disastrous.

"People who might otherwise have been behind such a measure have not only opposed the proposal to ban abortions, but also opposed the church. Why? Because it represents to them the same dictatorial demands as they knew under the Communists. They had no voice in this decision; it was ordered from above. The result has been, as I said, a very real calamity. The evangelists are saying that so long as the church tries to involve itself in politics, the danger of this schism deepening will continue.

"The fact is, church attendance is falling. The question is, how many of those who have stopped coming have lost a living faith, rejecting this new group that is attempting to become another authority over their lives, and how many came to church simply to escape the storm of life under Communist rule?"

That afternoon Jeffrey returned from a second meeting with Mr. Henryk to find Katya in her room surrounded by government forms, handwritten lists, and a Polish-English dictionary. He sat down on the floor beside her and began helping her with the tedious business of making a complete inventory for the export forms.

Once the forms were completed, they went downstairs for dinner, then returned and gathered up the papers, content to sit together and enjoy the feeling of a shared intimacy.

"This is the way I always thought a confessional would feel," he told her. "Quiet and intimate and protected. As though I could say anything I wanted and it would be all right."

"We all need a place where secrets can be revealed," she replied, setting aside her papers.

"We're not talking about the same thing, though, are we."

Katya shook her head. "I carry my place with me. Wherever I go, wherever I am, whatever happens."

"I used to feel that way."

"I know."

He leaned back. "That reminds me of something I haven't thought of in years. Back then, the greatest part of being religious for me was this feeling I had. I had a friend, somebody I could talk with about anything. I would talk with God and tell Him *everything* and He would always be there and everything would always be okay. He was my perfect friend."

She gazed at him with eyes more open than he had ever seen. "You really miss Him, don't you?"

Katya was too close to him for there to be any room for a lie. "I don't know if I really believe God exists. I miss the feeling, though. I see what I used to have there in your eyes, and I miss that."

She watched him, her eyes two gray-violet pools where he could lose himself for all his days. Jeffrey whispered, "I really love you, Katya."

She did not flinch, she did not draw back, she did not

belittle his confession with indifference. Instead, she cradled his hand in both of hers, bent down, and kissed it with the soft caress of butterfly wings.

Katya stroked his hand and murmured, "I've been so afraid."

"Of what?"

She kept her eyes on his hand. "Of falling in love. Afraid because it had already happened, afraid because . . ."

There was no longer enough room in Jeffrey's chest for his heart. "Because why?"

She turned to him in mute appeal, a yearning gaze that beckoned and pleaded for he knew not what. Slowly, very slowly she shook her head.

"Why won't you tell me, Katya?"

Her gaze did not waver as she asked, "What pushed you away from faith, Jeffrey?"

At that moment, in an instant of realization, he knew that the entire journey had been leading up to this question. Not just the evening. The thread leading to this had been woven into their relationship from the very first moment of their meeting. Some hidden part of him had been waiting for this, waiting and knowing that when the question came, he would tell her.

"When I was driving with Gregor the other day," Jeffrey began, "I was listening to him talk about faith and suffering, and at the same time I was going back over what happened to me. It was like being able to see it through his eyes and his perspective, which was totally different from how I felt about it at the time."

"How long ago was it? I mean, whatever happened to you."

"Hang on a minute, I'll tell you, I promise. But I want to tell you about this first." He related what Gregor had told him, then said, "As I was listening to him, I kept seeing things about myself I've never really understood before. Back when the problems all started, I'd get really mad and scream at God in my head, saying, you let my brother go through this and you let him hurt and you let him degrade himself, so to heck with you. But I was *really* thinking, you said I was special because I believed and I got baptized, but since you came into my life, it's been worse than it ever has before. That was why I left God behind, Katya—because He didn't do anything but make things worse for *me*, not for my brother or my parents or anybody else. I cared about them only after I'd finished caring about myself. He'd let *me* down. I didn't want to have anything more to do with Him."

The drawing away that he half expected didn't come. Katya's gaze remained open, her look filled with love. She said, "Tell me about your brother, Jeffrey."

"My brother. Yeah. The brother I don't have." The pressure in his chest built to an enormous bubble that *demanded* to be released.

"What was his name?"

"Is. What *is* his name. Charles. Chuckie was the kid; I don't know what he wants to be called anymore. My parents call him Charles. I guess they figure he's outgrown Chuckie. Either that, or they want to keep some kind of barrier between who Chuckie was and who this Charles is that he's become."

Katya's only movement was a soft caressing of his hand, one finger gently stroking out a reminder that he was not alone, that someone was there and listening and caring.

"Chuckie was a great kid. He was two years younger and I always felt like he was the kid for both of us. My mother used to say that I was born old, and that's the way I've felt. She has this picture of me, it was always the first thing she'd unpack whenever we arrived in a new home. My dad is sitting in his living-room chair, his slippers are on and he's got the paper spread all around him with the front section spread open and just low enough so you can see him frowning as he reads. And there I am, about four years old, sitting in this tiny little chair. I've got my bunny slippers on and I've got my legs crossed like Dad and I've got the funny papers spread all over me and I'm wearing an identical frown."

"It sounds adorable," Katya said.

"I guess so. Mom sure thinks it is. But that's the way I was. Chuckie, though, was always into everything. There was never anything steady or 'normal' about Chuckie. If he was happy you could hear him shouting and singing and laughing a block away. It was the same if he was sad.

He *hated* being sad. When he was down he'd become just as mad as he could, and let the whole world know it.

"Chuckie didn't get on well with all the relocations my dad's company put us through. When he was still little, he'd get sick—real sick. His favorite was bronchial pneumonia, but he pretty much covered the range from appendicitis to the bubonic plague. A lot of my first memories of a new place were of Mom dragging us around to different hospitals and doctors' offices—I was still too little to be left at home. And Chuckie was not exactly what you'd call an ideal patient. He didn't like the move, he didn't like the new home, he didn't like being sick, and he wanted the whole world to be angry with him. It was tough.

"Right after his fourteenth birthday we moved again. All I can remember about that first couple of weeks was unconsciously waiting for Chuckie to get sick, and then somehow not being happy when it didn't happen. Instead of getting sick, Chuckie sort of went away.

"The move was to Phoenix. I had just turned sixteen, and my dad gave me this clunker of an Olds, so what I really thought about was getting out and stretching my wings. So while Chuckie started fading into the shadows, I was busy being a teenager."

"You were a Christian then, isn't that right?"

"Yeah. I got baptized on my fifteenth birthday. I know, I know, a Christian's not supposed to be so selfish about himself, right?"

"That's not at all what I was thinking. Just because you're a Christian doesn't mean you're all of a sudden going to be made perfect. It just means you're called to work toward certain standards. Meeting these standards is a goal you'll be working for all your life."

"I like the way you say that."

"Why?"

"I don't know. You make it sound, well, approachable, as if I'm not being asked for the impossible."

She squeezed his hand. "Go on with the story."

"Mom was busy unpacking and getting us settled, and I was busy with this new school and new freedom, and Dad was busy with his new job. Nobody really seemed to notice that Chuckie had disappeared. His body was there, but he wasn't. He just left.

"We moved again at the end of the school year, and about that time we finally started noticing things—well, we finally started *talking* about things that we'd all been noticing for quite a while. Money was missing. Silver, too. And other things, little things like Dad's gold cufflinks that he wore only when he and Mom went out on special nights, and one of Mom's necklaces, and my new camera, and some other stuff.

"And the liquor was going down a lot faster than ever before, or so my Mom thought. They'd never really been big drinkers, but it was always there, and the bottles never seemed to be full anymore.

"First it was Dad who talked to Chuckie. Then Mom. Then Dad and Mom. Then me. Then all of us. It didn't do any good, though. Nothing at all. You can't imagine how sincere that kid was when he denied it. His pupils would be dilated to the size of bullet holes, and he'd be so sincere denying he was on anything that I'd go away believing him. Denial is the name of the game with somebody like that. They deny it to you, to themselves, to everybody who tries to get underneath the shell and make them face up to what they're doing. You don't know what lying is until you've tried to talk to an addict about his habit."

"Chuckie was on drugs?"

"Drugs, booze, anything he could buy or steal to stick down his throat or up his nose. It was like a metamorphosis in reverse. When we moved to Phoenix I had a colorful little butterfly for a kid brother. When we left there and moved to Philadelphia I had a worm.

"Philadelphia was the wrong place to take a kid with a drug problem. I guess we should have figured that out before, but Mom, Dad, and I never really complained about where the company was going to send us next. We knew without ever talking about it that this was just one of the prices we had to pay. And no matter how bad it was, we knew that it wasn't ever going to be for too long. But Philly was bad. Really bad. The only good thing I remember about Philadelphia was that as the problems with Chuckie got worse, my parents and I kept growing closer and closer together.

"Chuckie started selling drugs in Philly—or at least he

got *caught* the first time there. I don't know if he'd already started in Phoenix or not. Philadelphia was something from another world, though, with guys out of your worst nightmare hanging around the school fence, dripping with gold jewelry and selling everything. I mean everything. And Chuckie was into it all."

"It must have been awful for you," Katya said, her voice carrying a shared pain.

"You can't imagine. We'd get called down to the police station in the middle of the night, and I'd go down with Dad because Mom was having hysterics and I didn't want him to have to go alone. When my baby brother would come out, sometimes he was still drugged up. Sometimes he'd been sick all over himself, or had somebody else in the tank get sick on him. It seemed like we were in court almost every week.

"Finally the judge gave Dad an ultimatum. Either Chuckie went into a state-run rehabilitation program for under-age drug offenders, or he was going to reform school. I know it sounds strange, but that's really the first time that any of us admitted that the problem was out of control. Things like that happened to other people, not us. But this time it was us, and it wasn't just out of our control, it was out of our hands. Dad signed the papers and Chuckie went to a hospital for drugged-out teenage criminals.

"It just gets worse and worse," Katya murmured.

"That's the way it is with an addict. Alcoholic, druggie—they're all addicted, and the problems are the same. You wouldn't believe the letters we got from him in the beginning—how they were beating him and treating him horribly. Those letters just tore my mother up. The people we spoke to on the phone didn't help any; they all had the same deadpan delivery that made them sound like they'd do anything for a buck. Most of them were recovered addicts, and they knew all about the tricks the kids used to try and get out, or try and stay high.

"When we picked him up six weeks later, they warned us that Chuckie displayed all the symptoms of a recividist."

"Denial," Katya said.

"Right. They say that the biggest step to help a recovering addict is for the addict to admit that he or she has a problem. Chuckie never admitted once in all this time that he was taking *anything*. Not drinking, smoking, snorting, anything. Not even after we started finding his stash and pipes and empty bottles and roaches all over the house. Never. It was all a big conspiracy. And the people at the center were right. As soon as Chuckie got out, he started up again. Nothing at all had changed, except once he was back he stopped trying to hide it at all."

Jeffrey's mind went back to the uncounted days and nights—the sounds of his dad yelling and his mom crying and Chuckie cursing. At last his parents stopped trying to confront Chuckie at all, and the boy would come home late at night in a drug-induced stupor, crash around the house, and finally fall into bed, unchallenged.

In January there was yet another visit to the court, after his brother—still too young to have a license—tried to drive the family car through a concrete bridge support. The dust settled just in time for one more move, the last his parents would ever make. By then they were involved in Al-Anon support groups and classes on co-dependency, learning how to deal with their son's addiction, struggling to keep their marriage and their home intact.

There was none of the usual joking and half-worried excitement about this move. There was no time for that, no place, no energy. The three of them went through the accustomed motions with grim determination. Chuckie came and went like a wraith, occasionally sobering up long enough to realize that their world no longer revolved around him.

The day after they arrived in Jacksonville, Florida, they laid down the law to Charles—all three of them, together. They formed a united front and gave him the ultimatum in no uncertain terms. He was moving out.

Charles was told that an apartment had been rented for him near the university. A bedroom was going to be made up for him in their new house, but he could stay there only if he allowed himself to be tested for drugs and alcohol every day for two months. The only way he would be welcome in their home was if he was sober.

Charles whined and begged and pleaded and cried and

finally stomped his feet and screamed curses and punched a hole in the dining room wall. He spent only one night in their home; he came in around dawn, falling down drunk. Jeffrey and his father poured him into the new family car, drove him over to his new furnished studio, and dumped him fully clothed on the bed. They pinned a note to his shirt—since he was too drunk or stoned to understand what anyone was telling him—saying that if he was kicked out of this apartment, for any reason whatsoever, he was on his own. Charles missed seeing his father and his brother drive back home, both of them dry-eyed and grim-faced, neither having any more tears to shed.

"I left God behind in Philadelphia," Jeffrey went on. "I can still remember the exact moment. I was packing up Mom's porcelain figurines—she would buy herself one new figurine each time we moved. She loved them, she really did. She'd spend hours taking them out of this display case we had in the living room and dusting them off and just looking at them. It was her concession for having to move, and it gave her something nice to look forward to. She'd spend days and days going around all the shops in the new town, coming home with little pictures she'd take with her Polaroid. And the higher up the ladder Dad went, the nicer the figurines became. It was the one thing she always made us pack ourselves, and we always drove to our new home with them stowed somewhere safe in our car.

"So there I was, packing up the figurines, and I had this mental image of deciding it was time to stick God back somewhere in a box too—one that I never intended to open again. Nothing I'd heard in Sunday school or church ever got me prepared for what we were going through, and nobody was able to help me. The Bible sure didn't."

Katya did not contradict him as he expected. Instead she asked, "What happened to Charles?"

Jeffrey took a deep breath and steeled himself. "Charles wasn't exactly what you'd call pleased to all of a sudden lose his family. Only I doubt that he thought of us as family by then—more like a haven and a source of money and somebody to beat on emotionally."

Katya nodded.

"Anyway, we'd get calls from the landlord or the police

to ask if we knew that Charles had been here and done this or that. My parents absolutely refused to get involved. Every once in a while Charles would call and scream over the phone about abandonment and heartlessness, but they really stuck to their guns. Al-Anon had taught them how to detach from Charles' problems. After about nine months or so, just as I was getting ready to go off to college, I started seeing smiles around the house again, hearing laughter. You can't imagine how nice it is to hear laughter until you've lived in a house without it for a year or so."

"I can imagine it," Katya said softly.

He looked at her. "Yeah, maybe you can."

"What is that supposed to mean?"

"Ever since I've gotten here, I've been coming to grips with what lies behind that silent strength of yours."

This time it was different. This time the defense mechanism did not automatically freeze him out. There was no indifference, no denial, no drawing away. She simply said, "Finish your story."

"Okay. So Chuckie, I mean Charles, began going to greater and greater extremes. He got kicked out of his apartment, but by then he had a girl who took him in. Charles was growing up into this really good-looking kid. And there was something else about him, something other than his looks that drew the girls like a magnet."

"Certain women are attracted by guys with those kinds of problems," Katya said. "They usually have a tough external shell, and this type of girl wants to work her way inside. It's almost a motherly sort of reaction."

"You've met guys like this yourself."

"Every girl has. She can be attracted by the toughness, and maybe pride herself on her ability to understand this man that the rest of the world can't. Women in such situations put up with an enormous amount of abuse—physical or emotional—infidelity, unreliability, whatever. And still she works very hard to keep pleasing this man. She's never confident of her hold on him, except for this idea that she alone understands the soft, inner, hidden man."

"That's beautiful," Jeffrey said.

"It's tragic," Katya corrected.

"No, I mean the way you expressed it. Your insight."

She did not deny it. "Sometimes I feel as though I can see things and understand things that the rest of the world just keeps on trying to shut out. Maybe it's part of the gift of learning compassion, coming to understand more through trying to care more."

He turned and looked away.

"Did I say something wrong?"

"No," he sighed. "It just really hit home."

She waited a moment, and when he did not go on, she said, "Finish your story. Please."

"About two months after I started classes," Jeffrey continued, his voice a monotone, "I got a call from Mom. All the time she'd spent and the work she'd done to rebuild her life had been destroyed. She was crying so hard she couldn't talk, and finally had to give the phone over to Dad. He sounded worse than she did, really hollow. At two o'clock in the morning, Charles had gotten drunk at some party and climbed a tree. And he'd slipped out and fallen on his back and broken his spine."

"Oh, Jeffrey."

"He was paralyzed from the waist down," he went on, rushing now, pushing it out. "I listened to Dad tell me, and I wasn't thinking about Charles or Chuckie or whoever he was. I was thinking about my folks. And me. If they weren't strong enough to do the obvious, I was. I just cut him out. Right there. Cut him out completely. I didn't have a brother anymore. My folks were just too weak to do it. So I was going to do it for them. I told my dad I wasn't coming to the hospital, not then, not ever. And I didn't want them to mention his name around me ever again. As far as I was concerned, my brother was gone. Dead. Out of my life forever."

"What did your parents say?"

"That's a funny thing. Dad didn't object, and Mom never mentioned it. Not ever."

"And you never saw your brother again?"

"Once. I went to see him once more."

It was after his grandmother asked him, just before his departure for England. His brother was back in the hospital for surgery. All those years of sitting in a wheelchair had given him bedsores, and they'd become infected.

That was the worst part of going to see him, having to do it in the hospital. It was almost as though his grandmother's request had rolled back time, pushed him back nine years to the hospital visit he'd refused to make.

Charles was parked in a special air-bed, an incredible contraption with a pump built into its base. It pushed air continually up through a load of silicon sand into a bottom sheet of fine-mesh nylon; it let the air out in a continual cool blast that ballooned the sheet's slackness up and around Charles's limp body.

The years had softened Charles's features, but not as much as Jeffrey had expected. There was a slight blurring to the strong lines, but part of this was caused by the Demerol that Charles had control over. He had an electric pump connected to his IV, and every fifteen seconds or so Charles would push the button and give himself a dose. Jeffrey couldn't help but grin when he finally figured out why Charles kept such a grip on the button; at first Jeffrey thought it was for calling the slowest nurse in history. Charles would wait until a bleep announced that his next dose was up and charged. Knowing Charles, he'd have told the doctors he was in terminal pain. Giving that guy control over his own drug supply was the silliest thing Jeffrey had ever heard of.

That set the tone for their meeting, at least on Jeffrey's side. Charles acted as though he had seen his brother the day before—sort of bored and casual and not really concerned one way or the other. Jeffrey was standing there, trying to come up with something to say, when he caught sight of himself in the mirror across from Charles's bed.

His button-down Oxford shirt was crumpled from a day of running around, his top button undone and his tie at half-mast. His shoulders were hunched up as though he were getting ready to charge the line, and there were worry-frowns creasing his forehead.

Then his mother had appeared in the door, all bright and brown from her daily tennis and solid in her happiness. That amazed Jeffrey more than anything, how both his mom and his dad had somehow recovered from all the stuff life had thrown at them, and kept hold of both their happiness and their love for each other.

His brother took his cue like a consummate actor and folded inside the bed's balloon-sheets like he'd been hit with a sudden attack of real live pain. Jeffrey stepped back, watched his mother straighten her shoulders and take a breath and do the bravest thing he'd ever seen her do, which was meet her son with a smile. It was a forced smile, and the brightness had a brittle, lacquered quality to it. But it was still a smile, and the determination that she showed in not allowing Charles to drag her down into the pit again left Jeffrey speechless.

He left the hospital that day absolutely certain that his mom and his dad had found a strength that he didn't have, and hoped he'd never need. Not ever. For him the best way of dealing with his brother was by continuing to deny he even had one.

Katya drew him back with, "Do your parents believe in God, Jeffrey?"

"Not before all the mess with Chuckie started. Church was a place to go and make some social contacts, you know, help us get settled in. That's how I got into faith in the first place. I was just looking for a nice group of kids. Sometimes it was easier to find people to talk to a new kid at church than at school. But then I met this Sunday-school teacher who was really on fire.

"When I started reading the Bible and going to weeknight services and talking about getting baptized, my folks treated it like just another phase I was going through. They trusted me, and even though they didn't understand what I was doing, they figured it was okay since it made me so happy.

"The co-dependency group my parents started with in Jacksonville was connected to a church. The Al-Anon support group, too. And the more time they spent with the people in those groups, the more their conversation got sprinkled with these spiritual terms. Their new spirituality came at the same time when I was putting the lid on my box, so I made it clear that I didn't want to hear anything about faith. They still referred to it every once in a while, just letting me know it was there if I want to talk about it. But I'd just ignore it or change the subject, and that was it."

He watched her for a moment, savoring this feeling of closeness and friendship. This is what a true love ought to be, he decided. A best friend. He asked, "What are you thinking?"

"You probably won't like it," she replied.

"But it's something I ought to hear, right?"

"I can't decide that for you, Jeffrey."

"I trust you," he said. "Tell me."

"Somewhere along the way," she said quietly, "people have come up with the impression that if they believe in Jesus Christ, they won't have to suffer."

Her words did not need volume to have impact. Jeffrey shifted in his chair.

"Then when something hits them," Katya went on, "they question themselves and they question their faith: What have I done to deserve this? Has God found doubts in me, reasons to condemn me for my lack of faith, flaws in my beliefs that I have tried to hide even from myself?

"Then comes rage: I held up my part of the bargain, and look what you've done to me. But the Bible doesn't promise total protection, Jeffrey. Not even to the righteous man does it promise that. Look at Jesus Christ. Look at the apostle Paul. Look at Job. The Bible says that Job was an honorable, righteous man. A man who avoided evil. A man who honored God. And yet God allowed him to suffer terribly. There is no clearer message to me in all the Bible than this, Jeffrey. We see that even the most righteous man on earth is open to the pain of life."

Her eyes were wide open, her gaze seeking out the deepest wells of his heart. "Listen to me, Jeffrey. If we are faithful to Jesus Christ only when our lives are in the sunshine, then we do not truly love Him, no more than a true love on earth exists only when times are good and the couple live in harmony with each other. Genuine faith, and genuine love, does not always guarantee total protection from the risks and turmoils of life.

"Genuine faith consists of loving God *no matter* what the circumstances. We accept that our life is in His hands, *no matter* what the chaos of this world might bring, *no matter* what troubles confront us at the moment, *no matter* how we might hurt. We have placed our life in His hands and we *keep* it there."

She sat and watched him in silence, as though sensing that he had been stripped bare and needed time to put himself back together. When his eyes turned outward once more, and he truly saw her, she asked quietly, "Will you pray with me, Jeffrey?"

"Not now, okay? I want to think about this some first. Maybe later, but not now."

She did not try to hide her disappointment. "I will wait for that day as I have waited for nothing else in my life."

"When you talk like this you sound a thousand years old."

"Love is eternal, Jeffrey. Whoever loves in His name knows the gift of love's eternal wisdom. There is no other way."

CHAPTER
23

Jeffrey was coming to love these walks alone in early-morning Cracow. His days began with a quick breakfast, a telephone call to Katya's room to outline the day, and then off to Gregor's. On pretty days he stretched the walk by a dozen or so blocks, walking and watching and thinking.

This morning, however, a mist hung heavy over the city, muting sounds and closing off vision to ten paces ahead. People appeared first as gray-black shadows, firming into living shapes at the last moment, then disappearing just as swiftly. Jeffrey examined the faces and thought of all that had filled his past weeks.

Gregor greeted him with the casual air of a dear friend. Jeffrey pulled up a chair close to his. "I've been thinking about what you said."

"That is the best news I could possibly hear this morning," Gregor replied. "Except for the news of Christ's return."

"I was just wondering," Jeffrey said, "how you came to be religious."

"I don't know that I am what you would call religious," Gregor told him. "Being religious is in my view an external action, something I would do for the outside world. I find myself too busy to pay such things any mind."

He settled deeper into his pillows. "As for coming to faith, that happened in the darkness of the Nazi occupation. In those days, every Polish family had a Bible. And in almost every family, the Bible always remained on the shelf. I started reading the Bible during the war, not out of faith, but out of the need for distraction.

"I stayed in Cracow during the war. Our own house, quite a beautiful place, was taken over by the Nazis for use as a local office. We took what we could carry and moved to our cleaning lady's flat nearby."

"What happened to the cleaning lady?"

"She was there with us. She had two sons who were missing. Many young men simply disappeared during those dark times. We were all the family she knew, and when we lost everything, she simply took us in. She was embarrassed to have us stay there—after all, she had been the one who had scrubbed our floors. She treated us like privileged guests for more than three years. That was an eternally long period to a young teenager full of life and energy.

"I was fifteen when the Germans invaded, and it was dangerous to go out with the curfews and the uncertainty. Because all the schools had been closed by the Nazis, I finished high school by taking private lessons in a small group that met at the local seamstress' house. I felt a constant restlessness then, a frustration over not being old enough to fight, and not being well enough to rebel against my parents' wishes and fight anyway. Even then I had this problem with my joints. I would have liked to die fighting for my country, especially after Alexander was taken. It was very hard to stay home and hide and do nothing to bring Alexander back.

"Our cleaning lady, Pani Basha, was not an educated woman. In her house were only three books—the first and last volumes of Sienkiewicz's Trilogy, which is a sort of novelized summary of Polish heritage, and a leather-bound Bible. I turned to that book not out of faith, certainly not seeking guidance. What on earth could a book written two thousand years ago teach a young boy who was bored and distracted and worried and hungry and afraid? No, I turned to it out of restlessness.

"I read it like a novel, beginning with Genesis and finishing with Revelation. Then I read it more slowly. Then I began reading books out of sequence, and gradually I found myself absorbing different messages. The sheer *complexity* of the book astounded me. No matter how much I studied it, nor how often I read and reread a passage, there was always something which I had missed before. Another lesson. A deeper meaning that I only then was beginning to understand.

"When you have troubles, especially troubles which are so big that you know before you begin that you cannot conquer them, you feel as though you are the only one. No moment could be darker than the present moment. But I found the Bible to be full of war and destruction and hunger and suffering. And as I burrowed deeper and deeper into its pages, I also found that there were answers—not just to their pain and their distress and their distant troubles, but to *mine*.

"These men cried out to God, 'Father, do not forsake me.' And so, in my own small way, as a restless teenager caught up in a crisis not of my making and certainly out of my control, I too cried out. And God listened."

Gregor pointed toward his empty glass. "Do you think you might make me another tea?"

"Sure," Jeffrey said, rising to his feet.

"You are a good and honest man," Gregor said. "Alexander is fortunate to have you as an assistant, and a friend, if I may add."

"He is my friend," Jeffrey replied, hiding his embarrassment behind the alcove curtain. "Besides Katya, maybe my best friend."

"How wonderful for him. This makes what I am about to say all the more easy. I would like to lay my own responsibility upon you, if you will allow it." Gregor waited until Jeffrey reappeared. "You may call it a duty of our own partnership, if you will."

Jeffrey returned and set down the steaming glass. "Fire away."

"I want you to promise me that each and every day you will pray for Alexander's salvation."

Jeffrey hesitated. "After all these years, I would have

thought you'd have given up by now."

"One never gives up. One never loses hope. One continues to petition the Maker of all miracles, and one hopes for those who have not yet learned how to hope for themselves."

"After all that he's been through, I'm not surprised that he doesn't believe."

"That is indeed true," Gregor replied. "There are many people such as our Alexander, who have felt the need to cast away all semblance of faith in order to survive their ordeals. They have managed to survive where all but a handful were crushed and killed—or worse—because of simple strength of will. There is no denying the power and the self-confidence that they have earned. Yet I have also seen such people reach a crossroads where they come to recognize a need for power greater than what they themselves hold."

Gregor's eyes held a luminous quality. "There is always hope, my dear boy. Always. So long as there is life and the presence of the Lord in your heart, there is always hope. I am called to remain here with my arms outstretched, just as Christ did throughout His life and on unto death, and hope. And pray. Yes, that most of all."

Jeffrey found his eyes drawn to the simple crucifix hanging from the wall. "I've never thought of it in that way before."

"There are an infinite number of lessons to be drawn from the cross, my boy. Just as there are an infinite number of paths that lead man toward salvation." Gregor himself turned to face the crucifix. "All human hope lies at the foot of the cross. In the two thousand years since it first rose in a dark and gloomy sky, it has lost none of its luster, none of its power, none of its divine promise."

Jeffrey turned back to Gregor. "All right. I'll do it."

"Think carefully on this, my dear boy. This is a vital decision. You are accepting a duty that you will carry with you for as long as you or Alexander lives."

He nodded his understanding. "It's okay. I accept."

"Excellent." Gregor positively beamed. "I feel most reassured by your help."

Jeffrey rose to his feet. "I've got to meet our painter Mr.

Henryk again. He's supposed to get me some information Rokovski needs. When Katya gets here, tell her I should be back in an hour. We'll need to go straight on to our next buy."

"I will do so, my dear boy. And know that you go forth with my prayers accompanying you."

It was a moderate palace, as palaces went. The cream-and-white exterior gave it a fairy-tale lightness, accented by vast sweeps of windows. Dual exterior staircases with curving balustrades led around the ground-floor ballroom to a porticoed and pillared entrance on the second floor. The grounds were unkempt and barely a step away from forest, save for one sweep of still-green lawn directly in front of the palace.

Katya and Jeffrey entered through gates so rusted and decrepit that no amount of effort could close them. Jeffrey tried to focus his mind on the business at hand, but found it next to impossible. The information he had received from Mr. Henryk was nowhere near as complete as he had hoped.

"Gregor told me a little about this place while you were meeting with your mystery man," Katya told him. "He said it once belonged to an adviser to the king. After the Soviets installed the Communist regime it became an institute."

The closer they came to the palace, the more cracked and faded became the building's exterior. "An institute? For some disease, you mean?"

Katya shook her head. "Bunnies."

"What, raising rabbits for labs?"

"No, just to study." She smiled at him. "The National Communist Institute for Bunny Research."

"In a palace?"

"Don't expect Communism to make sense, Jeffrey. It will drive you to madness trying to apply logic to an illogical system. Just accept it. The former palace of a royal adviser is now a bunny farm."

"That's incredible."

"There were a lot of incredibles under Communism." Katya was no longer smiling. "The count who lived here was exiled to Siberia, and his children fled to Paris with the family jewels sewn into their clothes."

"But they could come back and reclaim the place now, isn't that right?"

"Gregor said they wouldn't because the government wants them to pay a maintenance fee for the past forty years, and they can't afford it. So I imagine it's like most other unclaimed properties. There's no for-sale sign out, but it's available for the right price. With the situation Poland is facing economically, they'd sell just about anything if the price was right."

The director appeared at the front door, a stocky woman in her early fifties, her hair chopped short and left in unnoticed disarray. She was dressed in clunky shoes and the inevitable white lab coat of authority. Behind stern square glasses, her eyes were intelligent, direct, impatient.

"This palace was built in the second half of the nineteenth century in the Italian style," she explained through Katya. Jeffrey listened and looked around as she led them into the upstairs foyer. Its mirrored ceiling, supported by interlaced girders, supported one of the largest chandeliers he had ever seen—perhaps eighteen feet high. The floors were inlaid with an intricately repeated Rococo pattern.

"It's all new," she told them. "Everything. The chandelier was brought in three years ago, before the Communists held a major function here. It is supposed to be a replica of the original.

"After the Nazis were driven from Poland and the Soviets took control," she went on, "the palace was repeatedly sacked by soldiers, the new Communist government, and by locals. Everything was taken. The floor and the marble fireplaces were chopped up and carried off. Afterward the government gave it to the institute because no one else wanted it. The palace was nothing more than a hollow shell. A bomb could not have done more damage."

"There must be a lot of money in bunnies," Jeffrey said, working to keep a straight face.

"I am not going to translate that, and you behave," Katya said sharply.

"Little by little we have repaired things," the woman continued. "We found good tenants to take over a series of rooms, and charged them a deposit large enough to make the initial repairs to that section. We arranged with the woodworking department of the local university to send up their best students. An office for the government agency responsible for lumber is here, and they made sure we could find enough wood. We fought our way through red tape for several grants from the government's historical society."

She led them through vast double doors into a formal parlor with a twenty-foot-high vaulted ceiling and rosewood floor. "Nine months ago we began work on the palace's final wing, and discovered a section of the cellar that the looters had missed. It was not surprising, really. In our own initial survey we missed it also. The door was more or less buried underneath a layer of soot, and was directly behind the old palace furnace. We found it only because we finally had enough money to repair the heating system."

Before Jeffrey stood a set of eight matching *caquetoire,* sixteenth-century Renaissance chairs. Originally of French design, they were also known as 'gossip chairs,' and had seats broad enough to accommodate a matron's multi-layered skirts. The legs were delicately turned, the armrests and connecting rails carved with *lunettes*—repetitive motifs in a semicircular pattern. The chairs' back panels were carved with *Romayne* work—oval-shaped portraits, probably of the original count who had ordered the chairs—depicting a stern-faced patriarch dressed in a Roman helmet.

"These are fantastic," Jeffrey said, kneeling before one after the other. "A major find."

"Yes, that is what we were supposed to think," the director agreed.

Jeffrey looked up. "What does she mean by that?"

"When we found them, we were naturally ecstatic," the woman explained through Katya. "But we wondered. Were they considered too old-fashioned and just stored away in a back room and simply forgotten? It was logical. But even someone such as I who knows nothing of antiques could see that they were of value. So why were they placed in a room with a door blocked and hidden?"

She walked to the side doors, opened them, said, "So we brought them out and began digging. And we found this."

Slowly Jeffrey rose and walked over. The doors opened into a small parlor, now set up as a conference room. The central table was intended to seat around twenty people, but all the chairs were gathered to one side. The long table was covered with green felt, and on its surface was displayed a complete formal dinner service.

"I imagine it was the most valuable item in the house besides the jewels," the woman said. "But far too heavy for anyone to escape with. It was packed in four great chests."

The plates, the serving dishes, and the silverware were all gilded. Gilding was accomplished by mixing a very fine gold dust with another substance that would make it adhere to a surface. Originally honey was used, then a century later an amalgam of mercury was substituted. While the mercury resulted in a finer and more consistent pattern, it was also highly poisonous, causing first sterility and later death. Apprentices to the gilders were encouraged to have children while still quite young.

The dishes were unadorned save for an embossed family shield. Jeffrey picked up one plate, turned it over, read, "Stuttgart, 1718." He set it down very gingerly.

"There are dishes for thirty and silverware for twenty-four," Katya translated. "They must have ordered replacements in case of breakage."

The director stepped around the table and faced Jeffrey. "This has become more than simply an institute. We house a conference center, offices, research labs, almost a dozen companies. We have turned one set of the old farm buildings into a distribution center, and want to do the same to the other seven barns. We, the companies who are housed here, are now the largest employer in the region, and people have come to count on us. But the government has no money, the historical society has been shut down, and the work yet to be done on this building is enormous. We need a new roof. I will not bother you with the figures for roofing an entire palace, but believe me, it is very high. The electrical system is antiquated and a fire hazard. We have two telephone lines and need fifty. The garden—you have seen our garden? It is turning into a jungle.

"The village school had a wall cave in two weeks ago, and now they are using the old palace greenhouses. They have no heat or running water, concrete floors, and lighting by an extension cord strung over from the main house. When we talk to the government we are rewarded with a lot of hand-waving and replies that there is no money, no money for anything."

She plucked a straight-backed chair from the tangle by the back wall, turned it around, and sat down facing Jeffrey. "So. You know our need. And now, young sir, we shall discuss price."

That afternoon the three of them—Jeffrey, Katya, and Dr. Rokovski—arrived at the Vavel Castle's central courtyard to be met by the museum curator, a nervous portly man in his late fifties who fussed about Dr. Rokovski like a mother hen.

"Ah, and these must be your guests from America." The curator's accent was far heavier than Dr. Rokovski's. His nervous eyes barely seemed to focus on them as he went through the formalities of bows and handshakes. "I understand you are experts in the conservation and storage of works of art."

Jeffrey showed momentary confusion before catching Dr. Rokovski's frowning nod from behind the curator. "Ah, yes."

"Mr. Sinclair is doing a preliminary survey to see if his company might be able to assist us in updating our methods," Dr. Rokovski covered smoothly. "This is his associate and translator, Miss Katya Nichols."

"Fine, fine. Well, shall I escort you down?"

"Oh, that will be quite all right, Mr. Stanislaus. I know how busy you are. And I do know my way quite well around here."

That was clearly not what the curator wanted to hear.
"I am sure it's not like in the West. We have so much to
learn here, and so much to do. My small staff has been so
busy, working day and night just in the viewing halls. The
special collections here in the West Wing, the permanent
exhibitions . . . well, you can imagine, so much has been
left undone in the cellars. We haven't even cleaned properly."

"We all certainly understand that you have tremendous
responsibilities," Dr. Rokovski replied, and avoided further protestations by blocking the curator and ushering
Jeffrey and Katya inside.

They passed under a stone archway, walked down a narrow corridor with a high vaulted ceiling and lamps set
where torches once had burned, and finally stopped before
a vast oak-beamed door lashed with rusting iron bands
broader than Jeffrey's hand. Dr. Rokovski spoke to an alert
guard and was given a ring containing a half dozen massive keys. He inserted a skeleton key almost a foot long
and weighing over a pound, and used both hands to grind
it around.

"This is the entrance to the vaults," he said, using his
shoulder to push the door aside. "We combine modern
alarm technology and video cameras with the best of ancient security."

They entered a small antechamber and descended down
a wide spiral staircase of worn stone. He fumbled in the
stairwell's murky half light. Fluorescent lights hanging
unevenly along the ceiling blinked on. A series of ancient
armored doors stood sentry down a long hallway. Each had
a small square window with iron grids set at eye level.

"We call them the museum vaults now," Rokovski said.
"But as you can see their earlier purpose was quite different. I shudder to think what might have happened here
centuries ago."

The dungeon's air was damp and close, and smelled of
nothing more sinister than cheap antiseptic cleanser and
old varnish. A wall apparatus kept constant record of
the temperature and humidity. Jeffrey reached into
his pocket and pulled out a slip of paper. It contained
the information from the latest meeting with the old

painter, Mr. Henryk. He handed the paper to Rokovski. "I think this is the chamber we are looking for."

Rokovski examined the paper, noted the hotel's imprint across the top, said, "This is your writing?"

"It is."

He turned and walked down the hallway, checking stenciled markings against the page as he went. They passed thirty doors, fifteen to each side, before the corridor opened up into what was clearly an unused workroom.

Dusty easels were stacked in two corners. Jars blackened with dust and old cleanser held scores of paint-smeared brushes. Floor-to-ceiling shelves built of warping plywood and covered with dust were filled to overflowing with chemicals and paints and rags and palettes and instruments whose use Jeffrey could only guess at. Set high in the wall to their right was one solitary pressed-glass window, giving meager light from the outside world. Jeffrey stood and looked up at it and wondered at the man who had called this place a haven.

In the far end of the workshop was a pair of doors. Between them stood the sort of old wooden card files that Jeffrey remembered from his high school library. Cards were crammed in so tightly that several of the drawers could not even be closed. There were further cards scattered across the floor, all covered with illegible scrawl.

Rokovski sighed and waved at the cards. "Our museum archives. It is shameful, *nie*?"

"Looks as if you could use the consultant I'm supposed to be," Jeffrey agreed.

Rokovski checked the page a final time, then fumbled with his keys and inserted a slightly smaller one into the left-hand door. The door groaned open. Rokovski reached inside and switched on the single bare overhead light bulb.

The entire room appeared to be carved from a single stone. The air was cool and stuffy. Stacked against all four walls were broad, flat wooden crates covered with dust and cobwebs.

Rokovski held up the sheet of paper. "This is all you have?"

Jeffrey nodded. "It is probably in this room."

"But all these crates are simply numbered. There's no

description on them, just on the archive card." The art director let out a groan. "This is impossible."

"No it's not," Katya said. "You two start opening the crates, and I will start checking the numbers against the archives."

Rokovski stared at her. "You don't even know what you are looking for."

"Something odd," Jeffrey replied. "Something that doesn't fit inside a museum vault."

"What if it is simply listed as a painting by another artist, one that does not exist?" Rokovski ran frantic fingers through his hair, gazed around the room. "Only an expert would know that the painting title is false."

"I don't think someone trying to hide the painting would have done that," Jeffrey replied. "There's too much chance that it would have been discovered." To Katya he said, "Look for something that doesn't fit."

"I understand," she replied. "Do you have a pen and paper?"

Rokovski fumbled in his jacket and handed them over. "I don't have time to spend days looking for a painting that might not exist at all."

"It exists," Jeffrey replied grimly.

"You had best hope so," Rokovski replied, stripping off his jacket and taking it back into the workshop. "You have the most at stake."

Jeffrey watched him disappear, then turned in silent appeal to Katya. She smiled her encouragement. "Something odd. Don't worry, Jeffrey. I understand."

Crate after crate was dragged out into the workshop, pried open, inspected, sealed shut again, and returned to the growing stack just inside the storage room door. Soon all three of them were sneezing and coughing from the dust that grew thicker with each disturbed crate.

Most of the crates were filled with bad portraits of arrogant-looking people, the kind of art even a close relative would prefer not to display. There were one or two passable scenes of war-time chivalry, and many paintings that were simply damaged beyond repair. Rokovski managed a few halfhearted jokes over the first few uncrated unknowns, but by the time sweat worked its way down both their faces, all attempts at humor had vanished.

While they worked their way down one wall, Katya started on the other side, listed a dozen numbers, then began painstakingly checking the files. Jeffrey struggled not to despair; they had managed to inspect only nineteen crates in the first hour, and the room held at least four or five hundred. The only consolation was that Katya appeared to be making three times the progress they did, although Rokovski greeted her each time their paths crossed with another derisive snort. It was clear he expected to have to go back and duplicate her efforts. Jeffrey was not sure the man was wrong.

Katya reentered the storage room chanting a number under her breath. Something in her tone made both the men look up from their labors. She fingered dozens of crates, examining the stencils. "Here. Check this one next."

"What for?" Jeffrey asked.

"How nice," interrupted Rokovski, fatigue giving rise to sarcasm. "Did you find that under 'R' for Rubens?"

"No," she replied, her poise untouched. "This number corresponds to a card labeled *Projekty Studenckie, Akademia Sztuk Pieknych.*"

"Student projects from the Academy of Fine Arts," Rokovski translated. "What on earth is that doing here?"

"It seems to me," Katya said, "that student work has no place in a museum vault. And anyone checking the inventory would open this crate last."

The crate was dragged out with renewed haste. Rokovski jammed the screwdriver under one corner, slipped, cursed and slammed it back into place with a vengeance. The wood creaked and complained and finally gave. Together he and Jeffrey pulled off the lid.

The first painting they lifted out was a mediocre pastoral scene. Next came two standard still-lifes, and under that a snowy landscape with a frozen river. Jeffrey reached for the next painting, the next to the last one, and as he pulled it out his heart lurched.

"There's something here," he said.

"It's too heavy by far," Rokovski agreed.

The painting was of dead hunting trophies. They turned it over, laid it flat, and saw that set into its back was a second, smaller, older frame.

"Bingo," Jeffrey said.

The student painting was just large enough to allow the smaller frame to fit snugly inside. They discovered as they tried to remove it that small thin nails had been hammered through the outer frame to seal it in place, to ensure that it would not be easily inspected. Because there were no nailheads, they used the screwdriver to probe between the frames, damaging the outer frame if necessary, and breaking the nails with a sharp upward twist. When all six were broken and the inner frame free, Jeffrey found his hands were shaking.

He turned to Rokovski, said, "You do it."

"With pleasure." He reached down with trembling hands, gently separated the inner frame, and lifted out the painting.

It was the Rubens.

They knelt around it in silence for a long, long while. Finally Rokovski stood, moved to the workshop table, cleared off a space, and gingerly set the painting down. He walked around it, inspecting it from various angles.

"I must say that when you told me about this," Rokovski said quietly, "I came back by the museum and looked carefully at the painting on exhibit. I inspected it as best I could without drawing attention to myself."

"So did we," Jeffrey replied.

"I could find nothing that left me thinking that here was a forgery. Nothing. But I am not an expert at classical painting, and I thought that perhaps I was wrong. Perhaps, you understand, just perhaps. And now that I stand here before this original, I see that indeed I was."

"It is a masterpiece," Katya agreed quietly.

Some of the other exposed paintings that littered the cramped little room were quality pieces, but there was something more to this one, something that drew the eye despite the room's poor lighting and the painting's relatively small size. The pale face framed a pair of dark eyes whose depths contained an unfathomable spark, a mysterious light that *demanded* attention.

It was indeed a master work.

That evening, while waiting to go to the airport and meet Alexander's plane, Jeffrey told Katya of his talk with Gregor. She listened to his account with the same absorption that she had shown him the evening before. At the conclusion she told him, "You're going to have to reach some decisions of your own before you can pray for Alexander, Jeffrey."

He nodded. "I've been thinking about that."

"What are you going to do?"

"I've got to get my own relationship with God back in order," he replied.

She reached across and took his hand. "It's the way I have always dreamed of our relationship beginning."

He stared at her. "This is what you've been waiting for?"

"I couldn't say it, Jeffrey. I couldn't ask. It couldn't be something you decided on because of me. It had to be something you did for yourself, for Him." She drank him with her eyes. "It's been the hardest thing I have ever waited for in all my life."

"All this time, all . . ." Slowly he shook his head. "This is incredible."

"My father became a Christian because it was the only way that Mama would marry him," Katya said. "Mama once told me she thinks making him give that promise was the greatest sin she ever committed. It kept him from ever finding Christ on his own, and in the end it drove him away from both of us, because he was living a lie, one she forced on him."

"So you waited," Jeffrey breathed, dumbfounded. "And hoped."

"And prayed," she added. "Prayed harder than I have ever prayed for anything in my entire life."

"But why the distance, Katya? Why the coldness? Was that because of your father, too?"

"No," she replied quietly. "Well, yes, I suppose in a way it all comes back to that first great hurt. But my first year at university, I met an older man. I gave too much too fast, Jeffrey. I didn't take time to see who it was that I was spending time with. I let myself be taken in by a lie, by a mask he wore because it suited him. I can look back now and understand that all he really wanted was to have me. When I refused, and explained that my faith didn't allow it, he tried every way he could to force me away from God."

She dropped her eyes to the hand she held in hers, her voice as gentle as the finger stroking his palm. "I was so busy trying to convince myself that deep down he really cared for me that I couldn't see the truth. And because of that I stayed around longer and let him hurt me more. I did not understand how a man could lie so, could care so little for me as a person that he would keep tearing at what was most important in my life, trying to destroy my faith just so he could sleep with me. Then one day I finally realized that he didn't care for me at all, just for my body, just for satisfying some hunger of his. It made me feel like dirt.

"After that, my life revolved around my studies and taking care of Mama. " She looked up, gave him the slightest hint of a smile. "And then this dashing young man came up to my table at the university, and he was neither a student, nor a believer. All the same problems, all the same mistakes, all over again."

She reached across and traced a feathery line down the side of his face. "And I could feel myself falling head over heels for him," she whispered, "like I had never fallen for anyone in my entire life. And I was so scared, Jeffrey. So very scared."

"There's no need to be frightened, Katya."

"I'm beginning to believe you," she said, and leaned forward to kiss him.

CHAPTER
24

Alexander was his normal silent self on the ride into Cracow from the airport that evening. Jeffrey played the patient companion and said little of his own activities, other than the fact that perhaps the solution to their export document problem had been discovered. Alexander replied to the news with a single nod of his head and the request that they go straight to Gregor's apartment instead of the hotel.

Gregor limped out to the landing, greeted his cousin with the traditional pair of kisses and the words, "You have been on my heart night and day, dear cousin. Night and day."

"I am grateful." Alexander seemed unsure of why he was there. "Is it too late for us to speak?"

"Of course not. I have just put on water for tea. Come in, come in."

Gregor led him to the apartment's only comfortable chair. "Pull it up close to the bed, cousin. I have perhaps done a bit too much today, and my bones are eager for a rest."

"Perhaps I should return tomorrow, then."

"Nonsense. I can rest while we are talking." He turned to the alcove and asked over his shoulder, "Will you take tea with us, Jeffrey?"

He looked uncomfortably at Alexander. "Maybe it would be better if I left."

"There is no need as far as I am concerned," Alexander replied. "You have walked with me this far; you may as well be in for the kill."

"No one is to be killed," Gregor replied, returning from the alcove bearing two steaming glasses. Silently he nodded Jeffrey toward a straight-backed chair in the room's far corner. "Although there would be no greater gift you could give me or your Maker than a decision to die to the things of this world."

Alexander sipped at his tea. "Even if I did consider the act as a serious possibility, I would find it positively mortifying to see the look of satisfaction on some priest's face. Imagine his pleasure at bringing a long-time offender like me to his knees."

It was one of the few times Jeffrey ever heard Gregor take a sharp tone. "If he takes pleasure for himself, then he is no priest, no matter what his earthly garb."

"Perhaps not, dear cousin. But your standards are sadly not held by all."

"They are not mine and they are not standards," Gregor replied hotly. He eased himself into a seated position on his bed and stretched his legs out with a sigh. "They are instructions, the first of which is true humility. You kneel to no mortal force when you cast your sins on the Savior. You bow your head to no mortal power."

Alexander smiled. "Do I detect an open wound?"

"There are some human failings I find harder to forgive than others," Gregor replied. "I do not ever want to think that a prideful Pharisee in priestly robes stood between you and eternal life."

"Eternal life," Alexander murmured. "There were times when I truly thought that I would live forever. Or at least that my days should never end."

"God willing, you shall have eternal life. He stands and knocks at the door to your heart. Will you not let Him enter?"

Alexander reached over and patted Gregor's shoulder. "You will be the death of me."

"The life, dear cousin. The life of you."

"An interesting concept. Quite an amusing change from the memories crowding up around me."

"Memories far easier to bear if you bore them not alone," Gregor replied.

"Yes," Alexander murmured, turning his gaze toward his steaming tea. "The burdens have become quite heavy."

"Do you wish to speak of them?"

Alexander hesitated, said to his glass, "It is so hard sometimes to understand how we feel. Our emotions are so very abstract. So we give them form, a name or place, and through this name an identity. For me, all fear, all dread, all hatred, is located at Florian's Gate. These feelings, this place, I have avoided all my life."

"Many of us have such a place," Gregor said quietly, "although it is not always something with a form as concrete as yours. To walk through this portal would be to confront these fears, to press through them, and to leave forgiveness in their wake."

"I could not," Alexander replied. "You are asking the impossible."

"Only because you insist on taking that walk alone," Gregor said. "You treat your fears and your hatreds as your most precious possessions. You allow them to define who you are, where you go, what you think. Imagine, my oldest and dearest friend, how life might be if love were there in their place."

Alexander gave no sign that he had even heard. He was silent for a very long time, the loudest sound in the room being the ticking of Gregor's bedside clock. Then he said, "I survived my time of suffering because I was *determined* to live. It was *my* strength. *My* will. And yet, as I find myself coming to face the same door which I escaped from so long ago, I wonder, my dear cousin. The past reaches up to surround me, and at times I feel that I have escaped from nothing at all. And the strength of my will does not appear to be powerful enough this time to save me."

Gregor shifted his head and looked upward, said to the ceiling, "It is possible to hurt so much, suffer so terribly, that life loses all meaning. This you know, my friend. You have seen it for yourself, and known its appeal. Death becomes not necessarily something welcome, but rather something *acceptable*. It can be a mental pain that pushes you to this brink, or emotional, or physical, sometimes even spiritual. Those who disbelieve the extent of another's suffering simply because the wounds are not visible are not only insensitive, they are dangerous. They literally push a sufferer toward death's door."

"That is one accusation I would never make of you," Alexander said quietly. "Your sensitivity is most painfully accurate."

"One basic element of suffering," Gregor went on, "is the way it makes time slow down. A sufferer finds it increasingly difficult to see beyond this moment of pain. He or she finds it almost impossible to believe that the suffering will ever end. It becomes the all in all of life. Pain is the start, the now, the finish."

"Indeed," Alexander murmured, his shoulders bowed, his head lowered almost to his hands.

"A sufferer comes to dread the night," Gregor told the roof above his head. "Once it arrives, it never seems to end. The darkness can become suffocating in its power to isolate, to smother hope, to increase aloneness. The person thinks, 'How long before I get up? The night drags on, and I toss till dawn.' Those are the words of Job, my old friend. He knew, and he said it well.

"Yet in the midst of this intense suffering, God's people have recourses that others do not have. In the thirty-sixth chapter of Job, the sufferer says to me and to all who know pain, 'But those who suffer, he delivers in their suffering; he speaks to them in their affliction.' Do you see, my dear Alexander? God comes to us in the midst of our pain. He promises to *be* there, to live through it with us. His presence is very real and very personal in such times."

He turned to Jeffrey. "Would you be so kind as to take the Bible from the shelf there and read from the first chapter of Second Corinthians?"

"Sure."

"Thank you so much. Begin with the second half of verse eight, would you, and read through verse ten."

Jeffrey fumbled with the unfamiliar pages, eventually found the spot, read:

"We were under great pressure, far beyond our ability to endure, so that we despaired even of life. Indeed, in our hearts we felt the sentence of death. But this happened that we might not rely on ourselves but on God, who raises the dead. He has delivered us from such a deadly peril, and he will deliver us. On him we have set our hope that he will continue to deliver us."

"In life or in death," Gregor said, "we are in God's strong hands."

CHAPTER
25

"Nova Huta was considered a Communist masterpiece," Katya told him the next morning as they drove toward their final appointment. "It was Poland's first planned city, built to staff the largest steel plant in the world, the Lenin Steel Works."

The driver turned off the main thoroughfare onto streets that were clearly not meant for cars. They were little more than broad sidewalks, about twelve feet wide. Graveled sections had been added at irregular points where cars could be pulled off and parked. Kerchiefed old women crammed together on a small front stoop and watched the car pass with grim suspicion.

"At the turn of the century, Cracow was once considered one of the jewels of Europe. Beginning in the year 900, it was the capital of one of the largest European kingdoms. It housed the third oldest university in the world. It had been Eastern Europe's center of intellectual thought and scientific exploration for over five centuries. But the Communists feared Cracow as a breeding ground for dissension, and worked to destroy its preeminent position. They decided the best way to do this was to change it from a center of intellectual growth into a worker's city."

The three-story houses looked like dark gray barracks. They stood in endless rows beneath tall birch trees, stretching out in every direction as far as Jeffrey could see. Their uniformity was jarringly oppressive, at direct odds to the summertime green.

"So the Communists chose a forest preserve outside of Cracow for the new factory, and razed it to the ground. Homes for the tens of thousands of steelworkers were built, and slowly the factory itself took form. They constructed the furnaces to burn soft coal, since that was what Poland had the most of, even though it is the most polluting fuel on earth, and extremely inefficient."

They pulled up in front of a building indistinguishable from its neighbors except for a faded number painted above the front door. The driver stopped the car.

"The result was that soon after the plant opened, it started raining black dust all over Cracow," Katya continued. "That is why these buildings are this color, Jeffrey. They were originally white. The dust is so thick in wintertime that people have to brush it off their car windows before they can drive. Nowadays rain here is so acidic that it is killing all the trees in Cracow and eating away at buildings that have survived almost a thousand years."

They walked up the cracked sidewalk, pushed their way through the front door, and followed Gregor's instructions to the second floor. The woman who opened the door was not extremely old—Jeffrey would have guessed no more than sixty. But unseen winds and burdens of a hard life had aged her. Her walk was labored, her hands palsied, her eyes weak and watery behind thick lenses. She led them into her sitting room, walking on legs that seemed to battle against her, forcing to throw her body around with each step. But the pain did not slow her down; she fought against her body with stubborn determination.

She seated them on her sofa, asked if they would take tea, and disappeared into the kitchen alcove. Her voice drifted out.

"She asked what we think of Nova Huta," Katya said.

Jeffrey hesitated, decided on the truth. "It's not as bad as the high-rises. But I'd imagine all these black buildings look like something out of a nightmare in the wintertime."

Katya turned and translated to the hidden woman. They were rewarded with a brief chuckle. "She says you are correct," Katya told him.

The woman reappeared, wiping her hands on the little

apron tied to her waist. "After the war," the woman told them through Katya, "when you finished your studies the central government gave you a paper called a Work Directive. This paper told you where you would work, what you would do, and which place you would live."

The woman pulled a straight-backed chair from the narrow dining table, turned it around, and eased herself down. With a deliberate motion she wiped one edge of her mouth with an unsteady hand. "You were expected to work and live in this place for the rest of your life.

"Nova Huta was a new development then. It was one of the few places where new housing was going up. New housing meant electricity and indoor plumbing, a toilet for every family, and heat. My husband and I were sent here.

"There were problems. There are always problems. My husband managed a tobacco factory which was next door to the steelworks. We both came from good Warsaw families. All of the other people around here were steelworkers. They wore overalls and helmets and had steel smut on their faces all the time. When we arrived, we were the only people in the entire area with a university education. I cannot tell you how alone it made us feel.

"But you learn not to think about happiness, or wishing you had a different job or a better place to live, or neighbors who could be your friends. You just get on. You survive. You protect yourself. You find something to live for. A purpose. A profession. Something. For me, it was my family and my God."

The teakettle began whistling; with visible effort she pushed herself from her chair and clumped into her little kitchen alcove. She continued to talk, her reedy voice holding an emotionless quality. "In the late forties," Katya translated, "many, many families in Poland began receiving Work Directives, notices that they were to be transported to Siberia. They had twenty-four hours to put their lives in order. They could take twenty kilos of luggage. My stepfather was a mining engineer, and one morning he received a directive to report to a mine in a village that no one could find on the map. He and my mother and my grandmother were sent. My name was not on the list, we learned later, because my birth records had been lost. Otherwise I would have been shipped off as well. My mother took me to my godmother's house, where I lived and waited for my parents to return.

"Fifteen years later, when Poland and Russia signed one of their Friendship Treaties, Poland asked them to re-instate the transportees, or at least those who had survived. My mother came home first. My stepfather had been sent to work in some other place and she had not seen him for seven years. He came home a month later and died three days after his arrival."

She returned and served them steaming glasses from a cheap tin serving tray. Through Katya she continued. "My grandmother had become sick on the trip to Siberia. They were traveling in cattle cars with no heat and little food. At one point the guards grew tired of her moans, opened the doors, and threw her from the train."

The woman went back to the kitchen. As she rummaged away from view she said, "Before she left for Siberia, my grandmother gave me her valuables. I was the only grandchild. Although I was quite young I knew that she was going and would never come back, so I didn't want to take them. I was hoping that if I refused she would have to either stay or return and give them to me later. But she insisted, and because I loved her I finally agreed. The jewelry I sell bit by bit, all except her wedding ring, which I wear as my own. That I will wear to my grave in memory of her and of my husband."

She returned with a crumpled plastic ice cream carton that she handed to Jeffrey. It still held the cold of the freezer. He hefted it, and felt the solid weight shift around.

The woman peered at him through thick lenses. "My son-in-law lost his job when his factory closed down, and my daughter is pregnant again." The edges of her mouth pulled up in a vague smile. "I am soon to take a trip to a place much farther away than Siberia. It would have been nice to leave these remaining pieces to my own granddaughter, but the money is needed. Perhaps she will remember me some other way."

"I am so glad you could join me," Dr. Rokovski gushed as Katya and Jeffrey entered the restaurant.

"What a charming place," Katya said, admiring the

beamed ceiling. "Isn't it, Jeffrey?"

"Mmmm." He shook Rokovski's hand and allowed himself to be ushered to a small quiet table upstairs in the Restaurant Wierzynek, one of Cracow's finest, located in a corner of the main market square. Jeffrey sat down, barely holding on to his impatience. It was not a good day for a three-hour dinner. Alexander had not appeared all day. When Jeffrey rang his room that afternoon he had received no reply. In a panic he had rushed over to Gregor's, fearing the worst, to find his friend limping about the tiny apartment, absolutely certain in his faith that Alexander was both all right and exactly where he should be—alone.

To top it off, the export documents had not been approved. Only Katya's insistence kept him from simply asking Rokovski for the crucial papers. He had held to his side of the bargain. There was work to be done. Too much for the time available. And now this.

"It is one of my favorites," Rokovski said. "I'm enough of a patriot to believe that history can add a special aroma to the best of food, and believe me, this restaurant holds claim to both."

"I love it," Katya said, clearly determined to retain her buoyant mood.

"I'm sure this has been quite a day for all of us," Rokovski said.

"And busy," Jeffrey added, jerking back when Katya kicked him under the table.

"No doubt. And I am indeed grateful that you would take the time to join me here. Some things, I am sure you will understand, are better discussed in the privacy of a public place." Rokovski showed pleasure at his own remark. "I am happy to report that the painting is now safely locked away in my own office cabinets."

"We are certainly glad to have been of some small assistance, aren't we, Jeffrey," Katya said.

After recrating the Rubens with the students' paintings, Rokovski scrawled a note on the archive card stating that the referenced paintings were being assigned to the ministry. Once they were back upstairs, he instructed the curator to have the crate delivered to his office. He wanted to use these relatively unimportant paintings, he explained, to test a new chemical conservation process proposed by the American group.

"Now then," Rokovski said. "If you would allow me to order for you."

Jeffrey waited through an endless discussion between Rokovski, a smiling Katya, and a theatrical waiter. Rokovski eventually turned back to him and said, "This restaurant used to be the private residence of Nicolaus Wierzynek, a very powerful member of the regional government. In 1364 Cracow was the site of the Great Conference of Monarchs, and Nicolaus was allowed to host the senior visitors for several dinners. Just think, my young friend, here in this very room sat the King of Denmark, the Holy Roman Emperor, the Prince of Austria, and the Polish King Casimir the Great. The food was so lavish and the service so faultless that it was decided then and there to make the place an eating establishment upon his death. And so it has been for over six hundred years, making it one of the oldest restaurants in all the world."

"How fascinating," Katya replied. "A bit of living history."

Jeffrey tucked his legs far under his seat and said, "Dr. Rokovski, we are now booked to leave Cracow for London the day after tomorrow."

"We will certainly be sorry to see you depart," Rokovski said.

"Yes. Thank you. The thing is, when I went by the ministry this afternoon, they said that my export license was still being held by your office."

"Ah," Rokovski smiled. "The license."

"Yes, sir. I was wondering if maybe I could come by and pick it up first thing tomorrow morning."

"Yes, of course. But I was wondering if I might impose upon you one further time."

Jeffrey felt his stomach sink a notch. "Impose?"

"Yes. Could you perhaps take along a little excess baggage?"

"How much is a little?"

"It would be quite a small parcel, actually. Perhaps the size of this table?" His eyes retained their smile. "Quite flat. Not heavy."

Jeffrey cast a glance at Katya, astonished to see that she was watching Rokovski with round eyes. "You mean the size of a painting?"

"Precisely." Rokovski leaned across the table. "Not offi-
cially, you understand. I want you to smuggle it."

"You want—"

"For the ministry," Rokovski went on, his voice pitched
low. "We cannot possibly be seen selling a Rubens masterpiece. We would be announcing to the world that we are
paupers. It would be taken as a willingness to exchange the
priceless for mere money. But we are, you see, truly bankrupt. Our coffers at the ministry are empty. Our roofs leak.
Our finest works are deteriorating so badly that some I fear
can never be restored. And so much more needs to be done.
You saw the condition of the museum vaults, our inventory,
our security, the primitive level of our efforts."

His voice was quietly intense. "And then there is my big
dream. No art in Poland has suffered so much in the past
fifty years as that of our churches. I have blueprints for the
renovation of an unused portion of Vavel Castle, which would
house some of the finest religious paintings and statuaries
in all of Europe. Of course, we could barely afford even the
blueprints, to say nothing of the enormous restoration required by some of these pieces. I will not horrify you with
stories of how they have been abused these past five decades."

They waited while the waiter arranged their plates; then
Jeffrey asked, "So how am I supposed to smuggle this out?"

"Your export documents will include a letter from my
office thanking you for the most kind offer to display some
of our students' artwork in your fine establishment." Rokovski positively beamed. "The painting in question has already
been placed back inside its home of the past forty years."

Jeffrey thought it over, decided it was workable. "How
would you like us to send you the money after selling the
painting?"

"You will not send it to me at all. A foundation has already been established for donations to the new museum
wing for religious art. I would simply expect to find one
morning that a large anonymous donation has been made to
our foundation."

Jeffrey looked around the restaurant as he ran the idea
through his mind. "I don't see any problem with that."

Rokovski visibly relaxed. "I must tell you, Mr. Sinclair, I
was most worried about taking up such a crucial and sensitive matter with someone I had only just met. But Mr. Kantor

spoke very highly of you, and I am beginning to see why."

"I think this is something that Mr. Kantor would agree with fully," Jeffrey replied. "It's a pleasure to act on his behalf."

"As it is for us to work with you. I need not tell you that a successful resolution of this matter will pave the way for our future assistance wherever and whenever you might require it. I think you will find us to be very good friends, Mr. Sinclair. Very good friends indeed."

CHAPTER

26

Jeffrey and Katya entered the hotel lobby on their final morning in Cracow to find Alexander seated near the front entrance, puffing contentedly on a cigar, looking positively peaceful. He rose to his feet, gave Katya a small bow. "Good morning, my dear. Jeffrey."

"Good morning, Mr. Kantor," Katya replied. "How are you feeling?"

"Better. I must say that I do indeed feel better."

"You look it," Jeffrey declared.

"Yes, I am happy to say that I rose with the dawn, ate a breakfast fit for a king, and have since been seated here thoroughly enjoying both the morning and this fine cigar."

"We have been praying for you," Katya said quietly.

Alexander looked at her for a long moment. "I cannot tell you how happy I am that my young friend and assistant has found you, my dear."

Katya slipped a soft hand into Jeffrey's. "Thank you."

"It is I who am grateful. To both of you." He looked at Jeffrey. "I understand from Gregor that you are due for a final meeting with Rokovski."

"In twenty minutes."

"Might I come along?"

"Of course."

"Excellent." He turned to Katya. "Gregor asked me to convey an invitation to accompany him to one of his orphanages. He thought you might like to have a chance to see his little charges."

"That would be wonderful. I imagine you two could use some time alone as well." She raised herself up on tiptoes and kissed Jeffrey. "Until later, then."

"Have an excellent morning, my dear," Alexander replied, bowing at her departure. He watched her leave through the front doors. "A most remarkable woman. Am I correct in detecting a change in the atmosphere between you?"

"This trip has been important in a lot of ways," Jeffrey replied.

"Indeed it has." Alexander gazed at him fondly. "I am very proud of you, Jeffrey. You have handled yourself tremendously well."

"Thanks. I've really enjoyed myself."

"One often overlooked element of success is the ability to enjoy your work."

Jeffrey shook his head. "I can't get over how much better you look."

"Thank you. Yes, I have indeed suffered through a very dark night. But I am allowing myself to hope that dawn has finally arrived." He leaned over, put out his cigar, said, "Perhaps we should be going, and you can fill me in along the way."

Rokovski was absolutely delighted to see Alexander enter his office with Jeffrey. "Mr. Kantor! How excellent to see you. I do hope that your health is better."

Alexander accepted the proffered hand, replied, *"Nie mozna narzekac.* I cannot complain. Thank you for asking."

"And Mr. Sinclair." Rokovski rewarded him with a genuine smile. "Would you gentlemen care for tea?"

"Well," Rokovski said once they were seated and served, "as they say in the spy novels, my friend, mission accomplished."

"Indeed," Kantor replied. "I have been most pleasantly surprised by the way events have unfolded."

"You have received copies of all the necessary export documents, Mr. Sinclair?"

"Everything is perfect," Jeffrey effused. "They were waiting for me at the ministry yesterday morning. Thank you again for your help."

"On the contrary, I am immensely grateful to know that we have begun what shall no doubt be a long and mutually beneficial relationship." Rokovski glanced at his watch. "I was informed that your shipment left on time yesterday, once the export documents were processed. It should be crossing the border at Frankfurt an der Oder just about now. No news is good news, so I'm sure all is well."

"Thanks to you," Alexander said. "We are very pleased to know that we have friends such as yourself upon whom we can rely."

"It is I who am pleased, Mr. Kantor. I cannot tell you how much this means, not only to me and to Cracow, but to all of Poland."

"It is always an honor to do something for Poland," Alexander replied. "There is one further point that my young associate thinks should be mentioned before we conclude our business."

"Of course," Rokovski replied, giving Jeffrey a sincere smile.

"We will naturally handle this sale of the painting in the most confidential of manners. My associate has an excellent working relationship with a major dealer. She has expressed a keen interest in acquiring items which are not intended for either public auction or display."

"An American," Jeffrey added. "Very professional, and very discreet."

Rokovski nodded approval. "Exactly what we require."

"But it is necessary to warn you," Alexander continued, "that with the same Rubens allegedly hanging in the museum of Vavel Castle, there is always the risk that at some time in the future an expert might be sent to inspect your painting. If he or she concludes that yours is indeed a forgery, it would be impossible to insure that the news will not leak out."

"Well, my friend," Rokovski replied, turning expansive, "I'm afraid it won't be me the expert will be visiting."

"I don't believe I understand," Alexander said.

"I told your young colleague about my big dream. I had a second big dream, which will come as no surprise to you.

And that is the accumulation of as many Polish works of art and antiques as possible to restore our heritage. I'm sure you are familiar that museums regularly exchange paintings to complete one special collection or another. For many months I have been negotiating with the state museum of Moscow for the return of a series of paintings by Matejko. These paintings, I might add, each occupy one entire wall of the exhibition rooms."

"Brilliant," Kantor murmured. "Absolutely brilliant."

"They disappeared from Poland just after the Red Army arrived in 1945. The Cracow museum authorities were given some lame excuse about their being transported to Moscow for safekeeping. I have been struggling to find something from our collection that they might be willing to take in trade, but was getting nowhere. Shortly after Mr. Sinclair met with me, it occurred that a Rubens might pique their curiosity."

"My friend," Kantor said, "you have made your country proud."

"Needless to say," Rokovski went on, smiling broadly, "they were absolutely delighted. Being the gentleman that I am, I insisted that they send their top Old Master expert to authenticate it. I mentioned to them on the phone that over the years there had been some rumblings about the painting's authenticity, and I would not want them to be disappointed."

"Of course not."

"The expert arrived here yesterday, and his initial report is most positive. It appears that Moscow is anxious to take advantage of our offer before we wake up and realize how one-sided it is. We have just this morning heard that the six Matejkos are already being crated for shipment. They will be unveiled at a special exhibition commemorating the Vavel Castle's thousandth anniversary."

Alexander returned his smile. "It is a pity that your coup will have to remain in secret. You deserve a hero's reward."

"I shall receive my reward every time I stand before the Matejkos, and as I watch my new museum wing for religious art take shape." Rokovski stood with his guests, walked around his desk, took Alexander's hand in both of his. "My friend, Poland shall never perish."

"As long as we are alive," Alexander replied solemnly.

They stood together for a moment before the director released Alexander's hand and reached for Jeffrey's. "Mr. Sinclair, I shall look forward to many further opportunities to work with you."

"Nothing could give me more pleasure," Jeffrey replied.

Rokovski ushered them downstairs, bowed them through the main portals, shut the door behind them. Once they were back on the street, Jeffrey stood and blinked in the sunlight, said, "I can't believe it's over."

"A job well done." Alexander's eyes were moist. He looked straight across the market square, a slight smile on his features.

"What's next?"

"There is a small church not far from here," Alexander replied. "My mother used to go there when I was young. I believe I might like to stop by for a moment."

"Sure. I love these old churches. Which one is it?"

Alexander motioned out over the square, out beyond the colorful market stalls and the throngs of people and the flower sellers, out across the expanse of history. "Just on the other side of Florian's Gate," he said.

Acknowledgments

While *Florian's Gate* is indeed a work of fiction, I have tried very hard to remain true to the actual situation I found in the newly liberated lands of Eastern Europe. The learning process that unfolded during my trips, as well as during the preparatory work done before traveling, was both challenging and rewarding. I found myself being forced to rethink much of the perspective I have inherited from my Western culture, and as a result I feel that I have been granted a unique opportunity to grow and develop both as an individual and as a Christian.

My research trips to Poland were made infinitely richer through the kind hospitality of Isabella's family. Their warm and giving nature come truly from the heart, and they shared with us the very best of both what they had and who they were. I am truly thankful to be a part of such a wonderful family.

Many powerful lessons came to me through these visits with my wife's family. Despite the pain that was recalled along with the memories, they shared a number of the events which they either witnessed or experienced themselves during the past five decades. What touched me most deeply, however, was not the experiences themselves, but rather the way in which they were described.

Virtually all the events woven into the Polish section of this book come from their experiences, and where possible are kept exactly as they were related to me. I say this so that there can be no question as to the reality of their suffering. And yet, throughout my visits with them, they never overcame their natural humility to the point of really believing that what they had to say was of any special significance, or could be of interest to others.

Isabella believes that there are two major reasons for this: First, *everyone* in Poland suffered horribly as a result of both the war and Stalin's subsequent domination of Eastern Europe. Because they have spent their lives surrounded by other families who experienced the same or even worse traumas, they cannot understand how great an impact their stories might have on someone from the West.

The second reason is that they see themselves as simple people—they are not famous, they have not conquered their difficulties, they have not made a great name for themselves. They have simply endured, and their life stories are nothing more in their eyes than struggling to live and to survive despite all that is placed upon their minds and hearts and shoulders. They shared their experiences with me in acknowledgement of my becoming part of the family. But they never could understand why I insisted on taking notes. They never could see why their stories moved me as they did.

My wife's assistance is found on every page of this book. None of her in Poland speaks English, so all of their stories and observations were painstakingly translated by her. She taught me constantly from the wealth of knowledge which she has gained through her travels and studies; Isabella attended the University of Cracow for a year, and has returned numerous times since then, including one visit just as martial law was imposed. It has been a very rewarding experience to work with her on this book. I feel that I have begun to understand a fragment of the beauty and the strength which is contained within the Polish spirit.

My wife's father, Olgierd Kaliszczak, was prisoner number 1914 in the Auschwitz concentration camp. All that is described here in this book—from being picked up during a random street search to being released because of his mother's untiring efforts—comes from his memories, and is written using his words. The only change I made was that Olgierd was actually arrested at a market square in Warsaw instead of Cracow. It was the first time that he had ever spoken of his experiences in such detail, and it was a tremendously difficult endeavor. I am extremely grateful to him, both for the painful act of remembering, and for granting me the gift of this sharing. I would also like to offer my heartfelt thanks to his wife, Danka, who gave me my first lessons in Polish hospitality at their home in Virginia. The key, I have learned from her and others, is to give the very best of what one has, and to give from the heart.

Janusz Zurawski is former director of one of Poland's largest construction engineering groups. He and his wife Haluta opened their hearts and home to us, and aided me greatly in gaining historical insight into the Polish character. Dr. Teresa Aleksandrowicz virtually took responsibility for us during our second visit to Warsaw.

Marian and Dusia Tarka shared numerous experiences that were truly difficult to relive, including the incident of the Siberian conscription—the woman who returned is a very dear friend of theirs. Their son, Slawek, was kind enough to spend several hours discussing the current crisis within the Polish police.

Olek Tarka and his wife Halinka were of immense help and support. From Olek I received much of the general economic perspective. Halinka personally took me around several villages near Cracow so that I might visit the homes and cottages which were described here.

Andrzej Koprowski, S.J., is the former head of media for the Polish Catholic Church, and currently directs programs on both national radio and television. Grzegorz Schmidt, S.J., is a rector of the Catholic University of Warsaw and editor of the Catholic magazine *Przeglad Powszechny*. Both of these gentlemen were kind enough to assist me in developing a perspective for the church's overall efforts.

Amid the incredible chaos of shifting from communism to capitalism (until recently, virtually no private commercial establishments were allowed), I found a number of people who were truly passionate about their fledgling antique trades, and who were delighted to speak about their experiences with a total stranger. Marck Lengiewicz is president of the Rempex Auction House. Barbara Zdrenka is owner of Warsaw's Antykwariat Dziel Sztuki Dawnej, a fine establishment with a remarkable collection of truly beautiful

small items. Monika Kuhne is manager of the Noble House
in Warsaw, a very up-market shop with some breathtaking
pieces. The staff of Cracow's Connoisseur Antyki were all
most patient with my endless questions.

Adam Konopacki is one of the few Polish art and antiques
consultants who has, in a short span of time, established a
name as a trustworthy evaluator. He was extremely helpful
in giving me an overview of the Polish antiques trade, the
characters involved, their backgrounds, and how the 'industry' is developing.

Waclaw Wlodarczyk is miner number 142 in the Wieliczka Salt Mines. When he learned the reason for our wanting
to visit the mines, he took it as a personal challenge and led
us down into the older unused areas—an exciting and somewhat frightening experience. Some of these areas had clearly
not been refurbished for decades, and the wood under our
feet and around our heads bore that strange hoary frost and
weak parchment feel. I am very grateful for an experience
that I will not soon forget.

John Hess is director of Youth With A Mission's efforts
in Cracow. It was from him that I learned of Father Bloknicki
and his Poland-wide mission project described in this book.

Rev. Konstanty Wiazowski is president of the Polish Baptist Union, and Rev. I. Barna is general secretary. They were
most kind in assisting me with my research; when our work
took longer than expected, they invited Isabella and me to
take part in a wedding celebration that evening. It was an
exceptional time for both of us, and we are truly grateful for
their congregation's open-hearted welcome.

The story of stealing antiques in East Germany by putting the owners into prison and sometimes torturing them
into signing the sales documents is true. The trial is currently underway for over a dozen defendants. The scandal
has now reached the top echelons of the former government.

Renate Trotz was co-founder of the Schwerin New Forum,
the nationwide democratic group whose peaceful protests
ushered in the fall of East German President Hoennecker
and the rise of democracy. She is also an attorney, and in
this capacity was most helpful in gaining background infor-

mation on the unfolding scandal.

Thilo Schelling and his assistant Kathrin Dobrowolski are responsible for working with West German and international companies who are starting up operations in the former East German state of Mecklenburg. He gave up a secure senior position in Dusseldorf in order to be a part of the rebuilding of new Germany. He provided a most enthusiastic and realistic overview, which helped tremendously in coming to understand the enormous problems—and opportunities—that face the new German states. His assistant deserves a special note of thanks for her open-hearted discussion of what it meant to live through the transition as a young woman professional. I am very grateful to both of them for their time and heartfelt assistance.

Help also came from the new Mecklenburg government's Secretary of State, Wolfgang Pfletshinger, and Minister of Commerce Lehman. Despite the enormous demands placed upon their time and energies, they stopped long enough to offer their perspectives with candor.

Rainer Rausch is a lawyer from Munich who has given up his practice, his home, and his former life in order to work with the evangelical church in Mecklenburg. He works both in attempting to regain assets stripped by the former Communist regime and in assisting people who have been persecuted because of their role within the church. He kindly assisted with gaining a clear perspective and with making introductions for me within the region.

Dr. Seyfarth is the head of Mecklenburg's only evangelical seminary, situated in Schwerin. He is a very deep-thinking, profound, and inspiring gentleman who grasps the problems facing his region with the gentle humility of one who truly loves Christ. I am indeed grateful for the insights that have gone into the making of this book, and for the lessons I gained personally from him.

Irene Heinze is the historian at the Castle-Museum of Güstrow in Mecklenburg. She spent an entire afternoon walking Isabella and me through their collection, explaining in detail the history and the significance of both the palace and the pieces housed there.

Several times a year, my wife and I try to schedule a four-day silent retreat at a Carmelite monastery near Oxford. During one of these visits we met a Polish gentleman,

Brother Jerzy, who became the basis for the character of
Gregor. He has remained a good friend and true example of
Christ's love at work.

My stepbrother, Lee Bunn, is a recovering alcoholic. His
story formed the basis for the character of Jeffrey's brother,
and I am immensely grateful that Lee feels confident enough
about his own past and recovery to allow me to use his experiences as a part of this book. Lee became a part of our
family several years after my departure for Europe at the
age of twenty-one, and we have never spent as much time
together as I would like. The segment about being moved
from place to place is fiction; the story of his fall from the
tree is sadly true. I am proud and happy to say, however, that
Lee is now a member of A.A., and has not only come to grips
with his own debilitation but truly grown in stature and
strength through his walk with the Lord. His mother, my
father's second wife, has taught me a tremendous amount
about strength through faith; it was Patricia who introduced
me to the concept of co-dependency, and to the healing power
of faith in such tragic circumstances. Her example has
proven to be a valuable beacon to others experiencing such
pain.

Seven weeks before I began work on this book, the pastor
of my church in Düsseldorf, Bill DeLay, entered the hospital
for what we thought was appendicitis, but what turned out
to be a tumor. He hovered at death's door for four days, then
two weeks into his hospitalization had a relapse and again
almost died. His four-month sojourn ended with a return to
full health, but during his recovery Bill suffered tremendous
agony. The result of this experience was a five-part sermon
series on the theme of suffering. Much of that has been in-
corporated into this book. Bill and his wife Cathy have continued to offer great assistance with both the scriptural messages required for my book, and the biblical wisdom
necessary for my own continued growth. I am very grateful
for their love and prayerful support.

My mother, Becky Bunn, is the former owner of an antiques gallery and has managed several others. I am indeed
grateful for the experiences and wisdom she has shared with

me, and for the appreciation I have gained through her for fine woodwork. She now leads her own church's Stephen Ministries Outreach Program; I have gained great insight in how to work with people in pain through our talks. Thanks again, Mom. Your words stay with me through the years.

Amelia Fitzalan-Howard is client services manager at Christie's in London. She was kind enough to spend several hours touring both the house's public showrooms and the underground treasure rooms. Edward Lennox-Boyd is manager of the furniture department, and explained the finer points of several pieces they had recently auctioned. These included the chest of drawers described during the Christie's scene near the beginning of the book; in this case I used the lowest initial estimate, because I feared the actual sales price would have seemed too unbelievable—the piece finally went for one and a half million pounds, over 2.75 million dollars.

Dr. Fabian Stein, director of Ermitage, Ltd., along with his partner, Alexander von Solodkov, runs one of the world's leading shops for Fabergé jewelry. He spent several days walking a total novice—me—through the artistic endeavors of one of the world's foremost jewelers.

Nancy Matthews, publicity director of the Franco-British Chamber of Commerce, received her initial training in antiques from the world-renowned Sotheby's School. Her assistance in making numerous contacts within the London antiques trade was invaluable.

Bryan Rolliston is co-owner of the Antique House on Kensington Church Street, and in the midst of a hectic day at the Grosvenor House Antiques Fair he took time to answer in exhaustive detail my questions about his pieces and the market in general.

Norman Adams owns the Adams store on Hans Road in the Kensington district of London, and is a passionate specialist in eighteenth-century English furniture. I am indeed grateful that he would share a bit of his knowledge and love of fine antiques with me.

The Grosvenor House Antiques Fair, under the patronage of Her Majesty Queen Elizabeth the Queen Mother, was for me something of a mind-boggling experience. I am extremely grateful to the staff of their very capable press office for treating a green newcomer with such tact and polite patience.

Working with the family at Bethany House Publishers continues to be a source of great joy. It means a very great deal to me that our professional relationship is enriched by growing friendships. I thank God for the opportunity to work with such fine and talented people. As it is not possible to name everyone who deserves mention, I shall limit myself to two very special individuals. David Koechel of the Koechel-Peterson studios designed and painted this book's splendid cover-art. Cindy Alewine is personal assistant to Bethany's Editor-in-Chief, and is very much responsible for the smooth running of our day-to-day activities. Cindy has been a true friend and highly valued confidant since the very first day.

As always, I close with an invitation for anyone who has questions or problems to feel free to write Reverend Paul McCommon. Paul has received a great number of letters from readers of my books, and always replies with promptness. He has been kind enough to share several of his less personal responses with me, and I have been deeply moved by his wisdom and gentle guidance. Anyone wishing to discuss a problem or question should please contact:

> Reverend Paul McCommon
> %Bethany House Publishers
> 6820 Auto Club Road
> Minneapolis, MN 55438